Dedicated to my sons, Thomas G. Hanna and Oscar R. Hanna. Without our adventures and the time we had, none of this book would have been possible.

Danny Hanna

A LEGEND CALLED TANNIV

The great gathering of Stormhorn

AUSTIN MACAULEY PUBLISHERS™

LONDON • CAMBRIDGE • NEW YORK • SHARJAH

A CIP catalogue record for this title is available from the British Library.

ISBN 9781398432154 (Paperback)
ISBN 9781398432161 (ePub e-book)

www.austinmacauley.com

First Published 2022
Austin Macauley Publishers Ltd®
1 Canada Square
Canary Wharf
London
E14 5AA

The Great Gathering of Stormhorn

Thomas would never forget the day his life changed. On the day that his life changed forever, he was a young boy, much like any other boy in England.

The year was 1984, and he was a small boy with light brown hair and blue eyes. Some would say a very cheeky face with a look of curiosity. He was a boy who treated the whole world as if it was a question; those questions were everywhere, and they needed to be answered. So you can imagine; he had a lot to talk about with whomever he came in contact with.

He remembered the day his grandmother came to pick him up. This was only days after the funeral of his late parents. He stood in the waiting room of the children's house, where he had been staying for a few days. It was necessary to stay here while the required paperwork had been officiated so that he could live with his grandmother.

The correct word for the house was 'orphanage', but he couldn't quite bring himself to say it or even recognise that he was in such a place or situation even though it was merely circumstance that brought him into a place like this. He was proud and would use the word 'circumstance' because using words like 'death' or 'dead' would have made people feel sad or sorry for him, and he didn't want anyone to feel sorry for him. In truth, he did not know what to feel.

In English culture in the 1980s, children were taught to deal with things differently.

The orphanage was a cold, detached residence. It was a tall Victorian building with a wooden floor painted with thick brown paint and looked like it was decorated regimentally every few years. There was glossy cream wall paint, which was painted so that it was easy to wipe clean for hygiene reasons. This was done for the benefit of the children who came and went, of course. It felt like a government building even though there was a splattering of children's toys and teddy bears, with pictures of dolls and trains on each wall.

The building had colossal cast iron radiators, with big metal pipes lining the inside as if a military contractor had done plumbing. The ceilings were very tall, and the hallway was grand with a sort of reception desk. The entrance and the main hallway had a massive front door with a large stained-glass Victorian door.

The door was memorable in itself; these were the types of things that curious boys remembered. It seemed at the time that it was massive and very wide in black gloss paint with two stained-glass windows, giant brass knobs and a thick cast iron door knocker. It was ornate as if the house was made for a loving, warm family at some point in its history. It was meant for a more comfortable lived-in home in London's Kensington district. Not the institutional sensations that the interior had taken on in its current function as a children's orphanage.

Thomas was at ease with the position because he knew it would only be for a few days. So he decided to take the attitude drummed into him at school, which meant only to answer when spoken to, smile, look cheerful, and give a happy veneer to his exterior.

He put his best foot forward and made his few days here go by as fast as possible. It was easier for him because he knew that his grandmother was coming to collect him.

He put on a front of a calm, even though his thoughts were about his future.

He had nothing but fond memories of his grandmother, a mysterious lady, who he saw two or maybe three times a year: once at Easter, once at Christmas, then a week in the summer. But he had never stayed with her alone. So despite his thin veneer of happiness, he was very apprehensive of simply everything.

He decided to keep to himself very detached and treat his stay at the orphanage just like a military operation. Only speaking when spoken to and timing his mealtimes regimentally to break up the days. He really wanted to get back to school, so his days went quicker to see his friends. But the children's authorities thought it would be best to have a rip-the-plaster-off attitude. The official theory is that visiting his friends or going back to school would only upset him. So, he waited out the three days in the house until his grandmother came to collect him.

Mealtimes felt like he was in an official government environment, just like school but not quite.

The house had a long mahogany table with benches on both sides and two chairs at the head of the table on either end. There was enough room to fit four children on each side. Then the house support workers, Mr Boggins and his wife, Mrs Boggins, came and sat on either end of the table with them at each meal.

Mr Boggins conducted prayers before meals, generally consisting of how fortunate the children were to be in such a lovely house. Also, how grateful they all should be, and how others were in much worse peril around the world, which he was probably right.

Mr Boggins said grace at each meal as if he had done it a million times before. Then again, in an army-like fashion, he passed out plastic plates, and metal knives and forks just like you would see at school.

He looked like a kind school caretaker. Thomas believed him to be around sixty years old. He was always fixing or painting something and continuously walked as if he had a job to do. He had an enormous round head with white hair and always wore a shirt, tie and trousers with a set of overalls. He was dressed for maintenance emergencies and for any official orphanage duties all at the same time. But he was always at his happiest in his shed, hammering away and doing jobs. The house was well-ordered and well-maintained, and nothing was out of place whatsoever.

Mrs Boggins was a large lady with a small nose, a big round face, and rosy pink cheeks. She did all the cooking and kitchen chores herself and volunteered the children to help each night tidy the kitchen after each meal.

Mrs Boggins would walk around the kitchen singing and humming music from her local church choir, which she attended twice a week; you could tell she loved it. She always tried to get the children to join in singing with her. They were both lovely people who had decided to dedicate their lives to helping small children. But Thomas kept his distance.

There was no point, he thought; he was only going to be in the house three days, he would say to himself over and over again.

At the time, there were only three other children in the house. Two girls, aged around ten or eleven, their names Beth and Stephanie, were equally friendly and polite, and they had been given the task of showing Thomas his room.

They were both tall and blonde with blue eyes; they even wore the same outfits, both wearing chequered dresses, the type that girls wore as summer uniforms for school. They both wore their hair in ponytails and spoke almost the same thing at the same time. He got the feeling that it was as if they had shown a child that room many times before.

They helped Thomas with his luggage and walked him up the old, creaky Victorian stairs to the first floor of this three-story Victorian house only days before. The room had brown curtains, glossy wipe-clean cream paint, a springy

7

metal bed, and a trains-and-cars bedsheet. The room was nothing special, and what did Thomas care about it anyway.

He simply thanked the two little girls and took his case and things. He looked around the room as they tried to explain the mealtime plan for the days to come.

"I understand that you are only here for three days, so I won't go into much detail," said Beth efficiently.

Beth was the older, more confident out of the two. "But when Mrs Boggins shouts, it will be to help her with a job—so listen out," repeated Beth offering friendly advice.

Thomas then understood why the other children had decided to take the second and third-floor bedrooms. Thomas would be the only one to hear Mrs Boggins shout, he thought.

There wasn't much point for him to make friends, so he was polite and nodded again, saying, "Thank you very much," and then he closed the door to be alone.

His reason for not making friends was simple; they went off to school for the day. While Thomas stayed in the house counting down the hours till meal times, in-between getting a shout from the kitchen to help Mrs Boggins with tasks.

He was old enough to understand that the tasks were just Mrs Boggins's attempt to bond with him, to get him out of his room and sing with her.

Which he didn't feel like doing; in fact, singing was the last thing he felt like doing. But he could sense that she was doing her best to cheer him up.

Each day, Thomas wore his school uniform, a dark grey Brummell blazer made of wool, with his red and blue striped tie, grey shorts, grey socks and scuffed shoes.

"Come on."

"Take off that tie and that blazer," Mrs Boggins said,

"That cap too. You're not at school now. Anyway," she said,

"You are going to be getting a new school uniform with a new school badge and a new cap badge soon," she added, looking down at Thomas.

But he didn't want to take it off. He was looking for security and refuge, and his school uniform felt comfortable. It was something he knew and something he remembered, so he kept wearing it every day.

In any case, he would be meeting his grandmother and wanted to be as smart as possible for her arrival.

This was part of his best-foot-forward attitude that he decided to assume each day with a chest-out approach and smile on his face. So while Thomas took his blazer off for chores.

He decided to tuck his tie into his shirt and rolled his sleeves with a slight sense of victory that he was maintaining his original plan. To be smart and wore his school uniform every day, and nothing was going to stop him.

It was only three days in total, but the evenings and nights were the worst. He hated going to bed. Not because of the bedroom or because of the situation he had been forced into. But because he simply missed his mum and stepfather in the evenings and in the dead of night, he thought about them the most. Not only did he feel it, but he knew his life had changed. He felt a horrible sense of uncertainty, doubt and insecurity.

On the day of the funeral, he was looking into the hole in the ground, wondering how he should act and hearing people say:

"What's going to become of poor Thomas!" the local gossipmongers whispered and muttered so that he would not hear. But like most boys, he could hear everything.

Thomas's grandmother, Margaret, was a strong lady. She was his mother's mother, and she said to Thomas that day:

"Don't worry, Thomas, you'll live with me now." It was as if there was no doubt in her mind whatsoever.

"We just need to get the official paperwork nonsense out of the way, and then I will come and get you," she said in a stern voice, smiling down at him.

He always loved going to his grandmother's house. She had the best food and the best home he had ever seen. But the only time he had spent in the place was at Christmas or Easter or the odd weekends or week during the summer. What would it be like to actually live there? Thomas thought to himself.

He was unsure about everything. Eating chocolate and cakes and having Christmas dinners with a sea of presents was one thing, but it won't be like this every day. Or will it? Thomas gently thought to himself with a slight smile on his face, thinking about it being Christmas every day.

He jumped into his very squeaky metal bed, shuffled into the itchy blankets and snuggled in for the night. Christmas, every day, gently resonated in his mind as he drifted off to sleep for the night.

Leaving Day

The following day, he awoke around seven in the morning. He could hear the three children running around the halls, the sound of water taps running, the sound of brushing teeth, the sound of doors slamming and showers hissing as the water came jetting out.

Then Mrs Boggins hollered, "KIDS! Come and get your breakfast, or you're going to be late."

"Thomas! Come down for breakfast!" called Mr Boggins.

Mrs Boggins shouted, "Oh, leave him be, Mr Boggins. He has no school, and he can come down later, and his grandmother won't be here till this afternoon."

He understood now why he got the first-floor bedroom. You get the racket of two girls getting ready upstairs and a din from Collin, the fourteen-year-old boy, stomping around on the third floor.

Then Mr and Mrs Boggins started bickering; Mrs Boggins shouted at Mr Boggins, who was getting under her feet, "Out of my way, you grumpy old man!"

Collin, the fourteen-year-old boy, kept to himself; he would come in from school, mutter a hello and eat his meals upstairs. He wasn't interested in mixing or becoming friends. So Thomas left him alone, and he left Thomas alone because Collin had seen hundreds of children come and go over the years.

As soon as Thomas heard the clatter of Beth, Stephanie and Collin leave the house, he listened out for what seemed to be a slam of the old Victorian door and jumped out of bed.

Today was the day his grandmother was coming to collect him. He could not say that he was excited, but then, she was family; and he could relate to that.

He laid out his school uniform; he got out a fresh, clean white shirt, with his grey blazer, with his gleaming red and gold school badge on it, his grey cap, grey shorts and new socks and shoes to wear.

He then rushed to the shower, taking his time to wash thoroughly; he brushed his teeth and combed his hair; he was average height for his age, thin with light brown hair, blue eyes and pale skin.

He was going to look his best, he thought to himself. He decided to put his best foot forward, be brave, and smile, which he was going to do.

After the shower, he went back to his room to get dressed, which he did faster than he ever had in his life.

Thomas was famous for not being the most efficient at getting ready. His mother, Alina, used to remark every morning,

"Thomas! You are so slow at getting ready every morning." He danced around getting distracted with one sock on and a shirt half fastened, and a school tie around his head. She would have been proud of him this morning.

Once Thomas had got dressed, he had two cases full of clothes and a holdall full of his favourite much-loved toys, curiosities, and other things along with stuff he wanted to retain. Things like a special stone, a unique shell, items that he had collected over the years.

He opened up his cases and bag and put things inside. Then he realised that Mrs Boggins had three shirts, shorts, trousers and socks that she was washing.

A loud shout came from downstairs. "Thomas! Come down and get your breakfast. And come down now!"

"Yes, Mrs Boggins!" he yelled back down the stairs. "I am on my way!"

He ran down the stairs as fast as he could. He was famous for this, too, running everywhere as if he was incapable of actually walking anywhere. He ran down the stairs and the hallway straight into the dining room.

"Good morning, Mrs Boggins!" He yelled.

"My word," Mrs Boggins said. "You are spritely this morning. Can't wait to get out of here, I bet."

"No, it's not that, Mrs Boggins," He said.

"Oh, it's okay,"

"I have seen many a child get excited about moving on from this house over the past forty years."

"Don't worry, I have seen it all in my time," said Mrs Boggins.

"Just make sure that you don't forget anything. I have put your clean washing in the side cabinet on the stairs outside your room."

"Thank you, Mrs Boggins," He replied.

After breakfast, which he finished in record time, he ran upstairs, stumbling, making a ruckus as he sprinted at lightning speed.

He grabbed his clean clothes packing his cases, ramming and squeezing, sitting and hugging the case to ensure everything was shut while stuffing in clothes that had popped out with his fingers, ensuring they were all fully inside correctly while his bloated cases barely remained closed.

Only a boy could pack as badly as he did. But he thought it looked fine, and it did the job. He didn't care; it was the day he was leaving. After washing, getting dressed, eating his breakfast and packing, he looked at the big clock in the hallway, and it was only mid-morning. His grandmother was not expected until three o'clock. It was going to be a long day.

He could hear Mr Boggins hammering, chopping and sawing something in the garden. He thought that it was only good and correct to go and say thank you and goodbye properly. So he sauntered downstairs and snuck through the kitchen very quietly and silently while Mrs Boggins sang hymns to herself loudly. This was to ensure that he was not roped into doing any more household tasks. He continued on and snuck into the garden without being noticed.

As he entered the garden, Mr Boggins popped his head up and said, "Hello, young Thomas. You make me laugh, boy! You have always got your school uniform on, hahaha. I could not wait to get out of mine when I was your age." Mr Boggins sniggered to himself and shook his head while he continued to cut some wood.

"The trick to life is keeping yourself busy, my boy. If you keep yourself busy, you won't be recruited to do anything you don't want to do," and by that, Thomas thought, he meant Mrs Boggins.

"I have come to say goodbye," said Thomas.

"Mrs Boggins said you are not leaving for another three hours, my boy. You can help me, and we can have some man time," he said.

This made Thomas smile because he wanted to help in the earlier two days, but he was not daring enough to ask or even venture outside the garden.

"Pass me that big hammer hanging up,"

"Here you go," said Thomas as he passed the hammer from the neatly placed tools on the bench.

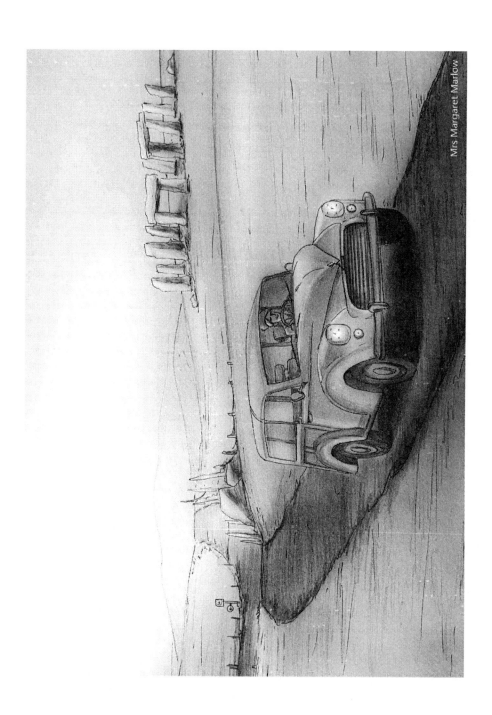

Mrs Margaret Marlow

The shed was immaculate. It was full of tools, gardening equipment and supplies that looked like he had been collecting forever. Everything had an order, and everything had a place. He had stencilled out the shape of each tool on the wall and painted the shape of each tool to ensure it all went back in the right place. Everything had a home. It was perfect.

"What are you building?" asked Thomas.

"I am not building anything. I am replacing and repairing the third-floor bannister and the handrail. It had come loose with Collin running up and down the stairs grabbing the rail as he goes… Well, it's actually not his fault; the house is a hundred years old, and that room has seen around fifty kids like you that run everywhere," said Mr Boggins.

Thomas smiled and acquiesced.

"Hold this piece of wood. We will fix this together, and Mrs Boggins will run us out a sandwich each for lunch at some point," he said with a smile.

Thomas didn't mind helping Mr Boggins, and he knew that the time would go much faster if he helped for the next few hours. Thomas's idea was to keep himself busy because he had already packed and done most of what he needed to do.

"So you're moving to the New Forest then, boy?" asked Mr Boggins.

"I think so, sir. My grandmother has an old stone house there, and it's a huge house from what I can remember," he added.

Mr Boggins replied, "I grew up there too, Thomas! You just be careful of those woods; some of those woods are the oldest in the world, and they hold countless secrets."

"What kind of secrets?" Thomas inquired.

"Well, you have the Stonehenge and Stone circles everywhere around that part of the world. And I mean Stone circles that they have not even found yet," said Mr Boggins.

"Then you have the legends of the shadow warriors."

"What are the shadow warriors?" asked Thomas enthusiastically.

"Legend says they are warriors stuck in the woods and move between time, space and the stone circles," replied Mr Boggins in a deep, growling voice.

"But they're just stories, Mr Boggins, aren't they?" He asked nervously.

"I am not so sure, my boy. I have heard strange voices and conversations whistling in the trees and wind in those woods when I was your age," said Mr Boggins.

14

"Lunchtime, boys!" Mrs Boggins cried as she toddled towards them with a platter of sandwiches and a huge jug of orange squash and cups.

"Mr Boggins has been telling me about the New Forest, shadow warriors and Stone Circles," said Thomas in a tense tone, wanting reassurance.

"Oh, I hope you haven't been scaring the boy," said Mrs Boggins in a very angry voice aimed at Mr Boggins.

"Take no notice, my dear. It's all nonsense. You just keep out of those woods and away from some of those Stone Circles, especially the Stone Circles in the woods," Mrs Boggins said in a speech sounding more like a warning.

"The problem is the Stone Circles move in those woods," said Mr Boggins.

"Oh, will you be quiet? Hush, Mr Boggins!" Mrs Boggins scolded as she swiped at Mr Boggins with the tea towel hanging over her shoulder, narrowly missing his head.

With that, a loud knock came from the old Victorian door. It was almost three o'clock, and it was grandmother; he was sure of it.

The door knocked again, and it was definitely his grandmother.

Only she would knock that loudly twice, and she was not known for her patience.

"You stay here. I will answer the door," said Mrs Boggins.

"I will come with you!" cried Thomas.

He jumped up and ran to the door with Mrs Boggins.

Mrs Boggins shuffled her way to the door with Thomas behind her. He was looking for a way past but couldn't find a polite way to barge past her, so he had to dig deep to adopt a bit of patience.

As she got to the door, she lifted her soft pudgy hands and began twisting the old Victorian doorknob and there she was, Thomas's grandmother.

She was a strong, stern lady, with dark brown hair and dark brown eyes, and a very serious face; when the door was open, she took the initiative to say hello first.

"Hello, Mrs Boggins. Have you got my grandson? I have the official paperwork for his release to me," she said sternly in a polite voice.

"I am here to take him with me back to Hampshire," she added.

He smiled as if he was being the most helpful boy in the world. "Hello, Mrs Marlow!" Mrs Boggins replied. "I have him right here. He's had his breakfast, and he's been helping out this morning. I even think that he has packed his suitcases," Mrs Boggins added.

With that, a small voice appeared, "Hello, Grandmother!" Thomas cried from behind Mrs Boggins's broad frame.

"I have been waiting for you all day!"

"Oh, he has indeed, and he's been no trouble whatsoever. He's been helping Mr Boggins in the garden fixing whatever it is he is fixing right now," Mrs Boggins said as if Mr Boggins was out there wasting time.

Thomas replied, "He's fixing the third-floor bannister, and I have been helping him."

With that, Thomas's grandmother Mrs Marlow said, "Well, that's good. A boy should always be busy. I don't want to be here long because we have a long journey back to Stoney Cross."

Thomas's grandmother was of average height, but you would think she was ten feet tall the way she carried herself. She always looked smart and immaculate. She always wore tweed, a long tweed skirt with sensible boots and a cream blouse with a matching tweed jacket. The type of hard-wearing clothes that you could do anything in, whether it was gardening or hiking. She wore proper country clothing and seemed to have an endless supply of tweed outfits.

She was of a stern appearance and always had glasses draped around her neck hanging from a cord. She was always terribly efficient and hated any sort of doddering or inefficiency.

"So what needs to be done for me to take the boy?" asked Mrs Marlow.

"Come in for a cup of tea. We need to do all the paperwork first, and it will take about an hour," Mrs Boggins said.

"Okay, well, if it takes that long, then that's what we will do," said Mrs Marlow.

As she passed through the old Victorian door, she said,

"Hello, Thomas, my boy! Why don't you run along and finish the job with Mr Boggins while I get the paperwork done? I will call you when we are ready."

Thomas about-turned and ran through the hallway, into the kitchen, and out through the back door into the garden.

"Ahh! Good Thomas, you are back! Hold this bit of wood while I get my drill," said Mr Boggins.

"He's always running," said Mrs Boggins shaking her head.

"That's my grandson," said Mrs Marlow.

"He's efficient; he gets that from me," she said with a very proud smile on her face.

Mrs Margaret Marlow

About an hour and two cups of tea later, all the necessary paperwork was finalised and completed to take Thomas and adopt him for good.

It was now time for Mrs Marlow to start looking after a boy full time as a mother, father, and grandmother. She did not seem to be phased by any of this whatsoever. She had a job to do, and she was going to do it to the best of her ability, no matter what.

Mrs Boggins could sense this, and she felt at ease as if her job was complete and that Thomas was going to be looked after. This was Mr and Mrs Boggins's only real quest to ensure each child that passed through their doors was left with the best chance in life.

"I will get Thomas," said Mrs Boggins.

Mrs Boggins got up puffing and mumbling and calmly shuffled out of the dining room where they had been doing what seemed to be an endless amount of paperwork. They went and stood proudly in the garden door frame to tell Mr Boggins and Thomas to go and fetch the luggage as it was time to leave now.

He shot up and ran towards the kitchen door from the far end of the garden.

Mrs Boggins chuckled and muttered, "He's always running. That boy! Always running, ha!"

"Okay," Thomas said eagerly. "I will get my bags."

He ran with such haste through the kitchen, down the hallway, and then with a sharp left skidding as he halted to change direction. He ran up the stairs with a thundering racket as each stair took the pounding from the most enthusiastic footsteps you had ever heard.

"Wait, Thomas! I will help you, you have three bags. You will need my help!" said Mr Boggins.

Mr Boggins stopped what he was doing. He promptly looked around for the correct place to lay his treasured drill down. Then looking around again to see if anything was out of place. He walked slowly from the far end of the garden to the kitchen door to go and help. Thomas was already on the first floor with his two suitcases and his holdall.

As suspected, when Mr Boggins arrived, he saw a boy trying every contorted manoeuvre possible to try and take on the two large suitcases and holdall himself.

"Come here, Thomas. I will help."

"Give me those cases, you take the holdall—we don't want any accidents, especially you falling down the stairs—do you realise the paperwork involved if you hurt yourself?." Mr Boggins said with great assurance.

Mrs Marlow punctually and sharply walked out from the dining room towards the big Victorian door. She stood patiently waiting for Thomas and Mr Boggins. Just then, they heard the shuffling of feet and luggage, taking each step carefully as they both walked down the stairs.

Mrs Marlow looked up with a small smile, locked eyes with him and said, "Not so fast, Thomas. We don't want any mishaps."

As Thomas ambled in the direction of his grandmother, she gave him her car keys, tapped him on the head and said, "Pop your luggage in the car and come back; we will say goodbye properly."

"Okay, Grandmother!" He cried.

Mr Boggins and Thomas sauntered through the door and down the old Victorian steps, through the small arrival garden to see the car parked directly outside.

Mrs Marlow had a blue Morris Minor Traveller. It had a wooden framed exterior, brilliant metal chrome bumpers and a shining metal chrome grill. These cars were ideal as they were like small vans and were perfect for living in the country.

Thomas looked for the keyhole on the right-hand door handle and pushed the keys into the grip of the boot. He shuffled and twisted the key as the holdall around his neck was moving around and getting in his way, further adding to the frustration of the stiff, awkward handle.

The handle opened at a right angle like a window to part-wooden part-metal stable-like doors on each side. He opened them both, stood back and thought,

"Wow, there is so much room for a small car. This is like a small van."

"Not that way, Thomas!" Mr Boggins said.

"Move the holdall out, and let me put these two cases in first. Then, I will jam and block the holdall into the side to stop the two cases from moving around on the journey," said Mr Boggins in an expert tone as if he had done this a thousand times before. Once the cases were in securely, Thomas closed the two doors, pushed the handle down and turned the key while juddering the handle vigorously to ensure it was locked safely and securely.

"Well done, Thomas! Let's go and say goodbye to Mrs Boggins," Mr Boggins said.

Thomas and Mr Boggins turned to walk the ten yards back to the house; Mrs Boggins and Mrs Marlow were on the doorstep talking and thanking each other for the time and the care taken for Thomas.

Mr Boggins walked back through the metal garden gate into the small garden entrance. The garden was excellently maintained with flawlessly pruned bushes and perfect flower beds.

Mr Boggins stretched out his hand to shake Thomas's hand and said, "It's been an absolute pleasure. I am going to miss my little helper, especially with the countless jobs I have to do around here."

Mrs Boggins rolled her eyes and winked at Thomas as if to say all these jobs are in his mind, and then gave a warm, loving smile.

"Come here," she said to Thomas. "None of that hand-shaking with me. Give me a big hug." She then grasped him and squeezed him for what seemed like days.

"Goodbye, Mrs Boggins. Thank you for everything, and goodbye, Mr Boggins; thank you for letting me help you with your jobs," He said.

"No, thank you!" said Mr Boggins with a smile and a wink and a pat on his head.

Mrs Marlow once again thanked them.

"I won't forget this and expect a card at Christmas!" Mrs Boggins cried.

"Come along, Thomas. Let's get in the car. We can wave goodbye as we drive off," Mrs Marlow said with an officiant attitude as if there was a schedule they all had to keep to.

I can see why Thomas runs everywhere, Mrs Boggins thought to herself, all this rushing around runs in the family. She smiled while waving her hands.

Thomas and Mrs Marlow gently turned around, walking towards the Morris Minor.

"Jump in the passenger seat," she said to her grandson.

"Okay," He said as he hurried around the car opening the chrome mental door handle while swinging the car door open and jumping into warm grey leather seats with stitched horizontal lines.

He looked across at the thin black steering wheel and the speedometer. The speedometer was unusual as it was positioned directly in the middle of the dashboard between the two seats.

He hadn't ever really sat in the front seat of a car, especially for a long journey, and the fact that he could see directly into the speedometer brought an exciting prospect to the journey.

Mrs Marlow coiled down the car window and then once again said thank-you to both Mr and Mrs Boggins, who had by this time strolled out onto the footpath opposite the house and positioned themselves to wave goodbye.

"Put your seat belt on, please, Thomas," said Mrs Marlow.

He fished his hands between the car seat and door, looking for the seat belt, clicking it into position and nodding his head as if to give the signal that he was all safe.

Mrs Marlow was feeling around for the keyhole to start the engine; she then twisted the key, and the car fired up, and the engine was running.

"Say Goodbye to Beth, Stephanie and Collin," Thomas said more out of politeness than anything else.

Then the car pulled away. "Goodbye!" shouted Mr and Mrs Boggins. A flurry of goodbyes seemed to be coming from every direction. As the car drove further and further away, Thomas twisted in his seat and waved goodbye from the back windows of the two-door wooden boot of the Morris Minor. He stayed as long as he could in this position to wave goodbye to them both. Until the car disappeared around the corner.

He then sat around facing the front, feeling slightly sad that he had to say goodbye and somewhat happy that he was with a family member.

He then looked up at his grandmother, who was concentrating on the road and felt a mixture of happiness and nervousness about the future.

His thoughts then turned to his old school friends and how he never really got to say goodbye properly and would he ever get the chance to see any of them again. These thoughts quickly turned to sadness about Mum and Dad and how he missed them dearly.

The Journey to Stoney Cross

"Put the radio on, Thomas, if you like!" Grandmother said loudly and sharply.

"Er er yes please, Grandma," Thomas said.

"Okay, sort it out then. We have a long journey, and there is nothing like music and the radio to pass the time," said Grandmother.

He leaned forward, jolting the seat belt safety mechanism, reaching out his hand to turn the radio on, then a blast of music came out of the tin sounding Morris minor speakers.

"Put the music on low; let's have it just as background music so we can have a good old chat. Next week is the start of the school summer holidays, so there is no point in putting you into school until September. So you can help me around the house." said Grandmother.

"Your mother used to love playing in the fields and running around the house in the summer holidays; you can look after the chickens and help me around the garden," she added.

"There is also a new boy who has moved to the house just down the road. He is from the village, so he knows the area well; they have just moved to our end of the village now."

"His name is Oscar. He is about your age and comes to the house often and helps out Mr Griffins, the gardener. I have told him that you are coming, and he seems excited." said Thomas's grandmother.

The houses in Stoney Cross were so far apart, and not many children in the village. Oscar was always hovering around working with Mr Griffins or chatting to Mrs Marlow and often popping into the house for lunch with Mrs Marlow, he was a cheeky chap, and everyone seemed to like him.

Mr Griffins, the gardener, was a lovely man; he'd been working the grounds of Mrs Marlow's for forty years, and he was also a woodsman for the local authorities, ensuring that the woods were looked after.

He was a tall, slender man always smartly dressed, with grey hair and blue eyes and a pale white appearance. Mr Griffins was always whistling and constantly pushing a wheelbarrow around. Thomas seemed to remember.

He was also fond of talking to Mr Griffins and often helped out whenever he came to stay at the cottage.

Thomas then drifted into a sleepy daze, still tired from a restless night, and he thought about his grandmother's house, which was enormous.

It was a big stone house with windows and different pitched rooftops all over it. It was filled with gabble rooftops, ridges and chimney stacks all over the top of the house.

Stonecross Manor had windows all over it with no actual uniformity, but it looked so beautiful it was so large. It was around three hundred years old and, it appeared that each generation had added to it over the ages, which gave it a unique charm and appeal to the building. Grandmother always said it had been in the family from when the house was built, and no other family had ever lived in it.

It had a long stone gravel driveway and garages on the left. From memory, there were big gates, the garages were once paddocks for horses, and these were huge buildings to explore.

He loved exploring the house in the past, and he loved the huge garden, grounds and buildings all over. The property and the gardens seemed endless the whole estate spread out over many acres of land. It had its own vegetable patches and huge lawns leading up to the woods, with the meadows and the fields in the distance. It was beautiful and a magical place to live.

If you looked left, there were woods and meadows, and if you looked right, there were woods and fields. The whole place was alive in the summer with flowers and butterflies and bees and green grass as far as the eye could see.

The house was positioned right at the end of Stoney Cross towards Lyndhurst, and a very short walk down to the Lyndhurst village shops. It was the most isolated house in the village, which took on the name Stone or Stoney Cross Manor.

The thought of spending the summer in the house was appealing to Thomas, but living there was slightly daunting; he had never stayed in the place on his own before, so this was another new prospect he needed to get used to.

He had fond memories of that house, but all memories consisted of his parents and their times—they had together as a family.

He gazed out of the window; while watching the English countryside go by at high speed, he wondered what the boy, Oscar, was like.

He wondered what kind of boy he would be and if they were going to become best friends. It would be nice to make a new friend, and to make a friend straight away would be even better, he thought to himself.

He had many thoughts, ideas and visions on this long drive with his head pressed up against the glass of the car window while listening to the music.

He thought more in detail about what Mr Boggins had said about the Stone Circles and the shadow warriors of the woods. What are they? He thought. Why has he never heard of them before? It was all extraordinary, and it added a layer of mystery to where he would be living.

After being in the car for hours and seeing Stonehenge as they raced past heading for Salisbury, he decided to talk to his grandmother about the Stone Circles and the shadow warriors and seeing Stonehenge was the ideal opportunity. But wary of what Gran would say, he would start the discussion off very softly and perhaps only talk about the Stone Circles this time. So talking about the Stone Circles would be a more straightforward approach because they are pretty standard in that part of the world. He didn't want to begin talking about shadow warriors with fear of sounding ill-advised with the information he had been told by Mr Boggins.

"Grandmother," Thomas said in a soft voice.

"Yes, my dear boy!" replied Grandmother enthusiastically. "What do you know about the Stone Circles?" Thomas said. "What do you mean?" asked Grandmother.

"There are many Stone Circles around these parts. You have Stonehenge and the Avebury Rings, Coate Stone Circle, and Ballymore Forrest Circle; there are many around these parts," said Grandmother.

"Okay, what about the Stone Circles in the woods."

"Also, the Stone Circles that move in the woods?" said Thomas.

"Who have you been talking to? Did your mother talk about this with you?" Grandmother said with a pressing apprehensive tone.

"No, Mother never once mentioned this to me. It was… it was… Mr Boggins mentioned this." Thomas said very timidly.

"Oh, well, take no notice then! It's just stories, old stories from the past," said Grandmother.

"There are many monsters, myths and legends. It's a very old part of the world, and with that comes myths and legends. Just you worry about normal stuff that a boy of your age should worry about," said Grandmother hurrying to move the conversation onto something new.

"I will introduce you to Oscar, the boy who lives in the house next door, tomorrow. He is a nice boy; he comes around the house all the time. He is eager to meet you because there are not many children around our end of the village," she added.

Thomas became suspicious because Grandmother was repeating what she had expressed to him early about Oscar being a nice boy who came to the house but in a slightly different way.

He decided not to continue the conversation and not press the discussion on more. He detected that the whole truth was not being told, and the way Grandmother had hurried the conversation on in such a rushed way also led to intrigue.

That's the second person that has shut the conversation down as soon as it started. Mrs Boggins did the same thing; she shut the conversation down and hurried to another topic, as soon as Mr Boggins began talking about the Stone Circles and the stone circles that move, and the shadow warriors too. Thomas wasn't sure why the conversation was being stopped. Perhaps the new boy Oscar would know something; he had been living there longer.

He sat back into the grey leather partly worn car seat, then faintly reclined the chair using a hand cranking knob; this was positioned down in the left-hand side of the chair, turning it back a few notched to make the chair recline.

He watched the world go by, thinking ever more about Stone Circles and the shadow warriors that Mr Boggins mentioned. He also thought about how Mrs Boggins shut the conversation down, then thought, why would Mum have known about this, and why didn't Mum tell me.

The whole conversation with Grandmother seemed to bring up more questions than answers, he thought.

He thought about his new home and about his new bedroom and his new garden. He'd stayed at the house many times before, but this time would be different.

He then thought more positively and started to think about new friends and again wondered what Oscar the new boy would be like. After five minutes of thought, he drifted off and fell asleep with his forehead pressed against the glass, then slumped diagonally in his chair with his arms positioned in-between the door and the seat; he fell fast asleep.

After a few hours, the car reduced speed and slowed, and the engine had become quiet, and Thomas could hear the tick-tocking noise from the indicator stalks from the old Morris Minor car.

His sleep was directly in tune with the sounds of the car. As soon as the car stopped, he started to stir and wake from his sleep.

Thomas knew he had arrived somewhere without the need to open up his eyes. Then again, without opening his eyes, he heard the clock like clicking of the hand brake pulling up to halt and to stop the car safely.

He could hear the noise of a button being pressed and the tic-toc sound from the car hazard lights flashing on and off. We've stopped, he thought, and his head popped up to look around.

Hello Thomas," Grandmother said softly.

"Where are we?" asked Thomas in a puzzled sleep tone.

"We're in Lyndhurst High Street, Thomas. Wait here, there are a few things that I need to pick up from the local shop before we get home. I will be back in five minutes," said Grandmother.

Thomas wound down his window and stretched his arms wide, and tried to outstretch his legs. The car was facing the footpath on his side, so he stretched his legs and got out.

It was a warm summer day, and the sky was blue. Many people were walking around up and down the bustling high street.

He looked one way and saw a bakery, a bank, newsagents, two grocery shops, two pubs, a café and two restaurants. It was quite nice and had everything that one needed from a local country high street.

Then a voice appeared over his shoulder. "Hello! I know this car; this is Mrs Marlow's car, and you must be her grandson, Thomas. Stand up, boy. Let me look at you," said an elderly lady of about eighty years old.

Thomas looked around and smiled. The lady appeared friendly, and it was pleasant to know that people were expecting him; it made him feel wanted and important. The lady was very small, had white hair and glasses, and walked with a cane, slightly bent over.

"Yes, my name is Thomas, and my grandmother is Mrs Marlow," he said.

"Pleased to meet you. I am Mrs Pucket," said the old lady. "Let me have a closer look at you; my eyes are not what they used to be," Mrs Pucket said.

He straightened his tie and blazer, stood upright in a military fashion, and looked directly at the lady.

"You're a special boy," said Mrs Pucket. "Has anyone ever told you that you are special," she asked as she stretched out her arm and bent her old fingers around Thomas's chin, pushing his face to one side into the sun. So she could look at his face from all different angles, then she moved his face backwards and forwards into the sun and into the shade.

"Yes, you are an exceptional boy. We will have to start work on you straight away if you are going to catch up with the others," Mrs Pucket said.

"Errrrrr! That's quite enough of that! Please, Mrs Pucket!" as the strong, stern voice of Mrs Marlow came into the conversation as if she had appeared from nowhere and right in the nick of time.

"Good afternoon, Mrs Pucket. We can't stop now; we need to be getting along. We have a busy day, and we need to get back to the house. Get into the car, please, Thomas," said Grandmother in a very hurried tone.

"You didn't tell me that the boy had the gift," said Mrs Pucket. Mrs Marlow walked around the back of the Morris Minor to put the bags of groceries she had just collected into the car.

"Now is not the time," said Mrs Marlow as she hurried and rushed back into the car, starting the engine as fast as possible. "Goodbye, Mrs Pucket."

Thomas, with the window, wound down, observed Mrs Pucket and waved goodbye with a smile on his face.

"What did she mean, Grandmother? Why did she say I was special?" He asked.

"Oh, Thomas, you are my grandson. Of course, you are special," Grandmother smiled and hurried the conversation onto another topic. "I've bought lots of food and groceries that I think you will like. You must write me a list of anything that you need and everything that you like in the next few days," Grandmother said efficiently and sternly. "Seat belt on, please, Thomas."

He clicked his seat belt on, sat firmly back into his seat, and went back to looking out of the window, again with a head full of questions regarding the fascinating encounter with Mrs Pucket.

Although Thomas was fascinated by the exchange of conversation with Mrs Pucket. He decided not to press for any more questions; he knew he would be at the house in hardly any time at all and started to think about his luggage, his new bedroom, and unpacking all of his things.

The car steadily drove through the village, past the Waterloo Arms pub, and out towards Pikeshill, then to the outskirts of town towards Stoney Cross.

Lyndhurst village was just like any other in England; it had pubs, restaurants, a small hotel and a small village supermarket with a huge church that you could be seen from anywhere in the village.

The car drove outside the main village road; they went up a small hill, then left, down a narrow lane for a mile past Emery Down, then down a road seldom used. "There's Oscar's house, you know, the new boy I told you about," Grandma said as the car raced by. Thomas shot upright and looked out of the window, thinking, Wow! That is not far at all, we are going to be neighbours.

Then with woodland on either side of the car, they drove down a narrow country road for a few hundred yards. Then with a sharp right turn, there it was, the main gates leading to the Stonecross Manor House. The car slowed dramatically and turned right onto the long gravel drive. On the right was a disused gatehouse, which was probably lived in when the house kept staff many years ago.

Driving very gradually up the gravel driveway, what sounded like a million tiny stones began hitting the underside of the car.

"Well, we're here, Thomas! That was good timing; there wasn't any traffic, and it didn't take as long as I thought," said Grandmother.

He stepped out of the car and looked around. It was early evening, and the sun was sitting low and directly into his eyes. He looked at the massive house with the many chimneys, smokestacks and windows of all shapes and sizes. The emerald green ivy ran all over the place, twisting and winding from bottom to top; he looked at the garage and old horse paddock areas and thought, so this is my new home. He was obviously sad but tried not to show it. He remembered his mum and father and how they often came here as a family, and now it was just him and Grandmother.

"Hello, Thomas," a voice came from the other side of the driveway. It was Mr Griffins, the gardener. He walked towards the car, and you could hear the crunching sound of the gravel with every footstep he took. Crunch-crunch-crunch was the sound the gardening boots made on the gravel driveway. He walked towards Thomas, and he could see him unpeeling his gloves one by one, stuffing the first glove under his arm-pit to take off the other.

"Hello, Thomas, my boy. Good to see you, lad," said Mr Griffins.

"You have a welcoming committee here somewhere, my boy," Mr Griffins said while looking around as if to search for someone. With that, you could hear the wooden scrapping sound of someone climbing the wooden gate that led to the back garden.

"Here he is! That boy pops up everywhere," said Mr Griffins. It was Oscar, the boy who lived next door. He had a cheeky face with brown eyes, blonde hair and wore shorts, a shirt, a dark green sweater and sturdy boots. He smiled over at Thomas, then at Mrs Marlow and Mr Griffins as he jumped down from the fence and ran towards Thomas.

"Oscar, gates have a wonderful way of working, as they open and close on hinges; you don't need to climb them," said Mrs Marlow to Oscar with a discerning look. He looked over at Mrs Marlow, smiled with his cheeky face, and gave the biggest smile. She pretended not to be influenced by his smile but couldn't quite mask her small smile at this cheeky but polite young boy.

In truth, she was happy that he had been waiting with such excitement. It was exactly what Thomas needed; a friend to help him settle in.

At lightning speed, he sprinted straight over to Thomas, skidding to a halt, making an outstretched line of skidding dirt in the gravel driveway as he stopped. He had even succeeded to get to Thomas before Mr Griffins.

"Hello, Thomas, my name is Oscar Williams. I live next door, and I have been waiting for you all day," He had an exciting tone to his voice as if he had been rehearsing the lines for days. Then, before Thomas could say anything, he talked again in a hurried sentence. "Well, I am not exactly next door. All the houses are so far apart here, but you know what I mean," said Oscar as if he had so much to say to Thomas.

You could tell that he was delighted to have a friend. Every day he helped Mr Griffins in the garden and talked to Mrs Marlow, so much that they had now become his friends. He worked and ate lunch every day with Mrs Marlow, and he had become a permanent fixture in the daily running of the house.

He stretched out his hand and said, "Pleased to meet you," shaking Thomas's hand vigorously.

Thomas replied politely, "I am very pleased to meet you, too, Oscar; my grandmother has told me so much about you."

By this point, Mr Griffins and Mrs Marlow were standing, observing the exchange between the two boys.

Mr Griffins stood patiently waiting for his turn to greet Thomas correctly, waiting for Oscar to finish his discussion. He looked at Thomas, smiled, patted him on the head and the back, and then shook his hand. "Good to see you, my boy, and it's good to have you here; we've all been looking forward to your arrival," said Mr Griffins.

"Come along. Let's get the luggage out of the car and up to Thomas's new room," said Mrs Marlow.

"I will help!" said Oscar with the most amount of eagerness and enthusiasm.

"I will help, too," said Mr Griffins.

"Oscar, can you stay for dinner tonight?" asked Mrs Marlow.

"Yes, I think so. Can I phone my mum?" asked the excited Oscar.

"Yes, of course, you can," said Mrs Marlow. "What about you, Mr Griffins? Can you stay for dinner, too?"

"I can't see why not; it beats having dinner alone with Meg," said Mr Griffins.

Mr Griffins lived on the Stonecross Manor estate; he had a small cottage close to the forests at the far end of the country estate. He worked as a full-time gardener and estate maintenance man. There were no actual words to describe his job or duties. His daily work consisted of gardening, chopping wood, tending to the vegetable patch, maintaining the car and all manner of things.

Mr Griffins lived in the small cottage with his sheepdog, Meg; she was always with him and never left his side. Meg had taken it upon herself to look after Oscar, and from time to time, she would spend her time with him, too.

Mr Griffins also separated his time as a local woodsman and spent a lot of time in the forests and woodlands, tending to the forest's needs. He ensured that streams and rivers remained unblocked and undammed and that seasonal wildflowers and plants all stood a chance. He correctly maintained and ensured that the local wildlife had the right environment and thrived by managing any imported plants or culling them to preserve the environment. So, the chance of a home-cooked meal with company and conversation seemed very appealing. This would also allow Mrs Marlow to break Thomas into the house gently and keep his mind from being upset about his parents.

Mr Griffins and Oscar took the two cases from the back of the Morris Minor, and Thomas grabbed the holdall. Then Mrs Marlow, Thomas, Oscar, Mr Griffins and Meg, the dog, walked to the oak front door of the Manor.

Mr Harold Griffins

"Wait outside, Meg!" Mr Griffins said to the very obedient and well-trained dog. Meg immediately sat down and readied herself for a wait outside the house.

Mrs Marlow, with one hand and two bags of groceries that were wound around her fingers in a wiry way that plastic carry bags get, fished around for the keys to Stonecross Manor; doing this with her right hand, she found the door key and in they all went.

The hallway was enormous; you could turn left or right or go straight ahead. It had wooden oak flooring and an Arabic style rug in the middle with landscape paintings on the walls with a grandfather clock and coat stand on the left-hand side. Thomas looked around at the familiar surroundings again, thinking, "Wow! Now, this is home."

"Let's go straight upstairs with the belongings! Thomas, you have the big room at the end of the corridor. Mr Griffins has given it a new lick of paint, so it looks great," Grandmother said.

The staircase was a dark, wooden winding staircase, and it led up to the upper floor in three stages. It had a big, round, wooden ornamental bannister post, which had been carved by a master carpenter and looked like a giant carved artichoke. Each portion of the wooden staircase had flair, and design and all the bannister posts had a twisted wooden elegance.

"You three go upstairs. I am going to the kitchen to unpack the shopping and organise dinner," said Grandmother.

Mr Griffins and the two boys walked up the creaky, squeaky stairs; they walked up towards Thomas's new room. He knew the way, so he led confidently; Oscar walked behind and talked to Thomas, explaining that he was glad to help and looking forward to becoming close friends.

Thomas could see his new room; the corridor was very long with several doors on either side, which consisted of other rooms, a toilet, and a bathroom and cupboard space.

"Here we are, this is my room," said Thomas.

He opened the door and walked into his room.

It was freshly painted and had three large windows, and he could smell the fresh paint. The curtains and the bed linen looked new. The bed was an old, wooden bed, and it was huge. The wardrobe was ample, and a writing desk and chairs had been set in the corner of the room.

"Where do you want these bags?" asked Oscar.

"On the bed is fine, please," he said.

Both Mr Griffins and Oscar walked over to the bed and placed the luggage on the bed.

"We will meet you downstairs for dinner," said Mr Griffins. "Come along, Oscar."

"See you downstairs, Thomas," Oscar said.

"Okay, give me ten minutes," he said.

He walked around in the room and looked out of the window at the vast stretch of land. You could see Mr Griffin's cottage in the distance. A perfectly manicured lawn with giant, pruned hedges, a big glass greenhouse on the left with the old farm building, and horse paddocks on the far left. He could see the forest in the distance beyond the lawn and beyond Mr Griffins's cottage; it was one of the most extensive forests in England, and he had never explored that far before.

"At least I am not going to be bored," Thomas thought. Oscar seemed like a nice boy, and he appeared to know the area well; and because the summer holidays had begun, they were going to have fun and explore the area further together.

He unpacked his things, mainly looking for his wash-bag, taking everything out, and placing them into drawers. He then took his wash-bag next door to the bathroom. The house had many bathrooms, and he already knew he would be using this bathroom independently.

His grandmother's bedroom and bathroom were at the other end of the house, so there would be the most amount of privacy.

After around ten minutes, Thomas was all unpacked and decided to walk downstairs. He wandered down the long creaky passageway and down the winding stairs and could smell dinner as soon as he got to the bottom of the stairs. As he walked into the kitchen, he could see his grandmother at the stove, at the point of dishing up the food.

"It's only sausage, mash, peas, and gravy," she said to everyone.

"That's perfect! Thank you, Gran. That's exactly what I need," He said.

A space next to Oscar was left open for Thomas to sit down. Mrs Marlow walked over with two steaming hot plates and put them down in front of the boys. "Thank you so much." Both Thomas and Oscar replied fervently.

"Here you go, Mr Griffins," Mrs Marlow said as she sat down at the long oak kitchen table. They all tucked in and ate.

"This is delicious," said Mr Griffins. I don't get a chance to cook big, hot meals like this with it being just me and Meg in the cottage. In any case, every evening, this time of the year. I am up in the woods and in the forest, walking Meg and taking care of the woodland.

"You go into the forests at night?" asked Thomas inquisitively.

"Yes, Thomas, it's my job."

"Especially at this time of the year."

"I need to ensure that some of the plants and weeds that don't belong here are kept at bay," he added.

"This ensures that the badgers and foxes and local wildlife are not too affected by these sorts of disruptions," replied Mr Griffins.

"Don't you get scared going into the forests at night?" asked Oscar as if he had asked the same question before.

Good question, Thomas thought to himself; Oscar is as inquisitive as me.

"I am not alone," Mr Griffins said.

"Oh," said Oscar." Who are you with? What do you see?

"There are all sorts of stories about the forest at night", he said, leaning forward as if to wait for Mr Griffins to give him an exciting answer.

"I will tell you why I am not alone up at those woods." Mr Griffins said in a mysterious voice, looking over both shoulders.

Both Thomas and Oscar stopped eating and leaned forward, looking at each other first, then turning their gaze to Mr Griffins.

Mrs Marlow looked at Mr Griffins in a cross, irritated way, thinking, what is he going say.

"I am not alone up in those woods BECAUSE MEG IS WITH ME!" With that, Mr Griffins leaned back in his chair and laughed loudly, and Mrs Marlow also chuckled and gave a small laugh while holding a stern face.

"Oh no, Mr Griffins, that's not what I meant!" Oscar said, irritated and deflated. He then started shaking his head and putting his hand over his face; he then laughed. Then, Thomas giggled, too. The whole table laughed.

"You boys are to be very careful going into those woods at day or night," said Mrs Marlow.

"I agree, Mrs Marlow. There's enough property and fun to be had on these lands; you boys have plenty of space between your houses, here," said Mr Griffins. "Oh, and if you boys get bored, I have hundreds of jobs you can do."

Mrs Marlow and Mr Griffins knew that the woodland could be very foreboding as it was full of cliffs, rocks and overhangs and a whole load of other dangers. The forest went on for miles in each direction; often, hikers could go into the middle of the woods and get lost and stuck for days and days, and each year, many rescues and search parties would take place.

"Who wants pudding?" Mrs Marlow interjected as if to have the perfect excuse to change the subject.

"Me!" both boys cried.

Mrs Marlow got up and looked directly into the eyes of Mr Griffins. Being a perfectly tuned-in boy, Thomas looked at their gesturing with their eyes and thought they knew something that he didn't. Oscar looked at Thomas, and he looked back as if they were on the same wavelength.

"Just you boys take the warning. I don't want to be on a child hunt going into that forest searching for any lost little boys," said Mr Griffins.

"We won't," they both said.

"Tomorrow, I can show you all the work Mr Griffins, and I have been doing in the vegetable garden," said Oscar.

"That will be fun," said Thomas.

Mrs Marlow looked at Mr Griffins as if her plan to find the boys a friend had begun to work and how they would be able to keep each other occupied all summer.

Oscar was particularly delighted as they had been growing all manner of things in the garden. He had been helping out for a few months now.

Oscar assisted with growing enormous pumpkins and peas, giant courgettes and leeks, and apples and rhubarb and had so much fun farming them. Now that the summer had arrived, he could visibly see the result of the hard work and efforts. Most of all, he could now show his new friend.

Thomas was also looking forward to the vast estate and huge gardens and the vegetable garden. In Kensington, he had a tiny garden, and he always enjoyed coming to Grandmother's house, mainly because the grounds were so enormous. Now he had a friend to have adventures with, too.

"Here you go, Thomas. Here you go, Oscar. A bowl of ice cream. Sorry, that is all I have right now. We got home so late," said Mrs Marlow. Both boys' eyes lit up as they grabbed their spoons to eat their ice cream.

"Thank you very much!" said Thomas to his grandmother.

"Yes, thank you, Mrs Marlow," said Oscar while eating a mouth full of cold ice cream.

As the dinnertime came to an end, Mr Griffins decided to leave. He got up, said goodbye to the two boys, and thanked Mrs Marlow for dinner. He walked back through the house to the front door, collected the obedient Meg at the entrance and walked to the other side of the estate. It was a five-minute walk back to his small cottage on the edge of the estate. It was in a perfect setting, and it was close to the forest and on the far end of the country estate. Mr Griffins had the best of both worlds living in the position that his jobs were in.

The two boys continued to talk about the property, where Oscar lived, and a shortcut across the field. They could meet at some point in the middle between the houses tomorrow morning.

"Come on, Oscar! We will drive you back," said Mrs Marlow.

By this time, it was getting late, and Mrs Marlow didn't want Oscar walking back all on his own. Even if it was a summer evening, and it was perfectly light outside.

"It's okay, Mrs Marlow, I can walk; it's only a run across the field," he said, wanting to prove to Thomas that he didn't live far, thus cementing that they were neighbours and about to become good friends.

"No, Oscar, I am driving you home; that's all there is to it," said Mrs Marlow.

"Okay," Oscar replied unenthusiastically.

Both boys got up from the oak dining table with chair legs screeching against the hard ceramic tiled floor and walked towards the doorway into the grand hallway towards the big front door.

"I'll get my keys. You boys go and wait for me by the car," said Mrs Marlow. Both boys walked outside to the huge courtyard driveway and walked towards the car.

"Did you know, Thomas, there's another girl our age who lives in the other big house on the other side of the estate?" Oscar asked.

"No, I did not know that," Thomas replied.

"Yes, she lives in the other big manor house, Tappington Hall. Her name is Holly. She's a good friend, and we should go and visit her at some point," said Oscar with a smile as if thinking he was putting a new gang together and how fun the summer was going to be.

"Yes, that sounds great. I would love to meet with the girl," said Thomas.

With crunching gravelly footsteps, Mrs Marlow came towards the car to drive Oscar home. That abruptly ended the conversation between the two boys, the way children do when an adult is coming.

The drive to Oscar's house was only three minutes by car, but driving a small boy home by car that time of night would make Mrs Marlow feel better, even though he had run across the flowering meadow a thousand times before.

"Both of you squeeze into the front seat together; it's not far enough to worry about getting into the back," She said. Both the boys looked at each other and squeezed into the front seat tightly, packed like sardines, sniggering to each other, and Oscar pulled the seatbelt across their two small bodies while they both laughed. Then with a blast from the engine firing up, the crunch from the hand brake, and the jolt from the car going into gear, they were off to Oscar's house.

It was a beautiful summer evening; they could see the sun beaming through the bright green shrubs and trees and millions of insects flying in the dusky evening rays.

It looked magical as they could see shards of light appear sporadically between the trees and shrubs, especially when driving in a car with the sun bouncing off the window like lasers. Then, practically minutes later, they arrived at Oscar's house, and as he had mentioned, it was no distance at all. Nevertheless, Mrs Marlow was happy that she had dropped him off safely.

Oscar's house was not small; it was a large country cottage with well-kept gardens and a well-maintained driveway. He lived there with his mum, Jane, and his father lived in London. They had decided to separate a few years ago, but Oscar's father Max still came to see him and stayed in the house regularly, mainly on weekends.

As the car came into the drive, there was a roundabout-style oval piece of grass so that vehicles could drive in and drive off quickly. Then, with the sound of brakes and the ratchet' sound of the handbrake, they arrived.

"Here you go!" Mrs Marlow said.

"Thank you," He replied enthusiastically. He jumped out of the car and stepped towards his front door. Thomas wound down the window down and shouted, "Goodbye, Oscar."

"Nice to meet you; Thomas and I will see you tomorrow in the morning. I will run across the meadow between our houses and meet you in your garden," said Oscar, excited and animated with a sunny smile on his face.

Mrs Marlow pulled away slowly. Thomas waved to Oscar, and he waved enthusiastically back. Then as the car drove away, He kept his hand out of the window, constantly waving until Oscar was out of sight. Then Mrs Marlow pressed on the car's horn, "Beep! – Beep!"

"He is such a nice boy; I knew that you would both hit it off!" said Mrs Marlow.

"Yes, he is a nice boy, and he's funny, too," said Thomas with a smile on his face.

Mrs Marlow drove the car back up the country lane with the sun beaming through the two back windows of the Morris Minor and back to the Stonecross Manor.

"Well, I think tonight, Thomas, it should be shower and bed. It's almost eight o'clock, and by the time you are ready, it will be past nine o'clock," Mrs Marlow said.

"Yes, Grandmother," Thomas replied.

He was keen to get back to his new room. He had not quite had the chance to see it or absorb it correctly as it was all such a rush.

Once back to Stonecross Manor, Thomas entered the hallway entrance and said, "I will go up now, Gran."

"Okay, Thomas. I will pop up and see you in a while to make sure you have everything you need, and you have fresh towels in the bathroom next to your bedroom."

He nodded politely and ran up the giant grand staircase up to his new bedroom. Mrs Marlow turned and smiled as she watched him run up the stairs. It was the sound of the boy' crashing his feet up each step like a herd of elephants—Bang Bang Bang—, and she thought to herself that this was a sound she would need to get used to.

After a shower, he got into his pyjamas and unpacked his things. He had a huge wooden wardrobe and two sets of drawers in each corner of the room. He had three large lead-piped windows with curly ornate metal handles.

He looked out at the new view. The view was spectacular and much better than the view he had in London. He looked out at a green-grass garden.

It was a gigantic, perfectly cut emerald green lawn with giant laurel bushes and cut flower beds overflowing with colours coming from the summer flowers, which had all come into bloom. On the left were the old stables in red brick with square old crooked clay roof tiles, and the brick garden buildings, which housed all the garden tools.

Behind the garden, buildings were giant evergreens perfectly trimmed and manicured ten-foot hedges. At the other side of that were the vegetable patches and greenhouses at the far end of the lawn, where the woods or the correct name Ballymore Forest. Then, to the right were ten-foot-high green laurel hedges and Mr Griffins's old cottage, which stood on the edge of Ballymore Forest. Then he could see rolling forest and meadows as far as the eye could see.

He peered out at the vast landscape surveying all he could see. He could see Mr Griffins and Meg, the dog outside his old stone cottage quite visibly from his window. Thomas watched Mr Griffins shut his front door, and with a whistle to get Meg's attention, he walked into Ballymore Forest. By this time, it was nine-thirty at night, and it was almost dark. Thomas thought to himself, what was Mr Griffins doing entering the forest at that time of the night? He thought maybe he was just taking Meg for an evening stroll and how brave Mr Griffins was to be entering the woods at night.

He was still thinking about what Mr Boggins had said earlier that day in the garden at the orphanage, about the stone circles and the strange goings-on in Ballymore Forest, and if anyone knew about this, it would be Mr Griffins. He has lived in Stoney Cross his whole life, and his father was a woodsman before him. So Mr Griffins knew the forests better than anyone.

He stepped away from his window and yawned and stretched. By this time, he had finished unpacking, had taken a shower, had brushed his teeth, and had got ready for bed.

Knock Knock Knock—the sound of a gentle knuckle tapping against the old wooden oak door.

"May I come in, please, Thomas?" asked Grandmother in a low-pitched whisper.

"Yes! Come in, please, Grandmother!" Thomas cried.

"Is everything okay, Thomas? I mean, do you have everything that you need?" she asked.

"Yes, thank you, I have been looking out at the view; I have just seen Mr Griffins going into Ballymore Forest," he said.

"Oh, he's always in those woods; it's part of his duties as a woodsman," said Grandmother. "Come along, let's get you into bed. I have brought you some milk."

Mrs Marlow peeled back the bed covers on one corner, and Thomas jumped into bed while adjusting his striped red and white pyjama shirt and trousers. Mrs Marlow leaned forward and kissed Thomas on the forehead.

"Goodnight, Thomas. Sleep well, and don't think you have to wake up early and rush around in the morning. You have all day," said Mrs Marlow.

"Okay, Grandmother. I am meeting Oscar in the morning," said Thomas.

"Okay, goodnight, and sweet dreams. I am just down the far end of the corridor if you need me," said Mrs Marlow in an easy-going manner. She gently closed the door and turned the light out as she left.

Thomas laid in bed thinking about Oscar, thinking about the long day and about Mr Griffins and the forest.

He gently drifted off into a deep sleep, thinking about meeting Oscar in the morning and what they would do all day.

Playing Around in Stoney Cross

The next day, Oscar woke and rushed all around his house. He got dressed as fast as possible, went downstairs to his mum, Jane, and sat for breakfast.

"Good morning, Mum!" cried Oscar.

"Good morning, Oscar," said Jane with a loving smile.

"How was everything yesterday with the arrival of Mrs Marlow's grandson?" said Jane.

"Thomas is a very nice boy, and we have arranged to meet in his garden this morning," He said, thrilled and excited.

Jane was delighted that he had a new friend. There were not many children in the area, especially as the houses were all so far apart. She was pleased that he would now have someone to spend the summer with and that he would be busy making friends, playing, and having adventures.

Both Oscar and his mother had cereal and toast with homemade strawberry jam for breakfast and drank tea and milk. Oscar explained that he was meeting Thomas and would spend the day showing him the vegetable patch and the area and the best way to run across the meadow to each other's houses. His mother sat and listened to her son and how enthusiastically he chattered about his new friendship. After breakfast, he kissed his mother goodbye and said, "It's almost ten, and Thomas will be expecting me."

He ran outside his kitchen backdoor into his garden to the very end of his wooden fence. He then climbed over and ran into the meadow. The meadow between the two houses had a trampled, dry, dusty one-tracked path that wound like a snake to the far end of the field. The meadow had long grass, and with it being summer, had yellow, red, and purple wildflowers everywhere. The grass was slightly wet from the morning dew, and the sun had begun to shine onto the meadow. He could see the buzzing and flying of millions of tiny insects.

He ran up the dirt track over a slight hill towards the property of Stonecross Manor to a well-kept and well-painted white fence, and as he had done a thousand times before, climbed over the nearest point of the wall instead of walking down to the corner where the gate was.

There was another bit of land Oscar ran through, which was just long yellow grass, with two massive mounds similar to two small hills, which looked like giant molehills but were actually two ancient burial mounds around four thousand years old. These were so common in this part of the world. The round barrows were positioned on either side of the meadow. The forest was close to the two-round barrows, and Oscar and hikers had used the path too. He then sprinted past the edge of the Ballymore Forest, past Mr Griffins's old stone cottage where he could see him outside with Meg. "Hello, Mr Griffins!" Oscar cried.

He seemed to run through at one hundred miles per hour in such haste, jumping over ditches and taking long strides when he needed to. Mr Griffins was out at the front of his old stone cottage working on some wooden sticks about one yard-long, and he waved, and Meg barked.

"Hello, young Oscar! Are you off to see Master Thomas?" asked Mr Griffins with a chuckle and a smile.

"Yes, Mr Griffins and I do not want to be late!" He shouted, breathless and dashing while running and gasping as he ran as fast as he could run.

By this time, Thomas had also woken up and walked around the house, got dressed, brushed his teeth, and sat with his grandmother having breakfast.

"What time is it, Grandmother?" Thomas asked while twisting and turning his head, looking for a clock in his unfamiliar surroundings.

"There's a clock up there directly above the oven."

"Also another above the fireplace," said Grandmother, wanting to show Thomas so that he knew for the future.

"It's 10," said Thomas anxiously. "I do not want to be late to meet Oscar because we said we would meet in the middle of the garden at ten. Do you think that Oscar will be there, Gran?" he asked.

"Most definitely," said Grandmother.

"Okay, well, I better go. Thank you for breakfast, and I will see you later!" Thomas yelled as he ran towards the kitchen door opening the huge cast-iron handle onto the enormous stone patio area, which was raised and overlooked the whole garden in an elevated way.

He stopped on the patio; he looked left, and the morning sun shone directly into his eyes. He then raised his right hand to his eyebrows to shade from the sun's beaming light. Thomas looked out at the area, looking left and right to see the direction of where he thought Oscar would come from.

Then from the corner of his eyes, he could see Oscar running out from the shadow the sun was casting on Mr Griffins's stone cottage, towards the centre of the garden.

Thomas raised his eyes with delight, and a huge smile came onto his face. He ran towards the edge of the elevated patio area, and instead of going left or going right using the stone steps on either side, he jumped off the patio onto the lawn. Then into the sun's rays and landing on his feet, he sprinted towards the centre of the garden with one continuous motion.

"Oscar!" cried Thomas.

"Thomas!" called Oscar.

They ran to the middle of the garden.

"Good to see you," said Oscar.

"Yes, good to see you, too," said Thomas.

"I just ran past Mr Griffins and Meg; he has a bundle of sticks in his hand," said Oscar inquisitively.

"Oh!" said Thomas, "What would you like to do?"

"I would like to show you the vegetable patch," replied Oscar.

Oscar had only lived in his house for five months and had been helping Mr Griffins out in the garden. So he mentioned this again this morning to show Thomas everything that he had grown and personally tended to. They ran across the lawn in the gap between the old stable barn into the vegetable garden. Thomas had been there many times before in his numerous stays at Easters, Christmases, and summer visits, but he let his new friend lead the way as he seemed eager to show him all his hard work.

Once they had run around the far side of the old horse paddock buildings, the partly shady and summer sun-filled vegetable patch came into view through the gap in the ten-foot hedges.

There was a series of eight square-cut soil patches, these were around three metres wide, and three metres long that had been cut into the grass.

These square vegetable patches were growing different things. Some had bamboo canes holding up runner beans like wigwam tents and peas winding straight up the trellised wooden fences that Mr Griffins had salvaged from somewhere. Others had wicker with dark green netting protecting them from insects, insect's intent on eating the newly grown luscious green shoots.

Thomas could see cauliflower, cabbages, carrots, rhubarb, and apple with pear trees in the corner of the fruit gardens, leading down towards Ballymore Forest.

To the left was another old, red brick wall, covered in moss and ivy. At the foot of the wall were metres of tomatoes and cucumbers. There was enough food here to feed an army, Thomas thought to himself, and it did look like fun.

"Here you go, Thomas. This is what I have been doing for the past few months; it's so much fun. Mr Griffins lets me use any tool in the tool shed, and I have been helping to grow all of these things."

"It looks amazing," Thomas marvelled.

Both boys walked around the garden and the vegetable patches and strolled through the small, fruit-tree orchards, exploring in and out of the old horse paddocks and brick buildings. Oscar walked with a new sense of permission as he realised that this was Thomas's new house, too, so if he was Thomas's best friend, it gave him extra permission to explore.

They spent time talking about the forest and the meadows and the local school and spent intervals asking each other things like when their birthdays were. They spoke about the local school. They also laughed and played while running around looking at anything and everything. Both boys giggled and shared stories, pushed each other around in the wheelbarrow, and had so much fun.

After a few hours, Oscar, who was lying in a wheelbarrow in the midday sun, as if not having a care in the world, said, "Shall we go and see Holly, the girl from Tappington hall? It would be nice to introduce you?"

Thomas asked, "Is it far?"

"No, it's a ten-minute walk across the meadow down by the river bank and onto the other side. And I know a shortcut," Oscar said proudly.

"Okay," said Thomas. "It would be good to meet Holly straight away."

The boys set out diagonally across the gardens of Stonecross Manor and walked past Mr Griffins's stone cottage along the edge of Ballymore Forest. They ran northward down the meadow where the hill stretched down along an embankment that led to a wooded area towards the River Avon. Together, the two boys had sticks and pretended to be warriors with swords, swiping and swinging at long grass as if they were slaying medieval monsters and beasts. Along the way, they sprinted downhill, giggling as they ran faster and faster

down towards the river as gravity took hold of their legs, and the hill became steeper and steeper.

As they reached the small woods which lined the river banks, Thomas asked, "Where now?"

"Well, if you carry on down this side of the river, then you come to Saxon Bridge, which is a ten-minute walk," said Oscar.

"If it's a ten-minute walk to Saxon Bridge, then it's a ten-minute walk back up the other side of the riverbank," said Thomas.

"Yes, but we are going to cross here," said Oscar.

He swiped his stick at the stinging nettles surrounding the green brush and revealed some rocks, and where the river was running shallow, he could see a series of quite tricky stepping stones, which reached from one side of the river to the other.

"Here is the shortcut I told you about!" the boys smiled at each other, and they both looked with telepathy and mentally agreed to cross.

One by one, Oscar jumped across the stepping stones and reached the other side of the river. "Yes! I made it!" he shouted.

Then, Thomas gently stepped down around the newly cut-down stinging nettles and held a branch as he made a leap for the first stone.

"That's it! That's the hardest one to cross; the rest are easy!" shouted Oscar.

Thomas then jumped and leapt to another, then another, and reached the other side. He yelled, "Yes!"

"That's saved us eighteen minutes!" Oscar said proudly.

They sauntered up the other side of the riverbank and reached an ancient flint rock wall. They both leaned with their chests against the stone wall and peered over at Tappington Hall. It was so huge and so grand, it was ten times the size of Stonecross Manor, and it was gigantic.

It was made from old sandstone in a muted mustard colour; it had castle-like turreted towers at one end and another building at the other end. It had fifty windows and massive collonades with the most amazing gardens that endlessly swirled along gravel pathways running between the pruned, clipped and trimmed bushes and cropped trees. It had statues, angels, and imps everywhere, with great stone vases or urns and giant stone statues nestled between the snipped shrubberies hidden like frozen forgotten people.

"Holly lives here, Oscar?" Thomas asked in wonderment and amazement.

"Yes," said Oscar!

"Come on, let's climb the walls and see if she is here," said Oscar hurriedly.

Both boys climbed the old rock wall, then crept and slinked around the vast gardens looking for Holly.

"This way, Thomas. She always plays over by the tree," said Oscar.

They both headed to the far end of the perfect striped lawn and over to the old, enormous yew tree. The yew tree could not be missed; it was the most giant tree with branches so big and so heavy that they had nestled onto the ground.

As they sneaked and slipped closer to the yew tree, they sauntered, creeping and hiding behind every bush, stone statue, and ornament. They got closer and closer without being detected. They could hear a beautiful girl's voice.

It was Holly! She was sitting on a rope swing with a wooden plank seat. The swing was attached to the rafters of the yew tree, seamlessly positioned inside the massive canopy of the tree.

She gently glided and swung back and forth as the sun's rays hit her face while singing what appeared to be hymns. She wore a white crocheted long flowing dress and was a pretty dark-haired girl with hazel eyes and a beautiful complexion with a small button nose and striking features. She seemed very happy with a beautiful smile and a kind nature and was glad to see the boys. "Hello, Holly!" said Oscar.

"Arhhhhhh, Oscar! It's so nice to see you!" said Holly.

"It's nice to see you, too," he replied.

"And who is this?" asked Holly.

"This is Thomas. He lives here now and has moved into Stonecross Manor just along the top meadow on the edge of Ballymore Forest," said Oscar.

"Hello, Thomas. I am very pleased to meet you," said Holly in a very well-mannered gentle way.

"Hello, Holly. I am pleased to meet you too," said Thomas.

"Do you like to play hide-and-seek?" Holly asked.

"Yes," he answered. "You certainly have the best garden in the world to play hide-and-seek."

"Let's play!" exclaimed Oscar. "I will count first; you two go and hide."

Holly grabbed Thomas's hand, and they both sprinted outside the umbrella of the giant yew tree into the sunshine and brightness of the central garden and hid under a giant statue surrounded by green shrubs.

"Shhhhh, Thomas. We can sit here and hide together," Holly whispered. They both sat down under the central plinth of the statue and with a shrub covering their existence and waited still, holding hands.

"ONE HUNDRED. COMING, READY OR NOT?" Oscar yelled at the top of his voice.

Thomas and Holly both sat still like figurines in the trunks of the bushes, smiling at each other, sitting cross-legged. They could hear the rustling footsteps of Oscar coming closer, wandering backwards and forwards. He had played this game before with Holly and systematically checked each statue, vase, and garden ornament; it was only a matter of time before he found them. Closer and closer, Oscar got, tilting his head, bending down on his knees and laying on his chest, checking everywhere. Then, he saw a glimmer of white; it was Holly's dress peering out from the shrubs beneath the statue.

"Ahhhaaaa! Got you!" Oscar yelled.

Holly screamed, Thomas yelled, and everyone laughed. These games went on for several hours, the three playing in the garden in the summer sun. After some time, they sat in the sun, crossed-legged, facing one another, talking. They sat by the old stone wall at the far end of the estate exactly where the boys had climbed over early that day.

Oscar talked about the stepping-stone shortcut that he had found and how he had shown Thomas the shortcut; then he jumped up, grabbed Holly's hand, and said, "Come on, I will show you, so you know the way."

Thomas shot up with enthusiasm, too, and said, "Yes, what a good idea; we can play down at the river for a little while."

Holly looked at both the boys and said, "No! I can't leave the grounds."

Oscar said, "It's okay; we are not really allowed down there too. No one will know; it's fun playing down at the river."

Holly once again looked at the boys and said, "No, I can't. I am not allowed to leave the grounds. I am sorry; I have had so much fun, and I hope you come to visit again soon," She smiled at the boys, "Nice to see you again, Oscar. It was a pleasure meeting you, too, Thomas," as she ran back towards the expanse of the gardens and the house.

Both boys looked at each other and decided that it was late, and they were both hungry. They headed back to the meadow. They both ran back down to the Avon River to the exact point they had crossed hours earlier in the day. With sticks in hand, they swung and swiped at the long grass and the nettles on the side of the river bank.

"Here it is!" yelled Oscar; he had found the stepping-stones. Thomas came running and spotted them, too.

"Here what is?" asked a mysterious high-pitched, very noble, very superior, and exquisite voice.

The boys looked around very sharply, turning their heads in all directions. A man not old and not young stood in a long black cloak, looking very smart, tall, and handsome. He was pale-faced with beautifully cut black hair and almost black eyes.

"Here what is?" he asked again.

"Er er er, we've found some stepping stones, which will take us across the river, and it saves us from walking down to Saxon bridge," Thomas, being the older of the two, decided to be the spokesperson.

"Looking to save time, are you? There are better ways to use these stones," said the mysterious man.

As the man came closer, they could see he was very handsome; his long black hair came into view from his sunny silhouette, a man with a white shirt and very beautifully dressed. "Well, you might be able to help me," said the mysterious man. "My name is Alwin, and I am looking for Harold, the Sceptre Man. Do you know where this man lives?"

"Er no," said Oscar.

"Well then, you boys are no good to me," said Alwin.

"How far down is this Saxon Bridge?" asked Alwin again in a hasty, annoyed tone.

"Saxon bridge is a ten-minute walk on this side of the river in that direction," said Oscar as he pointed down the river towards the Old Saxon Bridge.

"I will most definitely be seeing you boys around," said Alwin. Both boys looked at each other, confused.

"Good day to you both, and if you see Harold, the sceptre man, be sure to tell him that Alwin is looking for him—he's a dear old friend. He will know what I mean!" said Alwin.

The two boys looked and shrugged their shoulders as if to say what was all that about. They both headed down the bank across the stepping-stones and looked across; it was strange they seemed to come here on one set of stones and go back on another.

Oscar looked and said, "There are two sets of stones. I hadn't noticed them before, and they arched round in a circle."

Thomas looked over and nodded. Both boys headed back up the meadow towards Mr Griffins's old stone cottage.

"There's Meg!" Oscar shouted. They looked around as Meg came running towards them both, waggling her tail and licking the two boys as if she was the happiest dog that had ever lived. Then, two seconds later came Mr Griffins.

"Hello, boys!" he said: with a big smile on his face, grinning and shaking his head approvingly. "What have you both been up to?"

"We've been playing in the Tappington Hall gardens," said Oscar.

"I knew the orchard and vegetable patch wouldn't contain you both for long," said Mr Griffins.

"Have you had lunch?" he said.

Both boys shouted, "No!"

"Come up to the cottage. I will make some sandwiches," said Mr Griffins. They walked back up the meadow towards the cottage with Meg walking between the two boys, getting the most fantastic amount of attention from them both.

They sat outside the cottage in the sun on Mr Griffins's iron garden furniture. Which was solid and metal but very comfortable. Meg sat in-between the two boys and circled around until she found a comfortable spot to lie down. Mr Griffins went inside to make some ham and tomato sandwiches and to bring some water.

"Here we go, boys!" Mr Griffins, some minutes later, carried out a big tray of sandwiches and a jug of water. "There are six sandwiches there, boys! So tuck in," he smiled. The two boys leaned across and grabbed at the fluffy white sandwiches to eat.

"Mr Griffins, we met a man earlier today," said Thomas.

"His name was Alwin, and he said he was looking for the Sceptre Man!" said Oscar. Mr Griffins shot out of his chair, and Meg shot up, too.

"Are you sure he said, Alwin?" Mr Griffins asked, looking at both boys, concerned.

"Yes! Yes!" Thomas said, looking very worried and upset. Both boys looked at each other and started to wonder why his mood had changed.

"Where did you see this man?" said Mr Griffins. "Come inside the house and answer these questions, boys," he said as he ushered and herded the boys inside the stone cottage while checking over both shoulders.

"Let's start from the beginning," said Mr Griffins. "Are you sure he said, Alwin?"

"Yes," said the boys at the same time.

"Where did you see Alwin?" asked Mr Griffins.

"Down by River Avon, by the steppingstone crossing," Oscar cried.

"There are no steppingstone crossings; I have been working and playing in these lands for sixty years; there are no stone crossings," said Mr Griffins, bewildered, scratching his head.

"There is not one stone crossing. There are two," said Thomas.

Then it's a Stone Circle that's moved! And that's why Alwin was there, thought Mr Griffins. "Try and think, boys. Did he say anything else?" he asked.

"Yes, he said he was looking for the Sceptre Man."

"That he would be seeing him again very soon," said Thomas trying to think of every detail so that he could be as helpful as possible, recognising that it was important information.

"Okay, okay. Thank you, boys. He can't quite come to this side of the river yet," said Mr Griffins. "These are very peculiar times, and there's talk of strange things going on everywhere, boys. Promise me you won't go into the woods and that you will stay together at all times." Said Mr Griffins leaning down, staring at them in the eyes.

"What is a Sceptre Man?" asked Oscar nervously.

"A sceptre man is a wandmaker. Alwin needs a new wand, and I don't like making his kind 'wands,' but it's my job, and I am not allowed to refuse," said Mr Griffins anxiously.

"You make wands?" enquired Thomas.

"You know Thomas, you are just like your mother; she was always asking me about wands," said Mr Griffins. "In the current times, I think I better show you, boys, something."

Mr Griffins ambled towards the middle of the old stone cottage flooring and peeled back one corner of an old tattered Persian rug to reveal an old trapdoor with a brass finger hole for pulling it open.

Prince Alwin Aminoff

"Close that door, please, Oscar!" said Mr Griffins.

He bent down and opened the door, making it groan as it unfastened. The trapdoor revealed an old dusty and cobwebbed staircase leading down into the darkness. The boys seemed to be worried and excited about the prospect of going down a hole like this.

A few steps down was a rock wall and an old torch hanging up on a rusty old nail. Mr Griffins grabbed the torch and flicked the switch on. The staircase lit up. Thomas peered around Mr Griffin's tweed blazer, and he could see steps leading down but no bottom.

"Stay close, boys, eighty-eight steps are leading down here, and we don't need any accidents. These steps can be wet and slippery," said Mr Griffins.

Both boys walked behind the old man, going step by step into the darkness until they reached the bottom. Mr Griffins shone the torch against the wall looking for a light switch.

"Oh, here it is! The light switch!" he exclaimed. "I installed the lighting myself about forty years ago; my father used candles; there were candles everywhere at one point and his father before too." Mr Griffins said nostalgically.

The cave was incredible; it had stalagmites and stalactites, all glowing in the artificial lighting Mr Griffins had installed.

They were yellow, gold, orange, cream, and off-white, with crystals bouncing off the lights. The cave went on and on forever, and the boys could hear echoes of their voices in the distance getting ever fainter. They heard drops of water, could see ponds and lakes of water in the distance. This place was gigantic; it was like being inside a giant basilica.

There were rows upon rows of wooden bookcases and old, wooden shelves and hundreds and hundreds of polished wooden sticks. Some straight, somewhere twisted, somewhere thick, and somewhere thin. All were labelled with some sort of writing. They could see that each rack of sticks had been meticulously logged and recorded. There were thousands of them laying in batches in a well-ordered manner.

There were thousands of old paper scrolls, ink pots, and glass bottles filled with different coloured waters, with books everywhere. Books piled high with candelabras and old dripping wax on them. The old books were of all shapes and sizes.

There were labels on everything, again accurately logged and chronicled, so that all were written and well-ordered. The boys looked closer, and all the books were in a language that both boys could not understand. It was as if the shelves and bookcases went on for miles and miles and went ten-rows-high in every direction.

"Take a seat, boys," said Mr Griffins.

The boys sat down on two old leather green chairs opposite the oldest rock they had ever seen. It was piled high with books and with sticks and glass balls filled with fluid bubbling strangely. The two leather chairs had been worn at the arms and had seen better days, again looking like the oldest chairs they had ever seen.

Sitting down and watching across the rock at Mr Griffins, the two boys looked like they were at the desk of their headmaster or in a bank.

"Okay, boys, I need to give you a wand each, something simple that is not going to blow your head off, and something that is not going to get you into trouble," said Mr Griffins. "Wands are very personal; you can't just pick any old one."

Both boys looked around, still trying to take understand what Mr Griffins was saying. He shuffled some paper, put on his glasses and walked around looking at scrolls.

"Oscar, go to row twenty, down that way," said Mr Griffins, lifting his arm and pointing down one of the aisles in the distance. "When you get there, you will see hundreds of different wands. Pick them up, feel them, touch them and come back with one that feels comfortable. AND TAKE YOUR TIME!" Oscar ran down the passageway, counting up to aisle twenty.

Thomas sat patiently, observing Mr Griffins go to one side of the cave while running his fingers across the spine of the books. Then held up scrolls to the light, peering into the cylinders to read the letters as if he had read every single book and scroll in the whole network of caves a thousand times before.

"Oh! Here it is, Thomas, I have found it," said Mr Griffins. Thomas sat upright in a spritely way, as if eager to start his quest and hunt for his wand. "Go down to aisle ninety-nine, and again take your time; these things can't be rushed. You will know when you find the right one."

He jumped out of his chair, like a shot running down the caverns counting as he went and halted by the pond. He then came to bookcase ninety-nine, then bounding between the stalagmites and ducking underneath the stalactites, he searched, looking for his perfect wand.

Both boys had not asked the vital question, what were they choosing a wand for, and why Mr Griffins had a cave.

They were both excited and astonished at the prospect of everything going on; all questions could wait till later.

After twenty minutes, he could hear the first shout from Oscar. "Got one!" he said with an echo vibrating down all the caves over and over again till it went faint into the vastness of the cave network.

"Are you sure, Oscar?" Mr Griffins asked with a smile. In fact, Mr Griffins knew that you would only shout if you were absolutely sure. It's like that with picking wands or sticks in a forest; you always know which one you like.

He hurried back down the pathway dodging the small puddles and stalagmites carefully as he ran back to Mr Griffin's desk.

"Oh! You have chosen Betula Pubescens, an excellent choice, my boy! This is the perfect choice for a boy like you; this will do the job and not get you into too much trouble." He said with a meaningful expression on his face while holding the wand up to the light.

Mr Harold Griffins Great wand library.

Oscar looked pleased with himself while swinging his legs excitedly and impatiently under his chair backwards and forwards.

"We will wait for Thomas before we activate them; we need to do this together!" repeated Mr Griffins while looking down the shaft of the wand and rubbing it with a cloth.

After another five minutes, which to Oscar felt like an hour. You could hear the echoing yell from Thomas. "I have one! I have found one, Mr Griffins!" Thomas shouted enthusiastically.

"Are you sure, Thomas?" said Mr Griffins, smiling and winking at Oscar, knowing all along that Thomas's choice is always the right one when it comes to choosing wands. He came running up the pathway, bobbing and weaving through the rocky spikes, ducking underneath the stalactites, and jumping over the small puddles.

"Here you go, Mr Griffins, I have found one!" said Thomas as he panted and struggled for air, trying to talk and breathe at the same time with so much excitement.

"Another excellent choice, Thomas. You have chosen a Junipers Communis," said Mr Griffins with a proud, satisfied smirk on his face. It was almost as if he knew which stick each boy would choose and pick out before they made their decision.

He held the stick up into the light, squinting and peering with one eye and looking down the twisted shaft. It was a fascinating choice; this wand had a twist like a spiral and looked a tad knotted and gnarled. But Thomas was highly pleased with his choice.

Oscar's wand was smooth and straight, traditional, not too thick and not too thin, and he was enormously pleased with his choice, too.

"Come sit down, Thomas," said Mr Griffins. "I need to talk to you two boys. Before I activate the wands, I need to tell you both that these wands are not strong enough for anything other than defence and protection," He said sternly. Both boys were bursting with a million questions he could see on their faces. Nevertheless, they both sat and listened.

"They are never to be used for anything other than protection and defence. Do you understand?" Mr Griffins asked as he stood up, his deep voice echoing through the caves as he repeated himself.

"Yes, Mr Griffins!" Both boys yelled with confidence.

"Then let's begin," He said as he reached for his spectacles.

Activating a wand was easy; a magic wand was particular to the person. Each boy held their magic wands with both hands, and Mr Griffins said, "Repeat after me loud and clear, boys.

"Hoc magicum est multa sunt."

Each boy responded clearly, following each word carefully, grasping and holding the wands in the air. As they both said the words, the enchanted wands appeared an electric blue for a second and then went back to normal.

"Is that it?" said Oscar as he looked at Thomas.

"Yes, that's it! I didn't promise it would be glamorous and dazzling. They are both fully activated," said Mr Griffins as if he had heard that comment a thousand times before.

"What now?" asked Thomas?

"Now comes the hard work of becoming a wand owner and learning how to use it!" said Mr Griffins. "I am not a wizard nor an enchanted being of any description. I'm a Sceptre Man and wand-maker, a keeper of wands. Nor do I want to be a wizard or a magical being."

"So what should we do with them?" asked Oscar.

"I will show you now. Both of you stand up," ordered Mr Griffins.

Both boys stood and held their wands above their heads with both hands and closed their eyes in complete silence; they could hear the dripping of water in the caves.

"Now repeat after me," said Mr Griffins. "Umbraculum!" He shouted in a deep tone.

"Umbraculum!" the boys shouted.

"Again, say it," Mr Griffins ordered.

"Umbraculum!" Thomas and Oscar cried.

The wands gave out a fizz, and a hiss and each boy had a perfect purple spherical halo around them. It was electric blue and elaborate in appearance, and the spheres cracked, popped, and hissed. The boys opened their eyes and saw that they were in perfect protective bubbles. Thomas and Oscar were amazed and awestruck, and almost as fast as the protective bubbles came, they disappeared. Both boys' heads dropped with exhaustion as if they had both been holding something heavy.

"It's strenuous work, isn't it, boys?" said Mr Griffins.

"Yes, it's the most exhausting thing I have ever done," said Thomas, and then Oscar agreed, nodding, with both boys out of breath.

"Magic is exhausting, demanding and gruelling; magic is only as strong as the person holding the wand," said Mr Griffins. "Remember, boys, these are not powerful wands; they are only for self-defence, and I don't want you to use these out in the open where anyone can see. You must promise me, boys."

"Promise number one, keep these a secret," said Mr Griffins.

"Yes, Mr Griffins." Both boys cried.

"Promise number two, only use these for self-defence."

"Yes, Mr Griffins." Both boys cried again in complete agreement.

"I have a wand contract to be signed by each of you," He said. "This is standard wand administration work that my father, his father, and his father have been doing for nine hundred years."

The Griffin's dynasty kept records and archives of wands for centuries; it was one of the most important jobs a Sceptre Man could do. No one could walk out of the wand cave without signing a wand contract; it would render the wand useless without the wand contract signed.

Mr Griffins untied two contract scrolls and unfurled them, and asked each boy to sign. He pulled out a feathered quill and dipped it in a gold ink-pot, which sat on his desk. Both boys looked at each other, and without even questioning, signed each wand agreement. The ink began to sparkle with gusto and shine as bright as a star, then settled down. Thomas and Oscar looked at each other in utter disbelief.

"Remember, practice Umbraculum but only when you are on your own and in private. No one must-see," said Mr Griffins. Both boys nodded their assent and looked down at their new wands in astonishment and amazement.

"Come on, boys, let's go back up and finish off the sandwiches," said Mr Griffins. He turned the torch back on and switched off the lights. The cave then fell back into darkness. "Boys, hold up your wands and concentrate hard. You can light the way," said Mr Griffins. "Repeat after me. Lux splendida!"

The boys shouted, "Lux splendida!" With that, both wands lit up like a light bulb, lighting the way up the eighty-eight steps. They walked back through the trapdoor and put down their enchanted wands to stop the light; Oscar unbolted the door to the cottage and sat back down on the metal garden furniture to finish eating. Once again, Meg was pleased to see the boys, and she settled down between the two seats.

"So, you are Harold, the Sceptre Man that Alwin was asking about?" asked Thomas, glancing at Mr Griffins sideways.

"Yes, that is me," said Mr Griffins.

"What does he want you for?" asked Oscar.

"He wants a new powerful wand and probably not for doing good," said Mr Griffins.

"Can't you just say no?" asked Thomas.

"I can't say no. It is my burden and responsibility to supply wands to good and evil. My surroundings are considered sanctified grounds, and the wands do not work properly on my property. So, I am considered to be neutral," answered Mr Griffins.

"What do you mean, neutral? Neutral from what? And who is Alwin?" probed Thomas.

Mr Griffins looked at his watch and explained that it was a long story and very late. They finished up the sandwiches and jug of water, said goodbye to Mr Griffins, and they walked to the halfway point of the meadow between Thomas's and Oscar's house.

When the boys were in the far distance, Mr Griffins shouted, "Thomas, tell your grandmother I will come over this evening for a conversation after dinner at eight o'clock!"

"Yes, Mr Griffins, I will!" Thomas yelled from halfway up the meadow, cupping his hands around his mouth.

Mr Griffins hurried inside the stone cottage and began preparing himself for a meeting with Mrs Marlow.

The boys stood talking in the meadow, grasping their new wands and looking at each other in complete disbelief at the day.

"Well, this has been the craziest day ever," said Oscar, shaking his head in complete perplexity.

"I know, we met Holly today and Alwin, and now we have these wands," said Thomas. "We should hide them under our shirts."

"Good idea!" Oscar said as he began untucking his shirt and stuffing his wand in the waistband of his shorts.

"I better go back now; it's late. I think Grandmother will be worrying," said Thomas as he looked back at the Manor.

"Okay," said Oscar.

"Shall we meet tomorrow at the same time, in the same place?" asked Thomas.

"Yes!" said Oscar enthusiastically, nodding his head.

Both boys bid each other goodbye. Oscar ran down the dirt track and to the stone wall to his garden. He then jumped over his fence while Thomas ran the equal distance into his garden and up to the raised patio of Stonecross Manor through the back door of the kitchen in the house.

"Hello, Grandmother," said Thomas, puffing and panting. "Hello, Thomas! It looks like you have had a big day!" said Grandmother.

Mrs Marlow was facing the kitchen cooker, stirring a casserole she had just taken out of the oven. She then stopped suddenly, lifted her head, and squinted her eyes.

"I can feel that," Grandmother said.

"Feel what?" Thomas said nervously, not understanding what was going on.

Mrs Marlow turned around and, from the other side of the kitchen, said, "Lift your shirt, please, Thomas."

"How did you know?" He asked.

"Do you think I don't know the feeling of a wand coming into my house, young Thomas?" Grandmother asked in a stern tone, looking down at the boy.

"Let me have a look at the stick, please," Grandmother said as she held out her hand.

He handed over the wand and gave it to his Grandmother. Mrs Marlow looked at the enchanted wand and said, "What an interesting choice, Thomas. This won't do any harm to anyone; this is only for self-defence," she said knowingly.

"How do you know?" asked Thomas, confused, looking at the wand.

"You just make sure no one sees it, and I will have a talk with Mr Griffins," said Grandmother.

"Mr Griffins gave this to me because of Alwin," said Thomas.

"What do you mean, Alwin?" asked Grandmother grasping at the boy with both hands gripping his shoulders.

"We saw a man called Alwin today, down by Avon River and the stepping stones," said Thomas.

"What stepping stones? There are no stones down in Avon River!" said grandmother, all confused while looking out at the window.

"Mr Griffins said he would come over to talk to you after dinner tonight," said Thomas.

"Okay, let's just have dinner for now, and I will talk to Mr Griffins later," said Grandmother.

Mrs Marlow laid the table and started to serve dinner, all the while not concentrating on her job as if she had the weight of the world on her shoulders.

Thomas positioned his wand on the table in a delighted, pleased way, occasionally looking at the new magic wand, and started to eat dinner.

He talked about the day he had, and he chatted about the garden and talked about Oscar. He spoke about his day and did not mention meeting Alwin or Holly at Tappington Hall or the stepping stones.

Grandmother appeared to be listening but never really got involved, giving an occasional smile and agreement without engaging in conversation.

After dinner, it was around eight o'clock, and it was tranquil and bright outside, but the darkness of night was coming; Thomas decided to help in the kitchen and say goodnight to Grandmother and take a shower and go to bed. Clutching his new wand, he walked out of the kitchen down the hallway into the hall and walked up the grand wooden staircase looking at the paintings, landscapes, and portraits and swinging his new wand along the way.

Mrs Marlow said goodnight to Thomas, trying to give him attention and the appearance that everything was well, and she would be up later to say goodnight. She began to wipe the kitchen down and prepare for the arrival of Mr Griffins.

Knock Knock Knock—it was the sound of the back kitchen door; Mrs Marlow stopped what she was doing knowing that it was Harold and shouted, "Come in, Mr Griffins!"

He walked into the kitchen, took off his cap, and said, "Good evening Mrs Marlow."

Mrs Marlow replied calmly, "Good evening, Harold. Would you like a cup of tea?"

"Yes, please," said Mr Griffins.

Hearing the knock on the kitchen door from upstairs and the slam of the big oak stable door closing, Thomas snuck down the stairs and sat halfway up the enormous wooden staircases trying not to make the old oak wooden floorboards squeak; he tiptoed onto a step and sat down to listen.

Mrs Marlow fetched the tea, sat down at the long kitchen table opposite Mr Griffins, and poured the tea.

"Tell me everything you know," said Mrs Marlow.

"It's the two boys that know more than me. But from what I can gather, the stone circles have begun to move, and Alwin has appeared for the first time in years," said Mr Griffins.

"I didn't ask Thomas directly. That boy has been through enough," said Mrs Marlow.

"I gave both boys a wand for protection only," said Mr Griffins timidly.

"Yes, I could see that, and not very powerful ones, which was very wise. Thank you, Harold," she said appreciatively and with a small smile.

"There's more, Mrs Marlow," said Mr Griffins. "I have been going into the forest at nightfall, and there's talk of strange things with the woodland folk, birds have begun to fly in peculiar ways and avoiding certain parts of the forest, and the stone circles are beginning to move again."

Mr Griffins continued explaining that he had been back over the great library of books and scrolls dating back nine hundred years of Griffin's occupation. He had been reading through the archives and records. Frantically studying in the caves of Stoney cottage, and checked all the signs. The stone circles had been moving, even the sun was sitting differently at Stonehenge, and the deer and wild horses had begun to behave differently.

"What are you saying?" said Mrs Marlow running out of patience and nervously leaning forward. "Get to the point, Harold."

"I think there has been a movement of people between the circles again," said Mr Griffins.

"I can't be certain, but if Alwin was wandering through the circles, then others would be too," said Mr Griffins.

"That's it, Mr Griffins. I have no choice; it's time for a gathering," said Mrs Marlow.

Mrs Marlow explained that the shadow warriors had always been there watching over the circles guaranteeing that the gateways were managed, and it was her job to call them in for a gathering. It was the first gathering in years, and there was a lot to organise, and everyone who mattered would be summoned.

"I will need to see Lorsan Yeldrove. He will need to be contacted first," said Mrs Marlow.

"Lorsan?" said Mr Griffins in a surprising way leaning back on his chair.

"He's a shadow warrior, one of the old chieftains from Tanniv," said Mrs Marlow.

"I will send word to arrange a meeting with Lorsan," she said.

"I know the Stone Circles are moving, and Alwin has been seen. But are you sure at this point it's worth gathering? The kings, chieftains, shadow warriors and Woodland folk?" said Mr Griffins.

"What more evidence do we need?" said Mrs Marlow. "It has been our job to watch over the two realms like beacons, and although we had prayed this day would never come, it has begun."

"Alwin is no real threat here; he just wants a new wand from me," said Mr Griffins.

"It's not Alwin I am worried about. Yes, he can cause damage, but it's the Empress. She has wanted power for years. She has desired control over the circles and the gateways to both worlds, Alina is no longer here, and Alwin has seen Thomas," said Mrs Marlow, driving her fists down onto the oak table.

"Perhaps you're right," said Mr Griffins shaking his head in disbelief in a mournful way.

"I will do what I can when I can, but I must always remain neutral," He said.

"I know, my dear friend—I know!" said Mrs Marlow. "I must summon a gathering; I will get to work on this right away."

"Okay, I will get back to Stoney Cottage now, Mrs Marlow. I have a lot of reading to do; there will be things expected of me now," said Mr Griffins.

"Goodnight, Harold and whatever needs to be done needs to be done!" said Mrs Marlow.

Thomas was still midway up the staircase, listening, snooping; his mind was going into overdrive. "I will need to tell Oscar everything."

Thomas could hear the conversation coming to an end, and he could hear the dragging noise of the wooden chairs against the floor grating. He got up and tiptoed back to the top of the landing. Still not quite believing the conversation had ended, he hovered around, waiting to see what Grandmother was going to do.

He could hear the goodbyes from Mr Griffins and the closing of the kitchen door that led out onto the patio and back garden, and he edged back down the hall to his bedroom.

He could hear his grandmother rustling around looking for something. So Thomas stayed within earshot to find out what was going on.

Mrs Marlow was looking for a key that she found hidden at the back of the cookery bookshelf in a secret location. It was an enormous black ancient key that looked older than time.

She closed the curtains in the kitchen, walked into the hallway, and then closed the curtains all around the lower part of the house.

Looking over both shoulders, she slinked quietly towards the grand staircase to a cupboard door under the stairs. She unlocked the door, opened the creaking old door, and walked down to what appeared to be a basement.

She flicked on a light switch at the top of the stairs and carefully stepped down some ancient stone stairs. As she got closer to the bottom, the chamber was colossal; it went on forever. It was dark and black, and the walls were filled with books, bottles and jars of different coloured potions, and row upon row of old books, the walls were lined with huge rocks, and each stone had engravings written in an ancient language long forgotten.

In the middle of the chamber was a vast stone circle a fraction of the size of Stonehenge but still impressive. The henge looked thousands of years old and looked like the Avebury rings or the Stonehenge itself.

Mrs Marlow collected her wand, which was sitting on an old wooden desk, and repeated the words, "Tupel, Sathgang, and Yinfon" over and over aloud.

Thomas could hear something from the top of the landing he was unsure of and crept down the stairs to investigate further, skulking down the stairs one by one; the voice got louder and louder. He had reached the hallway and could see the doorway below the stairs was open; he turned and walked down onto the basement stairs. Thomas crept about halfway down, then sat just below the line of sight behind a rock that covered the chamber and the stairs. He could see the cave, and his grandmother, and the stone circle.

"Tupel, Sathgang, Yinfon; Tupel, Sathgang, Yinfon; Tupel, Sathgang, Yinfon; come to me my old friends. Come to me!" She bellowed brasher and ever louder.

A bright light emerged out from the middle of the stone circle, then it formed a gold ring, with scenery appearing and coming into focus. Then flying towards Mrs Marlow and into the cave came three great horned eagle owls.

"My old friends! You have come to me in my time of need," said Mrs Marlow with a smile on her face.

The three owls circled around the stone rings and each settling on a sarsen stone facing Mrs Marlow.

She walked over to each owl and stroked them as if she was stroking an obedient pet. The owls were enormous; each had bright orange eyes and speckled feathers with the largest eyebrow horned like feathers.

Tupel, Sathgang, and Yinfon The Giant Eagle Owls.

The birds looked wise and understanding, as if they knew what they needed to do and had done this before.

"Tupel!" called Mrs Marlow. "Tupel, go fly and tell of the gathering. Explain that a gathering has started on the Mountains of Stormhorn and all that the great lords, king, and chieftains will gather in the great halls of Stormhorn. Tell Lorsan Yeldrove his bloodline is needed once again."

"Sathgang," called Mrs Marlow as she walked towards the megalith that Sathgang had settled on. "Sathgang, go fly and tell of the gathering.

Go to the forest of Vakoborg, the Forest of The Great Oris Gorge and tell of the gathering at the great halls of Stormhorn. Tell the Disaris people, the king, and the mining Turgett's of Jandar."

"Yinfon," called Mrs Marlow as she looked around at Yinfon. "Yinfon go fly and tell of the gathering go to the Tarrenash plains and the rock mines of cloven town and tell of the gathering at the great halls of Stormhorn in Mountains. Tell the Turgett Lord in Qulan and deep in the mines of Jandar." Mrs Marlow tied a message to each of the owl's yellow legs.

The three owls stretched, hooted, and with their giant wings, they flew in a ring around the great stone circle in an energetic display.

Thomas gasped. Mrs Marlow looked around and could spot Thomas and his feet. Not wanting to break the concentration, she thought, I will deal with you later, young man. Thomas ducked down thinking, did I get seen, or did I bend down in time? Not really sure, he ran up the old damp stairs, up to the main hallway, up the staircase back to his room. He got straight into bed, buzzing from what he had just seen.

Mrs Marlow focused on the three birds of prey who flew back through the gateway portal and out into Tanniv.

Tanniv Land was not another world; it was the same world like Earth. The two places, Earth and Tanniv, existed side by side, and both places needed each other to survive. The Stone Circles existed as a portal between the two locations, and only very few people knew how to use the circles correctly. Different cultures buried their stone rings like in Göbekli Tepe to stop them from being misused, but Stonehenge, Carnac and Avebury were still very much open.

She closed the portal, safe in the knowledge that the messages would be delivered.

The great halls of Stormhorn were four days' walk through the Stone Circle portal in the Ballymore Forest, and there was a lot of work to do.

It was the first time in years that a gathering was called, and this was to be the most significant gathering that had ever been written about. If all the lords, stewards, kings and queens were to come, she would need to be organised, and many things needed to be done.

Mrs Marlow looked back towards the stairs and had realised that Thomas was gone. I will leave him till the morning now, she thought to herself.

That night, Mrs Marlow went to bed, and Thomas laid in bed thinking about what he had just seen. He thought about meeting Alwin and the hours spent wand-hunting with Mr Griffins down in the grotto of Stoney cottage; he thought about his new magic wand. Then about Oscar, about Holly and playing in the gardens of Tappington Hall. He was worried about what Grandmother would say if she did see him. He also thought about talking to Oscar in the morning because he needed to tell him everything he had seen.

Being a big day and having a lot to think about, Thomas drifted off into a deep sleep.

The following day, Thomas woke up to the faint sound of his grandmother in the kitchen. He got out of bed, opened his curtains and could see it was another crystal clear blue-skied English summer's day in the New Forest. What could today possibly hold for me? Thought Thomas as yesterday's events flashed through his mind.

He ran down the hall to his bathroom and brushed his teeth while getting ready for the day; he ran back to his bedroom and put on shorts, socks and a shirt. He then went to his top drawer, where he kept his socks and got his new wand.

He then walked down the stairs very timidly, not really knowing what Grandmother would say to him or how he would be greeted or if she had seen him last night underneath the house. So, he walked down to the kitchen with a sense of hesitation and uncertainty.

As Thomas ambled down the upstairs hallway towards the staircase, he wondered what conversations grandmother had in mind for him and prepared himself with different scenarios in his mind.

He walked down the old staircase gripping the handrails all the way down as his hand made a squeaking sound; he then jumped off the last step and walked past the door under the stairs where the newly discovered Stone Circles stood. He opened the door nervously, and he could see Grandmother at the stove.

Mrs Marlow looked over her shoulder and said, "Good Morning Thomas!" with a thunderous chirpy voice, as if she had planned to be overly happy to through him off the cent for spying. Thomas looked puzzled and thought, maybe she did not see him.

"Good morning, Grandmother," Thomas said with a surprised tone.

"Jam on toast and porridge this morning, young Thomas," grandmother said.

"Yes, please," He said.

"We have a hectic day ahead of us," said Grandmother assertively.

Mrs Marlow placed jam on toast in front of Thomas and a hot bowl of porridge.

"There's honey over there if you want it and some orange juice," said Grandmother as she patted him on the head. He was now feeling totally at ease, which is how Mrs Marlow wanted him to be.

"What are your plans for the day, Thomas?" said Grandmother.

"I am meeting Oscar in the meadow in a minute," He said.

"That's good because I will need both you boys today," said Grandmother. "Untuck that wand from under your shirt, Thomas. You can keep it out in the open, now," she said strictly.

"Okay, Grandmother," said Thomas.

"So first things first, young Thomas. I know you saw me last night, and I know that you saw everything. It's about time you knew everything; these are potentially dangerous times," said Mrs Marlow. "Go and get Oscar, and I will explain to you both."

After breakfast, he ran out of the back kitchen door across the lawn, down past Stoney Cottage and into the meadow between Oscar's and Thomas's house. He stood in the morning sun for several minutes until he could see a silhouetted figure of a small boy in the sunshine, climbing over his stone wall into the meadow.

"Thomas!" Oscar yelled at the top of his voice and ran through the meadow with his wand in hand.

"Oscar!" He shouted, waving his arms wildly.

"Oh, have I got a story to tell you!" Thomas said, shaking his head to animate the exchange. Oscar's eyes lit up as he eagerly anticipated the following words he was about to say.

Thomas explained what had happened. He described that Grandmother knew about the wand as soon as he walked into the house; he explained about the conversation with Mr Griffins, then about the cave underneath Stonecross manor and how there was a magic stone circle. As they leisurely strolled back through the meadow past Stoney cottage and towards Stonecross manor, Thomas managed to explain everything without hesitation. He described the three magic owls and everything that he saw in the cave and that Mrs Marlow was some kind of magic lady.

For the first time in his life, Oscar was speechless. He listened carefully as they slowly walked back to Stonecross Manor, nodding and walking sideways to capture all emotions on Thoma's face as he explained everything.

"So my grandmother has asked to see us both together; she wants to explain what is happening," He said.

"Okay!" Oscar said enthusiastically as they walked into the gardens and up to the house.

Both boys walked up to the raised patio area of the manor and into the kitchen.

As the boys walked into the house, Mrs Marlow was sitting at the kitchen table reading a very thick book that looked a million years old and had piles of books scattered all around her, with tall stacks of books spread all over the long oak kitchen table.

"Good morning, Oscar," She said, peering up to say hello.

"Good morning, Mrs Marlow," Oscar said with a smile on his face.

"Would you like a drink Oscar?" Mrs Marlow asked as she stood up to walk towards the far end of the kitchen.

"Just water is fine, Mrs Marlow. I will have some biscuits if you got them," said Oscar with a cheeky face.

Mrs Marlow grinned as if hearing something normal was precisely what she needed to hear after all the drama of the past twelve hours.

She filled a big glass jug of orange juice and some biscuits on a plate with two glasses. She then told both boys to take a seat at the kitchen table and explained the best way she could without scaring the two boys too much, fully aware that all of this may be a lot to take in.

Mrs Marlow explained to Thomas and Oscar that she was a White Sorceress and one of the guardians of the Stone Circles, and the family bloodline had been protectors of the Stone Circles for thousands of years.

The stone circle underneath the Stonecross Manor is five thousand years old and is one of the gateways to Tanniv Land.

Both boys sat with their jaws wide in total astonishment, and amazement both listening carefully but with more questions than answers filling up their minds; they both remained quiet to listen to every word being said.

"So the Stone Circle is a doorway to another land," said Thomas, muddled and confused.

"No, it's the same place, it's the same planet, it's just a different time," said Grandmother.

Mrs Marlow explained that time was an artificial concept; places like Stonehenge and Göbekli Tepe were built to manage time and the season and move through the portals so that people could learn from mistakes from the past for the benefit of the future.

Over time the knowledge of the portals had been lost. Many powerful stone circles like in Turley near the old Fertile Crescent had been buried thousands of years ago, and this was done to stop them from being used, but they have been found and dug up again. Only a few in this period knew of their existence and how to use stones circles around the world in England and Carnac France.

She explained that like present day-earth, Tanniv land had its wars and problems and conflicts, just like modern times; however, the new threat was more severe than anything happening in the world today.

A queen who called herself the Empress Aminoff of Tanniv and Earth wanted to be Empress of Earth and Tanniv and would stop at nothing to fulfil her so-called destiny.

She was banished to the far side of the Ilihorn Mountains, where she stayed with her army and allies and swore she would return one day to take the Stone Circles and the gateways and portals to reside in both times.

Years ago, the Armies of Tanniv gathered together on a field of battle west of the river Ailmar against the Aminoff Armies; during; the battle, the Aminoff had been driven back across the mighty river, back to the Mountains of Ilihorn.

As her armies were driven back into the dark mountains, the West Tanniv Armies and the shadow warrior clan followed in pursuit to finish the Aminoff's forever. But this was a deception, a trap. The pursuing army became imprisoned in a maze of canyons, and a great mountain battle took place for many months.

Countless soldiers from Tarrenash and the Disaris of Vakoborg, the Turgett people, and woodland folk lost their lives in this snare. But she was damaged, too, and many of the Aminoff Army died in the countless assaults they made on the West Tanniv Army.

The armies of West Tanniv lost many great warriors, but the troops of Aminoff were tremendously damaged and injured too. A truce or peace was never agreed upon; the battles and skirmishes became fewer as money resources and lives had run out.

Neither side has recovered enough to damage each other again or be a real threat to this day. Some of the warriors of West Tanniv remain to defend the last bastions and outposts against Empress Anastasia Aminoff.

These warriors are called shadow warriors. They set up a sequence of remote castles and fortifications along a thousand-mile line to hold off the threat of an Aminoff attack again.

The defensive line would be no real threat to anyone if the Aminoffs decided to rise again. The shadow warriors were an elite fighting force numbering in the thousands before the great Ilihorn trap, and now all that remains are a few hundred.

The shadow warriors wandered and travelled between circles in the great forests gathering information and intelligence are waiting for an attack to this very day.

All that separated West and East was a mighty river called the Ailmar River, and it is vast and is the clear distinction between West and East. It is the natural line that both armies fell back to, creating a West and East continent to this very day.

Queen Anastasia Aminoff

Queen Anastasia was not an authentic empress, but she called herself Empress Anastasia Aminoff of Tanniv but was an actual Queen of Moltenwing.

She lived in the great Capital City of Moltenwing.

This city is east of the river Ailmar, and the lords and nobles of Moltenwing were loyal to the Aminoffs.

Moltenwing was the capital city of East Tanniv and was strategically placed in the centre of Tanniv; it had control of the cities and towns from all of the surrounding areas.

The Aminoffs controlled all the wealth, prosperity, and riches throughout East Tanniv. Along with all the farming and the precious metals of Ilihorn.

It controlled the rivers and everything east of the river for thousands of miles in each direction; they held the Hiligor Sea, as the Aminoff had a mighty navy, which contained all the trade. It had set up an administration centre for counting and controlling the wealth and built up a reputation for managing prices and currencies, which also had its effects in West Tanniv.

The capital of Moltenwing is the most magnificent city in Tanniv. It was built to look imposing and intimidating; it was built to surprise and bewilder all that came to the great city; it was made from the wealth coming in from the great farming plains, from the slaves that died for it. The exploitation from all the cities and towns being taxed from thousands of miles around made Anastasia powerful. Moltenwing was built out of fear and serfdom and was a city created by bones. The bones of millions of serfs.

The city could be seen from every direction for hundreds of miles. Travellers could see the great walls that enclosed the city, and the mighty palaces inside were the most exquisite in the world. It was built so people would remember.

The Empress Aminoff

The lords and nobles of East Tanniv were loyal because she laced their pockets with trade agreements and dealt with any whispering of unhappiness with the most severe of punishments. No matter how rich or noble you were, if she had decided you were no longer helpful, she would march an army onto the land of the person who fell from favour. Then destroy their very existence and abolish the family, the family name, and any trace they ever existed. She would then divide up the wealth between her lords, nobles, and advisers. These acts kept everyone in her circle loyal, close and dependable.

She was the most beautiful, striking woman the world had ever seen.

She was tall and slim with eyes the colour of blue ice and hair so blonde it was almost white. Her jawline was perfect, and her skin was white and pale. She; wore a crown to perfection and held her head high in superiority to everyone around her. She was graceful and always wore flowing dresses, and when she walked, she cast a spell on all around her. Even the beautiful women of Moltenwing marvelled at her splendour, and all desired to be her.

She was able to talk and give great speeches to captivate and flatter everyone. She rarely used her magic as she was a master of manipulation and had the reputation of dealing out punishment and chastisement without being associated. But everyone knew it was her.

Queen Anastasia was a genuine threat to all of Tanniv. Everyone lived in fear that the Aminoffs were waiting for the chance to strike again. While her power grew, she expanded her lands. The Queen's ambition and desire for a unified Tanniv land were always on her mind.

Controlling the Stone Circles was an obsession that grew in her every day.

After the great battle of Ilihorn, the Aminoff armies took a long time to recover. But new alliances had moulded, and new trade agreements had been made. Some warlords from the North in the far reaches of Tanniv had made treaties to support the Aminoffs.

Prince Alwin was Queen Anastasia's only child and her prized son, and he had been making agreements and treaties for many years, further strengthening the armies of Moltenwing.

He had been made lord of Ilihorn and was given this kingdom as a young man. He loved to prove to his mother how loyal he was and how impressive he was. In truth, Prince Alwin of Moltenwing was a great tactical mind and helped administer West Tanniv to perfection.

The Ilihorn Mountains were rich in iron, steel, gold and silver, and the influential people in East Tanniv had gotten rich from the Aminoff reign of terror. The buying and selling of slaves was a popular method of trading up and down the River Ailmar. By using the poor slaves to excavate and mine ever deeper into the mountains, anyone who mattered in the Queen's service became richer and richer from the free serf economy that she had created.

The salves and the precious metals and resources allowed Prince Alwin to trade and buy many alliances; these alliances were made thousands of miles up the great river Ailmar.

Everyone was corrupt, the trade and prices were manipulated, and every now and again, Queen Anastasia would order the random levelling and burning of a town or village to show that she could.

Queen Anastasia and Prince Alwin knew that trade, commerce, and administration were the key to controlling Tanniv and did so with perfection. As long as the people that mattered remained rich and got more prosperous, the balance of power would be in the Aminoffs' favour.

Many of the countless towns and cities along the river Ailmar all traded with the Aminoffs in exchange for iron, gold and silver; they were not always administered most lawfully or most fairly.

The cities along the river traded grain and farming brought in from the expansive great plains and cornfields of fertile lands east of Ilihorn.

The plains stretched for four thousand miles, and the serfs were bound to the land by debt and cruelty.

The slaves came from far and wide, and many were captured from raiding parties that travelled across the River Ailmar into the towns and villages of West Tanniv.

Prince Alwin had built a great fleet of magnificent warships and merchant ships. He traded and developed a vast army full of alliances and swords for hire. The Queen was proud of her son; she often spoke of him to her lords as the master of all men.

The alliance's Prince Alwin made had all been bought with the enormous wealth that had come from the serf economy and the resources that poured down the river.

Prince Alwin was an excellent trader, a brilliant commercial man, and a master at controlling the towns and cities of the river.

He controlled them through fear, through manipulation, and through generous trade agreements that the lords could not say no to.

Prince Alwin knew that if he controlled the sea, the ports, and the river, he could control the lands of Tanniv east of the river, and he would worry about the west when the time was right.

Kings and nobles of different types controlled everything west of the river.

The Disaris people, The Turgett lords, and the ancient kings all lived in peace and relied on a system of trade and commerce but through a peaceful, independent central trade system coming from Tarrenash.

None of this meant that West Tanniv was without arguments, grievances, and disagreements; however, the country had not seen war or fighting for years.

The shadow warriors west of the River Ailmar controlled a thousand-mile border, which held back the Aminoffs. The peaceful King and lords paid for this in the West of Tanniv as it was a vital part of living so that the Aminoffs would not rise again to fight another great war.

West Tanniv was a peaceful place with vast woodland, hills, and huge mountain ranges in the North. The climate was sunny and had its correct seasons throughout the calendar year, and was bright with lush green woodlands and fertile farming lands.

The kingdoms that made up West Tanniv were split into regions, and while some areas had disagreements and differences, there was peace and trade between each town, and the provinces existed as a cooperative.

The Aminoffs didn't have access west of the river because of the shadow warrior border, but the threat never disappeared. Many people in West Tanniv knew that a peril would come one day, as many disputes from East and West never got forgotten.

Trade did get through as smugglers and cutthroats keen to make money lined the river on each side, and where there was a desire to make money, the resources to stop it was far weaker.

The scouts of the shadow warriors knew that this took place but turned a blind eye because the problem was too big to fix.

The significant difference west of the River Ailmar was the stone circles, and the Aminoff saw this as a major embarrassment and a constant reminder of what had been taken from them.

The Aminoffs were denied access to the Stone circles; no stone circle had ever been made to the East of the Ailmar River. This was a constant source of anger with Queen Anastasia, and she had never forgotten what she was denied, and her powers grew stronger every day.

But Prince Alwin had been seen in England, so the Stone circles had begun to move. One may have moved to the East of the Ailmar River.

Mrs Marlow explained that this was the only explanation because Prince Alwin was in Stoney Cross.

If it was him, and if he was here, it would only be to get a new wand for Queen Aminoff from Mr Griffins.

"Why can't Mr Griffins just say no?" asked Oscar even though he knew the answer.

"Mr Griffins is a sceptre man, a wandmaker! It is his job, and if he denies a wand to Alwin, then the neutral ground spell treaty would be broken, allowing Queen Aminoff to take over the wand library," said Mrs Marlow.

Mrs Marlow explained that there was no time to lose.

Prince Alwin was on the wrong side of the river Avon. He somehow had found his way from East Tanniv to Stoney Cross via a moving stone circle, explaining that this was why the stepping stones had appeared in the River Avon, which took them to Tappington Hall that day, and Prince Alwin was close.

He had not been to Stoney Cottage in a long time, so the landscape and the place must have changed dramatically; however, he would find Mr Griffins soon.

Queen Anastasia had not had a new wand in a long time, and to continue the threat into West Tanniv, she would need a new enchanted wand. This is the reason why she has sent Alwin. The wandmakers have an accurate record of her wand that Queen Anastasia needed, and all Alwin would need to do is ask for a new one. Then Alwin would return the same way he came.

Both boys listened and hung on every single word of the story, both with their mouths wide open; you could hear a pin drop.

"Then we are in danger," said Thomas in an anxious voice.

"Not at the moment these things take time, but we will need to act fast," said Grandmother. "So, boys! The reason why I have asked you to come and listen to me is simple. I must train you, boys, to use those wands. "So your training must commence at once," she said.

"I have summoned a warrior to meet me in the Grand stone circle in Ballymore Forrest. His name is Lorsan Yeldrove, and he is a great warrior and a leader of the Bastions of Yelcan, which separates the river Ailmar.

Lorsan Yeldrove will take me on a passage to the mountain halls of Stormhorn for the gathering. But I need your help."

"I am old now, and to open a portal powerful enough to get into Tanniv, I will need your wands and your strength," Grandmother added further.

"I saw you do it last night," said Thomas.

"You saw me summon Owls here for a few minutes, Thomas, not teleporting a person through time to Tanniv; this will take a lot of strength and power," said Grandmother.

"I will help," said Oscar proudly.

"I will help too, Grandmother," said Thomas equally eager.

Mrs Marlow explained that in the Middle of Ballymore woods was an old stone circle that was more powerful and commanding than the one underneath Stonecross Manor, and they would need to call on Lorsan Yeldrove to come and collect her.

Mrs Marlow went on to explain that the warrior Lorsan was an astonishing shadow warrior. Lorsan was a general in the great wars between East and West, and he had led the charge into the Ilihorn canyon; he was there at the time of the great deception.

Lorsan was a hero of many assaults on Ilihorn castle in numerous battles. He was to be trusted completely, and he would take Mrs Marlow to Stormhorn safely for the gathering.

The Training

Mrs Marlow got up from the kitchen table and walked to the hall. The three of them stood in the hall as she pointed at the paintings, and all the previous relatives, who were white wizards and witches, all had been guardians of the Stone Circles of England.

Walking around the grand hall, all looking at paintings and having each one explained, felt great to the boys; they both looked on in interest, taking in all the history and information.

Mrs Marlow then walked towards the door under the staircase and opened the cellar door with the massive iron key.

This was the first time Oscar had seen this room, and while Thomas had seen this room before, he never really saw it properly.

They walked down the damp staircase which had been carved into the rocks. Mrs Marlow flicked a light switch, and they could hear the tinging sound of lights going on as if hundreds of lights had all turned on.

When the boys got down into the room, they both looked around in amazement. It was a vast library with what seemed to be rows and rows of millions of books and bottles and potions. The entrance cave was huge; it had a stone circle in the middle, which Thomas described to Oscar on the meadow.

"Both of you stand in the middle of the stone circle and hold out your wands," said Mrs Marlow.

Thomas and Oscar walked into the middle of the Stone circle. They both were still in amazement at what was happening, and they looked around the room and could see a maze of bookshelves go on for miles in every direction.

"Have you read all of these books?" asked Oscar.

"Yes, I have had to read them all," said Mrs Marlow to both boys.

Mrs Marlow explained that she was going to teach defence only for now and how to hold open a stable portal for her to pass through. While a portal could be opened, time travel like this was very tough.

It took a lot of power to manipulate time and a lot of energy and strength, and quite often, you need more than one wizard or sorceress to do it. So friendship and alliances were the Stone circle's natural defence against time and the improper use of the circle.

"So you could not put an army through the portals?" said Thomas fretfully.

"It's never been done before, and I can't think how it could be done, but we must always be aware that anything and everything can be possible," said Grandmother.

Mrs Marlow stood up straight, walked over to her desk, got out an ivory white wand, and spoke, "Librorum Libros Pertinet Libri". And with that, the books flew across the room, coming from the far reaches of the great library. They flew from everywhere and started swirling in a circle. Faces with noses appeared on the books with eyes, and they flew into the faces of Thomas and Oscar. They began to insult the two boys and were very rude.

One book looked at Thomas in the face and said, "Look, it's a grubby boy," and began to flap its pages to ruffle his hair.

Another fat book flew into Oscar's face and said: "Look at this cheeky one," and clipped him around the back of the head and laughed in a deep laugh.

The books flew everywhere, calling the boys all sorts of names. They all had posh superior voices and acted like they knew everything in the world.

Mrs Marlow was busy looking for her glasses could hear the rude, impolite comments being made from the books, and she would deal with this promptly.

The books continued to smack the bottoms and pull their hair and their ears and continued to laugh and cackle and shriek at the two boys.

Mrs Marlow then waved her wand and shouted, "Prohibere!"

All the books stopped and hovered in front of Mrs Marlow in a line sniggering.

She then told each of them off for being so rude and so discourteous.

"No wonder people don't come down here to read you anymore; your behaviour is terrible," She said in an abrupt angry tone.

All the books looked down at the floor and looked sombre and sad.

"Now we have a job to do. We need to get these two boys trained fully in the next two days to help me create a portal for me to travel to Tanniv," she said.

"Tanniv!" One of the books cried.

"A portal! With these two boys!" another yelled.

All the books then looked at each other and again laughed.

"I am sorry, boys. Books are famous for thinking that they are better than anyone else. But in truth, they are limited to what is written inside them," said Mrs Marlow.

Mrs Marlow then waved her wand and bellowed, "Prohibere Statuam!"

The books hovered in front of Mrs Marlow, they all lined up, but they were frozen like statues this time. They had gags in their mouths, and they could not speak.

"I gave you all a chance like I do every time, and there's no point moaning now," said Mrs Marlow as each book looked with a frown and mumbled moaning tones from underneath their handkerchief gags.

"We have work to do and no time to waste," said Mrs Marlow.

Thomas and Oscar gasped in astonishment and sniggered and giggled at the telling off and gaging of the books.

One by one, the books hovered before the two apprentices. The White Sorceress removed the gags, and the books read themselves to the boys.

By this time, two small school-style wooden desks and wooden chairs had appeared in the middle of the stone circles, and each book presented itself to the boys.

Each book taught the history of the stone circles. Another book explained portals, and then others hovered around while the boys repeated and called out the names of the spells; this went on for hours.

The boys listened to the books as they taught them; they repeatedly waved their wands and lit up the room even more.

Another book taught how to hold a wand and the angles in which the enchanted wands worked with different spells.

Another book taught the boys were to stand in a stone circle while opening up a portal.

Another book taught the boys about Tanniv and another about the cultures of Tanniv.

Books flew everywhere backwards and forwards from the shelves. Mrs Marlow was waving her wand, repeating names of books, and sparks flew, and trails of lights glided about all around the cave. Big and small books, all with different voices and personalities, and colours sparkled, and light flew everywhere.

The boys took in all the information and were learning very fast. Mrs Marlow knew that boys and girls of this age had dynamism, energy, and the capacity to take in information quickly and loads of it.

"Enough!" roared Mrs Marlow after several hours. The books stopped and hovered, and while some stayed, others went back to their places back in the bookshelves in the great library; all the books looked at the boys and observed each other with their individual faces and eyes. The books hovered silently while Mrs Marlow spoke.

"Let's see what you have learned," said Mrs Marlow.

The two boys instinctively walked to a separate area of the stone circle, and it was as if what they had just learned was now automatic.

Mrs Marlow stood up from her desk waved her wand at the two desks and chairs, and they disappeared in a puff of glimmering radiant silver dust dissolving into nothing.

"We are going to open up a portal now. Don't worry; this stone circle is not powerful enough; it's just a test," said Mr Marlow.

The boys looked at each other and nodded. They gripped their wands tightly and held them high in the air. She stood opposite the two boys; the boys faced her, Oscar to the left and Thomas to the right, forming a triangle.

The books that were left flying around all looked at each other; some smirked, some leered, and others grinned, and a few looked severe, but all watched with great interest.

"Okay, boys," said Mrs Marlow as she took an intense breath. Thomas and Oscar looked at each other and nodded. Everyone looked nervous and tense.

The books all began to tighten up their pages and go apprehensive and rigid as they gazed down at the circle with curiosity.

"Repeat after me, aperta ianua—aperta ianua," said Mrs Marlow.

The three of them repeated over and over, "Aperta Ianua!"

"Concentrate boys, put all your energy into it!" shouted Mrs Marlow.

A wind whipped up inside the stone circle and the boys' hair began to blow all over the place. Thomas gasped and concentrated harder and harder.

Oscar gulped and concentrated harder, feeling the air pressure change around the room; a ball of light appeared in the middle. Oscar opened his eyes and looked around the room with interest and concern. Then with his break in concentration, the circle closed, the wind stopped, and Oscar stumbled back.

A great roar of laughter came from the books. They began to open up their pages and flap about, falling onto each other and laughing.

"Enough!" roared Mrs Marlow as she pointed her wand aggressively at the books.

"One more word from you lot, and I will take you down to the local library with all the other books, so you can be taken home, fingered and played around with by the general public!" screamed Mrs Marlow.

The books instantly closed up and looked frightened and stopped straight away.

"Keep reading and learning with the books, boys. We will try again in an hour," said Mrs Marlow.

All the books opened up and flew around the room, talking out loud and reciting their pages.

Mrs Marlow returned to her desk and again pointed to other books as they flew backwards and forward out from the grand library.

She conjured up the chairs and the desks back, and they arrived in the middle of the stone circle as they had done before.

She had a look of exhaustion and worry. But she needed the boys to help, and this was her only chance to get back to Tanniv. She had called a great gathering, and she needed to attend.

Lorsan would be waiting on the other side of the Portal in Tanniv with a small gathering of soldiers to take her on the long voyage to Stormhorn. Everything was in motion, and by now, the three Owls that she had dispatched to pass on the message would have arrived.

The training continued throughout the day. She made potions and labelled them and while packing a bag for her long voyage.

She left the cave to go back upstairs to the kitchen to organise lunch, leaving the boys with the books to learn.

She made some sandwiches and unpacked some fruit cake along with a large jug of water, and walked back down the cave to see the boys with an enormous tray of lunch.

"Let's stop now," Mrs Marlow said to the boys smiling and squinting scornfully at the books.

The books hovered around muttering and mumbling with the occasional giggle when Mrs Marlow said, "For heaven's sake, you lot, back to your shelves! I will call you back when I need you."

"Well, I never…" said a book.

"Have you ever been spoken to so rudely?" said another book.

"Come along books, I know when we are not wanted," said a very posh sounding book.

The books one by one returned to their respective homes back to the shelves leaving Mrs Marlow and the two boys to have lunch.

By this time, it was midday, and while the two boys had learned so much, there was still a lot to do.

"We will try again with the portal to Tanniv after lunch," said Mrs Marlow.

"Okay," said Oscar as he reached for a sandwich from the silver tray.

"Yes, we are learning a lot," said Thomas.

"We will train today and tomorrow and then early evening tomorrow, providing we can do this. Mr Griffins and the both of you will go into the Ballymore Forest Stone Circle and open up the gateway to Tanniv," said Mrs Marlow as both boys listened and nodded while eating and drinking.

She went on to explain, "While I am away, Mr Griffins has promised to come and stay in Stonecross Manor with Meg and, Mrs Pucket, the lady that you met in the high street is going to come and stay, too."

"I can ask my mum if I can stay for a few days too," said Oscar devotedly while looking at Thomas.

"That would be a big help Oscar," said Mrs Marlow as she smiled down at the boy.

The three of them sat and ate lunch and talked about Tanniv and the warrior, Lorsan Yeldrove. Mrs Marlow explained that she would only be a week or so, but she could come back, giving the illusion to everyone that she had not been gone at all.

"So you can effectively be gone for years and come back at the same time," said Thomas with an excited but puzzled look on his face.

"Well, I won't be gone for years," said Mrs Marlow.

As the keeper of the Stone Circles and as the white sorcerer, it was the job of the Stone Circle keeper to pass on vital information that would affect Tanniv. Usually, Mrs Marlow's owls would be enough to pass on messages, but Alwin and the moving of a stone circle were too significant; she had to go to explain in person.

She had called a great gathering in the halls of Stormhorn, and she would need to explain herself. She carried a historic bloodline of white stone keepers, and only a person from this bloodline could pass on a message like this or call for a great gathering.

The folk in West Tanniv were diplomatic and peaceful people, and like anywhere, they all had their differences. There were many regions of West Tanniv, and these districts were not without arguments and not without quarrels and disputes. Most common were disputes over borders and trading; there are always disputes like any other great land made up of many cultures, religions, and beliefs.

These differences were often squabbled about for generations. So most great meetings did not end well, which is why a gathering had not happened in many years. The great halls of Stormhorn had seen its fair share of arguments that often ended in meetings coming to a halt.

These days a great gathering could only be called upon by a trusted outsider, and the Marlow name was understood to be a reliable name and a name that could hold such a gathering. It was also understood that the Marlow Name and bloodline had controlled the Stone circles and critical circles like Stonehenge and Avebury for thousands of years without any faults.

So a Marlow name was well respected and not disputed by anyone.

Just the summoning of the great messenger owls was enough for the people of West Tanniv. The great owls would not fly to anyone and would not be controlled by anyone. The great eagle owls could sense the bloodline and would only trust a Marlow stone keeper. This was evidence enough for many of the clans and regions of West Tanniv because the great eagle owls of Tanniv neither answered nor trusted anyone.

The eagle owls symbolised peace and unification of West Tanniv, and the kings and chieftains of West Tanniv all carried the emblem and marched together under this banner. However, the borders were underfunded, and the shadow warriors held a defensive line that was far too long for its numbers.

The taxes subsidised the funding of the shadow warrior defensive line from the people of West Tanniv, and the funding amounts were out of date. The taxes for this were created when the Armies of Moltenwing were weak and did not carry a threat. But times had changed, and the borders would now need to be strengthened again.

Mrs Marlow sat at her desk for hours, reading the old laws and understanding the taxation of the borders and the complex cultural differences of all the people.

If she was going to get the people of West Tanniv to work together and reunite, she would need to be well versed in this information.

During lunch, Mrs Marlow passed as much information as possible to the two boys. She appreciated that there was so much information to take in, and she would do her best. She spoke about the great lands of Tanniv and the complex relationship between the Tarrenash, the Disaris, and the Turgett tribes.

Each region and country of West Tanniv had many resources like woods, farming, metals and orchards, and barley, corn, livestock, horse's pigs, and cattle. All this gave way to windmills, cotton, and precious metals, and all were being traded in market towns and great cities like in Tarrenash.

Tarrenash was a city and region ruled by King and Queen Drusunal and had ruled Tarrenash for seven hundred years.

Tarrenash was deep in the heart of West Tanniv and was a beautiful, prosperous city. It was rich from the trading that happened and supplied the coin and banking for the whole of West Tanniv.

King Drusunal had a daughter that ruled with her father her name was Princess Katya was beautiful with blonde hair and dark eyes with a beautiful sun-kissed complexion.

She was trained as a warrior and was highly proficient in sword fighting of all kinds. She had been trained in the art of war, as well as the art of diplomacy and kindness.

She helped her father, King Drusunal, administer the laws and regulations of the region and was seen to be very wise and very fair and a true diplomat in every sense of the word.

She was loved by the people of Tarrenash greatly. She was sent to many diplomatic conferences in Tanniv and inspected the borderlands in the east towards the river. She was not yet married, and no match had been found. Furthermore, she was one day to be the Queen and Ruler of Tarrenash.

Mrs Marlow went on explaining the geography and the economics of Tanniv to the two boys. She designated the information she thought was most relevant. The two boys finished lunch.

"No questions, boys!" said Mrs Marlow.

"We have a lot to get through; we need to continue the training," She said.

Both boys sat up straight, and she conjured the books back.

"Enjoy your food, did you?" said one book in a very posh ladies' expression.

"Would have been nice to get an invite," said another equally posh voice.

"Enough!" said Mrs Marlow; with that, the books looked around and went straight back to work.

The boys waved their wands, and different colour sparks and orbs lit up the room.

Mrs Marlow was old and really too old for this kind of adventure with this burden and pressure. Her daughter, Thomas's mother, was next in line, and she did not want the affliction of taking on the responsibility of being a white stone keeper, so she left for London only to return for Christmas and Easter.

Mrs Marlow saw that Thomas had the gift and saw that Oscar also had something exceptional and quickly picked this up.

Both boys were doing well. She could see that one of the boys excelled in something, and the other was surpassed in another magical discipline.

As the day went on, the books continuously taught the two eager boys. Mrs Marlow continued to beckon down books from the great library's far reaches filling the two boys' heads with spells and information and power that they never knew they had. They were both learning at a fast rate.

Mrs Marlow continued to pack her bag and felt ever more exhausted with the enormous task ahead.

"Okay, boys. Time to try again," said Mrs Marlow. It was now late in the day. The books stopped and gathered together in a row and looked down at the stone circle. Once again, the two desks and the two chairs disappeared, leaving the three of them standing in the stone circle in the corners.

They all stood looking at each other, this time with a sense of extreme seriousness; with deep breaths, they filled their lungs with air, and they spoke the words that would open up a portal to Tanniv.

"Repeat after me, aperta ianua—aperta ianua," said Mrs Marlow.

The three of them repeated over and over again, "Aperta ianua".

"Once again," She said. "Concentrate, boys, put all your energy into it."

A wind began to whip up inside the stone circle, but the wind was much stronger and more controlled this time.

The books that were hovering backed away, and they all excitingly looked at each other as if something was going to happen this time. The room was filled with confidence.

Then a tiny ball of bright light formed in the middle of the circle, and it grew bigger and bigger.

"Concentrate, boys!" shouted Mrs Marlow as she used all her energy to keep the portal light open.

Oscar gritted his teeth, then screwed up his face as if this exhorted all his energy into the middle of the circle. Thomas looked strained as the bright orb grew bigger and bigger. By this time, it was the size of a two-metre ball; the ball stayed open for ten seconds, then closed instantly and disappeared; the room fell silent, and the wind stopped.

A clapping noise came from the books as they applauded their hard-backed bindings against their pages. Then an enormous bright blue butterfly flew around the room.

"Did we do it?" cried Thomas as he eagerly leaned forwards, wondering if that was - what was needed.

"Yes, Thomas!" yelled Grandmother.

"Wahoo!" screamed Oscar as he jumped into the air. The bright blue butterfly landed on Thomas's hand.

"Is this from Tanniv?" said Thomas as Oscar strode towards him in total wonder and total amazement gazing at the perfect Blue Butterfly.

"Yes, boys, yes! That was the biggest gateway that this circle had ever seen!" she yelled.

Mrs Marlow then collapsed down into her chair in an exhausted slump. Thomas looked around at his grandmother, and Oscar looked too; both were surprised and concerned.

"Are you okay?" said the boys at precisely the same time.

"I am fine, boys. That took a lot of energy out of me," said Mr Marlow as she smiled at both boys.

"The point is we did it, boys; we opened up a large portal, and something came back from Tanniv," said Mrs Marlow reaching for her spectacles; she held out her hand, and the butterfly moved onto the back of her hand. "Yes, this is definitely from Tanniv," she said positively and confidently. The boys looked at each other and smiled.

"There is still so much to do, and we must continue," said Mrs Marlow as she got up from her chair, still a little out of breath while adjusting her blouse and tweed blazer.

Both boys returned to the centre and practised their defensive spells that they had learned the day before. Mrs Marlow and the talkative superior snooty books practised all afternoon. They repeated opening up portals and closing them in preparation for the following evening.

The plan was simple, early evening as the sun began to set; they would meet at Stoney Cross Cottage with Mr Griffins and Meg. They would walk with Mr Griffins's guidance to the centre of Ballymore Forrest to the stone circle. Mrs Marlow, Thomas, and Oscar were going to open up a new portal in the centre of the stone circle at Ballymore woods. Then Mrs Marlow would walk through to meet Lorsan Yeldrove in Tanniv, who would chaperon her on the journey to Stormhorn.

Later that day, the boys had spent six hours learning and practising their enchanted spells. Oscar had suggested going home to tell his mum he would stay at Stonecross Manor with Thomas for tonight and the next night.

Mrs Marlow, as promised, phoned Oscar's mother to ensure that this was okay. After she finished the phone call, she mentioned that he would have to go home to collect clothes and a toothbrush that day.

"I will drive you down to your house Oscar!" said Mrs Marlow.

"No, it's okay. It's faster to run across the meadow," said Oscar as he was already halfway up the stairs leading towards the cellar door.

"It's okay, Grandmother. I will go with him," said Thomas.

"Okay then, boys. Stay together and go straight there and come straight back," said Mrs Marlow.

The two boys sprinted up the stairs, out of the cellar door. Through the hallway, then out the kitchen door, onto the raised patio, and with a jump onto the lawns, they ran across the grass by Stoney Cross Cottage, both looking at the Cottage to see if Mr Griffins or Meg was home. As they ran onto the meadow and down the dirt track leading towards Oscar's house, they could see the Avon River and the stepping stones that they now knew to be a moving stone circle.

Their minds raced, and they began to think about Alwin and how they had seen him there only the day before. They also thought about Holly in Tappington Hall.

"Shall we quickly go and see Holly?" asked Thomas.

"What about Alwin and how your grandmother said not to go down there?" said Oscar apprehensively but agreeable at the same time.

"Come on, Oscar! We can run straight there, quickly say hello to Holly and then run straight back. We have our wands now, so what harm could it do?" asked Thomas being very keen and enthusiastic to see Holly again.

Thomas had a wonderful time with Holly the day before and remembered how she held his hand and how they played with her in the gardens.

"Okay, then Thomas, we do have our wands, and we have been training all day. So yes, let's go," said Oscar as he justified this to himself.

In truth, no magic was any match for Prince Alwin, especially two small boys who had defensive wands that had been training for just a few days.

They ran down to Avon River and saw the stepping stones, which they now knew to be a moving stone circle and crossed them one by one across the crystal clear sunny waters of the River Avon. With a jump up to the side of the river through the long yellow sun-bleached grass, they could see the perimeter flint rock walls of Tappington Hall. They both sprang up onto the walls and jumped down the other side, snooping around the gardens. Darting between the giant garden ornaments and perfectly pruned hedges, both whispering but shouting "Holly!" "Holly!"

"Let's look over by the Yew tree," said Thomas to Oscar in a very faint voice while cupping his hands around his mouth to muffle the noise.

They darted behind the hedge leading towards the wooded area of the gardens, and there she was. She was sitting in the sunny part of the garden just before the Yew tree branches that overhung and blocked out the sunlight. She had flowers in her hands that she had been picking and was humming and signing softly.

"Holly!"   said   Thomas.

"Hello, Holly," said Oscar.

"Oh! Oscar! Thomas! Hello! It's so nice that you are coming to see me. I have been thinking about you both all day," said Holly softly.

Thomas smiled pleasantly at Holly, and she smiled back. Thomas built up a fondness for Holly; he liked that she had been thinking about him because he had been thinking about her, too.

"We have only come to say hello. We can't stop," said Oscar.

"Yes, I am sorry, Holly, we are going to be busy in the next few days. So we decided to come and say hello we will see you later in the week," said Thomas.

"Perhaps you can meet us in the meadow next time," said Oscar. "The meadow seems to be in the middle of our houses!"

"I told you both that I can't leave Tappington Hall grounds," said Holly in a very sombre, very lonely voice. Thomas spotted that she was getting upset, so they decided to change the subject.

"That's okay," he said, "We can come here each time to play!"

"Yes, yes. We can come here, Holly. Anytime, no problem!" Oscar said.

"Well, I have something to tell you both!" She said.

"What is it, Holly?" Oscar whispered in a calm voice.

"Tomorrow night, I have to leave, and I will not be coming back," said Holly.

"Why?" said Thomas looking extremely disappointed.

"I thought we would be able to play all summer," said Thomas in a very gloomy voice.

"I have been here for a long time now, and all the signs are telling me it's time for me to go," said Holly.

Thomas, not really understanding anything Holly had just said, stood quiet, listening. Then Oscar broke the silence by saying, "We need to go, Thomas." Thomas agreed.

"Yes, we need to go, Holly," said Thomas.

Holly said goodbye to the boys and gave them a big embrace, wishing them both the best in life, hopeful that she would see them soon. She looked at both boys with a small smile, then ran back towards the great house.

"Goodbye, Holly!" Oscar shouted.

"Yes, goodbye, Holly!" Thomas cried, too.

Both boys watched Holly run off as she vanished from sight running behind one of the green hedges at the far end of the garden.

"Let's go, Thomas," said Oscar.

Thomas was wiping the tears from his face, not wanting to show any sign of upset, said yes in a faint, broken voice.

Both boys ran back to the stone wall out of the Tappington Hall estate, down through the long yellow grass to Avon River towards the stepping stones.

They leapt back across the river, Avon stepping on each stone carefully as they crossed the river. Then back up towards the meadow then down to Oscar's house. They got to the back of his garden, jumped the fence, and into the lawn.

"We will go in through the back door," said Oscar.

They walked into the back door where Oscar's mum Jane was sitting at the kitchen table.

"Hello, stranger," Jane said to Oscar.

"Do you know this boy leaves the house in the morning, then I never see him till the night? You must be the famous Thomas. I keep hearing about you, young man. Pleased to meet you," Jane said to Thomas.

"Please to meet you too, Mrs Williams," said Thomas.

"Did Mrs Marlow call you?" Oscar asked his mum, interrupting impatiently.

"Yes, I know everything about it," said Jane.

"I have left you a bag in the hallway with clothes and with your wash-bag and toothbrush, too!" said Jane.

"Okay, thanks, Mum," said Oscar. "I am staying at Stonecross with Thomas for two nights."

"Yes, yes, I know Oscar; Mrs Marlow phoned me earlier today."

Mrs Williams was so happy that a new boy had finally moved close and that he had a new friend to play with; she could see a marked improvement even in the past few days. Not that she was worried about Oscar, he always seemed a happy enough boy and was content running around everywhere. It was delightful to see him with a friend, and Thomas was a sweet boy from a lovely family, which is always a good thing with mums.

Oscar went into the hallway, collected his bag, and said goodbye to his mother.

"I will see you in two days," said Oscar.

"Okay, my boy," said Jane.

The two boys ran out into the back garden and up the meadow towards Stoney Cross Cottage. By this time, the summer evening sun was sitting very low and almost in the boys' eyes as they ran up the small meadow hill towards the round barrows.

Oscar had put his head through his bag strap and had one of the straps over one shoulder, and the bag pushed behind him, so he could run faster up the field. As they got closer and closer to Stoney Cross Cottage, the two boys could make out the sunny silhouette of the Cottage because the sun was striking directly in their eyes as they came up the hill.

Then a voice appeared from nowhere. The boys were partially blinded by the sun both had one hand cupped over their eyes to see where the voice was coming from.

"Hello again, boys!" said the voice in a superior, very aristocratic manner.

"Thank you for the directions yesterday; they were most helpful," the well-mannered noble voice said.

The boys adjusted their steps to come out of the direct sunlight. Then stood in front of them, coming into focus, was Alwin.

"You're Prince Alwin Aminoff," Oscar said in horror, realising what he had said as soon as he said it, holding his head and shaking.

"Has someone been talking about me, boy?" said Alwin slyly. "I don't recall being famous in these parts, and I can sense what you boys are trying to hide!"

"We are hiding nothing," said Thomas.

"Then why can I sense that you both have wands under your shirts, boy?" Alwin said in a more aggressive tone. It was as if he was gracing them with his patience and compassion, and they should be grateful. Thomas, detecting Prince Alwin's aggression, decided not to provoke or antagonise the situation.

"Oh yes, we have wands. I thought you meant something else," said Thomas.

"This is the last time I ask, and there will not be a third time. So be very careful with what you next say to me, boys," Alwin said as he sneered and leered at the two boys.

"Where can I find the Sceptre Man?" said Alwin.

Then another voice appeared from the silhouette of the sun, and it was a familiar voice.

"I will take over from here, boys!" said Mr Griffins with the loyal Meg by his side, looking dubious at Alwin.

"It's all threats, boys. This is neutral ground, he can't do anything here, and he knows it," said Mr Griffins as he stepped in front of the two boys making sure he was getting between Alwin and Thomas and Oscar, creating an obstruction. Meg sensed a problem and walked in between the boys creating an obstacle and protecting the boys.

"Now, is that any way to treat an old friend?" said Alwin.

"Alwin, we are many things, but we are not friends," said Mr Griffins.

"It's been many years we have known each other, and your manners have not improved," said Alwin.

"I know what you want, PRINCE ALWIN AMINOFF. So let's just get it done, so you can be on your way," said Mr Griffins in a nervous, stern voice as he kept the two boys firmly behind him and Meg between his legs.

He then led Alwin up through the meadow to his Cottage; Mr Griffins grabbed the two boys keeping them as far away from Prince Alwin as possible. As they got closer to the Cottage, Mr Griffins was thinking "how to solve a problem;" Alwin had seen the wands, and he knew that the boys were being taught by someone close, and he did not want to show Alwin the direction the two boys were going or where the boys lived.

So the four of them walked the twenty paces up to the Cottage. Mr Griffins invited Alwin Aminoff into the old stone cottage, and he gestured the boys on frantically waving behind his back, signalling to the boys to run home back to Stonecross Manor and take Meg with them. He went to bolt the door of the stone cottage with Alwin inside; Mr Griffins said, "Goodbye, Alwin and I have a business to attend to."

Alwin looked over Mr Griffin's shoulder and said, "Goodbye, boys. I will be seeing you soon." He grinned. "There is something about you two boys." He laughed and shook his finger at them.

The two boys left and walked alongside Ballymore woods with Meg. The dog looked highly stressed like she did not want to leave Mr Griffins's side.

Thomas got down on his knees to stroke Meg and comfort her and said, "It's okay, Meg. Mr Griffins will be fine. Come back to the house with us, and we will fix you some food," He said reassuringly to the dog who had calmed down.

Alwin was a handsome man, and you could tell he was influential and powerful and had a great sense of negotiation. He had confidence and presence.

"There is something about the tall boy," said Alwin.

"Let's just concentrate on the wand," said Mr Griffins.

The door closed on the Cottage, and again, Mr Griffins waved his hands in a restrained way to usher the boys back home from the window.

Mr Griffins said, "I suppose I should offer you a drink."

"A drink?" said Alwin as he laughed. "Mr Harold Griffins! My family has been keeping your ragtag family name in the business for hundreds of years. AND DON'T YOU FORGET IT!" Alwin said as he gritted his teeth with venom losing his temper slightly. Then with a gentleman's grin, he slipped back to being polite and gentlemanly with impeccable etiquette and manners.

"And my family have been providing you with the best wands, so it works both ways," said Mr Griffins, equally as annoyed.

"I will need no drink from you. Just get me my mother's new wand, and I will be on my way," said Alwin.

Mr Griffins pulled back the living room rug and opened the cellar door to the wand library.

The exchange was to be very simple. Mr Griffins walked down to the correct aisle in the grotto to the shelves' to the suitable row of wands and collected the wand. He would then walk back to his desk, filling out the paperwork to hand it over to Alwin.

Alwin sat down in a chair opposite the boulder, then leaned back in his chair and put his hands together, twiddling and drumming his fingers while humming a tune.

"Yes, you Griffins do a good job," said Alwin smirking at Mr Griffins; he could see that he had an accurate record of everything here. "One day, you will work for me," he smirked and sniggered at Mr Griffins in a very calm, charming way.

"This is neutral ground, and you can't break the peace treaty here," said Mr Griffins confidently and assertively.

"Yes, yes, yes, Harold! I know! Not yet, we can't," said Alwin as he drove his fist down onto the large oak desk, once again showing a side of his personality he was masking.

The treaty of the cave and the Griffins was fashioned hundreds of years ago. It was simple; the Griffins would supply everyone with wands no matter nationality or conflicts; this would be for an exchange for neutral ground. In return, the treaty was made that the Griffins could not choose sides nor aid or meddle in any affairs of a political nature. But the Griffins were clever somewhere deep in the small print of the agreement; there was a spell that would render all wands everywhere useless if the treaty was ever broken. The Aminoffs felt cheated with this law and would remain bitter about this restriction many hundreds of years later.

The Aminoffs governed East Tanniv and made the laws they did not abide by anyone else's law. Nevertheless, Alwin needed a wand and was sent by his mother. So he would need to be patient and show respect.

The Griffins had felt safe for the past one hundred years that all the Stone circles were in the West, and they were being correctly managed by the Disaris and Tarrenash Kingdoms. The shadow warriors of West Tanniv had defended this fiercely under the West Tanniv banner of the great eagle owls. Until now, somehow, a stone circle has turned up in the river Avon and then Alwin with it. So the Stone circles had started to move. This was the first time in hundreds of years the stones had moved. Both Mr Griffins and Mrs Marlow studied the library looking, and it appeared the last movement of the stone circles was around nine hundred years ago.

The fact that Oscar had first seen these Stone Circles and Thomas, too, still remained an unanswered question. Further study was needed into why the stone circles had moved and how Alwin had managed to travel through it.

Mr Griffins had Prince Alwin in front of him and could ask such questions very easily. But there was no point; Alwin would not tell the truth even if he answered. This would need to be figured out, and much more reading would reveal the answer from the thousands of books and scrolls.

Mr Griffins unfurled a wand contract for Anastasia Aminoff and handed it over the large Oak wooden desk to Alwin. "Sign here, please," said Mr Griffins.

"Certainly Harold," said Alwin; he leaned forward, and with a feathered quill and inkpot in front of him, he signed. The contract began to glow, and the ink became a brilliant golden yellow and brightly sparkled.

"Arh theatre! I do love theatricals," said Alwin. As he shoved the scroll back across the desk to Mr Griffins as if it was a complete insult to ask a royal Aminoff to sign something. So degrading the processes by being rude and dismissive made the Prince feel better about the process.

"See you in another few years," said Mr Griffins with a dry smile on his face.

"Or maybe sooner than you think," said Alwin looking back at the old man through the corners of his eyes with an uneven look and a grin.

"Yes, Prince Aminoff," said Mr Griffins, not wanting to argue, as he tried to get the whole procedure over as fast as possible.

The Prince griping the wand, made his way back up through the cellar door to the cottage's living room.

"How do you live in something so small!" said the Prince crudely. By this time, the Prince had got what he came for, so all the niceness he was falsely attempting fell away.

"It does us Griffins just fine," he said again, not wanting to engage further with the Prince in an effort to hurry Alwin leaving.

Mr Griffins walked over to the door, unbolted the huge iron bolt and opened the door while gesturing his hand and arm for Alwin to walk through.

Alwin walked through the door and took a look outside at the summer's day. "Maybe I will stay awhile. I am definitely interested in those two boys, especially the taller one," said Alwin with an intriguing voice while touching his chin as if to think deeper about what he had just said.

Taking a deep breath and rolling his eyes behind the Prince's back, Mr Griffins felt an enormous sense of dread as it was the sentence that he had feared the most that the Prince would say.

Prince Alwin Aminoff had seen the boys, and had seen the wands, and had seen the boys playing around the stone circle in the Avon River. He was bound to be deeply interested in the two boys, especially Thomas.

"Don't you have to get that wand back to the Queen?" said Mr Griffins.

"Don't you tell a Prince what to do or talk about my mother's wants and needs

again," said Alwin, slightly taken back as if no one had ever spoken to him like this.

"You talk to me like that again, treaty or no treaty, I will end you and this place," said Alwin.

"Now now, Prince Alwin, I meant no harm; I am in the service for both sides and getting wands back to their owners is an important part of the wand making process," said Mr Griffins. "You don't build up thousands of years of a wand-making business without running it efficiently."

"Perhaps you are right, Sceptre Man," said Alwin. He turned and walked down the meadow towards the direction of the river Avon and the stone circle. "Goodbye, Harold." He said when he was several metres down the meadow.

Mr Griffins said nothing; he watched Alwin disappear down the meadow towards Avon River then returned inside Stoney Cross Cottage. He bolted the door firmly again and went down the cellar hatch into the grand wand library to read his books and scrolls.

The boys had made their way back to Stonecross Manor; they had run across the lawns and had gone up to Thomas's room and were watching from the bedroom window that overlooked the garden, over in the direction to Mr Griffin's house and Ballymore woods.

"What do you think has happened?" asked Oscar to Thomas as both boys had the bedroom lights off and their faces pressed up against the window.

By this time, the sky was pink, and darkness was coming; the sun had almost set entirely on the meadow, and the sunlight on the lawn showed only a tiny patch of light slowly fading.

"I think Mr Griffins has handed over the wand, and Alwin has gone back to Tanniv," said Thomas.

"But how does he pass through the stone circles in Avon River when it takes three of us to open a portal?" Oscar asked.

"I don't know, but I think this is what Grandmother and Mr Griffins are trying desperately to find out," said Thomas.

"None of this makes sense right now. We should just concentrate on creating a portal big enough in Ballymore woods tomorrow for Grandmother,"

"I agree we should continue to practice our magic," said Oscar.

"Mr Griffins will come to no harm as it is neutral ground," said Oscar remembering what Mr Griffins had told them both several times.

They continued to watch out of the window until it got dark. The sun had firmly set on the surrounding area. They could see the dark outline of Ballymore Forest, and in the distance, they could faintly see Stoney Cottage.

"Let's go downstairs," Thomas said to Oscar.

"Yes, you can't see anything right now," said Oscar taking one last look as he cupped his hands around the glass window to look one last time.

"I am sure it will be alright," said Thomas.

They walked downstairs into the hall through the cellar door and then down to continue the lessons.

Mrs Marlow was still down in the cellar studying and cramming as much information as possible. These were potentially dark times, and the burden was put on her shoulders to help ease the situation; she was reading about the moving stone circles.

Anyone that knew about moving stone circles was long gone, and they moved so infrequently that there was no real experience in these phenomena. Mrs Marlow remembered reading about the moving of the rings in many books before. She studied books written in Saxony French and many references to the Carnac Normandy France standing stones and even as far back as Göbekli Tepe. But no firm writing was ever transcribed about this by anyone she could remember.

She called upon the books with her wand and went backwards and forward, only stopping to quiz them for short conversations.

The books would stop and give recommendations, books were generally known all's by personality, and they hated not knowing something.

"Hello, Grandmother," Thomas said as he walked into the cellar.

"Hello Thomas, hello Oscar," said Mrs Marlow to the two boys.

"What time is it?" Mrs Marlow asked abruptly as she stopped to look over at the two boys.

Thomas looked down at his watch only to be interrupted by a book who jumped into the conversation and shouted loudly, "It's eight-twenty!" looking at the two boys and laughing.

"You have to be faster than that said the big huge fat book," laughing.

"Yes, Grandmother. He is correct," said Thomas.

"I am never wrong," said the book in a superior manner.

"Well, let's stop for the day and get some dinner," said Mrs Marlow.

She stood up, and then she sent all the books back with a wave of her wand.

"Come on, boys, let's go to the kitchen," She said to them both.

"Why are books so impolite?" Thomas asked Grandmother.

"They think they are knowledgeable. That's all Thomas, it's in their nature, but you are right, they are extremely rude," said Mrs Marlow as she patted him on the head.

Mrs Marlow marshalled the boys up the stairs and through the cellar door, turning off the lights, then locking the door with the big iron key.

"This door should always remain locked, boys," Mrs Marlow said with a stern tone and voice and looked both boys in the eyes, so they agreed.

Thomas and Oscar agreed and nodded as if to let Mrs Marlow know how important the comment was, and they both agreed strongly, which was confirmation enough, and no more was needed to be said. They walked into the kitchen and sat down at the pantry table while Mrs Marlow prepared dinner.

"We will eat a big dinner tonight as we have much to do tomorrow," said Mrs Marlow to both the boys. "It's so late, boys. Go and take a shower, then come down in your pyjamas to eat dinner. By the time you are finished, we will be ready."

"Okay, Mrs Marlow!" shouted Oscar as the two boys raced out the kitchen into the hallway and up the stairs.

"Slowly, boys!" Mrs Marlow shouted. "You boys run everywhere."

"There is a camp bed that I will come and set up later, so you boys can sleep in the same room." Mrs Marlow said, this time raising her voice louder, so she could be heard over the din of the boys' speedy footsteps.

Oscar was particularly enthusiastic and excited because he had never stayed at Stonecross Manor before and had secretly wondered what it would be like to stay in the house and what it was like upstairs. The house was enormous, and he had always wanted to explore more.

They both ran up the stairs down the long corridor, and into Thomas's room.

"You can use the shower first," said Thomas to Oscar.

"Okay. Thank you, Thomas," he said.

Thomas decided to lay on his bed while Oscar got ready. He thought about Alwin and the exchange in conversation that happened between him and Mr Griffins. I suppose I was lucky it's neutral ground, thought Thomas, and he thought about how Mr Griffins got on finding a wand for the Queen Aminoff, too.

His thoughts then turned to Holly and how he was going to miss her.

He only met Holly twice, and he had grown to like her and, like the idea of spending the summer playing with her in Tappington Hall. It was an instant friendship that formed and an instant like of each other's company. It's strange how you can instantly like someone. He instantly liked Oscar, and he instantly liked Holly too.

Thomas could hear the shower turn off and shortly after listened to the creaking footsteps on the floorboards of Oscar walking back to the room. Thomas was happy to have Oscar back with him; it was nice to have company, especially after everything the two boys had to take in over the last two days. "All yours now," said Oscar, as he walked back with his hair a little wet and his striped pyjamas on.

"Okay, thank you," said Thomas as he gathered all of his night ware and towel and ambled towards the bathroom.

Oscar walked around the room then looked into the darkness towards Stoney Cottage then towards Ballymore Forrest.

He then lay on the bed thinking about Alwin and the lessons he had during the day. What an adventure, he thought to himself. His head was buzzing with information, and the encounter with Alwin left him thinking about Mr Griffins and how the exchange in conversation went. But he was left feeling satisfactory as the neutral ground treaty would mean no one would come to any harm.

Mrs Marlow entered with the camp bed so Oscar could sleep in the same room with Thomas.

"Grab that end, Oscar, and let's put your head in the same end as Thomas's pillow," she added.

"Okay," he said actively.

Mrs Marlow smiled down at Oscar and said, "You are always happy; it's good to have you around. You are going to go far in life, my boy. I can see that in your eyes."

They both straightened out the bed. Then Oscar jumped back onto Thomas's bed while Mrs Marlow organised the bed covers and straightened out the pillow and pillowcases.

"As soon as Thomas is ready, come straight down," said Mrs Marlow as she left the room and went urgently downstairs to check on dinner. Oscar shook his head positively and waited for Thomas.

Shortly after his shower Thomas arrived back in the room again; both boys had got ready so fast that they still had areas of their pyjamas slightly stuck to their bodies while still a little damp.

They ran down the long corridor, the grand staircase into the hall, and then the kitchen.

"Sit down, boys. It's almost ready," said Mrs Marlow as both boys pulled out their chairs to sit at the kitchen table.

"I have heated a chicken pie and boiled some potatoes with vegetables!" She added, half excusing that she has had very little time.

"Are these vegetables from the garden Mrs Marlow?" Oscar asked.

"Yes," She added while smiling at both boys.

A hot plate of chicken pie, vegetables with potatoes and gravy was placed in front of the boys, and they all sat down to eat.

Mrs Marlow sat down and went over the plan to go to Ballymore Forrest. Again she explained that Mr Griffins would escort them to the Stone Circle in the centre of Ballymore Forrest, it was around four hours of walking, and they would have to do it in the dark. But Mr Griffins and Meg could navigate through the forest in the dark no-problem.

Once the stone circle portal to Tanniv was opened and Mrs Marlow travelled through the gateway, it would close, leaving Thomas, Oscar, Mr Griffins, and Meg to travel back.

Mrs Mabel Pucket, a long dear friend and cousin of Mrs Marlow, would be coming tomorrow to stay at Stonecross Manor and, along with Mr Griffins, would take care of the two boys.

Mrs Mabel Pucket was also a white sorcerer and protector of the stone circles and would be arriving to assist in the further training of the two boys the next day. She was long since retired as she was far too old now but was a fully trusted friend of Mrs Marlow and was only too happy to look after Thomas at Stonecross Manor.

"But what about you returning?" said Thomas looking very concerned?

"Will there be enough people to open up a Portal in Tanniv!" said Oscar.

"You will not even tell I have gone. I will arrive back at more or less the same time," said Mrs Marlow confidently to both boys.

Thomas had met Mrs Pucket days before in Lyndhurst High Street. She was the very interesting inquisitive lady who talked about training and strange things like this. Suddenly everything became apparent, and Thomas understood the weird cryptic comments that Mrs Pucket had said days before.

Mrs Marlow opened up ancient scrolls, maps and very large old books and placed them onto the big Oak table in front of the two boys. These maps and books were all from Tanniv and explained the regions' complex geography and economics.

Mrs Marlow went on to talk about the voyage from the West Tanniv stone circle to Stormhorn and how it would take around four days. The stone circle was around four hundred miles away from Vakoborg City and Stormhorn. The terrain from memory would not be a pleasant journey as they would need to walk through forests and cross rivers, then walk through the foothills of Stormhorn to get to the Mountains. Thomas and Oscar listened as Mrs Marlow explained the plans and the expedition ahead.

She would then need to go in front of the great gathering and explain to the kings, queens, lords and nobles of West Tanniv. She would need to explain that there was a real threat and to try and reunite West Tanniv under the banner of the great eagle owls.

This would not be easy because most regions had indifferences, and many were more interested in the economics of trade and money. Going to war, reuniting, or strengthening defences would all cost time and money, and who would pay for that. These were all arguments stretching back hundreds of years, and Mrs Marlow knew that these quarrels could end in a stalemate conversation as they had done in the past.

East Tanniv was built as a dictatorship, so the uniting of East Tanniv was already done. The Aminoffs had bought the great alliances needed to create an army, and those who disagreed were destroyed. The Aminoff had control of the trade and the strategic cities, which further strengthened their forces. Some of West Tanniv had become dangerous, too.

So East Tanniv was already ahead of West Tanniv in many areas. The great trade deals created by Moltenwing had made an excellent economy, with the slave trade supplying free labour.

This ensured that East Tanniv would recover faster, and signs were showing that the East Tanniv Kingdom under the Aminoffs had been showing marks of recovery and great wealth. This bought alliances and persuasion even in areas of West Tanniv too.

The Aminoffs fleet of ships could be seen trading up and down the river Ailmar, and the Aminoff Navy also had control of the Hiligor Sea in the far south of Tanniv. The Hiligor Sea was seen to be neutral seas; however, it was under complete control of the Aminoff administrations coming from the city port of Elec.

The City of Elec was in East Tanniv and housed many of the great ships. It was the central trading point for merchant commerce and harvest crops coming from the river merchants. Both East and West traded in Elec, and it was considered to be a dominant trade point between the two kingdoms. It was a prosperous place, the architecture and beauty of the buildings were built out of a solid economic trade agreement with Moltenwing, and in the past, it also traded in Tarrenash and Qulan.

The City of Elec was not a safe place to be for anyone. Many people went missing and were sold to slave gangs for work. The slaves were sent to the great farming communities or the mountain mines of Ilihorn. Only the rich and the strong survived in Elec. It was a place that turned a blind eye to laws. The Pubs and drinking halls were filled with vagrant traders, smugglers of all types from both sides of the river.

The rich palaces and grand houses of Elec had been taken over by the new wealthy warlords and the new traders who ran the cities' wealth.

Some of the old Elec city Palaces still kept the old nobles in place. But these were noble families that were compliant with the Aminoffs' taxations and were seen to be of benefit.

Before the great Battle of Ilihorn, many residents from Tarrenash and Qulan also lived in the City and owned many trade merchants, Palaces, and grand houses. Now the City had turned lawless many of these traders had long gone. The Drusanal Royal family of Tarrenash had moved out decades ago and were once a prominent part of the history and reputation of the City.

Prince Aminoff owned the grandest palace in Elec and often visited the City and called many assemblies of the local lords and noblemen. He was also the Cities commerce minister and had the final signature for many of the essential tradings. This created an undercurrent of trade that did not pass through the central trade administration.

Prince Aminoff would manage illegal trade and meddle once the news had reached him. He had many networks of spies in Tanniv, and if deals were not going through the correct channels, this was met with the most severe consequences.

The City had also become famous for the largest slave market in Tanniv and had become extremely rich from the slave trade. This created a slave trade on both sides in East and West Tanniv.

This was why Mrs Marlow needed a warrior like Lorsan Yeldrove to escort her to Stormhorn.

Rogue bandits or huge threats did not overrun West Tanniv; however, the ever-increasing wealth and influence had stretched from Moltenwing and was beginning to find its way west into the many kingdoms.

The slave market had become an increasing profit-making industry, so kidnapping had become more apparent. Also, the Aminoffs had spies everywhere.

Mrs Marlow had called upon Lorsan Yeldrove to escort her to Stormhorn. He generally travelled with twelve to fifteen warriors of all types and had become a legendary figure for his bravery, and he could be trusted.

The four-day trip would take them through some hostile places through the forests of Vakoborg, where King Grusan Gilgamesh resides.

They would need to stop at the forest City of Vakoborg to convince King Grusan Gilgamesh to attend the gathering. He had not participated in a gathering for many years because of his distrust.

The Disaris were masters of the stone circles and could quickly move around the ancient circles, creating portals. However, they were suspicious of everyone and kept themselves in the forests.

Their religious beliefs were deeply entrenched in the Stone circles and the changing of the season. The Disaris were very private and would not allow other cultures to become Disaris citizens or be part of any religious ceremony. This meant very few marriages between Tarrenash and Disaris, and the Disaris that married others were banished from the forest City of Vakoborg.

Mrs Marlow and Lorsan Yeldrove would need to convince King Gilgamesh to attend first. Then, if the grand council of Stormhorn could see the King and Lorsan Yeldrove travelling together and with a white sorcerer, this would be a powerful statement to unite the regions again under the great eagle owl of West Tanniv.

Thomas and Oscar listened on and were deeply interested in everything Mrs Marlow said to the two boys. She continued to tell them about Lorsan Yeldrove. She felt that the more information she told the boys, the more at ease they were becoming about what needed to be done.

Lord General Lorsan Yeldrove

He was a tall, dark-haired, handsome man with dark eyes and looked strong. He wore a great warrior's uniform and looked like he had seen many battles.

He had an interest in the gathering at Stormhorn and was determined to be heard. His legions patrolled the borders and lined the river. He was always asking the Kingdom of Tanniv for more money and that a threat from the East would come one day. But it was widely believed that both sides were so impaired and damaged from the last Great War that no side would ever fight again. This would mean that the shadow warriors would remain underfunded and weak.

Lorsan Yeldrove was determined to make this gathering a learning exercise so the people of West Tanniv would understand the threat.

The Yeldrove name was a traditional noble family name from East Tanniv, and there were Yeldrove's still living in grand houses and palaces in the City of Elec and Moltenwing. Despite being utterly loyal to the Tarrenash and Qulan City councils for many years, numerous influential people would only see the family name and refused to listen to Lorsan.

So Mrs Marlow, the White Sorcerer, was going to be the key to making the people of West Tanniv listen.

The Marlow bloodline was essential to the regions, kingdoms, and countries of Tanniv. To be a Marlow was honest and impartial as the Marlow's had been taking care of the Stone circles without mistakes for nine hundred years.

Therefore, a Marlow calling the gathering at Stormhorn was considered to be the most important gathering. The great eagle owls would have passed on the messages by now, and the wheels were in motion.

"That's enough now, boys. It's getting very late; it's almost ten o'clock," said Mrs Marlow.

The two boys wanted to listen more as they found the whole thing so fascinating it was almost like a book from a fairy tale. By this time, they were both on the table studying the maps and books and understanding more and more with each passing minute.

"Come along, boys. I will walk you up to your bedroom," said Mrs Marlow.

Lord General Lorsan Yeldrove

The three strolled upstairs and along the corridor down to the end where Thomas's room was situated.

Thomas jumped into bed, folding his covers back in one corner; he stuffed his feet in and shuffled down the bed until his head was on the pillow.

Oscar carefully sat on the camp bed and trundled his feet into the bed as the springs from the bed creaked and squeaked.

"Goodnight, Thomas. Goodnight, Oscar," said Mrs Marlow.

"Goodnight, Mrs Marlow," said Oscar.

"Goodnight, Grandmother," said Thomas.

It had been such a long day, and Mrs Marlow knew it would not be long before the boys would be asleep.

She turned off the light and left the boys in the dark to fall asleep.

"Thomas," said Oscar in a whispered voice.

"Yes," said Thomas.

"East Tanniv sounds so amazing. Do you think we will be able to go when we get older?" Oscar asked.

"I hope so because it does sound so incredible," replied Thomas.

The boys fell silent, each in thoughts from their own sentiments of the day. At the same time, Mrs Marlow went back downstairs to tidy up the kitchen from all the maps, books, and scrolls.

The Stone Circle of Ballymore Forest

The following day Thomas woke up very early to the sound of crockery being moved around in the kitchen. So he ran downstairs to take a further look at the maps, scrolls, and books, and Oscar was still in bed and still fast asleep.

"Good morning, Grandmother," said Thomas.

"Good morning!" she said in a very alarmed and surprising way.

"What are you doing up so early?" said Grandmother.

"I wanted to ask you about my mum," said Thomas. "Did my mother know about you being a white sorcerer?" he asked.

Mrs Marlow stopped what she was doing as if the conversation was inevitable, and she had been expecting it.

She made a cup of tea for them both and began to explain. Your mother was a white sorcerer, and she was also a stone circle keeper. But when she fell pregnant with you, she decided to stop this part of her life and move to London.

"You were all that she worried about, and she made the decision never to involve you in magic or practise magic again. So, she gave up her wand and never returned to the stone circles again."

"Did mother ever go to Tanniv?" asked Thomas.

Mrs Marlow closed her eyes, not wanting to answer the question, and said, "Yes. Yes, Thomas, she was in Tanniv more than here most of the time. She loved it," said Grandmother.

His face lit up, and he was in complete disbelief that his mother, a very straight, quiet lady, was now a sorcerer and had travelled through stone circle portals to Tanniv.

"Did she go a lot, and was she well-known?" asked Thomas again, bursting with a million questions.

Not wanting to lie to Thomas and knowing that he would find out eventually, she decided to tell him the truth about his mother.

Thomas's mother's name was Alina Marlow, and she travelled to Tanniv all the time.

She was taught white sorcery from the age of three and became one of the most powerful sorcerers of the White Order of the Stone Keepers. Her father, Mrs Marlows Husand, and Thomas's Grandfather, Mr Thomas Marlow, was also a mighty wizard who died when she was twelve.

She would travel to Tanniv and had the ability and power to open up portals on her own. She would spend time travelling through Tanniv and was very well known and respected with the Disaris of Vakoborg.

She would spend time in the City of Tarrenash, and she had a job in the coastal trading City of Qulan.

The coastal trading City of Qulan is a famous port and is situated in the Hiligor Sea. It's renowned for the fishing trade and is also a central trading post for every type of dealing. The cities markets trade in spices and farming produce, with anything from precious metals and precious stones and fine jewellery being sold.

Alina Marlow, the White Sorcerer, was on the trading council and governed over trading and commerce, and was a signatory for many treaties and trade agreements in the entire region. The city itself was beautiful; it was near the southern Jandar Mountain where Turgett's lives, so you would fully expect to see Turgett trading and working in many of the restaurants, bakeries, pubs and alehouses.

The weather was always hot and sunny, and the surrounding areas were green with palm trees all fed from the crystal clear fresh waters running down from the Jandar Mountains.

A great fleet of merchant ships, fishing boats, and galleons were permanently moored in its harbour. It was a hustling city, sweltering during the summer, and there was always a deal to be had.

Alina Marlow, Thomas's mother, loved this city; the climate was pleasant, the food was terrific, and she had an important job signing trade agreements on both sides of the river. She got on well with the Turgett people, and many respected her.

The Turgett confided in her to always help with selling produce or mining and always got a fair deal. Many of the merchants from Ilihorn had an aggressive trading style and felt that because of the Turgett people's small size, they could push them around and give them bad deals on their goods.

Alina Marlow moved freely on both sides of Tanniv because you could move between East and West in those days with relative ease. She often visited the

City of Elec and traded directly with the trading council of Elec. She was very well respected and loved by all.

Then one day, at the age of twenty-five, she decided to go back to Stonecross Manor never to return and left for London to work as a school teacher.

This broke the bloodline of Marlow's white sorcerers, and Mrs Marlow, Thomas's grandmother, had held the position on her own ever since.

He sat and listened carefully to his grandmother as she talked about his mother, all the while Thomas sat in total astonishment. To Thomas, his mother, Alina Marlow was an ordinary lady that was just like any mother, his stepfather was also a kind man that worked in a bank in London Monday through to Friday, and they both spent time with Thomas each weekend. It was a perfectly ordinary life, and he had expected nothing like this.

Mrs Marlow looked at her grandson and ended the conversation explaining to Thomas that there would be more times for questions and that there was no rush, and over time she would explain everything.

Thomas, looking very sad, said, "Okay, Grandmother. I would like to know more, and I understand it will take time."

"Yes, it will take time because she did so much good, and in time people will tell you this," said Mrs Marlow.

"Why don't you go and wake up Oscar, and I will make some breakfast. We have a lot to do today," said Mrs Marlow.

"Okay, Grandmother," Thomas said as he hurried out the door into the hallway and up the stairs.

Oscar was already awake and in the bathroom, and he could hear him brushing his teeth. Thomas decided to make his bed and get ready and do the same. After getting ready, they both ran downstairs to have breakfast.

"Good morning, Oscar. Did you sleep well?" said Mrs Marlow.

"Yes, I slept very well. Thank you, Mrs Marlow," said Oscar.

"I have made some soft-boiled eggs, and there's toast, jam, and tea in the middle too," said Mrs Marlow.

"Thank you very much!" both boys cried.

"Mrs Pucket is arriving at ten-thirty today," she added.

She is coming to help take over the lessons. She was an excellent white sorcerer in her day, but she had been in retirement for many years. Mrs Pucket was a cousin of Mrs Marlow, so they were also related, making her and Thomas distant cousins.

Mrs Pucket was also coming to stay at the Manor to look after Thomas and waiting in the house when Mr Griffins brought the two boys back.

There was a knocking at the front door.

"That will be Mrs Pucket," said Mrs Marlow.

"Can you answer the door please, boys?" She said again.

The two boys got up from the kitchen table and ran to the front door, and there stood Mrs Pucket. She was a very old lady, and Thomas had met her in Lyndhurst high street a few days before.

Oscar also knew her because she often visited Stonecross Manor. So she was a face that both boys already knew.

"Hello, Mrs Pucket," said Thomas and Oscar as they stood in the doorway with big smiles.

"Hello, boys," said Mrs Pucket. "Mrs Marlow told me that you boys created a portal in the Manor Stone Circle yesterday." Both boys nodded.

Mrs Pucket walked into the hallway, looked around, and hung her small thin jacket onto the coat stand. She hung up her hat and said, "Let's get to work."

Mrs Marlow could hear the voices from the conversations coming from the hallway and decided to go and join the chat.

"Hello, Mrs Pucket," said Mrs Marlow. "Thomas, please can you take Mrs Pucket's bag up to the spare room? And Oscar, please take the key and open the cellar door; we need to begin as soon as possible," she said as she handed Oscar the enormous iron cellar door key.

Oscar opened the door and flicked on the lights, and walked down to the cellar. Mrs Pucket allowed him to guide her down even though she had been down into the Stonecross Manor caverns thousands of times before.

Thomas came running from upstairs down through the cellar door. Mrs Marlow also followed.

"We need to teach the boys about portals the books know where we finished yesterday," said Mrs Marlow. "If you could summon the correct books please, Mrs Pucket. This is where we left the lesson yesterday."

"Don't worry, boys, if these books are rude to you, I will give them a zap with my wand," said Mrs Pucket as she winked at the two boys. The two boys smiled back as they wanted the books to get zapped after the rude way they treated them.

Mrs Marlow sat down at her desk and went back to studying the scrolls, maps, and books that she had been walking around with for the past few days. The scrolls, maps, and books had not left her side.

Mrs Pucket started the lesson with the two boys, she conjured up the two desks and the two wooden chairs, and the two boys sat down in the same places they sat the day before. She began waving her wand and beckoning books down from the far-flung reaches of the cavern library. The books flew towards the two boys and saw Mrs Pucket. She gave them a squinting, angry look, and they knew that she meant business, so they decided to behave.

Watching the books behave and look scared of Mrs Pucket made Thomas and Oscar laugh.

The books saw the two boys laugh and gave them the most sinister look. All afternoon the books flew backwards and forwards. The boys would stop to move their wands and do a small spell. Mrs Pucket would also show them, and the books would start back up again; the books would talk to the boys and read out their pages, filling their heads with knowledge.

Once again, Mrs Pucket would order the boys to stop and then began teaching them how to hold their wands for portals, and she showed them how to create mini gateways. They would get up, form a triangle in the middle of the stone circle, make a mini-portal and then sit back down again. During the day, the boys became better and better.

Occasionally, Mrs Marlow would look up from her desk and peer through the top of her glasses to watch the lessons and experiments taking place.

"Both you boys are exceptional. Not everyone can do this type of magic, and you boys are doing so well," Mrs Pucket remarked with a very pleasing smile on her face as the lessons continued.

Mrs Marlow stopped the lessons to explain that they would be meeting Mr Griffins at Stoney Cross Cottage that evening at seven. By this time, it was one in the afternoon, and they had stopped for lunch. They all sat around eating sandwiches and talked about Ballymore Forest and the long walk into the middle of the Forest to the Stone Circles.

Mrs Marlow still could not find any great detail on moving stone circles; however, she had seen this mentioned in books many hundreds of times.

The Stone Circles were moving; the one in Avon River was evidence for this. Alwin turning up for the first time in years was evidence for this too.

Mrs Marlow was collating evidence for the great gathering. The Disaris King Gilgamesh would need to be convinced. Although the Disaris religion was very secretive, their fundamental religious belief was based on stone circles and the seasons. So if she could persuade King Grusan Gilgamesh that the stone circles were moving, this would be evidence enough to get him to the great gathering at Stormhorn.

She sat the two boys down and explained everything in detail. She explained the plan of the journey and how long the expedition would take.

By this time, it was late afternoon. Mrs Marlow instructed the two boys to put on some night clothing. Thomas was wearing shoes, long socks ruffled down at the ankles, shorts down to his knees, and he decided to wear a t-shirt, a shirt, a jumper, and a blazer. Oscar had almost the same clothing, a racing green coloured jumper, a shirt, and a blazer.

The two boys finished getting ready and walked back down the stairs to meet Mrs Marlow and Mrs Pucket in the kitchen.

Mrs Marlow went into a storeroom at the far end of the kitchen's dining area and brought out two large torches. She handed one to each of the boys and said, "We will need these, boys."

She picked up her thick green hessian satchel; it was the bag that she had been packing all week in preparation for the long voyage ahead. She was wearing trousers and walking boots along with a jumper and a thick coat, and she looked ready to leave.

"Goodbye, Mrs Pucket," said Mrs Marlow. "I may be a few days."

"Okay, no problem. We've done this a hundred times before," said Mrs Pucket as she looked at her old friend then winked at the two boys.

"Mr Griffins will walk the two boys back at dawn, so don't wait up," said Mrs Marlow. "Goodbye, Mrs Pucket," said the two boys.

"See you in the morning, boys, and we will keep up the lessons and the training late tomorrow afternoon," said Mrs Pucket as she looked at the two boys.

Mrs Marlow, Thomas, and Oscar set off across the garden lawn in the dark over to the Cottage. They could see the light on in the distance coming from the criss-cross window pattern in the old stone cottage.

They walked across the lawn while Oscar and Thomas had an excited, nervous feeling and an; overwhelming sense of adventure and unknown.

As they got closer and closer to Stoney Cross Cottage, they could see the silhouette of Mr Griffins and Meg, the dog, moving around. Mr Griffins could see the torchlights and the silhouettes of Mrs Marlow and the two boys too.

It was not completely dark; it was a bright evening with the moon shining bright yellow and the stars illuminating the night sky. It was a clear night, and there was not a sign of cloud cover or rain.

As they got closer, Meg began to bark faintly, it was a bark to say hello and was not a nervous yap, and they could hear Mr Griffins Muttering to Meg.

"Good evening, Mr Griffins!" shouted Mrs Marlow from several metres away.

"Good evening, Mrs Marlow. Hello, boys," said Mr Griffins.

"You couldn't have picked a better night for it," said Mr Griffins as his face came into focus from the dark of the night.

"Yes, it's a great night. I feel that luck is on our side," said Mrs Marlow.

"Now, I must tell you all. I am neutral, and I can't in any way take sides or be seen to be helping, and right now, I am going on a walk in the woods and to show you one of my favourite places," said Mr Griffins.

"But I can't help in any way," repeated Mr Griffins.

"Understood. The boys have had a full briefing, I assure you; it's a simple walk and a simple walk back," said Mrs Marlow.

"Mrs Pucket is at Stonecross Manor and will be expecting you around dawn," said Mrs Marlow.

"Right-o! Mrs Marlow," said Mr Griffins.

"We had better be off. It will take at least four hours, and Lorsan Yeldrove will be expecting us," said Mrs Marlow.

Mr Griffins and Meg began walking into Ballymore Forest, and Meg led the way. The forest was thick with trees, and the summer green leaves on the trees blotted out the light from the moon and the stars. So the forest was pitch black.

The forest floor was dense with pine needles and old crisp leaves that made a crunching sound and new leaves that felt soft, and partially rotting branches that snapped and popped underfoot when pressure was applied from their feet.

The forest smelt different too in the mild night air; they could smell almost spices from the rotting leaves and the soil and the fungus's and moss, all now being amplified by the limited sense they had in the dark.

"Be careful and watch your feet," said Mr Griffins.

"We will soon be on a smoother path, but this will take about an hour," He said.

Thomas and Oscar had not spoken for around thirty minutes, and they were occupied with the job in hand. Thomas walked through the woods concentrating on the forest floor, and thought about getting to the stone circle in Ballymore woods. Oscar focused on the forest floor; his mind would wander into the stone circles and even thoughts into thinking about Tanniv and the stories he had been told in the past few days.

They walked for miles avoiding fallen trees, logs, and piles of leaves and mounds. They could hear the night noises of deer in the forests and owls hooting in the distance. Step by step, they grasped tree trunks and branches to steady themselves and stooped underneath lower brushwood each time, minding every step they took. They walked deeper and deeper into the blackness of the forest. They tried to be quiet, but the crunching and snapping of trees and leaves underfoot were impossible.

Some miniature lights began to appear one by one, only tiny lights emerged by the hundreds, and they buzzed around them.

"Oh, here we go," said Mr Griffins while Meg barked.

"I wondered how long it would take..." he said again.

The two boys stopped and looked at each other in disbelief, then looked closer again, not believing their eyes.

"Fairies!" said Oscar as he looked back at Mr Griffins and Mrs Marlow.

"Yes, Fairies!" Mrs Marlow and Mr Griffins both said together, shaking their heads.

"Go away!" said Mrs Marlow angrily.

"They look amazing!" said Thomas.

"Don't engage with them, Thomas; we will never get rid of them," repeated Mrs Marlow.

The fairies were beautiful; they glowed a bright green, pink, purple, and blue. They buzzed all around, laughing and giggling in high-pitched voices barely recognisable. They had blond hair and blue eyes and had the most amazing translucent wings, which beat millions of times a minute.

"They come from Tanniv and have damn near infested the forest now," said Mr Griffins as he flapped his arms, wafting them away.

The fairies came from Tanniv and somehow escaped through portals and had formed colonies all over England for the past hundred years. They were impossible to catch as they move so fast and could appear then reappear.

"We really must get this organised and send them back; I had not realised it had become such a problem," said Mrs Marlow as she was quite crossly swiping her arms around.

Thomas and Oscar looked and giggled as the fairies looked lovingly at them and sniggered back.

"Oh, don't encourage them," said Mrs Marlow.

"If we ignore them, then we will get rid of them; they're just seeking attention. Fairies are like a needy dog, and they will follow us for hours,"

Meg yapped at them, jumping up at them while biting the air. But they were far too fast to catch. Sensing that they were not getting any attention, the fairies looked sad and upset.

One beautiful angelic-looking fairy looked Oscar straight in the eyes and smiled, but he reluctantly looked away; they could hear faint crying and the tears coming from the fairy as she flew off. Then one by one, the fairies started to cry and look sad, and their wings began to dip and look flaccid as they each stopped following the group.

"Just ignore them, Oscar. It's all phoney; they just want you to take care of them and do everything for them. They prey; on children's good nature as they're inherently lazy creatures," said Mrs Marlow.

As they walked deeper and farther into the forest, the fairies disappeared. Their eyes were becoming more used to the night sky, and they could see clearly into the woods.

"Not far now to the forest path," said Mr Griffins; then, after that, we have another two hours of rambling until we get to the Ballymore Stone Circle.

Each footstep required heavy concentration; this was so as not to step into something too dangerous, such as a foxhole or a rabbit hole, or to step into uneven ground twisting an ankle or worse. Looking down at their footsteps, they occasionally got a beam of light coming from a break in the trees overhead, and they could see instantly clearer from the bright moon shining down. They could see the never-ending forest in each direction and see silhouetted hills and slopes in the wooded darkness of the forest.

"Here we are, on the path," said Mr Griffins. The trail was not quite a path, but it was better than what they had been walking on for the past hours. It was a

Ballymore Forest Stone Circle.

minimal, very tight, one-person dirt track that hikers had mildly trodden in. It was not too prominent and would still require a great deal of concentration as it was full of thick tree roots and rabbit holes and slopes on each side with ditches that the rain had formed in heavy showers over the years. But it was better than the trek through the uneven forest floor.

"It's about an hour and a half from here," said Mr Griffins.

Meg led the way, followed by Mr Griffins, then Thomas and Oscar with Mr Marlow at the back. Everyone was in perfect silence as it was tougher to talk in one line, and the terrain was leading up steep forest hills and then down deep forest steps, all taking an equal concentration in the dark not to fall over, so talking would have been another hindrance. So everyone marched on in silence, and they could only hear the rustling of coats and clunking of footsteps in walking boots against the dry mud and chalk forest surface.

Marching on into the night, they were making good time. The boys loosened their coats to allow cold air in as they started to get hot from the strenuous walking. In the distance was a tiny clearing with a pronounced uprooted tree trunk that had blown over in a storm at some point. The tree trunk's roots were exposed and looked like barky wooden octopus tentacles reaching out in the night's sky. They could see the underside of the trees' trunk covered in soil and white chalky deposits. It sloped down, and the tree's roots, some thicker than others, created perfect seating for them to sit on.

"Let's stop here for ten minutes," said Mrs Marlow.

"Good idea," said Mr Griffins. "We have about another hour to go." Mr Griffins said again, feeling like he should keep everyone up to speed on timings.

Thomas found a knotted branch to sit on, and Oscar sat on a lower thick root poking out from the bottom of the upturned tree. Mrs Marlow sat opposite Mr Griffins, and Meg nuzzled between the two boys.

Mrs Marlow went into her bag and passed around two canteens of water. She also opened and passed around shortbread.

"These are full of butter and sugar and is precisely what we need," said Mrs Marlow to the two boys while smiling at them both.

The two boys stretched out their hands in the dark towards the shortbread, trying hard not to drop them, and started to eat and drink water.

"Here you go, Mr Griffins," said Mr Marlow as she passed a foiled tin parcel of shortbread over to her friend Harold.

"And there's one for Meg," said Mrs Marlow as she handed the fourth parcel over to Oscar. Thomas and Oscar unwrapped Meg's tin foiled parcel, and they both broke the shortbread and gave it to Meg.

Mrs Marlow wrapped up the tin foiled remains of the shortbread and said, "I have made the same amount for the way back, and there are apple slices chopped up in there, too."

"Thank you, Mrs Marlow," said Oscar. "Yes, thank you, Grandmother," said Thomas.

"Are you all prepared for Tanniv?" said Thomas.

"Yes, my dear boy, it's been a long time. I used to leave these trips to your mother, so it's been a long time since I last went back," Mrs Marlow said as she smiled at the two boys.

In truth, she was not prepared at all. Mrs Marlow was far too old for a voyage like this, and she was feeling worn out from this journey through Ballymore Forest, and just the thought of another four days of travelling to the Disaris Kingdom of Vakoborg was exhausting.

Mr Griffins, who was almost the same age, could see it on her face that she was exhausted and not up for the job. He feared that maybe she would not return. But he also knew that someone needed to get the message to West Tanniv and both worlds depended on this message getting through. A Marlow needed to deliver the message and unite the people of West Tanniv, and this needed to be done now before it was too late.

They finished up the shortbread and drinks and set out for the Stone circle once again. The path through the woods was very dark and carried up over huge hills leading to a valley clearing.

"We're about twenty minutes away," said Mr Griffins as Meg led on through the winding path leading down into the valley clearing. By this time, it was almost midnight, and it was getting a little colder.

The footpath led down to a small stream; they could hear the trickling jangle noise that the stream made as they walked down into the valley and over a small wooden footbridge which opened out into a grass clearing with no woods on either side. They could see the Stone Circle Silhouette and the shadows of the stones now.

The stones were magnificent; each was slightly different, but all stood upright and formed a perfect circle.

"Here we are, Ballymore Stone Circle," said Mr Griffins.

"I will need to stand way back. I can't be seen helping anyone," he reminded.

The two boys had not said much all night; they were quiet because this was all new and an adventure. As they hiked up to the stone circle, they looked at it and felt the stones; they could feel the energy in the centre of the ring.

Mrs Marlow stood to one side and silently caught her breath, reserving her energy for the task ahead.

The two boys continued to stroll around the circle together, touching each stone and feeling the moss and lichen on the stone surfaces. They touched the great stones in a way that they had never done before. After two days of learning about the stone circles and all the information the books had bestowed on the two boys, they strolled around with a sense of familiarity that these stones were far more than just an old monument now.

They had learned so much, and the stones were a far cry from what they thought; only days before, they thought old cavemen had crudely made them. The giant stones were a gateway and were sacred stones, and an entire culture and belief system depended on the stability of the stone circles.

Mrs Marlow stood up and looked over at Mr Griffins and Meg in the distance.

"Come along, boys. Stand in your places," said Mrs Marlow.

"Remember, this is a powerful circle and more powerful than what you are used to," she said.

Thomas walked over to the far side of the stone circle, and Oscar more or less stayed where he was but ensuring he was level with Thomas and shuffled back and forward in the damp grass to ensure he was precisely placed. Mrs Marlow walked to what would have been the third point creating a triangle between the three of them.

This was exactly like they had previously practised; they all stood looking at each other, again with a sense of importance, that this was no longer a rehearsal.

Mrs Marlow cleared her throat tilted her head back, and with a deep breath, she began to say the words that would open up a portal to Tanniv.

"Repeat after me, aperta ianua—aperta ianua," said Mrs Marlow.

Thomas, and Oscar, repeated the words over and over. They had the look of extreme concentration and seriousness. They started shouting and closed their eyes to focus harder.

Then, just like before, a mighty gust of wind began to lash up inside the stone circle again, only this time, the wind was much stronger than they had experienced before. The power was immense. The ancient Britons positioned the Ballymore stone circle to enhance the earth's magnetic field, giving this circle a vast amount of celestial energy.

Then just like before, a small ball of bright light formed in the middle of the circle, and it grew larger and larger.

"Focus, boys!" shouted Mrs Marlow. As the wind and the ball of light grew bigger, Oscar clenched his wand so tight and held it up with all of his might. Thomas also looked overwrought as the bright white circle grew larger and bigger, and again scrunching his muscles and holding up his wand, he closed his eyes tight to focus his power onto the bright light.

By this time, it was the size of a four-metre oval shape and almost ready.

Mr Griffins and Meg could see the great light and wind from afar as the surrounding trees all creaked and groaned and moaned, and the leaves of the neighbouring vegetation rustled and blew off around the swirling wind.

Mrs Marlow again repeated "aperta, ianua", and the wind got stronger and stronger. Then collapsing on her knees from extreme exhaustion, Mrs Marlow fainted and was out cold.

The oval began to oscillate wildly out of control. Mrs Marlow had passed out from exhaustion; the brilliant white Portal was bouncing around the circle frantically, getting faster and faster and more violently the portal span. Mrs Marlow's wands stream that had been stabilising the Portal had stopped.

This caused an uncontrollable spin around the inner circle. Thomas continued to hold out his wand and shouted at Oscar to do the same.

The boys ducked and bobbed the spinning Portal as it spun around, getting ever more unpredictable and still holding up their wands; believing that this was the correct thing to do, the Portal grew ever brighter and even more ferocious.

The erratic, unpredictable giant orb had now taken on a mind of its own and was spinning towards Oscar.

He was jammed up against a huge sarsen stone and had nowhere to go, so he held out his wand and concentrated hard on the portal to ensure it would miss him, but it was too late the course in which the orb was spinning was directly into the path of Oscar.

It swallowed him, and Thomas screamed, "NOOOOOOO!" Oscar was sucked into the path of the portal, and he disappeared. Thomas's face was a look of shock and horror. The portal was beginning to shut as it was only supported by one wand, and a novice sorcerer could not hold onto it much longer. Thomas looked left at his grandmother lying on the ground; he looked hard and could see that she was still breathing and her head was moving. Thomas decided to jump into the portal to rescue Oscar.

He looked directly into the orb then tried to predict its next move. Thomas, still having marginal control of the sphere from one angle, ran straight into its path; fearing that the portal was just about to close, he shut his eyes holding out his wand and sprinted directly into its way. Then there was nothing, the portal closed, and the wind stopped, and all they could hear was the dead of night.

Mr Griffins ran over to Mrs Marlow, and Meg raced to her aid. She stirred and became conscious. Mr Griffins bent down and held Mrs Marlow head as she tried to get up.

"You stay right there," said Mr Griffins while he was trying to figure out the next best thing to do.

"The boys, the boys," she said. Then again, "What happened to the boys?" she repeated.

"There's no easy way to say this; they both got swallowed by the portal and are now in Tanniv," said Mr Griffins in an anxious tone.

Mrs Marlow sat up and said, "I must go with them," and began fishing around for her wand in the dark.

"We need to rest and get you back to Stonecross Manor," said Mr Griffins. "I am not allowed to help, and Mrs Pucket will be the best person to talk to now." Mr Griffins scratched his head thinking about the four-hour challenging walk back to Stonecross Manor.

Still unsure of what exactly happened, Mrs Marlow started to think a little clearer. He's a Marlow, and Lorsan Yeldrove will look after him, she thought to herself. Mrs Marlow tried to reassure herself as much as possible.

"Yes, we must get back to Stonecross Manor; the great eagle owls of Tanniv can help," Mrs Marlow said to Mr Griffins.

"Let's wait an hour or so until the sun comes up. It will give you some time to rest and will make the journey far easier," said Mr Griffins.

Mrs Marlow, still sitting on the floor, went through her bag for some water; then, leaning up against a giant Sarsen stone, she rationalised the situation. Thomas is a Marlow, and if I can get word to Lorsan Yeldrove, King Drusunal, and King Gilgamesh, then the boys could deliver my message at the great gathering of Stormhorn. Still in complete shock, she knew the boys would be okay and that she would do everything she could to ensure their safety, which could work.

By this time, Oscar and Thomas were in Tanniv and surrounded by warriors and soldiers from Tanniv in the Great Stone Circle of Vakoborg Forrest in the middle of the night. They stood together in the centre of the stone circle in complete shock, looking out at the dark faces looking back at them.

Then a huge grey and white dappled horse came trotting into the centre of the circle with a great handsome warrior in full battle dress astride the magnificent steed. The horse and the outstanding-looking warrior circled the two boys.

"Who are you boys, and where is the White Sorceress Marlow?" said Lorsan Yeldrove in a strong deep voice while still circling the two boys.

"My name is Thomas, and this is Oscar," said Thomas as the two boys looked up at the glorious-looking warrior in a very soft anxious voice.

"Speak up, boy! And what of the great White Sorceress?" said Lorsan Yeldrove.

"She is my grandmother, and we helped open the portal with our wands, but she is old now, and she collapsed with exhaustion," said Thomas as he loudly blurted out one hundred letters in a second.

"The portal took us instead," said Oscar in a flamboyant voice.

Lorsan Yeldrove pulled the horse to a complete stop, looked at the boys in the eyes, swung his leg over the saddle, and jumped down from the horse in one sweeping gymnastic motion.

He then examined the two boys closer. Looking at Oscar first, he looked deep into his eyes, and seeing his wand, he said, "So you are a sorcerer, too."

Oscar, not wanting to say too much and a little prone to an exaggeration, said, "Yes, sir, we both opened up the portal to come here," Lorsan smirked and looked back at his soldiers who were all looking at the exchange, and liking the boy's confidence. He then turned his gaze to Thomas.

"So you are the Sorceress Marlow's grandson," said Lorsan Yeldrove looking down at Thomas as he examined him thoroughly.

"Yes, sir," said Thomas.

"And are you a great sorcerer like young Oscar here?" repeated Lorsan as he looked back and grinned at the soldiers all looking on while turning his gaze back to Thomas.

"We have only just started, and we both opened up the portal," said Thomas softly

"And what of your mother, boy? I knew Alina well," said Lorsan Yeldrove confidently.

"You knew my mother," said Thomas, a little shaken and surprised.

"Yes, I knew your mother; she is a great person," said Lorsan.

"I am afraid to tell you she is dead. She died in an accident along with my father a few weeks ago," said Thomas to the great warrior, trying not to look upset.

"I am sorry to hear that; this saddens me too—there will be time to mourn her passing, but the time is not now," said Lorsan as he patted Thomas on the head.

Lorsan turned to the soldiers and roared in a deep, confident voice addressing the surrounding troops, "These boys are Marlows and white sorcerers and have come to the great gathering of Stormhorn to unite the clans." The soldiers cheered and clapped and looked at the boys.

"Get these boys horses. Tonight we ride to the great Disaris City of Vakoborg!" shouted Lorsan.

Thomas and Oscar observed the magnificent-looking soldiers and warriors around them. Each warrior had sturdy-looking leather boots and the most impressive buckskin tunics, and hardened leather chest plated armour with the great eagle owls on West Tanniv embossed on their chests. They all had swords and a shorter sword on each hip; they all had long hair and beards and wore helmets with white feathered hackles hanging from the hardened leather helmets. They had shields again bearing different images of the great eagle owls hanging from the horses' saddles.

A warrior tall and slightly younger than the rest walked towards the two boys and said, "My name is Elaith Tarron from the Tarrenash region; here are your horses, and stay close to me."

"Pleased to meet you," said Oscar.

"Yes, pleased to meet you," said Thomas.

The young warrior Elaith Tarron looked at the two boys, smiled, and said, "Stay close to me and ride in the middle of the pack; you are both my responsibility."

The two boys climbed onto their horses; neither had ridden before, but both cantered horses a little and knew enough to know what they were doing.

Thomas looked around at Oscar and the brilliant, outstanding warriors and felt safe. Oscar looked around and had the same feeling.

"It is almost two days ride to the great Disaris City of Vakoborg—it's full of bandits, Disaris spies, and spies from Moltenwing are in this forest. So there will be no talking. And keep your eyes open; we ride at night and will sleep in the day somewhere safe," said Elaith Tarron, knowing that the more information he gave them, the fewer questions they would ask.

The Vakoborg Forest was so thick with Disaris spies. Word had probably reached King Gilgamesh by now.

Lorsan was right at the front of the throng of men, and each soldier stood by their horses packing and unpacking equipment and fastening pouches and leather bags while ratcheting buckles tight all on all sides of the horse's saddles.

Around fifteen soldiers joined the expedition to Stormhorn, and each one looked like a hardened warrior who had seen many battles and all had such discipline.

"Saddle up, men! Let's ride out!" shouted Lorsan with a ferociously impressive commanding voice. Oscar looked on at Lorsan in complete amazement that he was amongst a real-life warrior.

Each warrior mounted their horse in one motion and trotted out into the deep thick forest of Vakoborg.

"Just stay in the middle, boys and ride close to me," said Elaith as he leaned over to grab the bit of Thomas's horse, pulling the mount in closer to himself. Thomas nodded and carried on riding.

They did not go into a gallop; it was more like a brisk trot given that they were in a dense forest and the woodland floor was uneven as it was nighttime.

The forest was the same but slightly different from England; it was the dead of night, the outline of the trees looked somewhat different, and the species of the leaves and plants looked somewhat dissimilar, but it felt like a typical forest.

The group had been riding for hours in silence, and then in the clearings, the troop rode into a gallop, and all the while, the sense of being watched was apparent. The soldiers around them would be continuously looking up at the canopy of the trees and into the blackness of the forest and in the distance. All had a job to do, and you could see that they were all very well-trained and all watching out. Elaith leaned forward and grasped the reigns from Oscar, pulling them in tightly. He whispered quietly while raising his index finger to his lips to signal stillness, "We are being watched." With some hand gestures coming from Lorsan Yeldrove, the troops formed a tight circle.

Not yet drawing their swords, they all looked out into the darkness and reached down to get their shields. One of the soldiers who were always by Lorsan's side, Captain Darfin Norlen, whispered into Lorsan's ear, "It's Disaris up in the trees, and we are being watched by the Disaris."

"Don't worry," one of the soldiers said to Thomas and Oscar, "It's just the Disaris letting us know that they know we are here."

The troops stood for several minutes still with their defensive shields and, without drawing their swords, were signalling that they were not an enemy of Disaris or Vakoborg.

Lorsan signalled again by raising his leather-gloved hand and making a fist gestured; he then pointed, and the warriors to move out one by one. Each warrior was carefully ensuring that Thomas and Oscar were encircled in the middle of the riding huddle. If the Disaris watched the troops, they could see that these were West Tanniv warriors from the Tarrenash banners on their shields and clothing and could see that they were friendly.

Everyone by now knew that a gathering had been called, and there were bands of soldiers on the main routes travelling north to Stormhorn.

Bands of men did not belong to the regions passing through on their way to the great gathering.

But a group of soldiers moving at night through the Vakoborg forest was strange and needed to be reported to King Gilgamesh.

Although the Tarrenash soldiers could not see the Disaris, they were all highly trained hunters and trackers and could sense and see that someone was watching them. Their experience told them that they were friendly and probably Disaris warriors. So the squad moved in the dead of night cautiously and ever courteously so not to insult or offend any friends that could be watching them deep in the dark mists of the forest. It was not their land, and they needed to respect that they were trespassing.

The Disaris King Grusan Gilgamesh

The bloodline of the King had ruled the Vakoborg Kingdom for seven hundred years. The Disariss had lived in Tanniv for thousands of years, and they had seen many changes.

The stone circles were their main religious focus. No one knew more about the mystical elements and the secret enchanted magic surrounding the stone circles and forests than the Disaris.

King Grusan was a highly suspicious king; he had seen the forests plundered and had seen his lands shrink over the centuries and was not welcoming to outsiders. He had seen many wars and delivered an army into the great trap at Ilihorn and had lost thousands of Disaris warriors defending Tanniv rights.

The Disaris required and wanted nothing from anyone and asked for nothing in return. King Gilgamesh looked after his people, and his main concentration was the religious order of the Disaris and keeping his lands free from bandits and East Tanniv spies.

The occasional Bauk that would wander down from the north in the summer and the greed of the Bauk would be problematic from time to time, but the Disaris managed their own problems.

He loved the city and the forest, and the Disaris people were always his primary concern. His political policies were purely democratic, and a huge Disaris council made decisions.

The King trusted the Disaris council, and each law was passed by vote. This ensured that the forest and the stone circles were preserved for future generations, which was the main emphasis of the King and the Disaris council.

Vakoborg had a massive Disaris army, and it was legendary; it was famed in both West and East Tanniv.

The Disaris Empire was a military state, and from the age of four, both boys and girls were conscripted and enrolled in the Disaris military agoge school.

The Disaris army had no ambition for war, increased wealth, or escalation in power or trade. The mighty Disaris armies were set up to defend the religion first then the kingdom and then the forest.

Even the Disaris women were inducted into the armies, and all the girls from the age of four were taught the skills of war, with sword fighting and longbows, axe handling, and the art of mystical practice that would infuse them with their forest surroundings.

No matter boy or girl, no quarter was given to girls, and they were expected to be as proficient at fighting as the men.

The Disaris council was made up of almost half women, and age and gender were not seen to be a disadvantage by anyone.

The Vakoborg Empire stretched for thousands of miles in each direction, with hugely dense forests with incredible canyons and valleys all lined with forests and trees with the most diverse forest life.

The Great Forest City of Vakoborg was gleamingly white; made from marble, it had the most impressive towers and turrets all over the city. The towers numbered in the hundreds as it seemed the fashion to build houses and Palaces with magnificent turret dwellings and all looked exclusive and unique.

This was seen as a competition between the wealthy of the city as each looked more splendid than the other.

It was a walled citadel with a thriving, prosperous city inside.

The floors and roads were marble and were gleaming white with the green of forest vegetation everywhere. The city could be turned into a fortress within minutes if the horns were sounded. It was covered in ivy and was surrounded by trees; it was built on an ancient mountain spring, so fresh water and supply were plentiful.

It was full of Ziggurats and had massive platformed Ziggurats that could be seen for miles, and if you were a bird, you would see a sea of green then a gleamingly white city in a mass of pea and emerald green colours.

The city was filled with restaurants, Inns and Hotels, and colossal market squares, and the forest city was just like any other city in Tanniv.

The Disaris people were totally self-sufficient and never really traded with the other countries and regions of Tanniv and kept themselves to themselves.

No outsiders could live in the city, and if Disaris married Tarrenash or Turgett's, they gave up their rights for Vakoborg citizenship. This was not uncommon, and examples of Disaris and Tarrenash marriages could be seen all over Tanniv.

It was a very religious country with the most impressive monasteries devoting prayers and religion to the stone circles.

King Grusan Gilgamesh

The Disaris churches, abbeys, and Ziggurats were dotted all around the country, deep into the forests for hundreds of miles. This was a military state deeply enthused with religious belief.

King Gilgamesh had one daughter who was proficient in war, excelled at sword fighting, and was a master volley with a bow and arrow. His daughter was his only child. She, too, sat on the great Disaris council as a primary decision-maker, always by King Gilgamesh's side and would deliberate on any decisions. The Princess had the same amount of power as the King in many respects.

Persuading the Disaris King to go to the Stormhorn gathering would be a monumental task, and now the persuasion was going to come from a boy from England accompanied by young Oscar.

Making Camp for the Day

As they travelled through the night, many hours passed. Elaith Tarron took his job seriously and kept the two boys close to protect them as much as possible from anything that could arise.

The horses cantered slowly into the night, and the soldiers' vigilance surrounding them made the two boys feel at ease.

The forest was different, and the two boys could hear various noises coming out of the forest's darkness that they had never heard before.

The soldiers were not alarmed as the different noises were the calling from birds and other animals not native to England. So everything had seemed different throughout the night's riding.

They travelled through valleys and up very steep hills, all completely covered by a forest canopy of leaves and thick brush.

Occasionally they could see the stars and the moonlight beaming through gaps in the forest branches and trees. But with it being dark, there was not too much to see.

They could hear a slight rumble of thunder now in the distance, which appeared very faint and not too frequent but was getting slightly louder, and with the clear night sky, there was no real risk of rain.

The horses and soldiers slowed, and Lorsan commanded, "We will stop here to take on water for the horses." A small stream at the bottom of a small wooded hill had been chosen; the stream was wide and looked like it was running rapidly down from the mountains.

The banks of the stream were sharp and steep, and in some places, the tree roots were visible and exposed; it widened into a very small pool, and each soldier, in turn, dismounted from their mount and took the horse to drink.

Each soldier stroked and caressed their horses and would feed them. Every soldier got out food and fed their horses, ensuring they were lavished with affection. They could hear faint voices from the soldiers all talking and muttering to their horses and treating them, almost like royalty and certainly like people and all done with the most amount of respect.

Elaith Tarron

Elaith Tarron dismounted and started to stroke his horse, also muttering to the horse tenderly, "You've done so well girl, you've done so well," as he looked into the horse's eyes while feeding the magnificent looking steed.

"Thomas and Oscar, come on, it's your turn," he whispered. Both the boys carefully jumped off their horses, took them by the reigns then looked at Elaith for further instructions. Elaith smiled, realising that the two boys were doing their best and said, "In that pouch there—there's horse feed, and when it's your turn, go to the pool and take them for a drink." He pointed to the boys with affirmative instruction.

"Elaith, what is my horse's name?" whispered Oscar.

"Your horse is she and is called Sylvar, and she's a mighty horse and has seen many skirmishes over the years; she won't let you down," said Elaith in a strong, confident voice as he patted Sylvar and stroked her with love and affection.

"And what is my horse called?" asked Thomas, whispering to Elaith.

"Your horse is a stallion called Leokan, he's a strong horse, and he never gets tired and is very reliable, and he never forgets a kind person," said Elaith as he smiled at Thomas.

"In Tarrenash, we treat horses like we do people; they are cared for and cherished. So make friends with your horses, lads. It's the most important thing," said Elaith. The two boys nodded in total agreement took their horses down to the pool of water for a drink, each talking to their mounts and stroking the horses. When the horses were done, they stood to one side and followed Elaith back to where the rest of the troops were resting.

"Let's sit on the rocks here," said Elaith.

Thomas and then Oscar sat on some boulders partially covered in thick green moss, and not wanting to break the silence, they looked at Elaith again with some uncertainty.

Elaith fished around in his saddlebags and pulled out some bread and dried meats; he divided them up into three and handed a portion to Oscar and then to Thomas.

"Eat!" Whispered Elaith.

"It's only a little, but we will eat again later," said Elaith. "It's not good to ride with a bloated gut," he added as he winked at the boys.

Thomas placed some dried meat on a bit of bread between his thumb and finger he ate. He tore off a piece and then ate, ripping the tough meat and bread with his teeth as he pulled it down with his hand.

Oscar being slightly fussy, studied the meat first and sniffed at it while holding it up and rotating it in the moonlight; deciding it was okay, he ate. It was great, he thought with a smile. It was a dried ham and bread sandwich, nothing special, but it was a nice sandwich.

"Did you hear that thunder again?" said Thomas to Elaith.

"That's no thunder," said Elaith.

"What is it then? I have been able to hear that sound for a few miles now," said Thomas.

"That's the Bauk in the Mornala Mountains about three miles from here," said Elaith with a serious tone to his voice.

"Bauk!" said Oscar with a surprised voice.

"What are Bauk?" he said.

"Bauk are giant greedy creatures, and they care only for two things, food and jewels. They bang the rocks together looking for diamonds, rubies, emeralds, and gold," replied Elaith.

"Why do they bang boulders, and what are Bauk?" said Thomas.

"Is that the noise Bauk makes?" said Thomas.

"No, they are banging boulders together," said Elaith waiting for the following questions.

"But they are also fierce, giant violent creatures. They are convinced that everyone wants to steal their precious stones, and they eat almost anything."

The vicious Bauk of the Mornala Mountains; were very fierce and extremely violent natured creatures. But mostly, they brawled, fought, and quarrelled with each other.

They would steal each other's jewels when they were not looking and would try all manner of tricks to outwit and swindle each other or even fight and brawl with each other to death.

This was brought on by obscure Bauk coupling and mating rituals, which happened every summer, the male Bauk with the most sparkly stones would win the attention of female Bauk.

They very rarely ventured down from the mountains of Mornala in fear of losing their hoards. They were a stupid race only concerned with violence and fighting each other. They fed on mountain goats, bears, birds, and mountain lions. Each year the salmon would run up the rivers and fill the mountain lakes, so most of the year, they had food and no real need to venture down to the hills.

They were gigantic creatures and all bone and muscle, and they are grey-blue with a big, bold stupid head; they bounded around taunting each other, they had colossal thick teeth for biting down on rocks. They spent their time fighting, banging rocks in huge quarries, and eating.

Their nearest civilisation was the Disaris of Vakoborg, who had no interest in the precious stones, so the two civilisations lived in relative peace. But occasionally, bandits and the odd chancer wanting to make their fortunes would sneak up to the Mornala Mountains with their heads filled with the legends of the rich senseless Bauk. The chancers would try and steal the precious diamonds, rubies, and gold; with varying degrees of success, they would return with stories of riches or stories of woe.

The not-so-successful thieves became Bauk food, which spawned the taste and desire for humans, as the Bauk considered humans a delicacy and the tastiest thing they could eat.

However, Bauk being inherently lazy and never wanting to leave their hoards were never seen outside the Mornala Mountains but occasionally in the Vakoborg forests.

Despite the well-known fact that Bauk never left the Mornala Mountains, Lorsan and the troops would travel through the mountains, maze of valleys, and foothills to avoid confrontation from the fantastic beasts.

The troops fed and watered their horses, saddled up, and started to ride out. Again Elaith kept the boys very close and led them directly into the middle of the soldiers, so they would all gallop together and be safe.

"It's about another three hours until the sun comes up, then we will make camp in the Oris Gorge," said Elaith.

Captain Norlen looked over at Elaith Tarron to say stop talking but then realised he had the two boys.

Elaith looked over at Captain Norlen with an apologetic expression and tilted his head towards Thomas and Oscar.

The Captain nodded his head slowly, partially sympathetic to give a look of understanding while expressing to keep the two boys quiet.

One by one, the horses led out from the stream, and the soldiers crowded around Thomas, Oscar, and Elaith as if this was a very well-rehearsed military formation that they had done many times before.

They trekked around the mountain foothills, never venturing over but always around, this time only going slowly as the terrain had become very rocky and uneven. The thunderous din from the Bauk was getting louder, and they could hear the rocks and boulders being knocked around clearer now, but the noise was still two or three miles away.

After several miles, the troops started to descend downwards, and still covered in the thick, dense forest, the angle of the ground felt steeper.

The pace was slow now, but the landscape was highly hazardous and gave way to slippy rocks.

The further down into the valley they went, the colder it got.

Elaith leaned forward to the rear of Oscar's saddle and pulled out a giant sheep's wool fleece blanket so enormous it looked like the hide from three or four sheep. He looked at Oscar and gestured with his arms in a cold wrapping mimicking motion to wrap up warm.

Thomas watching the interchange, took one hand off his horse's reigns and began fishing his arm around the back of his saddle for his huge fleece too.

Elaith could see that he was struggling, so he leaned over to Thomas's saddle, and with a considerable jolt, Elaith pulled out the warm blanket, and he wrapped this around him too. Thomas Observed thick leather string on each side; he tied it around his neck and then noticed more strings lower down the blanket; he tied these onto his legs. Oscar, spotting this, decided to do the same. Elaith looked at each boy with his strong warrior face nodded approvingly.

As the troops and horses ambled further down into the gorge, the temperature did drop, and it became noticeably colder.

The route was damp and wet, and extremely dangerous. Lorsan could see that the sky had turned from black to a deep blue. It was becoming morning, and they could see daylight and could hear birds singing.

The route was so slippery and so treacherous that no one would endeavour down into this area of the forest. Thomas could see that this was a military strategy to be safe while all the soldiers and horses slept and rested.

Finally, they reached the bottom of the gorge; it was fully daylight by now, but the dark canyon still had an atmosphere of nightfall about it. It was covered in thick green moss everywhere. The boys could hear the sound of heavy running water in the distance.

They carried on through the thick green vegetation, which had changed slightly until they came to the most beautiful silver and white waterfall.

The waterfall was huge; it was as tall as a skyscraper, and the water ran into a vast basin-like lake and was so crystal clear.

It was like magic; the waterfall mist and the green vegetation made this look like a place of absolute paradise and tranquillity.

They cantered around the lake to a clearing of caves positioned behind the waterfall, and one by one, each rider disappeared behind the cascade of water.

The caves were hidden entirely. Thomas sat patiently on his horse, thinking that "you would need to know the forest very well to know that these caves existed."

"This is where we make camp for the day," said Lorsan Yeldrove.

"Tend to your horses first!" shouted Captain Norlen, looking at the troops then directly at Thomas and Oscar with a wink.

"We can talk normally in here; there's no need to whisper now. The noise from the waterfall will silence out our voices," said Elaith. "Are you okay, boys?"

"Yes, fine, thank you, Elaith," said Thomas while Oscar nodded.

"It's been a long night, so tend to the horses first; this is the Tarrenash way—horses always first," said Elaith to the two boys.

The horses were given hay, feed, water and were tied up close together at the back of the cave and safely out of sight.

They kept the saddles on the horses encase they needed to escape fast or go into combat. A layer of sheepskin was laid down on the bedrock first to ensure the horses were comfortable, then a layer of hay.

Each soldier brushed and laid the horses down into a sleeping position, scrubbed and cleaned the mount, and ensured they had everything they needed.

Captain Norlen marched over to the soldiers and organised them into century duties in strategic locations around the cave and canyon. He was organising tactical lookout points for any danger to alert the group.

Elaith arranged and organised his sheepskins, furs, and pelts into a bed and shaped it like a nest between some rocks. The two boys learning fast, decided to pull out the skins, furs, and hides and arrange them up against an enormous boulder in a similar fashion.

It was so beautiful looking around the cave; it really looked like paradise, and now they had a nice warm bed to climb into thought Thomas.

The sound of the waterfall was also a comforting factor and would send everyone to sleep very fast.

Lorsan sauntered over to the two boys standing tall with his swords and blades hanging and spoke to Elaith, "Elaith, how are these two young soldiers coming along?"

"They are learning fast, my lord, and have been no trouble," said Elaith while slightly bowing his head.

"Boys, make sure you sleep, eat and drink plenty of water. We will ride out again tonight and stay close to Elaith," said Lorsan.

"Yes, sir," said Thomas, and following Elaith's example, slightly bowed his head.

"Yes, sir," said Oscar as he observed Thomas, and he too bowed his head. Lorsan looked at the two boys and smiled at their ability to learn fast.

The general looked back at Elaith. "We have two strong soldiers in the making," then turned to walk away.

This time, Thomas and Oscar were given more bread and meat and a thick cut of pork and a whole round loaf of bread, each with an apple and some potato cakes.

They sat down on their new makeshift beds and ate; this was plenty of food and more than they had expected.

Ripping bread apart and biting into thick cuts of pork, they sat quietly and had dinner while gazing around the cave and watching the mighty warriors.

The rest of the soldiers did the same; there was not much conversation in the cave; everyone was exhausted and wanted to sleep and rest.

"There will be no fire! We can't risk the smell of the fire reaching anyone, so make sure you wrap up warm, it's cold and damp in this cave, but we will be safe here," said Elaith.

"Sleep now. I will check on you during your sleep," Elaith said, acting like he had been given an assignment, and as a good soldier, he was going to do his very best to ensure he completed his task.

The boys slept close to each other with Elaith close, and the remaining soldiers slept around Thomas and Oscar in a protective ring.

Some soldiers went on century duty in critical positions in the canyon and vantage points around the waterfall. Two of the soldiers slept directly in the mouth of the cave for extra added protection.

The two boys looked at each other didn't say much they were both fatigued and exhausted.

"I hope Mrs Marlow is okay," said Oscar.

"She will be fine; she will be with Mr Griffins and Mrs Pucket," said Thomas. "But I am worried too; it's just that there has been no real-time to think about it."

"I understand what you mean. I can still hardly believe what is happening and who we are with right now," whispered Oscar.

"I wonder when we get to Vakoborg if I can get a message back to Grandmother," said Thomas.

The two boys rested on their backs, gazing up at the silver granite cave roof. Some soldiers were now snoring and were fast asleep.

Thomas and Oscar could still hear a faint thunderous noise every five minutes or so from the Bauk. This was still the sound of the Bauk mining and fighting and arguing between each other. It sounded like they were very nearby now. In essence, they were above them, but about two miles above them, in the Mornala Mountains. None of the soldiers looked worried or concerned about the noises, so it put the two boy's minds at rest.

Gradually both boys fell quickly into a deep sleep, both nestling, snuggling down in a bed of warm, comfortable, cosy animal fur.

They drifted off into a deep yawning sleep until the faint noise of the boulders being smashed by the Bauk of the Mountains above them made them drift off into silence.

The Long Walk Home

Mrs Marlow and Mr Griffins had been well underway for some time, walking back through Ballymore Forrest.

The walk was four hours, and they had been walking for around two hours. However, due to Mrs Marlow's weakened condition, the hike was very sluggish.

They had made their way to the dirt track and stopped at the upturned tree; it was now the tricky walk back through the thick forest that was the difficult one. But Mrs Marlow was a determined lady, and getting back to Stonecross Manor was her only focus and concentration at this point; she never panicked at what had happened; she just needed to get back.

"I hope that they will be okay; I should never have asked them to do this," said Mrs Marlow.

"You had no choice, the Stone Circles are moving, and Alwin Aminoff was in Stoney Cross," said Mr Griffins. "There was nothing more we could do this is our job and our duty."

"The boys will be fine. I know they will—I blame myself," said Mrs Marlow.

They rambled on through the night and the darkness; by this time, it was early morning, and it had become much brighter and considerably lighter, making progress quicker.

They stopped in the middle of the forest only to drink some water and take in some shortbread. Keeping their energy levels up was essential, and Mr Griffins knew this, so he encouraged breaks regularly through the long walk back, whether Mrs Marlow liked it or not.

Meg led on in front, keeping a vigilant eye out for anyone, making the two feel safe as they marched through the darkness.

Mrs Pucket was up early and watching out of the window from the kitchen. She hadn't slept that night, so she was completely dressed and preparing for the boys to come home.

She had been expecting them to be home by now as it was now almost eight o'clock in the morning, and they should have been back by now.

Mrs Pucket had lived in and around Lyndhurst all her life, so she knew all the stone circles and the forests very well. So she knew that this was a very long demanding arduous walk to the stone circles, and when exhausted, it would feel like an even longer walk back.

They both carried on moving at a much faster pace; as it was now almost nine o'clock, they could see familiar signs that they were getting closer and closer to Stonecross Manor.

"Not long now, around thirty minutes," said Mr Griffins.

"Yes, we will need to send a message to Vakoborg as soon as we get back," said Mrs Marlow.

Not wanting to argue and knowing that there was no point in trying to get Mrs Marlow to rest first would be impossible; Mr Griffins nodded in agreement and carried on marching through the forest at an ever-quickening pace.

Mrs Pucket was still at the window, and by now the summer sun had risen and the morning dew on the green laws was drying out and creating a slight morning mist; she looked out at the lawns towards Stoney Cross Cottage and never took her eyes off the grounds and surrounding areas. She knew more or less which direction they would come from, so she kept watchful.

Meg began to bark at the distance; Mr Griffins and Mrs Marlow looked up and could see the light at the end of the woods. The perimeter of the woods led down to Stoney Cross Cottage, and now everything was becoming more familiar.

"We have made it," Mrs Marlow cried.

"Good work, Meg," said Mr Griffins as he leaned down to pat her on the head while reaching into his pocket for a dog biscuit for Meg to eat.

Mrs Pucket, still looking out of the kitchen window, could see black bodies coming out of the morning mist and could see Mr Griffins, then Mrs Marlow, and Meg trudging across the lawn.

Her heart jumped with an uneasy anxious, and joyous flutter; then, her heart sank knowing that something must have gone terribly wrong.

She opened the kitchen's back door, walked out onto the raised garden patio area, and waved frantically at the two hiking across the lawn.

They walked closer and closer and then up the stairs to the patio. They both looked absolutely exhausted.

"Good morning, Mrs Pucket," said Mr Griffins.

"What has happened?" said Mrs Pucket.

Mr Griffins, not wanting to say anything, decided to let Mrs Marlow talk. They walked into the kitchen and sat down at the large oak kitchen table.

Mrs Marlow explained while Mrs Pucket made tea. She explained that it was too much for her and that she could not stabilise the portal; the boys were not ready.

"I passed out with exhaustion—this is all too much for me now. I am far too old for this," said Mrs Marlow in a deeply saddened voice.

She explained how she collapsed through sheer exhaustion trying to open up the portal and that the boys did a fantastic job but were far too young and had no real experience.

"When Mrs Marlow passed out, the portal began to oscillate violently, first swallowing Oscar. The poor boy, not knowing where to go. Then Thomas, sensing that the portal was going to close, went in after to save Oscar!" said Mr Griffins.

Mrs Pucket made tea and some toast to keep everyone's spirits up. They sat around talking and discussing what to do next and what the plans were going to be.

"The boys will be safe with Lorsan Yeldrove and the Tarrenash, and when they get to the City of Vakoborg, the Disaris will take them in. The boy's a Marlow," said Mrs Pucket.

"He will be completely safe," she added.

"Yes, you are right. You are a dear friend."

"After tea, we will send a message to King Gilgamesh and ask him to take the boys in until it's safe to bring them back," said Mrs Marlow.

"All is not lost," said Mrs Pucket.

"There is always hope, and they are with some great people right now!"

"I better get back. I can't be seen to be helping," said Mr Griffins.

"I know, Harold. You have done far too much already, and I don't want to put the peace treaty at risk," said Mrs Marlow.

"I wish I could do more. I will come back late this afternoon to see how everything is," said Mr Griffins as he got up and walked out the door.

Meg was outside sleeping in the mid-morning sun and got up as soon as she heard the door open.

After Breakfast Mrs Marlow, and Mrs Pucket went down through the old Cellar door into the sorcerer library and the stone circles, and the two of them summoned a great eagle owl of Tanniv.

They took up their positions in the centre of the ancient stone circle. They held their wands aloft and together joined a small portal.

A bright light appeared out from the middle of the stone circle, and then it formed a huge gold ring.

"Tupel, Tupel, Tupel, come to me, my old friend, come to me!" She bellowed brasher, and ever louder then into the cave came the great horned eagle owl called Tupel.

Tupel circled around the stone rings and settled on a stone facing Mrs Marlow.

Mrs Pucket and Marlow went over to Tupel, stroking him with affection.

Mrs Marlow hurried over to her desk, writing a letter to King Gilgamesh of Vakoborg, explaining that Thomas was a Marlow and both boys should be protected under the banner of the white stone sorcerers.

She rolled up the letter and popped it into a small leather pouch, and tied it to Tupel's bright yellow limb.

"Go fly, Tupel, my old friend. Fly to Vakoborg and deliver this to the Great King Grusan Gilgamesh of Vakoborg!"

Tupel looked at the two ladies with his bright orange eyes, then stretched out his mighty wings of almost two metres, and gave out a huge squawk, and flew around the monumental cave in a majestic circle.

Both ladies held their wands aloft and reopened the portal for Tupel to fly back through to Tanniv.

The message of the two boys would reach The King later that day before Lorsan Yeldrove, the two boys, and the squad of warriors would enter the City of Vakoborg.

"That's all we can do now," said Mrs Marlow.

"I will stay as long as it takes. I don't want you to be here on your own," said Mrs Pucket.

"That would be a big help. I still have so much to read and study about," said Mrs Marlow.

"Then I will help you, and together we will find the answers and help the two boys," said Mrs Pucket.

The Bauk of Vakoborg Canyon

Several hours into a deep sleep, Oscar awoke to loud noises and could hear the most horrendous vulgar uproars; he shot up out of his bed of furs and pelts, then ran over to the waterfall and looked through.

He could barely see through the semi-transparent wall of water and could see some massive fuss happening.

He looked all around the cave, and the horses were all upright and looking very skittish, very anxious and worried. They were bobbing their heads, braying and neighing loudly, looking very edgy and upset at the noises and din happening outside.

Oscar looked everywhere and all around him, but the firs and bedding had remained. It was so strange, and things did not seem to be right. So with a worried, nervous feeling, he decided to investigate.

Great enormous roars and grumbles could be heard, and the ground shook while gravel and dust came down from the granite ceiling of the cave.

"Wake up, Thomas! Wake up!" cried Oscar panicking and shaking Thomas in his bed of fur and wool.

"What is it—what is it?" asked Thomas, wiping and rubbing his eyes, still half asleep.

"I don't know, but I can hear some dreadful-frightful noises, and the soldiers have gone!" shouted Oscar.

The two boys got up and ran towards to exit of the cave. Being careful not to slip on the wet rocks, they paced about them, trying to see through the wet wall of transparent water, barely seeing shadows and silhouettes moving everywhere. They still could not see what was making the noise, and nothing had come into view. So they jostled around to the cave entrance to walk out.

It was huge, around ten people tall. It was grey and blue with scars all over his body.

He had a huge giant, bold head shaped like a boulder and gigantic disgusting ivory white and slightly yellow teeth, with massive muscles and a cloth to cover his modesty.

He was swinging a huge wooden bulbous club, growling and moaning and groaning everywhere in a total fury and angry rage.

Lorsan, Captain Norlen, and the soldiers were fighting it from every angle. Elaith caught sight of the boys and ran towards them.

"Get back inside!" he yelled.

"What is it?" said Oscar.

"It's a BAUK! Now get back inside," said Elaith.

The Bauk swung his club at some rocks while moaning and groaning; he batted a bolder high into the air, and then a huge-sized boulder came hurtling towards Elaith as he had his back facing the Bauk, talking to the two boys he did not see what had happened.

"Look out!" shouted Oscar. He grasped his wand, shouted the words, "Umbraculum! Umbraculum! Custodire!" A giant bright red shield covered Thomas, Oscar, and Elaith, and the rocks hit the magical shield and bounced off and disintegrated, protecting the three of them from certain death.

Lorsan, the Captain, and the soldiers looked over at the boys with interest and then carried on trying to tackle the enormous, monstrous problem in front of them.

"Where's my treasure!" screamed the huge Bauk in a languid uneducated voice.

"No one steals my treasure!" repeated the Bauk over and over again. "I like eating humans. You all will taste so good." He said while licking his lips, fighting, and drooling at the thought of eating such a tasty delicacy.

Soldiers all around him strained to fight the mighty beast with giant long spears. They stabbed and poked the Bauk; with each pierced spear into his thick grey skin, the Bauk roared louder and moaned as he got injured with every stab of an arrow or spear.

A young soldier looking to prove his bravery climbed a colossal boulder and drew his sword, and as the Bauk swung his club backwards and forward, he pivoted, then timed a perfect jump and leapt onto the Bauk's back while holding onto his thinning hair he plunged a sword into his hind.

The Bauk yelled out while contorting his arms and hands around the back of his head and neck while roaring and moaning.

"My friends would have heard me by now and will come and eat you too," he laughed as if trying to think of revenge and a silver lining to his poor fate.

The Bauk

The Bauk slowed more and more, and as he slowed down, more plunges from swords and spears came from the soldiers surrounding the great beast.

Finally dropping to his knees, the Bauk's thick black tongue came out of his mouth, and with a final sigh, his eyes rolled as he fell to the floor down to his chest with his head hitting the rocks, shaking the earth.

The soldiers did not cheer, nor did they sound joyful about killing the colossal beast. They, one by one, honoured the creature by standing in front of him, saluting.

Lorsan marched down to the creature's head. He placed his hand on the Bauk and said, "You fought bravely, my friend. Today was not your day."

The troop marched back up to the cave and started to pack.

"We had better get out of here fast; the other Bauk would have heard the moaning," said Captain Norlen.

Everyone packed frantically, rolling up the furs, and Elaith showed Thomas and Oscar how to pack. It was almost nightfall, so it was time to move out.

"Oh, and Oscar," Elaith said with a strong voice. "Thank you for stopping the boulders," he said again while nodding and acknowledging respect. Oscar said nothing; he did not know what to say. He saw the danger and reacted, and it seemed like the logical thing to do.

Each soldier collected their horse, packed up their, belongings and walked out of the cold, wet cave.

"How did the Bauk know we were there?" said Oscar.

One of the soldiers on duty—a brave soldier named Vulen—leaned towards Oscar, "I saw a boulder came hurtling down from the top of the canyon. Several minutes later, a Bauk came looking for the boulder, and he could smell humans and the rest, you know." The brave soldier said while walking past with his horse.

It was still light, but it was twilight, and the sun was about to set on the forest again for the second night.

The soldiers all lined up in the clearing, and a yell came from Lorsan.

"Riders, saddle up!" each rider climbed up onto his horse.

Thomas climbed up onto his horse, then Oscar; Elaith looked at the two boys. "Make sure you keep close, boys." The two boys nodded.

The troop pressed on deeper and deeper into the canyon again; they could hear the thunderous noise from the Bauk. This time the Bauk noise took on a more frightening feeling of a genuine threat. Each soldier looked more observant and more attentive than ever; each rode with one hand on his sword pommel, ready to draw at any time.

Some of the soldiers carried a bow and had an arrows' fletching's half-cocked in the string ready to be drawn at a moment's notice.

The two boys set out on their horses Oscar on Sylvar and Thomas on Leokan; both horses were now getting used to the two boys' company.

Slowly and quietly, they made their way out of the forest canyon, climbing up a steep-sided valley back on what felt like flatter ground. By morning, they would be in the mighty Forest City of Vakoborg.

Some of the soldiers carried a bow and had arrows' fletching's half-cocked in the string ready to be drawn at a moment's notice.

The two boys set out on their horses Oscar on Sylvar and Thomas on Leokan; both horses were now getting used to the two boys' company.

Slowly and quietly, they made their way out of the forest canyon, climbing up a steep-sided valley back on what felt like flatter ground. By morning, they would be in the mighty Forest City of Vakoborg.

The Captain held out his hand to signal stop. Everyone stopped at once; they all looked around everywhere, being watchful deep into the forest. They could hear horses and the sound of men and soldiers.

The Tarrenash squad encircled the two boys and formed a defensive formation.

Louder and louder, the noise of men and horses became as the newly discovered horses took on the sound that they were galloping towards them.

"Keep your swords and your bows sheathed," said Lorsan Yeldrove.

A legion of forest troops came out of the forest darkness and rode at them from all angles. The riders who were now visible started circling the soldiers of Tarrenash in a show of might.

Round and round, the soldiers went the circle moving ever closer to the Tarrenash.

There were twenty gleaming white horses with twenty forest soldiers on them, all with bows pointing at the soldiers of Tarrenash. Dressed in green with grey hoods hiding their faces and camouflage paint on their white skin to hide their faces from being seen. The hooded warriors came at them, encircling closer and closer in the most intimidating fashion.

They stopped as a great warrior cantered forward towards Lorsan Yeldrove, gazing at him from his hooded face. The darkness of the night was now masking his identity as he trotted closer.

Thomas and Oscar, in the centre of the huddle, could only see glimpses of the exchange but moved around to see more of the encounter with this strange warrior of the forest.

The warrior put away his bow and refaced his sword back into its sheath safely.

"I saw the awkward, clumsy way you and your troops handled that Bauk back in the canyon. I do not need weapons, and I can use my hands," said the dark hooded warrior as the rest of his legion laughed.

"I remember the way you handled that maiden when her husband caught you," said Lorsan Yeldrove. "Remind me, didn't you run across the roof without your shoes?"

Everyone laughed; the Tarrenash troops and the Vakoborg forest legions all laughed and shook hands.

Removing his hood, the great Disaris leader held out his hand, shaking Lorsan's hand and looking at Captain Norlen and saying, "I can't believe you are still taking orders from this old pirate," said the Disaris general.

"I have come to guide you back into Vakoborg City we have been expecting you," said the Disaris general.

The Disaris general's name was Lord Halamar Yelfir. He was the greatest living soldier in the Disaris army, and he had come personally to meet his friend General Lorsan Yeldrove and escort them into Vakoborg.

"I don't do this for just anyone," said Halamar Yelfir.

"I know, my old friend, it is a great honour," said Lorsan Yeldrove.

"It's a time of many changes, I fear, my old friend," said Halamar Yelfir.

"Yes, Halamar, I can feel the change in the air," said General Yeldrove.

"How are things in Vakoborg right now?" said Lorsan.

"We are hearing stories of Aminoff spies all over Vakoborg," Halamar said with a sound of dread.

"Yes, it's the same in Tarrenash; right now, I fear we are all feeling the lash from East Tanniv," said Lorsan.

The two great warriors galloped into the forest, and the Legion of Disaris and Tarrenash troops followed on together side by side.

General Yelfir and General Yeldrove both fought together side by side at the great battle of Ilihorn.

They both understood what politicians did not. They knew that this was not a time of peace, and it was merely a lull; because of lack of resources, the cease-fire that has lasted many years could easily ignite again anytime.

They knew this day would come and that both sides' unfinished business of war would need to be settled one day.

Thomas and Oscar looked over each shoulder at the magnificent-looking warriors from the Disaris army and the Tarrenash army. They felt immensely proud to be marching into Vakoborg alongside these soldiers.

Several hours later, the forest started to look different, and they could see clearings of buildings in the distance in the dark. The sun was about to rise, and they could see signs of farming and life around them.

As the sun came up and morning broke, they could see a great monastery or church. It looked magnificent; the building was made of pure white marble and a gold-domed onion-style tower on the roof. It was huge, and the complex of buildings and walls went on for what appeared to be miles.

The Disaris General Lord Halamar Yelfir.

"Elaith, I have a question," said Thomas.

"Yes, Thomas," said Elaith.

"Is this Vakoborg City?" Thomas asked.

"No, Thomas, this is a religious settlement. We will need to change here into our parade uniforms and straighten out our kit. We can't march into Vakoborg looking like a mess. We need to wash here, change and look sharp," said Elaith.

The Tarrenash troops and the Vakoborg legion cantered on around the front of the bright white building covered in dark green ivy, around to the grand front entrance to the most enormous wooden doors the boys had ever seen.

They were at least ten metres tall with iron door fittings with Disaris writing carved and forged into the metal with blue lapis lazuli panels, and all over the doors were carved Disaris religious scenes and stone circles.

General Yelfir got off his horse and knocked on a smaller door.

A speaking hatch opened up on the door, and he spoke to the monastery's priest, asking to use the facilities for an hour to freshen up before they reached Vakoborg City for an audience with the great King Gilgamesh.

The hooded Disaris priest nodded and opened the mighty doors, ten metres high and ten metres across.

Both doors were heaved and pulled open by twenty male and female hooded religious monks from the order of the stone circles of Vakoborg. The two squadrons of soldiers cantered in through the great doors, which opened up to the most beautiful green gardens, set in collonades of white marble and a waterfall on each side of the garden, leading to a great central lake.

The Disaris legion and the Tarrenash troops dismounted and unpacked. Some monks came and guided the troops inside the building to use the washing and bathroom facilities.

A tall bearded Disaris priest with a white hooded gown and long white beard walked towards Halamar and spoke with him for several minutes while looking and watching Thomas and Oscar.

Lorsan beckoned Elaith over to join the conversation.

"Thomas, Oscar, come here. The head of the monastery would like to talk to you," said Elaith.

They sauntered over to the wonderful-looking white priest and stood in front of him. He bent down and looked the two boys in the eyes and said, "You're a Marlow from the White Sorcerers of Stoney Cross, aren't you?" in a very soft voice looking Thomas directly in his blue eyes.

"Yes, my name is Thomas."

"And you, what is your name?" the white priest said while looking at Oscar.

"My name is Oscar," he said while a little shy, looking down at his feet.

"My name is Elion, and I am a religious High Priest of Vakoborg, pleased to meet you. How are my stones doing in Stonehenge, Ballymore, and Avebury?" he asked.

"Er er, they're fine, sir," Thomas said not, knowing what to say.

"I knew your mother, and I know your grandmother,"

"After your visit to see the King, I would like you to come back to talk to you more," said the Disaris Priest Elion.

"Yes, sir, well, I think I can, but I think we are going to Stormhorn too," said Thomas thinking that he had said far too much.

Lorsan jumped into the conversation very fast, defending the boy, "The boy is tired from our journey; we are not sure of our next trip yet."

Elion stopped to think while gazing at the two boys.

"We have Disaris clothes that will fit those boys. They can't be travelling around Tanniv dressed like that; there are spies everywhere," said the wise High Priest Elion.

The Priest clapped his hands and beckoned two Disaris monks over, and the two Monks were instructed to bring suitable clothing for the two boys.

The rest of the two squads freshened up, ate a little, took care of the horses, and prepared for the short trip into the great Forest City of Vakoborg.

Thomas and Oscar walked over to their horses and brushed them down, then following the other soldiers, they fed the horses, gave them water, and spent time preparing them.

Two of the Disaris monks came with clothing for Thomas and Oscar, then were escorted to use the washing rooms on the far side of the garden.

The two boys got changed into the most stunning outfits consisting of leather trousers and tunics displaying the Disaris emblems of Vakoborg with the eagle owls of West Tanniv.

They kept their regular clothes and took them with them in a small leather bag. Knowing that they would need these for the way home, but for now, they looked like they belonged and lived in Tanniv.

Elaith was now dressed smartly in full parade dress, ready to enter the City of Vakoborg. Let's rest here for an hour; it's far too early to enter the city.

The three of them sat down in the enchanted green garden; it was so peaceful. They could hear the sound of the waterfalls and the birds flying overhead.

They could see the Disaris Priest and monks in their long hooded grey robes walking about doing tasks all around the gardens.

"It is so peaceful here," said Oscar as he broke the silence between Thomas and Elaith.

"Yes, it is Oscar," said Elaith.

"When we enter the city, what are we going to do?" asked Thomas.

"General Lorsan and Captain Norlen will be coming over to prepare us for the meeting with the Disaris King. They will be over shortly," said Elaith.

Both boys layout on the green grass directly in the sun warming and waited patiently and slept for a while.

Some Disaris came with water and some food. They waited while watching Halamar, Lorsan and Captain Norlen, and the Disaris as they deliberated the timings and orders of meeting King Gilgamesh.

Meeting a king was not as simple as just a knock on the door. There were rules and an order of service to obey too.

Thomas was very nervous; he knew he would need to pass on the messages and convince the great King Gilgamesh to go to Stormhorn, but he also knew it was within Lorsan's benefit to help Thomas persuade the King.

Lorsan knew that having a Marlow from the White Sorcerers' order in front of a very religious King would be all the convincing he needed.

Thomas was Lorsan Yeldrove's good luck charm, and he felt the same about having Lorsan as a companion. Together they would need to persuade the King.

Oscar was watching over at the table at the far side of the courtyard in the beautiful Monastery. He could see the four warriors talking and gesticulating.

The four men got up from the table at the same time; they then looked at each other for a second, then shook each other's hands and embraced each other. Knowing that this looked like the four men had come up with a plan or an agreement, Oscar nudged Thomas and said, "They are coming over."

Thomas looked over, and they could see that the four men were walking towards them.

He took a deep breath, and the two boys stood up straight as if they were lining up for a school assembly. Then Elaith looked over, jumped to his feet too, and was in full attention.

Oscar Williams

Elaith positioned himself directly behind the two boys with his chest out and arms straight by his side and stood to attention.

The four men marched towards them. He could see that Lorsan was smiling, and the Disaris warrior Halamar was pleased, too. Halamar spoke first.

"You boys look very smart in your Disaris clothes," said Halamar as he got closer and looked down at the two boys.

"We have come up with a strategy, boys," said Lorsan.

"Have you ever met with a King before?" asked Halamar.

"No, sir," said Oscar.

"No sir," said Thomas.

"I have sent a warrior to Vakoborg explaining that you boys are coming and need to meet with King Gilgamesh. He is expecting you, so we have planned to get to the palace by midday," said Halamar. "I will escort you into the Great Disaris Hall, and the six of us will talk to the great King," said Lorsan.

"Six of us?" said Thomas.

"Yes. Thomas, Oscar, Lord Halamar Yelfir, Captain Darin Norlen, me, and Elaith." Lorsan Yeldrove said, pointing his finger at the young soldier.

Elaith bowed his head, pretending not to look thrilled, and said, "Yes, my lord."

"You will now not leave these boys' side," said Lorsan looking directly at Elaith.

"The way I see it, Oscar saved your life back in Oris Gorge with that boulder, so you owe these boys the same."

"Yes, my lord," said the young Tarrenash warrior.

This was a great honour for a young Tarrenash soldier to be in a Disaris court in front of the King and a protector, a white stone sorcerer. As a young warrior, this is everything a soldier would want: to be significant, participate in diplomatic affairs, and fight for good.

Lorsan and Halamar were great men, famed not only for their fighting but for being leaders of men. They had a way of thinking about situations and bringing out the best in people, which was the mark of great leaders.

Captain Norlen looked on at Thomas, Oscar, and Elaith with a demanding stern face and said, "Go and saddle up; we ride out in ten minutes; you can't keep a king waiting,"

The Disaris Legion led on, and the Tarrenash troops cantered out of the beautiful Disaris Monastery with Lord Lorsan Yeldrove, Lord Halamar Yelfir, and Elaith Tarron, with Thomas and Oscar at the head of the mighty parade. They marched onto the great City of Vakoborg.

Looking all-around at the wonders of Vakoborg, the Disaris houses, villages, and the children came out to watch. The farmers stopped to look at the; Vakoborg and Tarrenash procession of warriors. Thomas and Oscar rode with their heads held high in brand new Disaris clothing and felt very special; indeed, like they were part of something as the Disaris people looked on.

Over the hill and through the clearing, they could finally see the Great Disaris Forest City of Vakoborg.

It was a mighty City gleaming white in marble with battlements and towers by the thousands everywhere. It was a spectacle to behold. Thomas looked in total astonishment, and Oscar looked in complete bewilderment. This was one of the most impressive sights one could ever see, thought Thomas.

As they travelled through even more Disaris, children, women, and men would wave and follow as they rode ever closer to the city gates.

The Great Disaris City of Vakoborg

The two squads stopped directly outside the vast white marble gates; the forest had been cut back everywhere not to engulf the spectacular citadel, which gave way to farming outside the city walls. The ramparts of the citadel had the most enormous deepest moat you could imagine. The Disaris Vakoborg City felt like the safest city in the world. Surrounded by forest at all sides, an army would have to know where they were going to find it. Then tackle the tallest walls with the most highly trained army in the world. It felt impregnable to any would-be attacker of this city.

As they entered the city more, Disaris looked on at the two legions of Tarreash and Disaris marching side by side.

Everyone looked like a great warrior here. Even the children and women looked like they could fight.

The Vakoborg Empire was a military state, and the military Agoge schools took both boys and girls from a very young age. Everyone in Vakoborg knew how to fight. But being a highly religious country, their spiritual practices and traditions took precedence.

As the squadrons marched on through the city streets, they headed for the palace. The boys still felt incredibly proud, and they looked on and observed the houses inside the castle walls and the pubs, bars, and restaurants.

The city had market squares and narrow streets. Everywhere they looked, there were churches on every street corner and more than one great Ziggurat in the town. The city was spotless, and everywhere green ivy and green plants against white clean marble walls decorated the streets.

The Disaris upper classes, nobles, and wealthy had palaces around Vakoborg, distinguishing between richer and poorer neighbourhoods.

In the more affluent areas, the Ziggurat took on a more spectacular feel, with the architecture looking distinctly different and better-off.

The Great Forest City of Vakoborg.

As the procession cantered ever closer to the main Palace of Vakoborg, the neighbourhoods became more beautiful and ornate. As they marched closer, they came to a checkpoint for entering the Palace.

Six smartly dressed Disaris soldiers came out of a guard room in gleaming silver armour with helmets and horsehair hackles on the helmets.

Lord General Halamar Yelfir rode a few steps forward to address the guardsman. The guardsman looked up at the General, saluted, and in an eager way opened the doors to the palace courtyard as if they had been expecting them.

The procession marched through the palace gates, and the soldiers of Tarrenash nodded with gratitude at the guardsman. The Disaris legion rode with eyes front proudly into the King's Palace courtyard.

They entered an incredible parade square full of cloisters and archways and carved pillars everywhere, all depicting Disaris scenes of some description from a time long ago.

There were green trees and a vast garden with four white marbles towers overlooking the colossal courtyard.

Some Disaris stable workers rushed out to receive the horses. Lorsan Yeldrove gave the order to dismount; then, general Yelfir gave the order to dismount. They walked their horses into the stables. The Tarrenash men knowing precisely what to do commenced taking care of the horses' needs first, this time removing the saddles and the kit from the horses' back.

Thomas and Oscar looked on at the soldiers and decided to copy them, with Elaith helping and showing them what to do. Oscar took care of his horse Sylvar, and Thomas took care of his mount Leokan, each time following precisely what Elaith did.

Lorsan ordered the men to fall into a parade line, so he could examine the troops before they entered the Palace.

Elaith knowing that he had to take care of the two boys, beckoned them to fall in next to him on the courtyard square. Elaith looked at the boys and pulled their clothes, straightening them out to get them as smart as possible.

Captain Norlen and General Yeldrove walked up and down the line examining the men, and once satisfied, Captain Norlen called out Thomas, Oscar, and Elaith to stand forward and follow them into the Palace gates.

General Yeldrove looked over at the Disaris General and nodded. General Halamar followed on with his Disaris Captain called Thalland Rothlan.

They all met at the foot of the marble steps, and they marched up towards the Great Disaris hall; each member of the precision marched in with General Halamar Yelfir leading the way.

As they entered the great hall, it was huge; it had colossal wooden rafter beams and marble columns and pillars holding up an enormous roof. Each wall had stained-glass windows depicting stone circles and Disaris religious practices, as well as great Disaris war victories.

There were paintings of religious rituals on each wall, too, with statues and carvings in marble everywhere.

On each side of the great hall were marble pews fifteen benches high on each side. These benches were filled with the great Disaris council. The council consisted of elected officials, nobles, women, children, and Disaris religious members.

The procession members marched through the great hall in total silence, with everyone looking on at them. They marched towards three wooden carved thrones at the end of the aisle raised high on the steps at the far end; on each side were Disaris royal servants waiting for the great King to enter.

As they got closer to the thrones, General Yelfir stopped just in front of the chairs. He looked back at the two boys and explained we will address the great King from here.

They stopped and waited in anticipation for the great King to enter.

King Grusan Gilgamesh

A master of ceremony walked out from behind a curtain by the two thrones with a huge ivory-carved staff. He crashed the butt of the staff on the marble floor three times, producing a huge, loud acoustic echo in the great hall; everyone in the great council stood up at once again, filling the quiet hall with noises of shuffling and stamping.

"His Majesty King Grusan Gilgamesh and his daughter, Princess Holly Gilgamesh of, the mighty Vakoborg forest and Mornala Mountains!" said the master of ceremony. The King appeared; he walked in very elegantly from a door on the left-hand side through a huge marble archway, then the Disaris princess walked through after the King. The princess was young but was treated every bit like a King.

As she came into view and stood in front of her throne, ready to sit down, Oscar and Thomas gasped in surprise and disbelief. Princess Gilgamesh looked closely at the boys squinting to get a better view, and looked on in disbelief. The great King noticed the exchange in mannerisms and faces then looked on at his daughter, the princess, then holding up his arms, stopping the dignitary and, pomp, he decided to halt proceedings, and the great hall fell silent.

All the while, General Lorsan Yeldrove and General Halamar Yelfir also took on a look of complete confusion.

"Do you know these two boys?" said King Grusan Gilgamesh, as he gazed down at his daughter in a puzzled way.

"Yes, Father," said Princess Holly Gilgamesh.

"Come closer, boys," said the great King.

"How do you know my daughter?" asked the King.

Thomas and Oscar nervously stepped forward and bowed heads.

"We used to play together in the gardens of Tappington Hall," said Oscar in a low voice.

"Explain to me, please," said the King to Princess Gilgamesh. "I used the stones circles to go to the ancient Disaris grounds of Tappington Hall in Stoney Cross, but father, I never left the grounds," said Princess Holly Gilgamesh.

"She didn't leave Tappington Hall once!" shouted Thomas.

King Gilgamesh and the rest of the court looked on. It was the most unusual start to a royal visit the great King had ever encountered.

"Now we have established who knows who, what have you come here for?" said King Gilgamesh.

"We shall continue this conversation later," the great King said to Holly.

Holly looked at Oscar and Thomas and winked; the boys looked up only to lower their eyes again in front of the King.

Lorsan Yeldrove decided to talk to bring some order back to the conversations. "King Gilgamesh, there is a great gathering that has been called from the Marlow Stone sorcerer, and the boys have come to talk to you about it," said Lorsan Yeldrove.

"I know of this gathering. I have been told, but Disaris do not attend such meetings anymore," said King Gilgamesh.

"Yes, but your Majesty, the boy is a Marlow, and he is asking for your attendance," said Lorsan Yeldrove.

"May I speak?" asked Thomas tenderly.

The great King looked down at the boy and said, "Speak."

Thomas explained to King Gilgamesh that Prince Alwin Aminoff visited Stoney Cross, a Stone Circle had appeared in the River Avon by his house, and how his grandmother had summoned the great eagle owls of Tanniv to call a gathering at Stormhorn.

Once Thomas had finished, General Lorsan spoke about the raids on Tarrenash lands and how Moltenwing and Ilihorn were orchestrating attacks and Pogroms in West Tanniv. Many West Tanniv people had been taken as slaves, and the border Bastions of West Tanniv were understaffed and underfunded.

The East Tanniv Navy had now overrun the River Ailmar, and they now had complete control of the trade-in Tanniv, the river, and in the Hiligor Sea.

The great King sat back and, not being rushed by anyone, looked slowly across at the great Disaris council and asked, "Is there any news from the City of Qulan?"

"Not yet, my King. We are hoping to all talk at the gathering of Stormhorn," said Lorsan Yeldrove. "No word from QULAN, and you are HOPING they will show at the gathering at Stormhorn," said King Gilgamesh.

"Yes, my lord, but everyone is going to go to Stormhorn, and we must act now before it's too late," said Lorsan Yeldrove.

The great King sat back on his throne and contemplated.

"What have you got to say about all of this, Lord Yelfir?" said the King looking at his Disaris general.

"The forest is not right, my King. There are spies everywhere right now in the forest of Vakoborg," said Lord Yelfir.

"But do you have any evidence?" asked the King.

The wise King sat back, this time looking at the Princess, and again over to the Disaris council.

"It will not be long before Vakoborg is affected. The Aminoff spies and raiding parties are everywhere, and now the great stone circles are moving too," repeated Lorsan.

"I do not see how any of this is Disaris business. However, I will sit with my Disaris council and consider everything that I have heard before today. I will consult my council before committing a Disaris to the gathering of Stormhorn," said the King.

Thomas, Oscar, Lorsan, Elaith, and Captain Norlen were dismissed and sent to the garrison quarters to rest until they were called upon again by the King and the great Disaris council.

Thomas and Oscar bowed their heads and said goodbye to Princess Holly directly; they turned and walked back down the great hall.

Lorsan also bowed to the great King with Captain Norlen and Elaith bowing directly behind him and walked back down the great hall towards the exit.

The King, along with Princess Gilgamesh and the Disaris, council stayed to discuss the great gathering of Stormhorn.

The Council members started to shout from the stalls.

"It's not our business!" shouted a wealthy Disaris merchant.

"We stay in our forest. We bother no one, even though our lands have shrunk by greedy Tarrenash and the Turgett," said a Disaris nobleman from deep within the gallows' of the council.

"We lost too many Disaris in the last conflict," said a high priest.

Princess Gilgamesh, who had said nothing all day, stood up: "Anastasia Aminoff has now started to call herself Empress; this means that she is no longer satisfied that she is Queen of East Tanniv. She is looking at building an Empire, and she will stop at nothing.

"Yes, we can sit here and do nothing, and we will be safe in our forest for a time, but who do we turn to if Tarrenash falls or Qulan City falls?" said Princess Gilgamesh.

"I know many of you still trade with Qulan and with Tarrenash and with the border towns, too." Princess Gilgamesh looked several Disaris merchants directly in the eyes.

"So don't tell me that we need no one," said the Princess angrily.

King Gilgamesh was seated and watched the conversations fly backwards and forward across the room, taking in all the information. He looked at his daughter as she conversed directly with Disaris elders and Disaris merchants, holding her own in the arguments that began to break out.

"Enough!" shouted the King, the whole court fell silent.

"I have listened to what has happened here today; I have listened to my council and my daughter and the Marlow boy. And I have listened to the General of the Tarrenash people," said the King. "I am still undecided, but what I know is that no one wants war, and I certainly do not want war, but I want to be a voice in a room, and I want to be ears in the room at Stormhorn."

The great council erupted into an outbreak of yells, screams, and shouts, with everyone shouting and screaming at the same time, it was a terrible commotion that filled the hall, and that could be heard from outside.

"I will send my daughter, Princess Holly Gilgamesh, and my Disaris General, Halamar Yelfir, to represent us at the great gathering of Stormhorn!" shouted the King.

Then silence fell upon the great Disaris council hall you could hear a pin drop.

"We cannot disregard that the Marlow boy has come from the stone circles, we can't ignore that the stone circles are moving, and we cannot ignore that Prince Alwin Aminoff has appeared in Stoney Cross!" said King Gilgamesh addressing his court.

He stood up and addressed the entire court like a King; he held his daughter's hand, pulling her to her feet. They both stood together. "I will not go to

Stormhorn; for a king to attend shows worry and aggression, but to send my daughter shows faith and diplomacy!"

"We will not go to war, but we will listen to what everyone has to say! And these are my final words," said the great King Gilgamesh.

After many hours, guards were sent to the garrison quarters to get Lorsan, Thomas, and Oscar. Like before, they started the long walk down the great hall with the Disaris council looking onwards at them as they walked through the mighty hall. King Gilgamesh and Princess Gilgamesh were sat on their thrones in reediness to tell them of their decision.

The three of them stood silent with their heads slightly bowed. King Gilgamesh and Princess Gilgamesh stood. The King waved his hand at the hall for everyone to be seated.

"I have taken all the information from you today to come to this decision," said the great King.

"It is not my wish to go to war," said the King. "It is not my wish to send money or fund a war. It is not my wish to send the wrong message and be seen antagonising a war. And it is not my decision to put any Disaris life at risk."

"However, I agree to send my daughter, Princess Gilgamesh, and my general, Halamar Yelfir, to Stormhorn to attend the great gathering to listen to what everyone has to say!"

Lorsan Yeldrove sighed with relief it was not the answer he was looking for because he wanted the King to attend the great gathering. However, sending his daughter Princess Holly Gilgamesh was the next best thing he could have wished for.

Thomas and Oscar also exhaled with relief that the gathering of Stormhorn was going to happen.

The King dismissed the three of them and sent them back to the garrison quarters to rest.

On the walk back, Oscar asked, "So what happens now? Can we go home now?"

"I will not tell you to stay a moment longer now that you have delivered your message to the King of Vakoborg; however, I will ask you to attend the gathering at Stormhorn. I will need a Marlow to attend, as there is more to do," said Lorsan looking at the two boys.

Thomas looked at Oscar, and he looked back.

"You can go back if you want," said Thomas.

"No, Thomas. We will go back together, and if it means going to Stormhorn, then this is what we must do," said Oscar.

Lorsan looked at the two boys as they spoke. Thomas looked at Lorsan and said, "We will come with you to Stormhorn, Lord Yeldrove."

"Thank you, my friends," said Lorsan as they walked back to the garrison quarters; they met up with Elaith, who gave them a short sword each.

"Do you know how to use a sword?" asked Elaith.

"No," said both boys.

"Then I will teach you, boy's, how to fight," said Elaith.

Elaith took the boys down to the gardens, and they spent several hours practising with their swords. Elaith taught them the basic moves and showed them how to swing the swords and use them defensively.

Princess Gilgamesh looked down at the two boys from her chamber balcony observing them, in astonishment that they were now with her in Vakoborg city.

She had only said goodbye to them days before in Tappington Hall. So it was strange how they were going on an incredible voyage to Stormhorn.

After sword training, the two boys returned to their new room to wash and rest on their bunks in the garrison quarters.

King Gilgamesh sent a Disaris ambassador to find the two boys inviting them to dinner with the King and Princess that evening. The Disaris messenger would come and collect them to take them to the King's dining hall.

The two boys rested on their bunks with their Disaris clothes on, resting looking up at the ceiling of their very simple garrison quarters. The soldier's rooms consisted of a room with two wooden beds and a small bathroom. It was okay, especially as they had slept in a waterfall cave with Bauk around them the day before.

"One of us should go and tell Elaith about our dinner with King Gilgamesh," said Oscar.

"I will go; I don't mind," said Thomas.

Thomas got off his bed and went to find Elaith; he spotted one of the soldiers outside tending to the horses.

"Excuse me, sir. Have you seen Elaith?" Thomas asked politely.

"You don't have to 'Sir' me," said the soldier. "He's over there." The soldier said, laughing.

He walked over to Elaith and explained about his new dinner arrangement with the King. Elaith told Thomas to enjoy himself, and he would communicate to the captain and to Lord General Yeldrove where both boys were going to be.

He went back to his bedroom quarters. Oscar was fast asleep, and Thomas felt tired, too, as they had not slept all night. So he took the opportunity to rest.

Both boys woke up that evening and got ready. By now, both boys were getting into the military-style of looking and behaving, and wearing a Disaris military uniform helped them feel the part too.

Using a bucket of water, they brushed themselves down and washed up in the bathroom facilities using the soap provided and some towels. Then turning to each other, they helped each other straighten their uniforms along with their belts and buckles, too, so they both looked smart.

They waited for a knock on the door, and a Disaris soldier came to collect them to take them to dinner. They walked across the courtyard; by this time, the sun was shining on the white marble, lighting the buildings in a peachy pink colour from the dusk sun.

They marched up an ornate set of steps, which led up to the Disaris council hall, but then turned right up to another set of steps into a more furnished part of the palace. It was beautiful, and the hallway into the court was filled with paintings, murals, frescos, and ornate palace furniture. They could smell the aroma from dinner down the far end of the hall. They passed by what seemed to be a corridor of infinite doors, with doors on the left then another passageway with a never-ending amount of halls on the right.

This Disaris palace was colossal. Finally, they reached the end of the corridor into the royal dining room. The dining hall was so big and filled with antiquities and religious monuments and statues with grand paintings.

King Gilgamesh and Princess Gilgamesh were sat at the end of a long, highly polished wooden table that looked like it could seat a hundred people.

Massive white chandeliers were hanging from the ceilings, and staff stood everywhere. The servants had set four places for the meal. Holly got up from the table to run around to hug them both.

"It's so nice to see you two, and you can imagine my surprise," said Holly as she smiled fondly at the two boys.

"It was a surprise for us too," said Oscar.

King Gilgamesh stood up and, looking down at the two boys, offered them a seat. Two of the staff strode forward to pull out the chairs, and they both sat down to eat.

"So you are a Marlow, young Thomas," said King Gilgamesh.

"My grandmother is, and my mother was before she got married," said Thomas.

"And you, Oscar, you have that wand. Are you a sorcerer?"

Not wanting to bend the truth to a King, Oscar replied honestly, "We received our wands days ago, and we are in training." The King nodded and looked back at his daughter Princess Gilgamesh.

"I knew your mother, Alina Marlow; she was a wise woman. She helped mend the bridge between Qulan and Vakoborg, and she was a great ambassador," said King Gilgamesh.

Thomas had only just learned about his mother's life in Tanniv. In truth, she was a great diplomat. She lived in the city port of Qulan and stood on the merchants' council, ensuring that everyone got a fair trade deal, and she provided peace between the many regions and countries. Alina knew that this was the most important thing.

She spent much of her time in the port of Elec in East Tanniv, and the Marlow family name was of absolute influence in Tanniv.

So King Gilgamesh knew the importance of having a new Marlow at the table.

They sat and ate a beautiful meal of fresh vegetables cooked ten different ways, with a main course of potatoes and a pastry-wrapped deer's meat. The King talked about Tanniv and how Vakoborg lost thousands of lives in Ilihorn, and for many years the kingdoms lived in peace.

"I am sending my daughter to Stormhorn to listen and listen only, and I have no desire for a war," said the King.

Thomas looked at the King and nodded; he could see that he was not going to influence the King otherwise, and how would a boy from Stoney Cross manage to convince a King anyway.

"Yes, we will travel out together in the morning; it will be two days hard ride up to the Stormhorn Mountains we will travel by day," said Princess Holly Gilgamesh.

"I will call a meeting with General Yeldrove and General Yelfir tomorrow before we ride. I will commit twenty riders to match the twenty Tarrenash riders," said the King looking directly at Princess Gilgamesh.

"The route we will take will be through a passage under the Mornala Mountains and the Northern forest of Vakoborg; we have a Monastery there, and we can rest there on the first night." The Princess said affirmatively, acting more like a stern warrior princess.

The two boys listened, not knowing if they could add anything to the conversation.

"I have sent a Legion of Disaris riders to the four corners of the Vakoborg forest for an inspection and examination of the monasteries, the villages, and the Stone Circles; I need to gather the information for myself," said the King this time directly aiming the conversation at the two boys.

King Gilgamesh had a reputation of being a stubborn King, but none of this was true. He was highly intuitive and did not rush into decisions, and looked at every option. It was just his desire not to go to war unless it was necessary.

King Gilgamesh had vast forest lands with millions of Disaris to take care of; he was head of the religious order of Disaris too. King Gilgamesh had a responsibility not to go to war.

The King looked at the two boys and said, "I have had a message from the White Sorcerer Marlow."

Thomas and Oscar looked at each other Thomas asked, "Is she okay?"

"The White Sorcerer Marlow dispatched an eagle owl to me yesterday and wanted to pass on the message that she was okay and to go to Stormhorn to talk to the gathering and to return home after this," said the King.

"So you already knew of our arriving and of our mission," said Oscar.

"I would not be a great King if I did not know what was happening in my kingdom," said King Gilgamesh.

"We knew, but we did not know who was coming," said Princess Holly.

The conversation appeared to be fully orchestrated by the King. The topics and themes were going as the King intended at the pace the Great King envisioned. Oscar watched how the King faintly controlled the conversation with great skill and almost knew what would be said before it was told.

"Now tell me of Prince Alwin Aminoff," said the King to the boys.

"We saw him by the new Stone Circle that appeared almost overnight. He was very polite and very charming," said Oscar.

"But you could see behind his elegant nature, he had a fierce temper," said Thomas.

Thomas explained that the encounters with Alwin were brief; he had no genuine interest in the boys and that he was in Stoney Cross to see Harold Griffins, the sceptre man, to get a new wand for Queen Aminoff of Moltenwing.

The King and Princess sat back and listened to the two boys, all the while gathering information. Princess Gilgamesh was a pupil of her fathers and would one day be Queen of Vakoborg, and they could see that she was under the spotlight from everyone in Vakoborg and was expected to listen and be fair and objective.

"So Father, we have Prince Aminoff, a new wand for the Queen, supposedly moving stone circles, spies everywhere, and raids happening to towns and villages in the East of West Tanniv," said Princess Gilgamesh to her father.

"It is still not enough indication many of the findings are still circumstantial, and the gathering of Stormhorn is just a listening mission," the King said but this time directing this at Thomas and Oscar, too.

The King explained the difficulties they would encounter trying to reunite the regions, countries, and cities of West Tanniv.

It was going to be challenging to get the regions of West Tanniv to listen. The Disaris Council needed more convincing, and this was a fair assumption because war is always the last result, and the Disaris kept themselves to themselves.

Tarrenash and Qulan had been more affected given the geographical positions of the two regions; they were by topography closer to East Tanniv, and they were divided only by the mighty river of Ailmar. But they also had benefited from money made by trading from East Tanniv for centuries.

The Tarrenash and the shadow warriors were prone to exaggeration to get more taxes. More taxes for men to be paid and more bastion defences built along the Ailmar River. The levies paid by the regions of West Tanniv were already under strain, and the King of Vakoborg felt that he had given enough already. The general feeling from all regions of West Tanniv was that the armies had been given plenty, and there was no real threat of war.

There were many serfs inducted into the working camps of East Tanniv, and many slaves worked in the City of Moltenwing, where serfdom had become a fashionable commodity to have. Serfs worked on labour camps in farms all around the great plains of East Tanniv; this gave trading port cities like Elec incredible amounts of wealth, money, and power. Many merchants and profiteers from Qulan and Tarrenash still traded illegally, giving way to an undercurrent of black market business.

"So all was not as it seems. The greediness of merchants with lords and nobles on each side were willing to turn a blind eye," said the King to his Princess and the boys.

The Turgett of Qulan only wanted money and trade. They would live under relatively difficult circumstances providing money, and trade was to be made, and it would be difficult to unite the Turgett or the merchantmen that ran the port.

"So I am being cautious for many reasons."

"Since the war, Tanniv has become a complicated place, no longer do the great trade agreements of West and East exist, and it has forced an undercurrent of business and trade that are far too complicated to decipher," said the King.

Each region and town had a quarrel and argued with each other because all tried to undercut each other in trade deals that were not legal, so many arguments and old scores needed to be settled in Stormhorn.

"These are the kinds of conversations and complications that you will face in Stormhorn at the gathering, and the Disaris cannot be seen to be the aggressors," the King added.

"Do you think everyone will show up?" Thomas asked the King in a lowered voice.

"Yes, they will show up; many of them will see this as an opportunity to meet on neutral ground to trade and make money. So they will show," said King Gilgamesh.

"I will go, Father, and I will listen, and I will make a calculation on all the information I gather," said the Princess to her father. The King smiled at his daughter, who had been very quiet to this point.

"You will make a great Queen one day," said the King.

It was getting late, so the dinner ended; Thomas and Oscar said thank you for the dinner and goodnight to everyone. A soldier was called and accompanied the boys back to the garrison quarters.

The two boys got back to their room in the garrison. They rested on their beds, both thinking about the meeting with the King and the Princess. The session was so informative; they had learned so much from a very wise King, a wise King that refused to rush into decisions, and he shared with them all the politics of East and West Tanniv and what to expect.

The Great Gathering of Stormhorn

The following morning the boys woke up to doors slamming and heavy footsteps on the wooden floors coming from each room of the garrison quarters. They woke up and shot out of bed to get ready. After five minutes, both boys were washed and prepared for the day, proudly wearing their Disaris uniforms.

They followed some soldiers down to the central garrison mess hall, where breakfast was served for the Disaris Legion and the Tarrenash squad. They could see Elaith sitting at a long table with benches on either side.

A line for breakfast was served by staff, and Disaris girls served hot drinks and water at the table.

"Good morning, Elaith," said the two boys.

"Good morning, boys," said Elaith.

"The King had a lot to say last night over dinner," said Oscar, not wanting to hold anything back from Elaith.

"Let me stop you, Oscar; what was said between you and a private meeting with the king is for you only," said Elaith.

The two boys nodded in an understanding way and joined the line for breakfast. There were eggs with meats and sausages with different freshly baked bread and small cakes, all fantastic smells.

The hall was vast and could house hundreds of hungry soldiers; on the white plastered walls were hundreds of shields and coats of arms with swords that had been mounted on the walls for decoration. There was a tremendous roaring open fire at one end of the mess hall warming the building, and it looked like it remained burning no matter what the temperature was outside.

Both boys got their food and returned to the table to eat it with Elaith. Over on the far table was an officer's table with General Yelfir, General Yeldrove, Captain Norlen, and the Disaris Captain Thalland Rothlan. There was no sign of Princess Gilgamesh, but Thomas thought that she would appear at some point during the morning.

The officers looked deep in conversation and looked like they were planning a route to Stormhorn.

Princess Holly Gilgamesh

Lorsan locked eye contact with the two boys and gave a military-style bowed head back to the boys, and the boys nodded quietly back.

"Eat up, boys; you will need your energy today; there will be a parade and a full briefing," said Elaith.

Everyone ate and finished up. The garrison staff cleared away the plates and food, and one by one, Disaris soldiers and Tarrenash soldiers assembled themselves outside in the central courtyard.

Captain Norlen called the Tarrenash soldiers into a parade line. Elaith ushered the two boys into line alongside him.

Then a smartly dressed royal Disaris staff member sounded a horn to announce that the King and Princess were arriving to examine the parade. General Yelfir, General Yeldrove, Captain Norlen, and Captain Rothlan stood out front addressing the men and stood calmingly waiting for the King and the Princess to arrive.

The plan had been made to ride for one day to the monastery north of the Mornala Mountain.

All the troops stood to attention with a thunderous noise coming from the soldiers' boots when the King and the Princess came into view.

The Princess was in full riding dress, which included light armour with a tough leather helmet and full toughened leather light armour. She had a long sword and a short sword, and a longbow around her chest. These weapons were not for show; the Princess was a warrior in every sense of the word and was highly proficient in sword fighting and bow shooting.

The King strolled down to the parade at his own pace, looking left then looking right down the line of men in the parade.

He then addressed the soldiers, "This is not a forceful mission, and you are travelling together in peace, and no one is to become an aggressor on this mission. We are on a peaceful fact-finding assignment, attending the great gathering of Stormhorn!" bellowed the great King so that everyone could hear him.

Not wanting to say anything more so that he left that very clear message in everyone's head, he looked over at the Disaris Captain Thalland Rothlan and said, "Over to you.

"Captain Rothlan stood in front of the troops and ordered the soldiers to get the horses and saddle up. Captain Norlen gave the same orders to the Tarrenash soldiers too.

The courtyard was crowded with the bustle and commotion with stable hands, creating an order to which the horses led out from the Vakoborg Palace stables. It felt like electricity and positivity were in the air.

Each rider walked to their steed and organised their saddles and pouches, meticulously checking that each piece of equipment was packed correctly and then rechecked it again.

Elaith walked over to his horse with the two boys.

Oscar strode over to Sylvar and Thomas over to Leokan. Elaith helped them pack the horse and strapped down the saddle, ensuring their bedding and firs were rolled up on the saddle, which acted as a comfortable cushion. They all mounted up and sat on their horses, waiting for instructions.

Princess Holly Gilgamesh was already sitting astride her gleaming white horse, waiting with General Yelfir, also waiting for the Disaris Legion and the Tarrenash Troops to ride out.

King Gilgamesh said goodbye to his daughter, and the rest of the troops rode past to acknowledge their great King.

"Goodbye, Father," said Princess Gilgamesh the King Bowed his head in acknowledgement to the Princess.

Thomas and Oscar cantered past King Gilgamesh and bowed. The King then acknowledged with a smile and nodded back.

The Great Disaris Pass of Mornala

The newly formed procession of a Disaris legion and a Tarrenash squad galloped out of the courtyard and through the city streets of Vakoborg. Everywhere Disaris, young and old, lined the streets to watch as the new procession charged onto Stormhorn. They galloped out of the citadel walls and into the forest. They headed for the Mornala Mountains, all hopeful for an uneventful prompt journey to the Fenfir Monastery.

As the forest got denser and thicker, the galloped became a canter, and each rider cantered two by two into the thick Disaris Forest brush.

Princess Gilgamesh glanced over her shoulder to see Thomas and Oscar and decided to manoeuvre down the line to ride alongside them both.

"Thank you for your attendance at dinner last night," said Princess Gilgamesh.

"It was our pleasure, Holly. I mean, Princess," said Oscar.

"It will have to be Princess now, I am afraid, boys. I am sorry because I know that you know me as Holly," said Princess Gilgamesh.

"It's okay. We understand, Princess. We know that you are significant. I hope that we can deliver the message at the great gathering. I am very nervous, and I understand that everyone is expecting a Marlow to deliver the message," said Thomas.

"Don't worry, I will help you, and you have General Yeldrove and General Yelfir to help, too," said Princess Gilgamesh of Vakoborg.

Thomas cantered on with Oscar on one side and Princess Gilgamesh on the other side and felt more confident that he would not be delivering the message alone.

They spoke about Tappington Hall and Stoney Cross, and Princess Gilgamesh proudly pointed out regions within the forest of Vakoborg. As they got closer to the Mornala Mountains, they could again hear the Bauk on the mountains thunderously roaring from arguing. Oscar's face looked worried and concerned, and the Princess could see their concerns.

"Don't worry about the Bauk. We have a secret passage that will take us directly through the Mornala Mountains. Then four hours after that, we will be at the Fenfir Monastery," said the Princess reassuringly.

The Disariss have always tried to leave the Bauk alone, but they wander down from the mountains to the city and cause complete havoc. They are not famed for their honesty or their cleverness, but the forest Disaris try and leave them alone, and they live in relative peace.

They cantered deeper and deeper into the forest, and as they rode closer to the Mountains, they took a detour down into a small gully.

The Disaris legion, being led by Captain Rothlan, made his way down the single track seldom used into the thick forest. The rest of the procession also followed down into the small ravine travelling right the way through to a vast arched cave covered in ivy and trees, and unless you knew it was there, you would not see a cave existed.

"That's the Disaris pass; this will take us directly underneath the mountains," said Princess Gilgamesh.

The pass looked incredible but seldom used and showed signs of neglect and decay. The cave had massive pillars carved out of the granite rocks and magnificent statues of Disaris everywhere. There were Disaris carvings that looked like herculean, statuesque carvings with strong muscular Disaris holding up the roof of the pass. It also looked like a religious settlement had lived there many hundreds of years ago and had long been forgotten.

The horses showed signs of stress and apprehension as they got closer to the cave. The Disaris dismounted, calmed the horses, and made lanterns from rags, and with long baton-like sticks, they poured an oil sap substance onto the rags and soaked them. Another Disaris pulled out a fire lighting flint and lit one of the rag torches. One by one, a baton was lit and passed around to every member of the procession.

"It's okay, it can get pretty dark and gloomy in there, and this pass will save us almost two days," said Princess Gilgamesh looking at the two boys to alleviate their fears.

All the torches had been passed out to the Tarrenash troops and the two boys. Elaith kept Thomas and Oscar close, showing them how to wrap the reins around one hand while holding a lit torch, and the Disaris led on into the dark mammoth cave.

The cave was colossal, and all around, they could see almost cathedrals and palaces and grand houses had been carved into the granite rock.

"What is this place?" asked Oscar.

"This was an ancient Disaris settlement many years ago; it has not been lived in for hundreds of years," said the Princess.

"Why did people leave?" asked Thomas as he gazed around the cave in pure wonder at the magnificent engineering and decorative carving details that had gone into the cave.

The procession carried on into the pass leading deeper into the maze of caves. General Yelfir and Captain Rothlan lead from the front, having used the passage for many years. Again, the horses appeared more nervous and skittish Elaith leaned forward, putting his chest onto the horses' neck; he talked to his horse, calming her down as they navigated further into the network of caves.

Noises in the far reaches of the pass came from what sounded like every direction of the cave. Thomas looked at Elaith, and he had tied the rains around the grip on his saddle, keeping one hand free to hold the torch and another on the pommel of his sword. Looking around at the Disaris and the Tarrenash, they all appeared to be doing the same. Thomas tied his reins to his saddle and held onto his wand with his other hand. Oscar, still looking around at the vastness of the cave network, noticed too and did the same.

No one appeared too alarmed by the noises, but everyone was on full alert or in a heightened state of awareness.

One of the Disaris passed a message to the troops and explained that they were now halfway through the pass. By now, they had been in the passage for hours. But this would bring them to the other side of the Mornala Mountains and within hours of the Fenfir Monastery.

The strange noises persisted, and among the sounds, drips coming from the stalactite and stalagmite, everything seemed to feel a little less threatening.

They cantered on slowly through the caverns and hollows, now feeling every minute that passed would be one less minute in the caverns. Being this deep under the mountains felt unnatural; the Tarrenash were from the open grasslands and plains of Tanniv. They did not feel at ease in such an environment. The Disaris also did not feel comfortable in a dark cave as it was not the best fighting environment. From a tactical military point of view, it was not the best place to be, and they felt strategically exposed. However, this would save the troop days in getting to Stormhorn. So using the Disaris Pass was a risk that was worth taking.

As they progressed further and further into the caverns, the noises grew louder, and glowing yellow and orange lights appeared; the Disaris stopped, as did the Tarrenash. The highly trained warriors from Tarrenash and Vakoborg could now sense that they were being watched for sure, and there was imminent danger.

Elaith manoeuvred his horse closer to Thomas and Oscar. Two of the Disaris guard scuffled their horses back towards Princess Gilgamesh. Princess Gilgamesh tilting her head forward, prepared her bow.

Lorsan looking at Halamar looked at each other and said, "Tundra wolves."

"Yes, Tundra wolves, but hold. They may not attack," said Halamar.

"Wolves!" said Oscar looking at Princess Gilgamesh.

"These are not wolves like you get in England; these are four times the size and four times as deadly," said the Princess.

Suddenly, the cave filled up with yellow and orange glowing sets of eyes, and everywhere around them, the noises of profound snarling growls, rumbles, and barks filled the cave from every direction, with the noise bouncing off the many miles of caverns.

"Tarrenash! Ready weapons!" said Captain Norlen quickly but firmly.

Elaith drew his sword and, with his other hand, pulled the boys in closer. Princess Gilgamesh moved towards the front of the precision alongside Halamar and Thalland Rothlan.

"Disaris! Bows ready, and hold until I say," said Captain Rothlan. The Disaris positioned themselves, and all instinctively pointed a bow in the same direction creating a halo of arrowheads outwards towards the darkness.

"Pick a target and again hold," said Captain Rothlan.

By now, the snarling and growls got louder. The Wolves were huge and were four times bigger than any wolf in Europe. Tundra Wolves wandered with supreme confidence, especially in a well-established pack.

The troops could now make out the noise and see the eyes getting closer and the snarls getting louder. Lorsan Yeldrove fixed on one set of eyes and watched and watched carefully until the gigantic wolves came into view. The giant wolves looked directly at the Disaris and Tarrenash bearing their teeth, and the pack of wolves surrounded them on all sides.

"How many, General?" said Princess Gilgamesh?

"Maybe twenty-five," said General Yelfir.

"Just hold your arrows, Disaris," said Thalland Rothlan.

Thomas looked at Oscar, and they both looked at each other in doubt about what was going to take place. These wolves were colossal and looked like they had the upper hand. They were spread out around the surrounding higher rocks and adjacent caves; they were all poised for fighting as they came into view.

The wolves moved in ever closer, and they could see them salivating and coiling and furling their legs in readiness to pounce. Fresh Disaris meat and fresh Tarrenash meat were risks that the wolves would calculate, and it was a risk worth taking.

"Stay close," said Elaith Tarron to the two boys. The rest of the Tarrenash huddled around the two boys.

Another wolf that had locked in on Princess Gilgamesh walked crab-like in a sideways motion towards the Princess while snarling and salivating at the prospect of a Disaris meal and horse meat.

General Yelfir looked at the Princess and calmly said, "When you are ready, your highness," giving the order to fire when she felt the danger was imminent.

Princess Gilgamesh looking calm, pulled back her bow, and looking directly down the arrow with her squinted eye, she tracked the wolves' movement with the point of her arrow, now everywhere a wolf had chosen a soldier to pounce on. The wolf edged closer and shuffled his giant padded paws across the flaw coiled and ready to pounce. He sniffed the air to smell his victim, and as if he could no longer hold his tolerance, the tundra wolf pounced metres in the air with teeth showing and mouth wide open ready to bite into the Princess's neck.

Princess Gilgamesh calmly released her bow, and her arrow flew directly into the eyeball of this magnificent but deadly beast stopping it in the air from reaching its fatal objective.

Everywhere wolves pounced and attacked. The Disaris let out a volley of arrows, hitting wolves everywhere; they could hear the yelping from the injured wolves. The determination of the pack to get their meal and revenge made sure they would keep trying; again, the wolves attacked, not allowing time for the bows to be reloaded. Close fighting broke out everywhere horses lurched up onto their hind legs. The Tarrenash warriors used their swords and flamed torches while letting out a torrid of blade and fire at the beasts, stabbing and thrusting blades into wolves everywhere.

Again the wolves tried, and the arrows flew in defence. One of the wolves jumped from a rock, attacked a Disaris soldier, and knocked him off his horse; a Tarrenash warrior jumped off his steed to help with the fight fending off another wolf.

Princess Gilgamesh was unleashing arrows everywhere while Lorsan fought with his long sword at two wolves attacking from the front.

Elaith, still close to the boys, thrust his sword into wolves as they got close to the inner circle of Tarrenash warriors; however, his main concern was the boys.

Captain Norlen rode down to the central pack of the precision line, swaying and swinging his blade at the mighty wolves as he rode, cutting them down as he charged.

In the middle of the skirmish, more and more wolves jumped from the higher ground to corral and spook the horses, breaking up the defensive formation.

The wolves were as big as horses so getting in between them while thrashing violently was a straightforward strategy. Now clearly seeing the action as the formation broke, Oscar held his wand aloft and shouted, "Illuminare! Illuminare! Illuminare!" his wand lit up with the brightest light beaming outwards from the tip of his wand. The wolves stopped, and some unsure of the blinding light ran off into the darkness; some stopped and got distracted, giving time for the soldier to reload their bows and fire a volley of lethal arrows into the remaining wolves. The encounter had stopped, and with complete attention, each Tarrenash and Disaris reloaded or repositioned their sword for combat again; the yellow and orange eyes retreated into the darkness.

"Let's ride out!" cried Captain Norlen to the top of his voice, ensuring that he was going to be fully heard.

The Disaris Legion and the Tarrenash troops galloped out in a blaze of horses and cheers underneath the blinding bright light of Oscar's wand.

"Better stop that light now," said Elaith to him in a very proud way.

"Oh, yes," he said as he stilled the light from his wand.

The procession galloped wildly and faster out of the caverns until they felt safe. The Princess trotted over to Oscar and said, "Well done, Oscar." And he bowed his head, a little embarrassed.

Lorsan Yeldrove also manoeuvred over and said, "The Hero of the Disaris Pass, well done, my boy." Oscar smiled, and Thomas grinned back at him.

"Let's pick up the pace and get through the pass as fast as possible. If I know Tundra wolves, they will not give up that easily," said Halamar Yelfir.

Several hours later, they could see the daylight from the other side of the Disaris pass through a small cave tunnel in the distance. They galloped hard and rapidly out to the other side of the Mornala Mountains.

The forest this side of the mountains looked much greener, and while their eyes adjusted back to daylight, it was late afternoon.

"One more hour to the Fenfir Monastery," yelled Thalland Rothlan.

As they rode down from the Disaris Pass, a small river in a clearing on the left and the troops stopped for the horses to take on water.

"That was very tricky; I have never seen wolves that size before," said Thomas to Elaith.

"Yes, they were big wolves, but they didn't stand a chance against a Tarrenash blade, a Disaris bow, or even Oscar's wand," said Elaith as he winked at the two boys.

Princess Gilgamesh looked over at the two boys as she stood in the creek feeding her horse and letting her glorious white steed drink water.

The late afternoon sun was peering through the forest, lighting the small woodland river, which gave the river the appearance of silver mercury.

The Disaris Legion and the Tarrenash troops saddled up and rode out for the final few miles to the Fenfir Monastery.

The Fenfir Monastery

The Fenfir Monastery was positioned on a waterfall in the middle of a sea of emerald-green woodland. The monastery stood directly next to a massive Stone Circle, and this was on an ancient Disaris pilgrim's route, so many Disaris would come here to pray and take a lodging for the night.

The Fenfir Monastery was one of the final stops on the Pilgrims route. The final destination was an ancient order of Nuns in Disaris religious grounds of the Leoven Abbey. The Leoven Abbey was so deep in the forest that very rarely any Disaris went. The hooded Nuns were of great importance to the Disaris and Vakoborg forest empire, as they believed that they had found inner peace by living for hundreds of years deep in the forest.

They were a symbol of everything that the Disaris had lived for and were a symbol of Vakoborg. To live in peace in the forest symbiotically with the animals and seasons was of great importance. By legend and myth, the Nuns of the Leovan Abbey had achieved this state of excellence and perfection, and the Fenfir Monastery was the final stop before entering deep in the forest to search for the Leoven Nuns.

The religious order of the Fenfir monks and nuns was peaceful. Like all Disaris, they walked around in hooded robes, and out of manners, would remove their hoods only to talk.

The religious practices and faiths of the Disaris religious order were profoundly and firmly rooted around peace, love, and positivity to all things living and the Stone Circles. All Disaris across the whole of Vakoborg practised deep religious beliefs, and some lived for hundreds of years because of the inner peace they had found.

The treaties signed by East Tanniv after the great Ilihorn war ensured that sacred grounds were neutral ground and no war or disputes would take place on sanctified Disaris grounds.

As they arrived at the Fenfir Monastery, Princess Gilgamesh rode into the grounds of the Abbey first. Her father, King Gilgamesh is the head of the church of Disaris, so naturally, Princess Holly Gilgamesh was the second most important person to the Fenfir Monastery. She was one day going to be Queen and head of the church.

As they trotted into the square, the troops were met with hooded Abbots. They greeted them with fruit and water and a very warm, friendly welcoming.

The Tarrenash men took care of their horses, first stripping the horses of the saddles and equipment to leave them to rest for the night.

A Disaris High Priest named Lugella greeted Princess Gilgamesh and General Yelfir and welcomed in the procession bound for the great gathering of Stormhorn. This being a royal visit, a grand banquet had been prepared in honour of Princess Gilgamesh, with music and entertainment.

The troops and legion were shown to their quarters and freshened up for the night's banquet.

The high Priest Lugella wore black hooded robes with seven thin red rings on each sleeve indicating the seven stone circles of Tanniv. He was tall and robust with a solid, mature face and commanded respect. He was one of the most important Disaris in Vakoborg and took direction from the King himself. He knew a day in advance that the procession was arriving so organised a banquet.

An enormous long table had been laid out. The table was short in height and was for sitting on cushions without chairs. The Tarrenash troops and the Disaris troops sat together in no particular order and sat side by side.

Princess Gilgamesh assembled at the head of the table; she insisted that Thomas and Oscar sat with her. So she could introduce them to the high Priest Lugella who was head of the Fenfir Monastery, General Yelfir, Captain Rothlan, General Yeldrove, and Captain Norlen also sat with Princess Gilgamesh.

The atmosphere was one of celebration for the royal visit, and Disaris musicians played woodwind instruments and guitars with a cheerful, upbeat tempo to the music.

They ate and dined and talked, the soldiers spoke of battles, skirmishes, and loved ones, and the Disaris and Tarrenash soldiers teased each other about the cultural battle difference but all in good friendly nature. The Disaris and Tarrenash had been friends and allies for hundreds of years, and a great many treaties were signed by the two empires ensuring peace and aid in times of trouble.

Princess Gilgamesh introduced Thomas as the son of Alina Marlow, the White Sorceress, who was on the head of the trading council. "I knew your mother, and she was a great woman; I was sad to hear of her passing," said the High Priest Lugella.

"Thank you, sir," said Thomas.

"We said a prayer for her here in the Fenfir Monastery, and she was not forgotten," said the High Priest.

Thomas nodded gracefully and made a point of saying thank you again.

"What message will you deliver for Vakoborg at the great gathering?" said the high Priest directing the question at the Princess.

"No message from Vakoborg. In the discussions with the King and the Disaris council, we are to sit and to listen," said the Princess.

"Very wise, Princess. This is a difficult time, and we need to think about every decision we make," said the Priest Lugella looking at all the guests at the table.

"And you are to deliver the message on behalf of the Marlow, the White Sorcerer?" said the High Priest Lugella, looking at Thomas.

"Yes, sir," said Thomas, not knowing what to say to the high Priest as he still felt highly apprehensive about addressing a large number of people.

"And you intend to deliver this message wearing Disaris clothes, do you?" asked the Priest again.

Lorsan Yeldrove jumped into the conversation "The boy speaks for Tanniv and speaks for Tanniv, East and West. I will help this boy deliver the message."

"Then I would prefer he did that in neutral clothing. I will supply the two boys some clothes that would send a neutral message," said the very wise High Priest while tapping his fingers on the table.

The High Priest conversed more and enlightened that he meant no harm; he had been a high priest for many years.

The Priest understood the multifaceted conversations that would be held at Stormhorn. Some of the region's kings and lords would need no excuses in creating an argument, and wearing clothing from Disaris might cause political disruption.

The High Priest Lugella was very wise; he talked about listening and spoke about the Turgett people and the fortress towns along the river Ailmar and how each town would have its own agenda and reason not to reunite.

"You have a very challenging mission ahead of you tomorrow, and I will be interested in hearing what has been said. Would you mind if I send someone

The Dasaris Fenfir Monastery.

from the Fenfir Monastery Princess Gilgamesh to accompany you?" said the High Priest Lugella.

Not wanting to be rushed or forced into a decision, Princess Gilgamesh looked at the Priest and said, "I will discuss this with my Generals and give you an answer by morning. For now, let's enjoy the night."

"Yes, my Princess," said the High Priest.

The Priest Lugella looked at Thomas again and said, "Who was your father, Thomas. Anyone from Tanniv?"

"No, nothing as exciting as that, sir. He was an accountant from London," said Thomas.

"I see; I was sure I knew him," said the High Priest looking at Thomas in the eyes.

The Priestess Sana Norbella

"And they are amazing warriors too, with this one here being the hero of the Disaris Pass," said Lorsan Yeldrove jumping into the conversation and grabbing and clutching Oscar around the shoulders while laughing and deflecting the conversation.

The High Priest was a high priest for a reason; he was of very high intelligence and was a master at conversation and extracting information.

The night went on, and the music played. The two captains wandered around the Disaris and the Tarrenash soldiers and explained that this was not a late night. The Soldiers drifted back to their rooms provided by the Fenfir Monastery and the night came to a close.

Princess Gilgamesh thanked the Priest Lugella for his hospitality; she would call a meeting before they left in the morning. The Princess said goodnight to everyone and was escorted to her quarters by her guards.

Both boys followed the troops back to their lodgings in the Monastery and rested for the night.

The following morning, Disaris horns sounded for the Monastery to begin morning prayers. The horns were soft, welcoming; the noise of the horns rang out all over the cloisters and loggings and for miles around.

Breakfast had been called in the same room the banquet was held in last night. A soldier thumped on the door to the boy's room, and they were asked to attend a morning meeting with the Princess.

They got ready and realised that a sack had been placed on the door handle with new clothing. They opened it and were given white tunics and black hooded gowns with no markings. They changed the Disaris tunics, still keeping on the leather trousers, boots, and gloves, and they took off the Disaris tunics and replaced them.

The Disaris guard waited and escorted them down to a room in the Monastery for a meeting with the Princess. Already at the meeting were General Yelfir, Captain Rothlan, General Yeldrove, and Captain Norlen.

Thomas and Oscar walked into the room while the Disaris soldiers closed the door and stood guard.

"I have brought you together to discuss our meeting at Stormhorn.

"The High Priest Lugella has asked to send a representative of the Fenfir Monastery. I want your views on this," said the Princess looking at everyone.

"I see no problem, providing they are there to listen only. There are to be no interruptions," said General Yelfir.

"Did your father, the King, mention that he would like a representative of the Church present at this meeting?" asked General Yeldrove.

"No, he did not, General Yeldrove; however, not all things were discussed in the meetings," said the Princess.

"I see no harm, and it would show that we are taking the gathering seriously," said General Yelfir.

"Then I agree. The Fenfir Monastery can send one representative to conduct themselves under my supervision and to report directly to me," said the Princess addressing and nodding at everyone in the room.

"Captain Rothlan, can you talk to Priest Lugella and explain the conditions to which we agree?" said the Princess.

Captain Rothlan agreed, nodded, and left the room to tell the Priest. This brought the meeting to a close. Once again, the Disaris troops and Tarrenash soldiers assembled with their horses in the courtyard.

The High Priest Lugella stood in the courtyard, and stood beside him was a beautiful blonde Disaris priestess with blue eyes and wearing a Fenfir black hooded gown with the seven red rings on each sleeve.

She was tall and beautiful, and the Disaris and Tarrenash men looked on at her as she climbed upon her dapple grey steed.

Princess Gilgamesh looked at the young Disaris Priest and nodded. The young Disaris priestess bowed in recognition.

The Princess looked over at Captain Rothlan and said, "Find out her name."

Captain Rothlan went over to the young Disaris priestess.

"Good morning," said Captain Rothlan.

"Good morning," said the young Disaris priestess.

"May I have your name?" asked Captain Rothlan.

"Yes, my name is Sana Norbella, and I am of no significance to anyone. I am to be an ear for the Priest Lugella and not a voice," said the beautiful Disaris Priestess.

"It is simply, so we know your name, my lady," said Captain Rothlan.

Thomas climbed upon Leokan and Oscar upon Sylvar, everyone had a great sleep, and even the horses looked fresh and ready to go.

It was a bright blue sunny day and not too hot; the ride would be a steep climb up to the great hall of Stormhorn in the mountains. Both the Tarrenash and the Vakoborg had brought camping and tent equipment to ensure they had loggings. The gathering could last many days or could be a short discussion no one knew.

General Yelfir looked over at the Princess, who was saying goodbye to Priest Lugella, and nodded; she nodded back in recognition for General Halamar to give the order to move out.

General Yelfir looked at Captain Rothlan, and a great roar came from the captain, "Riders, saddle up and move out."

Each rider and its horse cantered past Priest Lugella and the Disaris abbots. All the soldiers tipped their heads, thanking the Disariss of Fenfir as they trotted past.

Princess Gilgamesh and her General were the last to leave, again thanking the High Priest for their hospitality.

"Look after that Marlow boy. He could be the biggest mystery Tanniv has ever known," said Priest Lugella.

The Princess looked back with a surprise and confused at the comment made with a disoriented look and wondered what the Disaris High Priest meant. The Disaris Priestess Sana Norbella locked eyes with Thomas as they both jogged past, causing a sharp pain in his temples which came and went.

The Final Push to Stormhorn

Elaith assumed his expected responsibility ensuring the two boys were huddled in the middle of the riders and well protected. While Princess Gilgamesh and her General trotted on towards the front.

Elaith was an excellent soldier, and looking after the two boys had now become a well-ordered regimental part of his daily duties.

It would be a flat route through the forest for a few hours, then a slow, challenging ride up to the mountains of Stormhorn.

The procession was now more than forty persons strong, with the newest member Sana Norbella quietly and silently riding alongside in her black robe, keeping her hood firmly up so as not to engage in conversation.

They rode on through the thick forest and could noticeably see hills in the distance, and as they gained higher ground, they could see through the dense forest and see rolling hills that led into huge mountains.

The Mountains were a natural barrier that ran east to west through West Tanniv; the mountains divided the very north, which was considered nomad country, and the far northern farming towns and outposts. Many lords lived in the far north, but not many would venture down into Tarrenash.

Many of the northern tribes would now trade heavily with the City port of Elec with reindeer, livestock, and meat along with furs and pelts. The northern tribes had huge trading ships, and once full of tradable goods, they would sail down to port Elec regularly. Often, they made the much longer voyage down to Qulan City, but the City of Elec was now gaining most of the trade.

The Nomads of the Northern territories of West Tanniv were not aggressive tribes. The Nomads had been called and would be making their way from the other side of the mountain divide.

The procession galloped high up into the mountains; they stopped at a clearing, and with it being a clear day, they could see the forest of Vakoborg in all its glory, and they could see the foothills leading down to the great plains of Tarrenash. The view down onto Tanniv looked magnificent and wonderful. In the far distance, they could see the opposing mountain range of the Jandar

Mountains and the blue snake meandering, twisting, and winding River of the mighty Ailmar.

They could see processions and lines of horses and troops from other regions, countries, and tribes of West Tanniv snaking their way up to Stormhorn.

Thomas and Oscar looked on as this was the first real evidence that the other regions of West Tanniv would be attending the gathering.

They also looked on in amazement because they had never seen Tanniv, and they could see the geography and typography that Mrs Marlow had been explaining to the two boys.

The two boys were happy to see the continent, and they were taking everything in and processing everything; however, the burden of responsibility on Thomas to deliver a message to kings, lords, the Disaris, and Turgett people, weighed heavy on his mind. The closer he got to Stormhorn, the more he thought about this. Mrs Marlow had prepared the two boys to help open a portal into Tanniv; she gave no training or instructions on delivering a message that war was coming.

As he cantered further up the mountains, he tried to remember the politics of Moltenwing and that Prince Alwin Aminoff was the son of Queen Anastasia Aminoff, and how Elec city was overrun with Moltenwing soldiers and was now flying the Aminoff flag.

He remembered how he would need to explain the moving of the stone circles and how he met Prince Alwin also, that his mother was Alina Marlow and grandson of Margaret Marlow.

At this point, he had not mentioned war, not even to the Princess or King Gilgamesh, but he would need to deliver the strong message of war at some point.

More doubts crept and tiptoed into his mind. He wondered how a boy could deliver a message to unite the continent of West Tanniv. The doubts got more significant in his mind with each step of his horse Leokan.

The banner of West Tanniv had not been united for decades; however, Thomas had Oscar with him, and Princess Gilgamesh, and Lorsan Yeldrove. He was not alone, he thought to himself, and he could somehow feel that his mother was with him too.

He had the backing and support of King Gilgamesh of Vakoborg and the City of Tarrenash, with Lord Yeldrove being the direct voice of King Drusunal.

Thomas had the support of many but would he be able to deliver the message, he thought.

Stunning views of West Tanniv.

He started to practice speeches in his head about how he was going to deliver the message. Over and over again, he remembered King Gilgamesh's advice and advice from the Disaris Priest Lugella. The Legion and troop's edged closer and closer to Stormhorn; they were now walking along a hazardous and treacherous pathway and mountain pass.

The trail was only suitable for one horse at a time and was a single-horse pathway that led out around the mountain and was one-metre wide with a colossal sheer drop running down into a canyon.

"Just around this corner, and we will be in the Stormhorn Plateau, leading into the mighty great hall," bellowed Captain Norlen as the troops navigated slowly around the small trail to safety. It took a while, but every person on the procession passed through securely, and as they rounded the corner, there it was, it was the great hall of Stormhorn.

It was long and tall and resembled a thatched roof barn but an immense-sized barn. It was made out of giant oak timbers and wattle and daub walls. All around the Plateau were campfires, tents and tribes of soldiers, and flags flying everywhere.

Unmistakably they could make out the nomadic tribes from the north, and they could make out the small Turgett from the Jandar Mountains.

There were banners from the City of Qulan and banners from the regions within Tarrenash. Even tribesmen that had come down from the trading towns from the north had arrived.

The Merchantmen and noblemen who controlled the farming and the buying and selling of goods across the many towns and cities of Tarrenash had presumably come to protect their trading and pay fewer taxes.

Everywhere everyone spoke of taxes and increases to protect the border bastions from the Westside of the river. These rumours came along with murmurs, whispers, and complaints that the shadow warriors would ask for more funding and more troops meaning higher taxes.

It appeared that everyone was coming from far and wide, and everyone speculated on what decisions would be made, or conversation would come out of the great gathering.

A Marlow had not been seen in Tanniv for years. Many remembered the head of the trading council Alina Marlow who signed many significant trade agreements on both sides of the river, and now a new Marlow had come and called a gathering.

The Great Meeting Hall of Stormhorn.

Unsure of the conversation ahead, many speculated about trade deals, the stone circles, and the shadow warrior bastions in the east. Many had never seen a Marlow and did not know what to expect.

General Yeldrove spotted a clearing among the hundreds of tents to set up camp. He then set the horses into a gallop to the spot he had chosen. The gallop was more for show than anything else; he wanted the people of West Tanniv to see the Tarrenash soldiers sporting their banners of the shadow warriors from the Yelcan bastion.

General Yelfir and Princess Gilgamesh also galloped into a spot close to the Tarrenash to make camp.

The people of Tanniv looked on at the beautiful Disaris Princess and whispered, she's the Disaris Princess from Vakoborg.

A greedy merchant commented that the Vakoborg forest was too big and needed to be chopped down as the Disaris hooded riders rode in. The Priestess Sana Norbella stood out with her black robes, and she stood out for her uniform and for her beauty too.

Everywhere people looked at everyone, many had read books on Disaris and Nomads and the smaller Turgett but had never actually seen each other until now.

Thomas and Oscar were in blind bewilderment at the colours, the flags, the different tents, and grand marquees. Oscar could not keep his eyes off the Nomadic tribes and their colourful pageantry. Everywhere they looked was the hustle and bustle from the building of tents and from the smells of different exotic foods being cooked and the sounds of conversations, fires, and erecting of tents.

The Tarrenash dismounted and immediately went into the work of taking care of the horses first. Oscar and Thomas, by now, instinctively looked after Leokan and Sylvar under the careful guidance of Elaith.

The Tarrenash soldiers drove iron stakes into the ground, building tents. Each soldier fed and watered the horses spending time with them to ensure they were happy.

Then instantly, they began working on fabricating tents and marquees.

"What can we do to help?" said Oscar; Elaith looked over both shoulders and said, go and talk to Princess Gilgamesh; she is looking over at you.

Princess Katya Drusunal

Princess Gilgamesh stood watching and overseeing the work from the Disaris soldiers with her guards standing on each of her shoulders; she looked magnificent. But she was looking for Thomas and Oscar.

Both the boys walked directly over to Princess Gilgamesh and bowed their heads; they; had gotten into the habit of doing this because everyone else had been bowing but somewhere in their minds, she was still Holly from Tappington Hall.

"I think it is wise to have a meeting tonight with the generals," said Princess Gilgamesh looking at both boys directly. Both boys nodded in agreement.

Thomas was feeling relieved to hear that a strategy meeting was going to take place. He had been practising speeches in his mind.

With the chaos of seeing the gathering, it had taken his mind off it for a while.

The great hall was a purpose-built building used only for council meetings and the gatherings like this. It had been largely misused as this was the first gathering for decades. Everywhere tents and flags were being pitched at every available spot.

In the far distance, another team of horses and riders with banners entered the encampment area. The flag seemed familiar to the two boys, and as they came into view, it was the banner of the Eagle Owl of Tarrenash.

Oscar yelled over to Lorsan, who by this time was looking at his fully erected tent. General Yeldrove looked over and instantly recognised the banner of Tarrenash.

The new horses and riders jockeyed over to the tents of the Disaris and Tarrenash procession.

A rider in full light armour with a full-faced helmet with a white horsehair ponytail attached to the helmet galloped ahead, aiming directly for Lorsan Yeldrove. Then circling him, the magnificent-looking rider turned and kept eyes fixed upon Lorsan.

The rider stopped in front of Lorsan, confident and magnificent in the sunlight as she jumped off her horse in the dusk, looking directly at Lorsan. The General got down on one knee and bowed his head. Everyone was looking at the exchange, and Thomas and Oscar looked on in complete excitement at the conversation. Here was someone so glorious and so important.

The rider took off her helmet, and with a gracious glance, she turned her head, adjusted her hair, and smiled. It was Princess Katya Drusunal of Tarrenash.

"I thought you might need my help," Princess Katya said as she smiled at her General.

"My Lady, your help is always welcome and can only strengthen our cause," said Lorsan.

She had come to aid Lorsan and the shadow warriors and to support in the conversations. The mighty City of Tarrenash was the central accounting and commerce capital for all agricultural regions and countries in Tanniv.

All monies flowed through the cities banking system, and all trade deals on both sides of the river Ailmar ended up in Tarrenash.

It was said that nine out of ten coins passed through Tarrenash. If there was going to be a complex conversation about funds and taxes to support the Bastions in the East, then the City of Tarrenash needed to send a Royal representative.

Now Thomas had two princesses, further adding to the support in reuniting the great banners of West Tanniv; this made him feel more confident.

Princess Katya Drusunal was beautiful and had dedicated her life to the successful running of the Tarrenash Kingdom. She had been sent by her father, King Drusunal, to reunite West Tanniv at all costs and had the look of determination in her eyes.

She surveyed the surrounding camps looking over at the Disaris, the Jandar mountain tribes, the Qulan City merchants, the Northern tribes, and the Nomads.

"We've had a great turn out, and you have done well to get the Disaris princess here," said Princess Katya to Lorsen.

Princess Katya and her elite guard made camp and erected tents right away, and among the hustle and bustle of the work General, Yeldrove made introductions.

Thomas and Oscar were introduced first, and both had a conversation with the Tarrenash Princess.

"So you are the Marlow boy," said the Princess as she stood tall in front of the two boys.

"Yes, my lady," said Thomas apprehensively.

"I knew your mother; we were great friends, and I was sad to hear of her passing," she added.

"And you are a stone circle wizard," she said, looking at Oscar and observing his wand that was neatly tucked into his belt.

"Yes, my lady," He said. Oscar was adapting a little better than Thomas to this new military-style, and he was learning fast with the customs of addressing royalty and generals.

Princess Katya smiled and moved to inspect the other Disaris troops and over to the Disaris General.

"Princess Gilgamesh has invited you to dine in her tent tonight, my lady," said General Yelfir.

"Then would you please tell Princess Gilgamesh of Vakoborg I would happily accept," said Princess Katya.

By this time, the fields and Plateau surrounding the great hall were full. Old friends reunited and plots, and discussions were being had from all areas of the field. It was not a gathering with one topic; this was a unique chance for merchants to make money, cut trade deals, and everywhere people had trade conversations. Old stories were being told with laughs and whispers, the din of work being done to the camps at every angle could be heard, along with fires being ignited and tent posts being hammered into the hard ground.

Thomas and Oscar marched back over to Elaith and waited for instructions.

"This is your tent for the night; you have one on your own. Now, what are you doing for food tonight?" added Elaith.

"We have been invited to dinner with Princess Gilgamesh," said Oscar.

"Okay, so we have a fire going for the Disaris and Tarrenash soldiers tonight; you are welcome to join us later if you wish, but for now, get some rest and check on your horses again later," said Elaith.

The day was late, and they knew they were expected over in Princess Gilgamesh's royal tent sometime soon. The sun had fallen, and the temperature faded very fast and descended into a mild but breezy night.

All around them, they could see the fires glowing bright orange in every direction and could smell foods from different cultures and regions of Tanniv. The two boys were too agitated to rest.

"Did you see those Nomad tents?" said Oscar.

"Yes," said Thomas.

Both boys were buzzing with excitement, so they strolled over to the royal tent; two royal Vakoborg guards stopped them in front of the pavilion entrance. The guards had seen the two boys many times but stood with tradition and would not let the boys pass.

Captain Rothlan came to the entrance and permitted the boys to enter. Already in the tent stood; General Yelfir and Princess Gilgamesh. The tent was covered with furs and pelts. It had a small fire in the centre, and food was being prepared by her Disaris guard.

"Come in, Thomas and Oscar," said Princess Gilgamesh warmly to the two boys.

The boys were seated on the floor covered in furs, with the Princess, The Disaris General, and the captain.

Shortly after sitting, Princess Katya arrived with General Lorsan Yeldrove and Captain Norlen.

Princess Gilgamesh stood up to greet the Tarrenash Princess, and a warm greeting was exchanged between the two Royal Princesses of Vakoborg and Tarrenash.

A long and peaceful alliance had existed between the two countries for centuries, and the two were great associates, having attended many royal occasions and dignitaries together. However, the significant age gap between the two could be seen with Princess Katya's age experiences and prudent nature being evident.

Everyone seated, while pieces of bread and meats were passed around on cooking trays, and while everyone was eating, respect was given to the two princesses; however, the conversation of the gathering had not yet been broached.

Princess Gilgamesh decided to talk first; it was her tent, and it felt within all etiquettes to be the first to speak officially about the looming topics.

"Thank you to everyone that has come tonight. Especially Her Royal Highness Princess Drusunal," said Princess Gilgamesh. Everyone around the table stopped to pay attention.

"The Disaris are here to listen. My father, the King, and I feel that we need to collate all the evidence and to support Thomas Marlow during this time before the Disaris of Vakoborg make a decision," said the small Princess as she addressed the tent most confidently.

"While you are here to listen, Princess Gilgamesh, it is our wish to support Thomas Marlow in his speech, but we also need action and commitment," said Princess Katya Drusunal in an elegant soft voice.

"I think that it's wise to call the meeting tomorrow at ten o'clock in the morning," said Lorsan; his reasons were simple it was going to be a long day.

Not everyone would agree, and it would be tough on the boys, and Lorsan knew this.

"We should also walk into the hall individually not to show any signs of partnerships," said Princess Katya.

Everyone agreed. Princess Gilgamesh sent a Legion of Disaris, and Princess Drusunal sent troops from Tarrenash to each tent to send the message of the ten o'clock to start in the great hall.

The group had dinner and continued to talk strategy around the table. These were difficult conversations; while there had been peace in the regions and countries of Tanniv, the times were still difficult as there were still social and political upheavals after the great battles of Ilihorn.

A gathering could hold the key to a more prosperous and peaceful age if everyone agreed.

The theory being a counterweight of a unified power in the west may deter Moltenwing and Ilihorn from striking again.

The night was filled with conversations of a lighter-hearted note based upon the Tanniv principles of free trade and peace. These types of conversations were golden age conversations, being spoken about in a reminiscent way. All free trade had been made impossible between West and East, with the divide being made ever more prevalent after the war of Ilihorn.

These were just conversations to fill the night; the actual point in the discussion was to warn of war coming from the Aminoff's. But none of this was spoken about. The only thing agreed upon was the time the gathering was to commence in the morning.

Thomas and Oscar sat and listened to the stories, and Thomas felt that these stories of peace and prosperity helped him forget about the message he had come to deliver.

The night came to a close, and all goodbyes and goodnights were said in the most well-mannered way. Everyone returned to the tents to sleep and rest.

Delivering the Message

The following morning the sun came up on the cold mountains creating a mist, and minute by minute, the sun's rays filled the grasslands of the Plateau. Each tent became bathed in the sun and created small shadows over the next tent for only minutes at a time until the sun was fully overlooking the Plateau.

Slowly each tent awoke with the sign of daylight, all preparing hot drinks and food for the morning breakfast in readiness for the gathering.

A steady stream of soldiers, lords, merchants, Turgett, and Tanniv people of all cultures, all made their way up the hill to the Great Hall.

The conversations filled the morning air, with chatting but no one saying anything meaningful.

Everyone was in a hurry to get the best seats. The keepers of the hall opened the doors, and everyone flooded in.

The hall was colossal and could easily house five hundred guests. With benches filling each side like a stadium, the spokesperson could stand in the centre and deliver the message to hear. The floor was made with great stone pathing slabs of granite rock, and the roof was an open-beam oak roof with giant oak rafters crisscrossing from all corners to keep the mighty thatched roof aloft.

Early that morning Princess Gilgamesh and a small procession of Disaris walked up to the hill to the Great Hall. The Princess of Vakoborg walked to the hall and was greeted with a shallow din of muttering as she entered with her Disaris guard. The Princess of Vakoborg took a seat at the far end of the Great Hall.

General Lorsan Yeldrove went to see the boy's tent before walking up the hill with the Tarenash princess.

"Good morning," said Lorsan to the two boys.

"Good morning, sir," said the two boys.

"My-self, the Princess, and the captain will walk up now. If you walk a few metres behind and make sure you enter on your own and take a seat near us," said the General.

"You will be fine," said Captain Norlen as he winked at the two boys and patted them on the heads.

Princess Katya walked over to the two boys and said, "Good luck. Speak clearly and loudly, and we will be right with you, so don't worry."

Elaith had been waiting for the Princess and General to say their good lucks. He walked over to offer advice, "Be calm. Remember to breathe. You're a soldier. Think of the Bauk you defeated and the Tundra wolves you conquered; this should be easy."

So be brave, and you will be fine," said Elaith.

Both boys looked at each other, and Thomas said, "Here goes nothing." They took a deep breath and marched on. They stopped to straighten each other's uniforms out. He remembered what a good idea it was to wear neutral clothing.

As the two boys walked up the hill, several metres in front of them, marched Princess Katya, Lorsan, and Captain Norlen with two Tarrenash guards.

The camp was deathly silent; they could faintly hear the campfires, the soldiers and staff that waited behind to guard and keep the fires burning.

Step by step, they march up the muddy hill getting ever closer to the enormous old, badly weathered doors. Captain Norlen looked back and gave the boys a signal to wait.

Thomas felt faint and slightly dazed, and looking puzzled, he stumbled, and an arm came out to grab him. It was Priestess Sana Norbella; she looked at him with her deep blue eyes and said, "Thomas, be calm and breathe.

I am with you now, and I will always be here; remember the air and the breeze; you are in total control," Sana gave Thomas some water and put her hands on his temples, saying a prayer instantly, making Thomas feel better. She pulled down her black hood and once again said, "You will be fine. I am with you," then walked into the hali with her black robe pulled back over her head.

Oscar looked up and said to Thomas, "It's our turn," everyone was now in the building and was waiting.

They walked into the Great Hall together; an older man with a staff stood to one side. He banged his staff on the floor five times, creating the most deafening noise.

Two men came and closed the old weathered doors behind them. The man then pointed towards the centre of the floor.

All around, people muttered, whispered and conversations were heard faintly in every direction. Every seat was packed, and the whole circumference of the hall was filled with the citizens of West Tanniv and most likely East Tanniv spies.

Thomas looked into the masses and fixed his eyes on the Priestess Sana, who had calmed him only moments ago. Her hood was still up, but he could see her blue eyes. She gazed directly at Thomas, which again settled him instantly in the most mesmerising way.

He stood up straight with Oscar by his side and spoke, "My name is Thomas Marlow. My mother was Alina Marlow. I am a sorcerer from the White Order of Stone Keepers," he bellowed out to everyone in the enormous hall in a strong, confident voice.

"I have come here today to tell you that the ancient Stone Circles are moving and to tell you that Alwin Aminoff was seen in Stoney Cross!" he shouted.

The masses became restless, especially at the name of an Aminoff being mentioned. The noise got louder and louder as the nervous conversations and energy rang out around them.

Then the older man with the staff banged it on the floor again five times to silence the angry onlookers. The great hall fell silent again. Thomas looked for Sana to help focus him. She again looked into his eyes and calmed him; it was as if she had a telepathic ability to reach and feed him confidence in his time of need.

"So I have come here today to say that war is coming," the crowd roared up again, this time even louder and more aggressive.

Again, the old man banged the staff, this time making ten bangs on the floor to silence the crowd. The hall again fell silent, wanting to hear what was next.

Then people shouted out.

"Slavery and serfdom are already in East Tanniv; you expect us to take up arms and become slaves in West Tanniv," said a wealthy merchant.

"We've seen no signs of war!" shouted a small Turgett from the Jandar Mountains.

"War! Never again!" shouted a town's lord from East Tanniv.

A merchant shipbuilder from Qulan City Port shouted, "They stay to their side of the river, and we stay on ours!"

All the people that yelled and made comments were not speaking the truth. They had all felt the long arm of the Aminoff now penetrating deep into West Tanniv for many years. There were countless kidnaps into Serfdom and corruptions in trade agreements; the Hiligor Sea and the river Ailmar were no longer safe.

Thomas and Oscar stood looking anxious, hearing the endless comments.

The old master of ceremony again banged his staff to try and retain order by hitting his staff, this time in rapid-fire until the din was silenced.

"I am asking you to reunite West Tanniv under the great eagle owls of Tanniv and arm the Bastions of Yelcan once again!" shouted Thomas.

Again the excuses and insults were made across at each other, but this time louder. The Tarrenash had been silent to this point, but they started to shout back across at the Jandar tribesman and the Qulan traders, all the while the Disaris sat quiet listening.

While the arguments loomed over the hall when it looked like everything had failed, an enormous shadow came over the skylight; everyone looked up as the dim lighting appeared to darken the hall.

A giant Tanniv eagle owl flew in from the roof, spiralling down with its huge wingspan casting a moving shadow, and landed on Thomas's shoulders, flapping and looking at everyone.

The court fell silent once again at this well recognised and highly respected omen.

Thomas looked across at Princess Gilgamesh and Lorsan as everyone was silenced and stunned at what they saw. Eagle owls didn't land on anyone, and no one had ever seen such behaviour. The eagle owl looked around at everybody, then flew high up into the hall, circled, landing on Thomas again, then flew off into the skylight.

"The boys speak the truth," bellowed Lorsan Yeldrove to the court.

The rest of the court, still bewildered, started to take notice.

Then a prosperous merchant that had interests in Qulan City and the City of Elec shouted, "Lorsan Yeldrove is from Moltenwing and wants more money for his ragtag border patrol in Yelcan!"

Once again, the court ascended into arguments, shouting and aggressive comments flying everywhere.

Princess Katya beckoned the boys to come and sit.

Then she stood up to say, "If war is coming, and I think we all know that it is, aren't we better to be prepared."

"But who will pay for all this?" asked a wealthy Turgett Lord from Jandar. The Jandar Turgett tribes only thought of money and would live in conflict if it meant they could still trade.

"Wasn't it a Marlow trade agreement that made the Jandar Turgett rich, under Alina Marlow, with the City of Elec?" said Princess Katya, aiming towards the Jandar Turgett tribes.

"How many of us can tell a story of slavery or kidnapping or ships going missing on the Hiligor sea, or cargo going missing in Elec or of raids coming from East Tanniv?" shouted Captain Norlen of the Tarrenash. The whole court fell silent.

"He just wants to raise taxes for the bastions in the East," said another trader from the north, also notorious for trading on both sides of the river.

The arguments flew backwards and forwards all day. The quarrels of serfdom and trade agreements went back and forward. Accusations flew wildly of trading with Moltenwing and Ilihorn. Agricultural contracts that were administered in Tarrenash were complained about.

Then Princess Katya stood up and said, "We are not asking to go to war, and we are asking for more money and more taxes to defend ourselves."

"We are asking for the regions to unite so that we are the counter-threat for peace in Tanniv," said the Princess of Tarrenash as she gazed at everyone and every tribe in the building.

The court stopped to listen, but again the arguments flew repeatedly, not getting anywhere. The hours passed, and tribes began to leave.

The Disaris sat back and listened. Princess Gilgamesh listened and said nothing.

They listened as accusations came from Qulan and Jandar.

The Tarrenash tried to assure them by offering declarations, but the mistrustful Turgett and Qulan traders refused to listen.

A single-bannered Empire of West Tanniv would not mean war; it would mean there would be no war, shouted Princess Katya.

It was hardly likely that the existing settlement agreements of Tarrenash Vakoborg, Qulan, and Jandar would mean peace; they were simply not strong enough, and the border defences were weak at best.

But by this time, the Disaris and Tarrenash feared that the Moltenwing secret trade deals were too appealing, inviting, and lucrative to reunite West Tanniv.

The Aminoffs had already set a cancer upon the population. The rot had set in as Qulan, and some of the Northern tribes had already made agreements with Moltwenwing.

For hours and hours, the arguments grew, and other quarrels repeated themselves over and over again. More and more tribes, lords, and nobles left the building, and the corrupt ones showed their hands by leaving early.

The Disaris remained all day until early evening, as the popularity of the Tarrenash relinquished, and the energy for arguments grew weary.

Princess Gilgamesh stood up, convinced she had heard everything she needed to hear, decided to leave. The court had fallen apart, and it descended into chaos.

Thomas and Oscar sat and watched as the court emptied. Princess Gilgamesh looked at the two boys and said, "We will get you home and back to Stoney Cross. I suggest you leave with us now."

Princess Katya looked at the Princess and said, "Is that it? You are going to ride away?"

"It is not a Disaris problem. My mission was to listen, and there is no evidence here today to suggest West Tanniv will change," said Princess Gilgamesh as she marched out the door.

The procession walked out to the campsite, and the soldiers from Tarrenash and Vakoborg had packed away, preparing to move out that night.

General Lorsan spoke to Princess Katya, "I need to go with the Disaris to ensure the boys get back to Stoney Cross. After that, I will ride to see the King in Tarrenash City."

"Yes, I will ride directly to Tarrenash, now. My father will want to know," said the Princess of Tarrenash.

The gathering disbanded as fast as it was gathered. Thomas looked in disbelief. Oscar ran around, watching everyone go.

"This has all been for nothing!" yelled Thomas.

"This has not been for nothing, Thomas; there will be no war, and peace will continue," said Princess Gilgamesh.

"Yes, but for how long and who will free the serfs in East Tanniv?" said Oscar.

A wind blew in and howled as late afternoon turned to dusk with cold grey skies and blustery winds. The soldiers struggled to pack away the tents all around; the wind blew stronger and stronger they could see in the distance the

Nomads struggling in the wind and lines of people in all directions leading out of the mountains. The whiff of failure was in the air as fires were stamped out, and a mess was left for the Stormhorn workforce to clean up.

"Riders, saddle up!" shouted Captain Norlen trying to yell over the howling sound of the wind.

"Disaris, saddle up!" cried Captain Rothlan.

The Disaris and the Tarrenash saddled up and galloped out of the Plateau Thomas, and Oscar looked stunned Elaith grabbed them and said, "come on, boys, we need to get out of here."

Princess Katya circled back and galloped towards the two boys looking them in the eyes through her helmet; she bowed and saluted them and said, "I will see you again, boys. Real soon. It is not over."

The Massacre of the Leoven Abbey

The Disaris rode out first, and as they galloped across the Plateau, the Tarrenash procession under General Yeldrove and Captain Norlen followed as they rode through the night.

Thomas galloped on Leokan and Oscar on Sylvar while Elaith was close, and the formation of Disaris and Tarrenash protected them.

The priestess Sana jockeyed close, ensuring a safe night ride.

A few hours went by; riding at night was difficult especially coming down the mountains. General Yelfir stopped riding and halted the procession; they could see a trail of flames in the distance coming from the north Vakoborg forest deep below in the pass.

The Princess stopped to look, then turned to Halamar and asked, "What do you think it is?"

"No one rides with flaming torches at night. Something has happened," said Captain Rothlan.

"Let's carry on," said the Princess.

The procession carried on hurriedly into the night but this time towards the flaming torches coming from the Northern Vakoborg forest. Sana Norbella galloped on then stopped and turned to look at Thomas; they both stopped and held their heads simultaneously as if something had happened that only they could feel.

As the procession rode faster and faster on the flattened Vakoborg forest floor, they aimed for the torches they could see in the distance like little spots of orange lights. Within an hour, the torches came closer and closer to the procession.

"Stay close to me!" shouted Elaith as he grabbed at Leokan and Sylvar to pull them close to him.

A horn let out, resounding through the forest; it was a Disaris horn. The flaming torches were friendly; they were Disaris.

The procession rode closer and closer to the flames, and the horns let out noise through the darkness of the forests to guide Princess Gilgamesh in.

They finally reached the Disaris with the flames. "Who are you?" shouted Princess Gilgamesh into the darkness of the forest.

"We are Disaris soldiers from Vakoborg city; we bring news," said the warrior as they got closer.

"What is it?" said the Princess in a hurried voice.

"The ancient order of Disaris Nuns"

"In the grounds of Leoven, they've all been attacked and killed," said the out-of-breath soldier.

"How do you know this?"

"How do you know this!" exclaimed the Princess in a horrified voice resounding through the rest of the troops and legions.

"A pilgrim who escaped told us," said the soldier.

"Disaris, tonight we ride to Leoven!" shouted the Princess Gilgamesh impatiently.

"Tarrenash, this is not your business. You do not have to come," said the Princess as she cantered the horse around.

General Lorsan Yeldrove rode around to talk to the Princess and said, "My lady, if it is a Disaris problem, then it is a Tarrenash problem, and we ride with you."

Looking over at General Yelfir and nodding, Lorsan let out a scream, "Tarrenash, tonight we ride with our Disaris brothers to Leoven!"

The Priestess Sana Norbella wearing her black abbot's robes, galloped to the front, looking everyone in the eyes and said, "I will lead the way."

The procession now, taking on an urgent unrelenting feel, galloped on into the night with the bright orange burning torches riding ever faster deep into the largely unknown darkness of the twisted forest.

The Disaris Nuns in the religious grounds of the Leoven Abbey were considered to be the most religious grounds in Vakoborg. All festivals of light and earth and seasons came from this ancient order of nuns on the sacred grounds. It was also considered neutral ground, so the Disaris had to see this to believe what had happened; it was not confirmed until they could see it.

The priestess Sana Norbella rode and rode hard, galloping over boulders and across streams.

Sana had built her life around religion and grew up with the Nuns. She was in shock at what may have happened. They rode hard, only stopping for water and food for the horses; they galloped for two days and two nights until they reached the grounds.

They could smell the smouldering fires from a few miles away; every soldier, whether Disaris or Tarrenash, could smell death in the air.

They cantered slower into the convent religious grounds. The peace-loving Disaris Nuns had been murdered and maimed. Riding around, each Nun looked like they had been through the worst atrocities that could be dealt out. The Disaris among them said nothing; each Nun looked like they had been harmed much worse than the one before.

The Tarrenash dismounted, trying to show respect to the Disaris. A Tarrenash soldier started to investigate who would do such a thing. Black arrows were laid everywhere. "These are Ilihorn arrows," said a soldier as he stood in a pool of blood, showing the arrow's fletchings to the rest of the procession.

The Priestess Sana looked around, trying to count the numbers of the dead "it looks like they have all been murdered, and none have been taken as slaves or will be sold into serfdom," said Sana.

The Disaris looked dejected but never cried or showed any emotions aside from rational thinking. They cantered around, some walked around, some prayed privately, and others decided to organise the mess.

"Can we organise a funeral?" asked Princess Gilgamesh, looking at Sana Norbella.

"Yes, I will organise," said the Priestess Norbella.

"Sana, you are in charge here now; tell us what needs to be done," said the Princess.

The High Priestess Sana Norbella nodded gently and began to organise the Disaris legions and Tarrenash troops into cleaning teams and creating religious funeral pyres. Thomas and Oscar helped tidy, clean, and kept themselves quiet.

This was the wickedest atrocity the Disaris had ever seen in nine hundred years, and the Nuns looked like they suffered most horrifically.

All around, paintings had been slashed by swords and sculptures pushed over and smashed. Books were burned, and no respect or mercy was shown to anyone. Everywhere lay victims and, no one had survived.

Peace-loving religious Nuns from a hallowed, sacred order had suffered in Vakoborg, and whoever did it wanted to send a message. It appeared that the barbarism had been done a week ago. Tarrenash and Disaris walked around gathering evidence trying to collate and record what had happened.

The Massacre of Leaven Abbey.

The Priestess Norbella continued to give orders and organised the convent's cleaning and restoration the best they could for now.

Funeral pyres were arranged in the fields in the surrounding areas, and one by one, the Priestess Norbella blessed and prayed, giving each of the eighty Nuns the best blessing that she could.

The Disaris and Tarrenash lit each one, and the orange flames lit up the black night skies.

The Disaris soldiers stood by each funeral, helping the Priestess Sana any way they could; they prayed with her at each burning mound. The Tarrenash prayed in the Tarrenash way down on knees with hands cupped together.

Princess Gilgamesh and the two boys followed and prayed and did what they could to help ease this massacre and atrocity.

Lord General Halamar Yelfir of the Disaris army looked angry and spoke to Princess Gilgamesh.

"We must ride to the City of Vakoborg and report what has happened here," said Lord Yelfir.

"No, we must wait for the Priestess Sana Norbella to finish her burials. Then we ride for Vakoborg to see my father; right now, this is The Priestess Sana Norbella's time, and we will leave once she sees fit," said Princess Gilgamesh.

The burning continued through the night; no one slept, and no one rested until each Nun had been put to rest in the proper Disaris way.

Everyone looked shocked and stunned and covered in black soot from the fires; it looked like a burning, seething mess. The mood was one of great sadness and tremendous anger. Sana Norbella prayed over each burning mass in an ancient Disaris tongue. Her lily-white skin was covered in black burning ash; she prayed for each victim, remembering each Nun with her soft Disaris tone and piercing blue eyes.

Princess Gilgamesh stood in front of the procession, directing a speech at everyone present; she stood on a nearby boulder high up to hear her; she stood with gigantic flames rising high behind her.

"Today will be remembered as the Massacre of the Leoven Abbey. Every Disaris and Tanniv man, woman, or child will be told of this massacre in both East and West Tanniv alike. A great monument will stand here so no one will ever forget this day," said the Princess in a deep, noble voice.

"For now, we ride to Vakoborg! Who is with me?" she bellowed, holding her Disaris sword aloft as if she had transformed into a warrior princess, and she appeared to grow up overnight into a mighty Disaris leader.

Everyone cheered.

Thomas held his wand aloft, and Oscar did the same.

The Tarrenash held their long swords overhead, and the Disaris blades were held upwards, all yelling and cheering.

Sanna looked up, covered in black soot, and the reflection of the bright orange flames against her skin gave her a determined look, and a knowing look that everything had now begun and nothing would ever be the same again. Sanna stood high up on a boulder looking over the bright orange fires with her sword in one hand and bow in another; she stood in the blackness of the night listening to her princess talk.

Everyone knew that nothing would ever be the same.

They saddled up and galloped out deep into the blackness of the forest for the City of Vakoborg, occasionally looking back to see the brightness of the flames burning behind them.

Praying for the Dead.

The Uniting of the Banners

During the failure and collapse of The Great Gathering of Stormhorn, the meeting of the regions seemed to do more harm than good.

The breakdown of the Gathering served as valuable propaganda for the Empress and Prince Alwin that West Tanniv was weak, and now due to the failures in the foundations of the West's social system, Moltenwing found themselves with many strategic victories and many diplomatic advantages.

The warring tribes from the north of Tanniv that held no political convictions continued to cross the Ailmar River, raiding towns and villages in the Northern territories of West Tanniv. They terrorized farming communities with atrocities and bullying without any opposition. It appeared that whole towns and villages were freely being raided, and the occupancies were being sold into the East Tanniv serfdom system.

These raids were coordinated not so Moltenwing could benefit from money or riches or even benefit from serfdom, which of course, you could never have enough serfs. But these were territorial and political games that Queen Aminoff and her administration were playing.

Moltenwing was testing to see what the West government would do under the collapse of the Stormhorn Gathering.

Serfdom was the backbone of the Moltenwing economy, and Queen Aminoff and The Nobles relied solely on the free work and labour of slavery to prop up the thriving nation. Whereby West Tanniv relied on cooperation and the sharing of liberties such as fair prices and free trade.

In Moltenwing, the aristocracies and high society used the quantifying of serfs to be seen as social standing. The more serfs a Lord, Noble, or Merchant had, the higher up the social ladder one was viewed.

It was estimated that many of the Nobles and Merchants had millions and millions of serfs working in farming on the Great Plains or in the mountain mines of Ilihorn. The figure could never be fully known as no census ever reached as far as the Rovalur Mountains in the far East of Tanniv.

Some individual Lord bragged that he had one million serfs on his lands on his own and would use this boast to increase high social status in Moltenwing.

Moltenwing's social events of the year comprised of such self-important bragging at grand balls and parties, and the whole of society seemed to be wrapped up in grand balls and social affairs that would be the chance to show off one's riches and wealth.

The Grand Palaces that sprung up all over the city would be evidence enough that the economy was prosperous, booming, and thriving, with ever-growing bigger and bigger palaces and grand houses being built in every direction.

East Tanniv was around fifteen times bigger than West Tanniv but lacked diversity in weather and culture. This would always be of great jealousy to the occupancies of the East; it would play into the hands of the Empress.

She would use these inferiorities to persuade the Nobles that the administration needed to take a hard line against the West.

Sending paid mercenary soldiers to raid West Tanniv towns would be a great way to experiment and assess the strength of Tarrenash.

Word reached the Aminoff administration that the Gathering of Stormhorn had collapsed. This type of information proved to be very useful, as this kind of valuable material helped to encourage the Kingdoms of East Tanniv and its influencers.

Queen Aminoff, who had been composing and orchestrating these territorial games of deceit and lies, would do so from Moltenwing and could easily deny any blame.

She could refute this had anything to do with her and blame the northern tribes on pretty much anything.

Many Northern occupied towns and villages from West Tanniv came under the protection of Tarrenash or the border forces from the Bastions. Still, after the collapse in Stormhorn, these fell into an ever-decreasing decline, making the borders weaker.

This was political chess being played by Queen Aminoff and her son Prince Alwin Aminoff, knowing that the Tarrenash could not constabularies the districts this far north anymore.

Dark days were upon West Tanniv, and the whole world could see the damage that had been caused due to the collapse in the Gathering. It opened up many doors and many avenues for East Tanniv to exploit.

The Capital City Moltenwing

225

The Annual Moltenwing Assembly

Each year the Capital City Moltenwing had ten days of parties and political meetings. These would take place in the East Tanniv Capital at various palaces across the City.

These parties would occur after the annual harvest, so the government and administration would have an accurate census to base any conversation on finances and political manoeuvrings.

These were thriving times in Moltenwing, and the free people of East Tanniv had never had it so good, and judging by the palaces and the way the rich were dressing and the lavished gold stage coaches buzzing around the cities streets, thriving times were being had in Moltenwing.

The annual assembly was a time to quantify and assess the year and make plans for the coming years.

It was a chance for merchants to trade and sign business treaties across the regions, and in every direction, large quantities of money were being made.

It was a time to show military might and for the many generals and commanders to get together and discuss strategies and future budgets.

It was a time for grand balls and parties to take place across the capital, with each party and prom more magnificent than the next.

It was a chance for Queen Aminoff to call an assembly of Commanders, Nobleman, Council Members, and Rich Merchants to all meet in the great meeting hall in the grand Moltenwing Palace.

The meeting hall of the Palace was an assembly hall; it had an enormous round table that could seat hundreds of people and was used every year to house the conversations and to admit policies.

The Queen was beautiful and radiant, and she walked around the envy of everyone in Moltenwing, her splendour and fashion were famed, and each girl tried to emulate her style and grace. If you were in favour of The Queen, the whole of Tanniv would be in your favour. If you fell from grace, you would be left with nothing.

It was well recollected that at a Royal social gathering in the Moltenwing Royal

Palace, one of the Nobleman, a man called Itham Sanev, remarked about the power and wealth of Queen Annastasia Aminoff.

During a grand Royal dinner, Itham drank too much wine by the bottle; he laughed at her new tittle and ambitions of being an Empress.

The Queen looked at the Nobleman with a beautiful cordial smile and gently bowed her head in a courteous motion.

The Queen stood up and walked around the table as the guests drank wine and ate dinner; the then diners realised she was strolling around the dining hall, and the whole table fell silent.

Queen Anastasia strolled around the table, talking to no one in particular, looking at the guests, and smiling; she began to speak.

"Everyone around this table is rich and wealthy," she said in a soft gracious tone.

"Everyone around this table has a grand palace and stately homes," as she sauntered around the room, brushing her elegant fingers on the shoulders of the aristocracy as she walked. The atmosphere by this time changed to deathly silence.

"Everyone around this table has fine jewellery; some would say finer than mine." As she looked across at the beautiful young girls sat beside their much older nobleman or commander husbands. She walked over to one of the beautiful Moltenwing girls and gently reached out her hand, and examined the diamond necklace the young lady was wearing around her neck, and she peered into the young lady's eyes.

"Everyone around this table trades with Qulan City or even in Tarrenash, but I say nothing,"

"You all do well and make money and collate power," she added again, walking diplomatically and graciously stepping around the elegant dining table, still touching everyone with her long striking fingers on the shoulders.

"I gave Tanniv my only son,"

"I sent him to live in the cold dark mountains of Ilihorn to trade with the greedy merchants in Elec."

"I did this to keep you all safe and well here in Moltenwing," she said as she continued to walk around the room looking at the grand frescos on the walls, this time with her back towards the guests, she addressed them and looked out at the cityscape.

"But I am too kind, and I am weak, and I turn a blind eye as I do not like confrontation."

"I am guilty of always thinking of others first; it is a fault of mine," she said, looking at everyone around the table, which by this time had all eyes fixed upon her.

Everyone was feeling nervous and anxious at the Queen's speech.

Prince Alwin Aminoff was the only person you could see around the table posed normally and sat calmly listening to his mother speak.

"But if someone around this table wants to laugh or thinks my ambitions are too much, I will erase them, I will erase their families, and their very existence, and set them to work in the fields and mines with the Serfs," she added, but this time you could feel the pressure in the room building.

Then walking around the table, she came to the Nobleman Itham Sanev and his beautiful young wife. With a gentle, slender lean in-between their heads, she whispered into their ears so that the whole table could hear. "if someone did not show respect or at least gratitude, I will divide up their wealth and share it with the vultures around this table."

Looking at her Elite Moltenwing Guards in the room, she gave the slightest of nods. The guards rushed towards Itham Sanev and his wife and dragged them out of the palace dining halls with hands around their mouths and necks. So swiftly that the chairs tilted and were lifted out of the grand dining hall with them in it.

The Queen's most faithful minister hurried swiftly towards her, and she whispered in his ear, "Never do I ever want to hear his name or be reminded of his name ever again."

This was enough information for the minister to understand what needed to be done. The Nobleman Itham Sanev and his wife and their families and lands were erased forever, never to be seen again.

Some say they continue to work in the slave mines of Ilihorn to this day. This was seen as typical that one of the wealthiest Nobles in East Tanniv could fall from grace in such away.

The Queen continued to walk around the table, every bit as beautiful and gracious as before.

"Every single one of you is here because I allow you to be here! I allow you to be rich, and I allow you to be in my company, and all I ask is respect, nothing more just respect!" She said in a very courteous, tactful, gracious, beautiful manner.

She laughed and looked directly at her son, then returned to her seat while the Prince made a series of tributes to end the evening.

The Annual Assembly was called that week, and hundreds of Commanders and High-ranking Generals came from all battalions of the armies. The Nobles, Lords, and wealthy merchants came from the far reaches of Tanniv.

They sat around the huge round table, each with their caddie or assistant standing directly behind them.

The Commanders and Generals looked magnificent in their gold-gilded, highly decorated uniforms, and the Nobles and Merchants were astonishingly dressed in finery with great gleaming jewel incrusted medals.

Sat at what could be described as the head of the table was a throne carved ornately in redwood with red velvet seating for the Empress. Then to the left was another slightly smaller throne, and the second was for her son Prince Alwin.

The Prince would earn the respect of the court by being The Queen's son. However, he also gained admiration with his public speaking, confidence, ability to govern, and being as persuasive as his mother.

Prince Alwin had also earned respect with his heroics and decisive decisions made at the battle of Ilihorn with many victories. He was a Prince and commander, chief of the armies at Ilihorn, and a politician.

He was also Vice-Admiral of the Navy and controlled the fleet in the Hiligor Sea, and as a successful warring veteran, he had the experience to keep the respect of the court.

The Prince was also an astute merchant trader and an excellent reader of people. He always knew who to have around him in specific meetings, who to brief, and who to keep onside.

He had single handily invigorated the economy of Port Elec many years before. Elec City was almost raised to the ground in the last great battle. Alwin rebuilt the City with the serfs and the riches from the Ilihorn Mountains and with trade deals done with The Qulan City trading council, which Alina Marlow set up.

He was well respected in the City Port of Elec and had a summer palace residents in the middle of the City.

He had a vast network of spies everywhere and had earned the approval of Moltenwing at a very young age, as he was head of the secret police too.

He may have been the Queens son, but he was powerful and well appreciated everywhere.

Most conversations between Prince Alwin and Empress Anastasia Aminoff would be made in private before such an assembly. The two would sit in secrecy, planning discussions, diplomatic strategies, and working out territorial policies.

They would sit for days working out who would attend, where they would sit, assessing one's riches and powers to have the measure of everyone around the table.

The Empress would often say nothing at an assembly, letting her son do all the talking and the work. This was because they had already agreed and had the meetings many days prior, and this would merely be a puppet assembly just for show.

The Princess would stand and address the court to speak about the merchant fleets and The Navy in the Hiligor Sea, discuss the Merchant riverboats in the Ailmar River.

As Commander and Chief of the Armies in Ilihorn, he would discuss the vast number of troops stationed in the mountain garrisons and the Armies stationed in the Elec districts.

The Prince would then generate an accurate census.

The armies the other commanders and generals could raise in the far-flung regions were of great interest and discussed at the week's annual meeting.

Most nobles counted millions of combatants as conscripts from the serf labour forces. These serfs counted as soldiers but were useless ill-equipped soldiers, most unwilling to fight.

The assembly would be a general meeting about armies and taxes and serfs and the quantification of troops stationed in areas of the country. This was vital information for the Empress as she was keen to begin invading areas of West Tanniv. However, a well-laid plan would need to be put in place, and the testing raids by the Northern tribes were important information and statistics that were being gathered and measured.

A silent war was being waged against Qulan and Tarrenash City. The consumption of the trade agreements, which was starting to destabilise the economies in the west.

There was no opposition in East Tanniv; everyone would agree. No one wanted to end up with the same fate as the Nobleman Itham Sanev and his family.

The result of this great assembly from a dictatorship would be an agreement on everything. So the silent trade wars and merchant blockades would continue to weaken West Tanniv further.

The East Tanniv spies would continue to cause disruptions, and the raids on the towns and villages would continue.

The atrocities caused at Leoven Abbey would never be mentioned, written about, or even ever discussed. This was orchestrated directly from the war administration in Moltenwing, and although no evidence would ever be seen, everyone knew it was an order that came from Anastasia Aminoff herself.

The Empress was also a great sorcerer and had much hatred for these ancient orders, which coveted the Stone Circles in the West.

The might and power of The Old Aminoff Empire centuries ago occupied the territories in the North Forest of Vakoborg. But now, the Stone circles were denied by The Disaris.

King Gilgamesh called these stone circles the Disaris Sanctified Lands, and it sent fury through her blood, and she would never forget this.

The arguments of who would own the circles and whether they were ancient Disaris Holy lands would be why the Disaris needed to blame Moltenwing.

The Empress had never made this a secret that she wanted the Northern Vakoborg Forest territories back in the Moltenwing Empire.

However, the question was how King Gilgamesh of the Disaris would react to the Massacre of the Leoven Abbey.

East Tanniv had what seemed to be the perfect administration and government. Prince Alwin controlled the fortress in the Mountains of Ilihorn. Prince Alwin commanded the armies and the Navy with his Commanders, and he positioned all troops strategically.

The merchant fleets had Moltenwing Naval support, and the thriving City port of Elect was busier than ever with trade and commerce. This kept the many towns and districts content as all the local economies in the regions thrived.

The funds from Moltenwing were now paying bribes for senior officials in Elec, so everyone was directly under the complete control of the Aminoffs.

The trading council of Qulan and Elec had been set up by Alina Marlow many years before. However, it was now so corrupt it was unrecognisable from its origins.

The Empress seldom left Moltenwing, but she would go to the Port of Elec for the annual regatta each year. This event was another important high society social occasion in Tanniv.

In the far south of Tanniv on the Hiligor Sea, another grand town called Port Elleth sat in the much warmer sub-tropical climate. Port Elleth was in the warmer temperatures of the south, with beautiful beaches and bustling pubs and taverns during the summer.

In the warmer months, the grand palaces and grand houses housed most of the aristocracy and wealthy inhabitants of Moltenwing as they would stay in Port Elleth during the hot summer months.

Port Elleth also contained the Moltenwing Navy, and colossal wooden sail ships would birth and could be seen for miles around.

It was a busy Port, not a thriving commercial centre, as it mainly survived as a Port full of sailors during the winter. Many of the Pubs and restaurants would be full of sailors at port for short periods before patrolling The Hiligor sea right up to the mouth of the mighty river Ailmar.

Like any port, this would also give way to bandits and smugglers of all types trading black market goods from the far reaches of Tanniv.

The upper side of Port Elleth housed the Grand summer homes and palaces of the rich from Moltenwing. This is where many royal summer parties would be held each year.

An entire garrison of soldiers would be stationed in port Elleth all year to safeguard the wealthy of Moltenwing.

Port Elleth also served as a meeting point for the wealthy aristocracy of East Tanniv to meet at grand summer parties and discuss matters that they would not dare to consider in Moltenwing.

Prince Alwin also held a grand residence in port Elleth and as Vice-Admiral of the Navy, one of his many titles. The Prince would often reside there to hold Navel meetings with his commanders and admirals.

Although East Tanniv was a dictatorship, the Empress would still need to keep her council and government onside. Hence, the annual Moltenwing assembly, which was a necessary entity, and the small town of Port Elleth would serve as a further stronghold for the Moltenwing Navy.

Anastasia understood the power of a good bribe, and everyone who needed to be paid was paid handsomely.

This unique way of functioning was seen to be of great importance because when the time was right, anyone and everyone could be conscripted into the armies. This secured The City of Elec and the town of Port Elleth, which would stay firmly under the control of the Moltenwing government.

Stonecross Manner

Back in Stonecross, Manner Thomas and Oscar had been back for many months. The two boys were now even more inseparable; they sat together in class, walked to school together, ate together, and stayed around each other's houses as much as possible.

Both Thomas and Oscar were now at Stoney Cross School, and winter had set in for the year.

The fields in the surrounding areas were now covered in thick white frost, or rain would sheet down; such is life in England.

The green flowery meadows and fields turned into yellows, ambers, and browns, and the English skies were mainly grey. But the evergreen trees of Ballymore Forest would still be a dark green sight among a palate of winter colours.

Mrs Marlow continued to care for Thomas, and both boys now had almost daily lessons in wizardry and sorcery.

Mrs Pucket had moved into Stonecross Manner permanently to help with the sorcery lessons for both boys and was a general source of help for Mrs Marlow, who was responsible for raising a boy.

Both boys were full of questions and often spoke of Tanniv and the gathering, and they both had an air of frustration that they could have done more to make the gathering a success.

Thomas was enormously frustrated that they had left Tanniv in such a hurry and such a mess, and the last few days after the Massacre of the Leoven Abbey, he had felt that all seemed to be lost.

He attended the local school with Oscar, and both boys would sit with the frustration that school seemed pointless after experiencing problems that Tanniv had.

All around, Stonecross Manner laid books and maps on the subject of Tanniv, and both boys would compulsively study.

The giant oak table in the kitchen housed books stacked high like skyscrapers on a city landscape. Books would be face down open like butterfly wings, ready to be picked up and studied at a moment's notice.

They studied books on Qulan City and Elec City and Moltenwing.

They read the warring chronicles of Ilihorn and soldiers' accounts of the Great War on both sides.

The Stonecross library in the caverns underneath the Manner had millions of books, and the two boys wanted to read all of them.

Oscar was mainly interested in the Disaris religion. He studied this often while Thomas was taking after his mother by understanding her work that went into the complex setting-up and management of the trade council between Qulan City and The City Port of Elec.

They read books on the Tarrenash and the Great Grassland farming communes and books on serfdom. They were trying to understand everything they could about Tanniv.

Mrs Pucket gave them a strict timetable for sorcerer lessons, and both boys were doing well.

However, Oscar appeared to be grasping the magic and spells much faster than Thomas. Thomas always looked like he had something on his mind.

They would often be in the cavern library reading or at the Kitchen table eating and reading. They always had their head stuck in a book about Tanniv.

The winters around Stoney cross were particularly hard as the cold winds would blow in from the Salisbury Plain, and the thick, dense forest created cold mists which kept everyone shivering.

There was not a lot else to do other than to go to school and study. However, the two boys had replaced play with sorcerer studies and studying about Tanniv.

One School morning, Thomas got ready, took a shower, and ran downstairs for breakfast; it was a strange day. Mrs Marlow was down in the caves already and had left a note on a box of cereal saying, "Make yourself breakfast. I am busy in the cave."

He made breakfast and immediately got stuck into a book on the table. After he ate, he got ready for school; he walked through the kitchen door, which led onto the grand hallway, then shouted under the stairs, "Goodbye Gran, I am off to school!" as he bellowed down the stairs.

Grandmother shouted back from down in the cellar. "See you tonight and have a good day," said Mrs Marlow, and off course, the sniggering and chuckle from the books came from the caves too as the books would laugh at anything.

He strode down the gravel drive; it was a cold day, and he wrapped up in his thick grey blazer and his thick black duffel coat with a striped scarf, grey school trousers, and his satchel around his shoulder and neck.

He took the three-minute walk down the road to Oscar's house.

Oscar was just leaving, and as Thomas turned the corner, he was shutting his front door. Thomas waited at the top of the drive to save walking down.

"Good morning Thomas," Oscar said with no genuine enthusiasm because it was a school day, and still, with a slice of toast in his mouth, he mumbled something else.

"Good morning, how are you today?" said Thomas adjusting the strap from his satchel around his neck.

"I am ok I have been reading about the Moltenwing capital, and it kept me up at night worrying," said Oscar.

"You shouldn't read about the Aminoff's before bed," said Thomas looking at him smiling.

"Yes, you are right. I should carry on my studies of Tanniv religions," said Oscar looking at Thomas and kicking stones.

"Grandmother was down in the caves when I woke this morning; it was strange," he said in a puzzled voice.

"Has she ever done this before?" said Oscar.

"No, I mean she's normally there to fix breakfast," said Thomas. "Where was Mrs Pucket?" said Oscar.

"I am not sure," said Thomas shaking his head and shrugging his shoulders. Both were running as they could hear the school bell and the din from schoolchildren all going into class, and they did not want to be late only to be kept behind after school.

After what they had witnessed, the school was a tough place to be. Battles with Bauk and gigantic tundra wolves, seeing Vakoborg, and the atrocities at the Leoven Abbey. Seeing all of this and then going back to school for maths and English lessons seemed to be boring in comparison.

Thomas missed Princess Gilgamesh, and he missed the importance of being a well-known name like Marlow.

He kept his mother's name as he never really knew his father; his father died in an aeroplane accident before he was born. So being Thomas Marlow of Tanniv meant something, and being Thomas Marlow in school meant nothing at all.

Both boys sprinted across the cold, wet playground as fast as they could, with their school satchels hampering their speed, bouncing around frantically.

As usual, they were the last to run in the door.

Mr Bird, the boy's teacher, stood in the doorway, propping it open with one arm and the boys ran under his arm like a tunnel.

They hung their coats on the pegs, sat down at their wooden school desks next to each other, and sat facing Mr Bird.

School days were dull to the two boys now that they had travelled across Tanniv as Soldiers of Tarrenash had been to Vakoborg, banqueted with Kings, and now they were learning in a cold classroom.

School went by like any other day, and the two boys went walking back up to Stonecross manor.

On the walk back up the hill, it was late and dark. Thomas walked slowly, talking to Oscar about school that day, and Oscar held on the straps of his bag while kicking the bag more or less up the street. Their ties were wonky, and their shirts were untucked.

Oscar looked up, spotting something out of the corner of his eye, moving fast in the sky.

"Look, Thomas, Look," he cried as both boys looked up at the dark skies.

A huge flapping shadow was circling and spiralling down to the two boys; it was an Owl but no ordinary Owl; it was a Giant Eagle Owl.

It was Tupel, one of the Grand Eagle Owls from Tanniv.

Tupel was the owl that landed on Thomas during the gathering of Stormhorn. A connection had built up with Tupel and the boys.

The giant bird flew down and landed on Thomas's shoulders; he was hefty with massive talons but was gentle.

Both boys stroked Tupel, which he loved and adored.

The great owl curled his head around the boy's stokes and purred with satisfaction.

"Look, Thomas, a Message," Oscar looked at the bright yellow talons and saw a letter around his claw.

"What is it?" said Thomas adjusting his neck to look around.

"I don't know, but there is a small scrolled-up paper in a ring," he said as he was trying to force the scroll from the ring.

Oscar prized the scroll from the talons of Tupel's ring. "Got it," he said.

Tupel looked at the two boys with his bright-orange eyes, and he nuzzled his head at the two boy's faces, then opened up his giant wingspan and pushed off for flight. The leap from Tupel Almost pushed Thomas to the floor, causing him to stumble slightly. The owl took off high into the cold night's sky, and gave several hoots, then flew off into the distance.

Struggling to find the light to read the scroll, the boys ran up the hill to Oscar's house to read the message properly.

In Oscars drive was the old garage, and using a torch that his father kept in the garage, they both sat comfortably in the dark ready to read.

Sitting comfortably on an old wooden workbench with a vice grip, both boys sat easily side by side. Oscar shone the light over his shoulder, and Thomas unfurled the scroll.

It was from King Gilgamesh of Vakoborg.

Thomas read on, "To the White Sorcerer Marlow, we ask for your help once again, we ask that you come to Tanniv in our time of great need."

The two boys looked at each other with a combination of astonishment and excitement.

Thomas read on with the letter; it explained that after the great Massacre of the Leoven Abbey, The Disaris were in a state of mourning.

They took time to deliberate with the Disaris council and had gathered significant information, and that now would be the time to reunite West Tanniv under one banner again.

King Gilgamesh explained they would need a Marlow to attend a roving campaign to travel around Tanniv to The City of Tarrenash, the City of Qulan, and every town in-between to coordinate a gathering and funding and support for reuniting West Tanniv.

The letter explained the attack on the Leoven Abbey needed to be known, and the story needed to be told.

The boys could not understand some strange Disaris letters and numbers at the very bottom of the note.

They sat in the dark garage with just a tiny light discussing the letter for some while, and they knew they had to discuss this with Mrs Marlow and Mrs Pucket, so they ran into Oscar's house, "wait here while I get changed. I will come to your house tonight."

He opened the door and shouted, "Mum, I am home, and Thomas is with me; I'm going to Thomas's to play tonight," he kicked his shoes off with his feet pushing down the backs of his boots to shuffle out of them he bellowed and ran up the stairs as fast as he could to get changed.

Thomas stood in the doorway when Jane came to the hallway to find out what was going on.

"Hello Thomas," Jane said with a smile on her face.

"Hello, Mrs Williams," Thomas said.

"Oh, Thomas, call me Jane," she said as she folded her arms and stood listening to Oscar thumping around.

"Ok, yes, Miss – I mean Jane," said Thomas, who was also looking upstairs, listening to the thumping and stomping around from a very excited Oscar.

"So, what is the plan? I only heard half of what he was saying," she said with a mystified look on her face.

"We are going to my house for a few hours," said Thomas.

The racket of Oscar got louder, and he was at the top of the stairs.

"Hello, Mum," he said hurriedly.

"Hello Oscar did you have a nice day," said Jane as she looked at him.

"Yes, Mum, it was great; I am going; I will be back in an hour," he said as he was tucking his arm into his duffel coat.

"Well, let me drive you," said Jane.

"No, we will run across the meadow; come on, Thomas," said Oscar.

"But it's too dark," she said, and by the time she had finished her sentence, the two boys took off across the meadow around the back of the house like rockets.

"Call me when you want to come back; I will drive round to get you," she shouted.

"Ok, Mum!" he bellowed as the two boys sprinted into the dark.

It was completely dark outside, but the guiding light was the lights coming from Stoney Cross Cottage, where Mr Griffins lived.

The two boys rushed fast and aimed for the cottage, then sprung through the hedges onto Stonecross Manner. They could see the light from the Kitchen and Mrs Marlow and Mrs Pucket in the pantry.

Bounding through the door like a herd of elephants, the two boys came into the kitchen with such enthusiasm. The ladies looked around as the two boys came bounding into the door full of excitement and information.

"Boys, you have to stop bouncing through in such a hurry," said Mrs Marlow angrily.

"And I take it we have got Oscar for dinner tonight," said Mrs Marlow.

"Yes, Grandmother and I have got something to tell you too," said Thomas gasping and out of breath.

"Boys, calm down, take your coats off, then come and sit down," said Mrs Pucket.

"We have an hour before dinner," said Mrs Marlow.

The boys placed their coats in the hallway on the coat stands and walked back into the kitchen to sit down slightly calmer this time.

"Now what is it," said Mrs Marlow.

Thomas explained that they were walking back from school, and they saw the great Eagle Owl Tupel and that he had delivered a message from King Gilgamesh directly to the two boys.

The two boys explained the letter and showed the note directly to the two ladies, who both studied the dispatch in detail, passing it backwards and forward while they peered through their glasses.

Both boys sat on their knees on the chairs and leaned into the middle of the table.

Thomas leaned across with his fingers, pointed to the letter, and said, "What are these numbers and letters?"

These are Disaris proto runic coordinates to get back to Tanniv for The Oris Monastery, "There's a stone circle there."

"Yes, we met the Disaris Priest Elion," said Oscar.

"Yes, that's his name, Priest Elion," said Mrs Marlow as she looked down at the letter with a low-spirited look on her face.

"Are you going to go, Grandmother?" said Thomas.

"Can't you see boys?"

"They are asking for you boys to go," repeated Mrs Pucket looking dejected about the burden of such a difficult task.

"They know that you are Alina's son now; they will need you to travel to Qulan and beyond to reunite the banner," said Mrs Marlow.

She explained to the two boys that the trading council of Qulan City and Elec City would need to be convinced and who better than the founder's son to reunite this banner.

Thomas, the Vakoborg, and The Tarrenash people know this now, and they want you to go.

He rested back in his chair, feeling the same burden of the gathering and how this was an unsuccessful attempt.

He always blamed himself. But he witnessed the Massacre of the Leoven Abbey and felt that something had to be done. For the past months, both boys walked around with the sense of emptiness and how they left Vakoborg, not knowing what would be done. Or if anything was going to be done.

Although the Disaris did not show emotions, the atmosphere in Vakoborg for those last few days was terrible, and the air was filled with uncertainty and doom.

Oscar had been studying Disaris religious life and spiritual practices, and the massacre that happened on sacred, sanctified lands was the worse crime imaginably and was an act of war and the utmost provocation.

Mrs Marlow looked at her grandson, knowing that he was to carry the load again. She knew that this campaign could be longer.

She looked at the two boys, took a deep breath, and said, "Well, we had better prepare you both then."

"Are we going back to Ballymore Forest stone rings?" said Oscar.

"No! This time we will go to The Avebury rings," said Mrs Marlow.

"It's too dangerous you will be seen," said Mrs Pucket.

"We will drive in the middle of the night perhaps at two o'clock in the morning we will raise a portal," said Mrs Marlow.

In truth, the walk to Ballymore Forest was too arduous and exhausting for Mrs Marlow; she never really recovered from it, the only real option to send the boys back was Avebury or Stonehenge.

Stonehenge was patrolled at night by security guards, so the only natural choice was The Avebury rings. The Stones at Avebury were large enough to support a portal between Mrs Pucket and Mrs Marlow, sending the boys back one at a time.

Much was discussed that night, but all agreed that going back was the only option.

The Avebury Rings

The Avebury rings would be easier to get to; however, one slight drawback was a village had been built in the centre of the rings over the past few centuries, and residents lived inside the circle.

This meant there was a good chance that the boys would get caught, but a portal being raised at two o'clock in the morning would minimise getting seen.

Maps of Avebury were laid out on the table, then moved again over dinner.

The four of them sat and talked about the plan during dinner.

It was Thursday in Stoney Cross, and the proto runic coordinates meant that they would leave Friday night.

Mrs Marlow looked over at Oscar and said, "Are you ok with this? It's a lot to deal with?"

Oscar looked at Mrs Marlow, then Mrs Pucket, and smiled; he lifted his wand and shouted, "volantem tapete," and the map began to fly around the room like a magic carpet.

"You try and stop me," He said with a beaming smile on his face.

Mrs Pucket looking at him, smiled while Mrs Marlow and Thomas laughed at the cheekiness and the map flying around the room.

Mrs Pucket observed Oscar's excellent magic looked cross but also looked admiringly as he was an exceptional student of magic and had come very far with his spells over the past many months.

Mrs Marlow looked at Oscar and said, "You are a good friend."

After dinner, she did what she always did and drove him back home.

In the car on the way to the house, Mrs Marlow guided Oscar to pack a bag for tomorrow night, as they would be leaving for Avebury late in the evening and try and rest as much as possible.

"Ok, Mrs Marlow," he shouted as he left the car.

"Good night, try to get some rest," She said with a smile on her face.

She had grown fond of him. He excelled in magic, and Mrs Pucket said he had shown a natural ability for the art.

Thomas did not have the same enthusiasm for magic. However, he had only just started a new school and lost his parents a year before and then the failure of the gathering; he never really got over the collapse of the gathering or seeing the Massacre of the Leoven Abbey.

It was as though Thomas knew he had to return to Tanniv and Mrs Marlow knew he would have to return too. She was too old now, and he was too young, but the balance of Tanniv and The Stone Rings would need to swing in favour of good, and only a Marlow could help restore the balance.

Moltenwing and The Aminoff's reach was stretching ever further. The economic and social balance of Tanniv was now so far in favour of Moltenwing, only reuniting the regions and countries that would save them now.

The following morning the boys got up for School Oscar had explained to his mother that he would be staying at Stonecross manner all weekend and after school that night.

It seemed unnecessary that the two boys would be going back to school. It was a cold winter's morning; thick white frost lay on the ground everywhere.

Thomas got ready and went downstairs for breakfast. Mrs Pucket was in the kitchen making tea and breakfast.

"Good morning," said Thomas stood in the kitchen all ready with his school uniform on.

"Good morning. I have made some porridge and some toast."

"Thank you, where is Grandmother," said Thomas.

"She's downstairs preparing your trip," said Mrs Pucket.

"You know she's very proud of you, and she understands that you are too young for this," said the old kind lady.

"I know, and I understand that I must reunite the banners of West Tanniv," said Thomas.

"Both you boys have done so well, and your magic is coming along very well," She said as she sat across the table with her cup of tea.

Thomas and Mrs Pucket continued to sit and have breakfast and discussed Tanniv and The Avebury Rings plan later that night.

After breakfast, he ran out to the hallway to get his coat and shouted down the cellar door, "See you tonight, Grandmother."

"Yes, you boys come straight home after school," shouted Mrs Marlow from down in the cellar.

He ran out of the door and was instantly hit with an icy winter wind. Everywhere he looked was a thick crystallised white frost on everything he could see.

The morning was cold and grey with a silver sky where the sun was trying to shine through. There was ice on puddles and ice on the hill leading down to Oscar's house.

Thomas skidded on the ice as much as he could, crisscrossing the road, sliding as much as possible. Skidding on ice are the types of things a boy should be doing with his life.

Thomas had studied so much on his mother's work, and learning about the multifaceted trade agreements with Qulan, Tarrenash, and Port Elec had taken a lot out of him.

His mother, Alina Marlow, was head of the Trading Council of Qulan, and many Lords of The Turgett mining communities of Jandar had become extremely rich because of Alina Marlow. Before these trade agreements, The Turgett were considered to be lower in the social system.

Reading and studying hundreds of social movements and trade agreements had taken its toll on Thomas, and while Oscar excelled in Magic, Thomas had fallen behind. Because he had felt picking up his mother's work would serve him well in future meetings.

In truth, the residents of The Jandar Mountains had attended the gathering. Along with the residents of Qulan, and they had chosen to be silent in the great hall that day.

When the talk and topics of increased taxes and funds to supply the border warriors came up, they were first to leave the great hall that day.

It seemed that Ilihorn was now pulling the strings in the trading council Of Qulan. The city was becoming rich and economically strong because of illegal dealings with East Tanniv. But at what cost, people would go missing almost daily in Qulan City, and the people of Jandar would often turn a blind eye for money, and the city was virtually running purely on corruption now.

Thomas knew he would need to enter Qulan and sit in the Marlow chair in the great trading council. While Thomas was not magically strong, he was becoming politically shrewder.

Thomas was still slipping down the icing path to Oscar's house and could see Oscar almost doing the same on the corner of the lane waiting.

He was skidding backwards and forwards in an ice patch he had now worn down to a black patch of ice but was having fun.

"Good morning," Thomas said from afar, skidding down the street.

"Good morning Thomas! Are you ready for tonight," said Oscar with a cold pink nose breathing out a puff of cloudy condensation vapour from the cold air.

"Yes, I can't believe we are going back!" said Oscar.

The two boys walked down the hill with a combination of skidding and walking down the icy road to school.

"Do you think the princess will be there?" said Thomas.

"Yes, I hope so," He said.

Then, like always, the school bell was ringing in the distance, and the two boys looked at each other shocked and started a mixture of running and trotting carefully in the icing conditions so as not to be late.

"Come on, Oscar, we can't be late then held back after school, not tonight," shouted Thomas.

The rule for this being as long as the pupil would be in the door by the time Mr Bird closed the door, they were not officially late.

The boys could now see the lines of children going into the school, with Mr Brid ringing the bell and holding the door open with one foot watching for stragglers to catch them out for being late.

The two boys ran and ran and were now in the playground, running and slipping all over the place.

Oscar was struggling as he had a rucksack on his back with his overnight and travelling things.

Thomas looked back at Oscar and grabbed the top of his bag handle on his back to steady him.

Thomas started a mixture of dragging, running, slipping, and skidding. Mr Bird could see this and stopped ringing the bell, knowing that Thomas and Oscar were the last two in, "It looks like you boys will be staying after school tonight for a few hours," shouted Mr Bird with a chuffed pleased look on his face.

Oscar looked up and could see the door moving and Mr Bird carefully removing his foot.

Thomas looked at Oscar with a disappointed look on his face with the thought of having to stay behind.

Oscar closed his eyes, gripped his wand in his coat, and muttered, "aperire venti, aperire venti, aperire venti" with that, an unexplainable gust of wind came from inside the school's corridor, pushing the door open and knocking Mr Bird off his feet. Onto his bottom, the bell fell out of his hand and rolled across the playground directly to Oscar's feet, and he stopped it with the bottom of his shoe.

He picked up the bell, and the two boys rushed over to Mr Brid.

"Are you ok sir," said Thomas.

"Yes, I am ok now; get in there, you two, you just got lucky today," said an angry teacher who had for sure thought that he had caught two detention fish in his net.

The two boys walked into the corridor and over to the pegs to hang their coats. "I can't believe you did that," said Thomas excited but shocked.

"I know! We couldn't be late tonight, though. I had no choice," whispered Oscar while stuffing his wand back into his inside pocket.

"Come on, you two into class! You had better impress me, today boys," said a grumpy Mr Bird who was still furious at what had happened but not entirely understanding why or who to blame.

Both boys with stooped heads looked at each other in a sideways glance from the corners of their eyes, hunched up their shoulders, and sniggered.

The day went pretty fast; it was another uneventful school day.

Each boy got on with his work with neat handwriting and straight backs in chairs, making sure Mr Bird did not have the excuse he was looking for.

The school bell rang and the two boys set off into the dark, cold late afternoon back up the icy hill to Stonecross.

They ran out of the playground and up the icy hill.

"Have you ever been to Avebury," said Thomas.

"Yes, a few times it's a strange place," Oscar said.

"Is there a village in the middle of the stone circle," said Thomas.

"Yes, and the stones there are huge, much bigger than the stones at Ballymore Forest," said Oscar remembering the out-of-control portal that sucked them into Tanniv the last time.

They ran up the hill past Oscar's house then into the drive at Stonecross.

The driveway light was on; a blinding light came from the overhead floodlight that filled the driveway with beaming lights.

As the boys rounded the corner, the light dazzled them.

A thick dark shadow came running towards them.

All they could hear was the sound of crunching stones from the driveway gravel getting faster and faster and aiming at the two boys.

Thomas lifted his arms and cupped his hands around his eyebrows to assess the situation.

Oscar, blinded and confused, was doing the same thing and tried to see who it was. The boys stood with hands around their eyes, disorientated and confused.

The sprinting got louder and louder, and the shadowy silhouette got darker and faster towards them. It was all happening so fast, and there was no time to react.

"Hello boys!" shouted Mr Griffins as Meg, the dog, sprinted towards the two boys wagging her tail and rubbing herself around them, weaving in and out of their legs in the most exciting way possible.

Both boys bent down, both patting and stroking the dog. Meg was filled with excitement, not knowing which boy to turn to first; she clawed away at the boy's legs and feet affectionately.

"It's Meg," shouted Oscar.

"Hello, Mr Griffins, we passed your house last night," said Thomas.

"Well, you should have popped in for a tea," said Mr Griffins.

"We will next time," said Thomas.

"I hear you boys are off on another adventure," said Mr Griffins.

"Yes, we are," said Oscar, half excited and half nervous.

"Well, the two ladies have asked Meg and me to visit tonight, so perhaps we had better talk inside," said Mr Griffins.

Thomas opened up the door, and everyone walked in.

The Cellar door on the right was closed, so they hung up their winter coats and walked into the kitchen.

The two ladies were preparing dinner; as everyone walked in, they turned and smiled and said hello.

"Come in, Mr Griffins and take a seat; you will be staying for dinner too," said Mrs Marlow.

"Hello boys take a seat," said Mrs Pucket.

"Where's Meg?" said Mrs Marlow as she looked around the kitchen.

"Oh, I have left her outside on the front porch; she will be ok," said Mr Griffins.

"Nonsense, bring her in; it's far too cold out there for her! I will give her some food too; she can curl up next to the fire," said Mrs Marlow.

"I will go and get her," said Oscar.

Everyone sat down for dinner and ate beef stew with mashed potatoes.

They discussed the plan to drive to Avebury to open up the portal to Tanniv.

Getting there at two o'clock in the morning would be fine as the village residents would be asleep.

Mr Griffins would not be going this time. Mrs Marlow thought it would be kind to involve him because he had been such a big help the last time, and after all, he was a wandmaker, and wandmakers should always remain neutral.

Mrs Marlow went over the arrangements for The Avebury rings to send them back to Vakoborg and the Oris Monastery.

"I am not sure who will be at The Oris Monastery, but I imagine you will have Princess Gilgamesh waiting for you two," said Mrs Marlow looking at the two boys.

Mrs Marlow knew that this time the boys would be away for a long time.

Tanniv was the size of Europe, and like Europe, it had many kingdoms, many countries, many regions, and many languages. To embark on this campaign was going to be dangerous and may take a long time.

They all ate and talked while the fires in the kitchen burned, keeping everyone warm.

Mrs Pucket insisted on everyone now having second and third helpings of the stew to ensure no one would be hungry later.

She had also made fruit and nut-filled flapjacks so that the boys had plenty of food for their journey into Vakoborg.

The two boys would be better prepared this time as they were going by invitation and not by mistake.

After dinner, Mr Griffins and Meg said their goodbyes to the two boys and wished them the best of luck and that he would be seeing them soon.

It was almost time to drive to Avebury.

The two boys with packed bags full of food and water made their way to the car with their wands. Both were wearing hard-wearing trousers with walking boots, vests, jumpers, and duffel coats.

It was almost sure that they would be asked to change their clothing when they got to the Oris Abbey by the Disaris, but for now, this icy, freezing cold night would need warm clothing.

The two old ladies who were equally dressed for the cold came out from the house covered in hats, scarfs, and gloves, with tweed country outfits and walking boots, too, looking very well-prepared for the activities to come.

"Come along, everyone in the car!" said Mrs Marlow.

Thomas opened the car door nearest to the drive while Oscar walked around to the door on the far side of her beloved Morris Minor Traveller.

Both boys clambered into the back seats of the car while Mrs Marlow and

Mrs Pucket waited for the boys to buckle up. They got into the car while Mrs Marlow started the engine.

The Morris Minor struggled to start a little bit with the cold temperature outside, but after a few turns on the ignition, the raspy sound of the engine fired up and turned over.

By now, it was midnight; it was an hour and thirty-minute drive to Avebury through the New Forest via Tidworth.

Oscar looked out of the window at the night skies thinking about the trip back to Tanniv.

He was a happy boy and nothing ever really deterred him – Mrs Pucket had taken a natural shine to the boy. He was easy to get along with and was a very relaxed character.

He had shown particular strengths in using his magic in tight, challenging situations. Although he should not have used his magic in the playground with Mr Bird earlier that morning, he could think quickly and use the correct type of spell to get him out of a fix.

As Oscar was looking out of the window at the flashing street lights speeding past like laser beams, he was thinking about Tanniv and the journey that lay ahead.

He was thinking about Princess Gilgamesh and The Warrior Elaith and who would meet them at the Oris Monastery.

The last days in Vakoborg were not great, as the mood of the whole city was low and melancholy.

The Disaris Churches and Disaris ziggurats rang out their bells all over the city in tribute and honour to remember the dead Nuns of Leoven Abbey.

Oscar laid in the garrison quarters in the Vakoborg Palace, wondering what was going to happen next. But the Disaris did nothing.

The Disaris way was to live in peace, but this could no longer be disregarded.

The political games and atrocities were now reaching deep into the heart of Vakoborg.

Oscar had been studying Disaris history and beliefs. He had been learning in detail about the Disaris social system.

They did not believe in war or conflict. But this was something that could not be ignored; how long would it be before this happened again.

The Older Disaris from the monasteries knew of The Empress Aminoff's desire to own the Stone Circles, and they knew that The Empress saw this as her mark by birth to own and run the circles.

The Aminoff armies had never managed to come this far West until now, and attacking a peace-loving abbey sent the message to King Gilgamesh that he needed to act now.

No words were being spoken in the car heading the Avebury rings; Oscar thought about what needed to be done.

Driving into Avebury was like going into a typical Village. It was strange there were Pubs, shops, a Hotel and houses lining the streets like any village in England.

Mrs Marlow parked in a quiet spot just before the Stone Circles, and as she drove into Avebury, she turned off her headlights and lifted off the cars' accelerator pedal to quiet the engine to drift and coast into the village. She then lifted the handbrake quietly as the car came to a stop.

It was very late, and the village was completely quiet with all the lights off in the houses.

The homes were made from flint rocks and some with old horsehair and plaster, better known as wattle and daub. Most of the homes had a thatched roof and were ancient houses; the village looked hundreds of years old.

Mrs Marlow stopped the car and prepared herself. She looked over her shoulder at the two boys and said, "we will get out now, but no talking we need to get through the village, then over the field without being seen," said Mrs Marlow to the two boys.

"It's not far, boys; let's just keep quiet then; once we are out in the field, we can talk but only at a whisper," said Mrs Pucket as she smiled at them both.

Both boys were now looking like young men; they looked at the two ladies and nodded in agreement.

Everyone got out of the car as quietly as possible.

Mrs Marlow had parked under a huge Oak tree just outside the village and had parked on a frozen mud patch around the back of the tree.

Both ladies closed the car doors as quietly as possible. Lifting the handle to the door and applying pressure with their hips, they closed the door until they heard a click indicating that it was now closed.

Mrs Marlow led the way through the centre of the village; not a word was spoken.

They marched down a road called Church Walk, which curved around to the left and led onto the village high street. Passing through a narrow road with the

Piskies of The Avebury Ring

ancient stone cottages on either side, they walked onto the narrow high street. They could see the Red Lion Pub in the distance and a small light coming from the lead piped windows of the landlord's private quarters.

On the left was the old Church with its Church Tower and graveyard, the centre point to the village.

It was a cold night, and the skies were so clear the moonlight was bright, and the stars lit up the night sky.

There was a small alleyway sandwiched between an old stone barn and some Victorian red brick houses. There was a gravel path alleyway that led directly onto the stone circle its self.

"Ok, boys, we are here; let's not talk just yet; we will aim for the bigger stones on the far side of the circle which comes away from the houses," said Mrs Marlow, whispering but annunciating at the two boys and Mrs Pucket.

Walking further down the dark, cold alley, they came to a clearing that led them out onto the stones. They could see shadows and silhouettes of the stones against the cold night's sky.

The ground was soft wintery, and muddy but still slightly frozen in areas. Mrs Marlow marched on, aiming for the stones in the far corner away from the houses.

Mrs Pucket, who was walking next to Mrs Marlow, said, "Do you remember when we used to come here?"

"Yes, my old friend, I do," she said affectionately to her dear old friend.

As they got closer, Mrs Marlow said, "We can talk now, boys, but only whispers," both boys nodded.

"Oh, No! I thought they had all gone!" said Mrs Pucket.

"Mrs Marlow look-look over there," said Mrs Pucket in an annoyed but hostile voice.

"Hello, hello, what you doing here," a voice said in a West Country old English accent.

Thomas and Oscar started looking around everywhere for this voice and could just about make out a very small shadow only around two yards tall.

"What is it, Mrs Pucket?" said Oscar in an anxious, nervous voice.

"Piskies!" said Mrs Pucket as she put her hand on her face.

"Piskies!" The boys said together in chorus.

"Yes, Piskies! And they are the most curious nosiest creatures known to humanity; tell them nothing," said Mrs Marlow with a frown on her face as if this had scuppered the plans.

"What you doing here then," said a little chubby-looking Pisky.

"Yes, what you doing here then – this time of night," said another Pisky as they all looked down and around.

"We will need to know the purpose of this visit," said yet another Pisky.

"Yes, we need to keep a log of these sorts of visits," said another Pisky as Mrs Marlow looked around, realising that there were five or six of them around them by now.

"It's two old ladies and two boys," said another cheeky Pisky.

"Less of the Old Ladies," said Mrs Marlow furiously, looking at the Pisky.

"We are just here to look at the stones, and if you don't mind, we are busy. Can you leave us alone," said Mrs Marlow, quickly looking at the eyes looking up at her.

Piskies were funny creatures, they had been hanging around the stone circles for centuries, and somehow they had got the notion that they were now in charge.

Piskies were inquisitive and nosey by nature, so this was all the excuse they needed to ask questions to satisfy their natural curiosity.

They were small about hip-high, with dark green and sometimes brown skin; they had big eyes and enormous round noses that looked like an aubergine on their face with funny shaped heads. They slept all day and came to life at night.

They didn't care much for exercise or running, so often, they were chubby or even fat. This was because they sat down gossiping all the time.

Pisky's loved to chinwag about each other, and it was their favourite pastime.

They would form social groups based on talking about each other. The more information a Pisky had, the higher up the social order a Pisky would be.

The head Pisky looked at Mrs Marlow with a book in his hand and a feathered quill. He was dressed in brown tartan trousers with a grubby white shirt and a waistcoat looking official.

He had a book and could write too; this Pisky was in charge as he looked like he wrote down everything.

"Come on! I need this information for my log – I keep a log, you know," said the Pisky. The rest of the Piskies stood behind him, nodding and agreeing.

Thomas and Oscar were fascinated by these little creatures; they were so funny and demanding, especially for information.

Thomas looked puzzled at how on earth they were going to get rid of them. Mrs Pucket looked over at the head Pisky and then at Mrs Marlow with a knowing look.

Mrs Pucket swiftly held out her wand and said "statuam", "statuam", "statuam", "statuam" ", statuam" "statuam" pointing at each Pisky, she turned each one to stone.

"That's dealt with that," said Mrs Pucket.

Oscar looked at Thomas and said, "Oh, I really liked them; they were so funny," and they both sniggered.

"Come along, the spell will only last an hour or so, and there will be more of them, no doubt."

"The whole place looks like it's infested with Piskies," said Mrs Marlow.

Walking further across the field to the far end of the circle stood some large Neolithic stones. These stones were ideal; they were far enough away from the village and powerful enough to create the portal.

Mrs Marlow organised the boys to help open up the portal. It would be easy enough with two experienced sorcerers and two apprentices; this would be simple.

"This is nothing we have not done hundreds of times before," said Mrs Pucket as she winked at Mrs Marlow.

The four of them stood facing three large stones.

Mrs Marlow straightened and pulled down her tweed jacket, and stood up straight.

"As soon as it's open, you go first, Thomas, and then you Oscar, do not delay just go when I say" ok Grandmother, Thomas said.

"Goodbye, Grandmother; we will be back as soon as we can," said Thomas taking a deep breath.

"Yes, goodbye, my boy," as she grabbed for Thomas, hugging him then reaching for Oscar, she grabbed him and pulled him for a hug.

Mrs Pucket, sensing a moment, patted both boys on the head, came in the hug, and said her goodbyes.

Mrs Marlow stood up straight and repositioned everyone.

The four of them stood with their wands aloft and again said "aperta ianua" "aperta, ianua", and the wind got stronger and stronger.

"Repeat after me aperta ianua – aperta ianua," said Mrs Marlow.

Thomas, Oscar, and Mrs Pucket repeated over and over again "aperta ianua" – "aperta ianua" – "aperta ianua," shouting this and closing their eyes to focus harder and harder.

Then just like before, a mighty blast of wind began to lash up inside the stone circle again. Only this time, the wind was much stronger than they had ever experienced before in Ballymore Forest or In Stonecross manor, as the power of the Avebury ring was so powerful.

Then just like before, a small ball of bright light formed in the middle of the circle and grew larger and larger.

"Focus, boys!" She shouted as the wind and the ball of light grew bigger.

Oscar clenched his wand so tight and looked at Mrs Marlow, waiting for the signal.

Thomas also looked at the bright circle and watched it grow larger and bigger, and then looking over at his grandmother and Mrs Pucket, he waited for the signal.

By this time, it was the size of a four-metre oval shape and ready and looking very stable.

"Now go – Thomas go! We will keep the portal open," Mrs Marlow shouted at Thomas over the noise of the brutal wind lashing up.

Thomas looked at the two ladies and jumped inside, disappearing into the bright white glow of the portal.

The gateway this time was utterly constant, and Oscar could see that everything was entirely under control.

"Now Oscar – you can go!" Repeated Mrs Marlow while concentrating immensely on the portal.

Oscar looked at the two ladies and jumped inside, disappearing into the bright luminosity of the gateway.

They were gone, and the portal abruptly closed, leaving Mrs Pucket and Mrs Marlow exhausted.

"Well, we did it," said Mrs Pucket.

"Yes, we did, but we had better go that was both noisy and bright," said Mrs Marlow, and they hurried off into the darkness.

Back in Tanniv

Both boys were now back in Vakoborg at The Oris Stone Circles in the Disaris Monastery and surrounded by warriors.

Their eyes were a little blurred from the portal travel, and as their eyesight came back into focus, they could see familiar faces.

The Priest Elion was standing in front of them with his bright white hooded robe; Princess Gilgamesh sat proudly on her horse, looking every bit like a warrior Princess.

The Priestess Sana Norbella stood quietly in her hooded robe, covering her face, looking fantastic.

There was a Disaris Elite guard everywhere, and everyone was wearing a more combat-style attire than before.

Oscar looked around, there were Tarrenash warriors too, and Elaith Tarron was standing there holding the reins of Leokan, and Sylva the boys' horses.

Thomas and Oscar took comfort in the familiar faces present and received a very warm welcome from everyone.

Tupel, the Eagle Owl, let out a loud squawk and could be seen flying overhead.

Smiles were coming from every direction as if an expectation of hope had now arrived.

Thomas instantly felt the same pressure from this hope that he felt at the Gathering of Stormhorn.

The Priest Elion greeted the two boys and thanked them for coming to the aid of Tanniv.

"Hello, boys,"

"We have prepared a feast for tonight, and we must get you out of those clothes," The Priest said while smiling at the two boys standing in their English clothing.

Princess Gilgamesh cantered closer to the boys in her brilliant white grand-looking horse. "Hello, my friends, my father and I thank you for your aid in our time of need."

"You are welcome, and it's so nice to see you, Princess Gilgamesh," said Thomas enthusiastically. Thomas made himself stop talking, remembering that she is a Princess and there would be time for the royal dignitaries to stop for a much less formal hello and conversation.

"Hello, Oscar! It's so nice to see you; you look different now; you look like a man," said the Princess. He smiled back and nodded his head again, knowing that there would be time for conversation later.

Thomas locked eye contact with The Priestess Sana Norbella, and he smiled and nodded. Sana bowed back with the shadow from her hooded robe partially covering her face. Sana was also dressed in a black combat-style uniform with light armour and two short swords holstered to her back, forming a cross, and he could see the sword pommels on each side of her head. She bowed and smiled at Oscar while he gave her a gentle nod back.

Elaith smiled at the two boys while gently lifting his hand in acknowledgement to say we can talk later, and like a good soldier would wait for his turn to speak to the boys.

"My father, The King is here now waiting to see you," said Princess Gilgamesh.

"King Gilgamesh is here?!" said Oscar with a small gasp.

"Yes, he has come to discuss with you about our assignment," said Princess Gilgamesh.

"We will show you to your quarters for the night we must get you out of those clothes; we do not know who is watching," said Priest Elion.

"We will send for you at dinner," said Princess Gilgamesh.

Thomas and Oscar settled into their room, washed up, and got changed into their Tanniv clothing. The room was simple two wooden beds with a small wash area, and the room was clean and comfortable.

A Vakoborg guard came and collected the two to meet and dine with King Gilgamesh.

Dinner was had in the cloisters of the central garden among the colonnades. A meal table was set up, and the King was sat at the head of the table.

"Hello, my boys – you are both men now; you have grown so much," said King Grusin.

"Hello, King Gilgamesh," said Thomas and Oscar, both bowing their heads.

In attendance at the meeting was Captain Thalland Rothlan of the Disaris army, The High Priest Elion, Lord General Halamar Yelfir, Princess Holly

Gilgamesh, and the Priestess Sana Norbella.

"Come and take a seat," said Captain Rothlan as he shook both of the boy's hands.

Pleasantries were exchanged, and food and wine were consumed over dinner. Many stories were told, along with jokes and tales. All the while, Thomas could sense a serious conversation was coming as the atmosphere in the monastery was tense from the time they had arrived.

As the evening continued, King Gilgamesh turned the discussions onto the present situation in Vakoborg "I have brought my most trusted Generals, soldiers and associates here with me tonight to share with you what our inquiry has concluded."

After the Massacre of the Levan Abbey, they were piecing together evidence of what had taken place in Leoven.

King Gilgamesh, and the High Priest Lugella, had sent Disaris to the four corners of Vakoborg and beyond. They sent them to gather the confirmation for who did this atrocity. For the past many months, the Disaris had collected the evidence needed.

The evidence had pointed towards Prince Alwin and Moltenwing.

Prince Alwin had been seen in Stoney Cross, and he had taken possession of a new wand from Harrold Griffins, the sceptre man. The only way he could have made the journey to Stoney Cross is through the Stone circles in Leovan.

The Leoven Abbey was captured, and for many days the Nuns were trapped by a mix of Northern raiders from East Tanniv, Ilihorn Dragoons, and potentially the ancient Drachen warriors.

Prince Alwin then used the Stone circles, and from what The Disaris could gather, the Nuns at Leoven had been tortured to help open the portal.

He had influenced the Nuns to help under the condition that no one would be hurt. After his return, he ordered everyone in the Leoven Abbey to be murdered and remove all evidence.

The other findings the Disaris had discovered was that one of the Stone Circles was now missing. Everyone around the table sat very quietly and listened. Most of this conversation was making sense to Oscar, as he had been reading about this.

The massacre of the Leoven Abbey was enough to break the peace treaties on its own.

These treaties had been laid out after the great Battle of Ilihorn and the

Tarrenash war. But now, a stone circle was missing, which meant the religious balance for the whole of Vakoborg and the Disaris belief system was now under threat and peril.

"This was an act of war," cried King Gilgamesh as he thumbed his first on the table.

"Never in nine hundred years have any such raids or armies dared to enter Vakoborg forest," said the King in a deep, loud gravelly voice.

"But we will not go to war, we will not react, we will wait until the time is right," said the King in a Calm voice. Princess Holly was by his side the whole time.

"I will send all of you on a crusade, a crusade to reunite West Tanniv under one banner," the King said again, looking at everyone in the eyes.

"You must visit Tarrenash and gather a great crusade."

"Then, visit every major town and village to tell what has happened at the Leoven abbey."

"We have Thomas Marlow and Oscar Williams, two white sorcerers from Stoney cross, to further strengthen our arguments."

Everyone around the table applauded as they talked about the strategy to travel to The City of Tarrenash to link up with Lord General Yeldrove and Princess Katya. They were already waiting for the crusade to catch up in Tarrenash City.

The rumours of the Leoven Abbey massacre by now had made their way through the small towns and villages in West Tanniv, but a travelling crusade to tell the world what happened would be more effective than stories.

As the night drew to a conclusion, Thomas and Oscar strolled back to their room in the monastery. They had been instructed to be ready in the morning to ride out at first light.

The boys took to their bunks to sleep.

It was a strange feeling being back in Vakoborg. But it made more sense to be in Tanniv than to be at School.

Studying the Tanniv social system and the commercial trade system had taken priority over any other thinking. So being at School taking maths lessons and breaks in playgrounds had made the two boys think about the world differently.

The way they left Tanniv under the black cloud of the Leoven Abbey made Oscar and Thomas feel that there was unfinished business in Tanniv.

Then the failure of the gathering left its own brand of disappointment deeply rooted in the boys, which left them thinking about it every day. So right now, to be back in Tanniv made more sense than to be in Stoney Cross.

The Black Ilihorn Palace

Prince Alwin was now in the Black Palace at Ilihorn.

The Palace was massive; it looked over a vast forest-covered canyon.

It was high up in the Ilihorn mountain ranges, and everyone could see the grand castle palace from everywhere.

The Palace had been made from the black granite rocks of the Mountains; it stood above a thriving mountain walled city made up of centuries of thatched housing built in every direction.

Prince Alwin was with his warring council discussing strategy with his generals and the Armies positioned along the Ailmar River down to the Hiligor Sea.

The Prince had called a meeting with his council not to discuss war but to size up which General and Lord would be with him when the time was right to invade the West.

His spies were now firmly in West Tanniv in every town, city, and village listening to conversations in Pubs and Traven's gathering intelligence.

The Prince understood that information was critical, and with his complex network of spies in Tanniv, he understood the public opinions on both sides of the river.

By this time, the information of the Disaris and Tarrenash Crusade to reunite West Tanniv had begun filtering its way to Prince Alwin. He needed to devise a strategy to stop this at all costs.

It was too soon for Moltenwing to attack West Tanniv.

The Moltenwing assemble would never agree to this just yet, and the Ilihorn armies made up of loyal Ilihorn Dragoons, Elite soldiers, and conscripts were not yet ready. So the Prince had no choice.

Deep in the mountains of Ilihorn were a tribe of Horseman Warriors that rode giant Ilihorn Mountain horses much like shire horses but bigger.

The ancient mountain tribes were called The Drachen Riders.

The Drachen riders were loyal to Prince Alwin; they were feared and considered sub-human monsters and more legend than real.

The Black Castle Of Illihorn.

They were often two and a half metres tall; they had black skin, with a crown of small horns on their heads and fang-like teeth.

Their eyes were yellow, and their customs and social traditions were focused on warrior craft, fighting with swords, wrestling, and all types of combat were drummed into them from birth. They wore black armour and were highly skilled swordsmen.

They lived high up in the mountains, herding giant cows, fiercely defending their territory, and hunted any trespassers in packs.

Prince Alwin went looking for the legendary tribes many years before, and after gaining the trust of the tribal leaders, an alliance was formed.

The alliance was ultimately moulded by the offering of horses, cattle, gold, diamonds, and an ancestral land and regions were created for them.

Prince Alwin quickly became comrades with this hostile tribe, and they now had a governed region within Ilihorn. This twisted form of bribery and diplomacy was one of Prince Alwin's primary skills; he could bring people close to him and offer riches and loyalty in return.

These Drachen Riders were driven to near extinction over the past hundred years, and they had a particular hatred of Disaris.

The Prince later fashioned an Elite Rider Drachen Guard and now had thirty Drachen Riders and a Platoon based in Ilihorn. Often a Platoon of Ilihorn Dragoons would have several Drachen Riders conscripted as they were unafraid and fearless.

The Drachen would follow orders relentlessly and would cut down anyone in their path.

They had a track record of consistently completing missions and were seen as Prince Alwin's Pride of the Army.

The primary talent of a Drachen Rider would be to sword fight on their horse, cutting and swiping at foe as there rode, and with their giant horse, they could ride hard at any Enemy.

During the assembly week in Moltenwing often Prince Alwin would be seen with two Drachen Riders as his guards.

The magnificent tall, striking brutes would produce the image he was looking for as a unifier of Tanniv.

The ladies of Moltenwing and other fascinated spectators would gather to watch these beasts march alongside the handsome eligible Prince.

Prince Alwin called for his warring council to meet at The Grand Ilihorn

Palace, high up in the mountains.

The warring council was made up of Lords and Generals from The Port of Elec. It was made up of Moltenwing high-ranking Officials, the Naval Admirals of Port Elleth and Merchant council members, and the various warring tribal leaders deemed highly important.

They studied great maps of Tanniv, deliberated on the positioning of troops and armies, and debated transportation and other military activities vital to moving large numbers of troops around.

It was not a council assembled to talk of war; Prince Alwin had other plans.

The Prince sat back in his chair and listened to the conversations and the arguments. He even listened to the old stories across the table when the Prince stood up to talk.

"There is talk of a Crusade of Disaris and Tarrenash being assembled to reunite West Tanniv," said the Prince as he smiled and looked up at everyone seated around the table.

Everyone in the room stopped to listen to the Prince speak.

"I am going to send twelve Drachen Riders to intercept this rabble and end this before it begins," said the Prince in his elegant regal voice.

"And what does intercept mean said a Nobleman from Moltenwing," as he stood up to address the Prince in his striking blue army uniform gilded with gold epaulettes, brassards, medals, looking at the Prince with his grey hair and curly moustache.

"Intercept means intercept… I don't think the Drachen Riders are famed for their conversation or diplomacy," said the Prince as he smiled and looked directly into the eyes of the nobleman that questioned him.

Everyone in the room roared up and laughed and looked at each other.

"I was not going to invite them for dinner," said the Prince as he stood up to walk around the room again, filling the hall with laughs.

"Many of the people, if not all the people in this room, are extremely wealthy and rich through the trading that is currently happening in Qulan right now."

"We would not want to disrupt this lucrative time for anyone," said the Prince as he paced up and down the floor and around the grand table.

"Would we all agree these are very prosperous times?" said the Prince. Everyone in the room looked at each other and nodded in agreement, and muttered yes.

"Then isn't it wise to protect this?"

"And a small crusade being lost is not a lot to ask for in the grand scheme of things, is it?"

Said the Prince as he stood back at the head of the table, with his knuckles on the table, leaning forward-looking at everyone in the room directly. Everyone again nodded in agreement, with warm sounds of mumbling happening at the same time.

"Good, I am glad that we all agree, the warring council shall agree together; to send twelve Drachen Riders to intercept and discuss the crusades directly with this rabble of Tarrenash and Disaris," said The Prince as he smiled at everyone down the table.

"Oh, and I will pick out the Drachen Riders that are most diplomatic!"

"Just for you, my Lord," said the Prince as everyone in the room laughed as the Nobleman fell silent and sat back down in his seat with embarrassment.

Getting the High Command to agree with this was the true reason for the warring council being together, and the Prince had achieved what he set out to do.

Now the Prince could say that the high command took the agreement for this action.

It would now be adopted as a council idea, not as Prince Alwin's idea; therefore, if something went wrong, the council would be to blame and not the Prince.

Prince Alwin sat back down in his chair while drumming his fingers together, pleased at the complete agreement.

The Prince smiled, nodded his head, and allowed his warring council to carry on talking about soldering and the quantifying of resources.

The Road to Tarrenash City

The following daybreak Thomas and Oscar were getting ready in The Oris Monastery courtyard. Elaith Tarron, to who they had not yet said hello properly, was readying his horse at the far side of the spectacular gardens.

As the two boys marched over to the far side of the courtyard, they could see the Priestess Sana stood in cloisters waiting for her horse to be ready. She always remained on the outskirts of everything, watching closely over everyone in the most mysterious way. Thomas was fascinated by the way she operated.

"Good morning, Elaith," said Oscar and then Thomas with smiles on their faces.

"Good morning, Thomas, and Good Morning, Oscar," said Elaith as he bowed his head.

"It looks like I have the honour of looking after you two again," said Elaith.

"That's great news," said Thomas.

"What are those pips on your shoulders, Elaith?" said Oscar being as curious as ever.

"I have been promoted to Lance-Corporal, but I insisted on having you in my command," said Elaith proudly.

"I have your horses Leokan and Sylva, and I insisted on this too," said Elaith.

"Thank you, Elaith, you made our last trip safe and unforgettable. I hope we have another safe adventure together," said Thomas.

The two boys were issued with light armour, hardened leather chest plates, and shoulder plates with riding thigh plates, and shin guards, all embossed with the Tarrenash eagle owl emblem on them.

The boys were given two short swords with Tarrenash light brigade helmets, again in hardened leather, and two hooded cloaks.

Elaith brought over Leokan and Sylva, and the two boys mounted the horses and waited patiently.

The horses looked pleased to see the two boys, and much love and affection were exchanged between the horses and the boys.

Sana cantered over to the boys; she looked glorious as she trotted over and nodded to the two boys as if to say hello, but no words were exchanged. She did not say much but had a full warrior dress, with her distinctive black hooded cloak and her dapple-grey horse.

The Priestess gained the respect of Princess Gilgamesh because of the way she handled the Leoven Abbey incident, and she was attending the crusade as a representative of The High Priest Lugella. She kept to herself, and everyone left her alone in return.

You could see that Sana had pain in her eyes from the massacre and was a vital person in helping spread the message of what had happened.

Princess Gilgamesh was on her spectacular white horse, getting ready to give the signal to ride out.

The Princess was astonishing, dressed in light armour of dark green with leather patens like dragon scales all over her Disaris armour and helmet.

Beside Princess Gilgamesh stood General Yelfir and Captain Rothlan, all in armoured uniform.

In addition to the Princess, The General, The Priestess Sana, the Crusade had fourteen Disaris and fourteen Tarrenash soldiers, making the number of the crusaders almost forty souls.

King Gilgamesh and The Oris Priest Elion stood together to wave out the crusaders.

Princess Gilgamesh placed her helmet on her head and looked back at her father with a slight nod, then a look back at the crusaders. She shouted, "Crusaders, let's ride out for Tarrenash."

She galloped out of the Oris Monastery into Vakoborg Forest, and the rest of the Crusaders rode out two by two through the courtyard gates.

It was one and a half days ride to The City of Tarrenash; however, the crusade's route would take three days.

They did not want to take any of the normal roads leading to the City because the villages and towns along the way would have spies.

Everyone in the newly formed crusade was under the impression that Moltenwing was waiting for a Disaris reaction for The Leoven Abbey, and now that one of the stone circles was lost, the whole of Tanniv could feel tension. But Disaris and Tarrenash were not eager for war, and the timing was unsuitable for such hasty reprisals.

The crusade would go around the Great Oris Gorge and use tunnels and caves further south of Vakoborg.

The Goathards, an ancient people who lived in South Tanniv, would take the crusaders through the cave network out to the pinnacles of Cloven Town.

Cloven Town was a small town very high up in the Jandar Mountains and completely out of the way from The City of Tarrenash.

The outpost town of Cloven was a minor trading garrison very remote and high up in the mountains of Jandar on the Tarrenash border.

It was a dangerous town filled with miners from the pits and a Tarrenash trading stronghold that administered trade and kept law and order on the border.

The Cloven Trading Town was famous for the Gold, Diamonds, and iron coming out from the mines for cash deals in the pubs and Traven's.

So it attracted the dangerous, the vagrant, the wanted, and the warlords, looking for money, for weapons and slaves to sell in Qulan to East Tanniv.

It was a town that a Princess or Crusade should not go near, but it had a fortress and a Tarrenash garrison expecting them.

The unimportant Town fortress would be the first resting point for the crusade and would be where they would spend their first night.

It was so dangerous that it was the last place anyone looking for the crusades would think to look.

It would appear that the crusade would be circumnavigating the City of Tarrenash to come in from the South.

The shortest route into the City of Tarrenash could be galloped in a little over a full day's ride from west Vakoborg. But Moltenwing spies would heavily track this route. Everywhere was danger now, and it felt like a tinderbox waiting to ignite.

The Crusaders cantered through the thick forests of Vakoborg; the further South they jockeyed, the wetter and rainier it became.

It was a challenging ride when riding in the rain. The troops could not hear correctly because of the sound of the rain on the leaves and branches of the trees.

It meant that silence was necessary, and to look upwards and out to the forest from all sides was a direct order from Captain Rothlan.

The warrior's archers and bows were half-cocked and half-loaded with sword pommels griped at all times. Thomas and Oscar were surrounded by

Tarrenash and Disaris troops, with Elaith close to them. So they both felt very safe.

Princess Gilgamesh was surrounded by her Disaris guard with her Captain riding close to her too.

Princess Gilgamesh looked different; something about her had changed after the Gathering and the Leoven Massacre.

Something changed in everyone that day; it was as if everyone was altered or transformed overnight. War was coming now, and it appeared that no one could avoid this. She carried her Disaris swords and bow and sat on her steed with great royal confidence, and in her green Disaris warrior armour, she looked every bit the warrior Princess she was bred to be.

The crusaders cantered on into the South Vakoborg forest, and everywhere was green, thick evergreen trees, and thick green moss as far as the eyes could see. The Oris gorge was not far, and they could hear the rumbling of the gorge waterfalls.

The Goathards were not Disaris and not Tarrenash; they were an ancient civilization that had been isolated for centuries. They lived in The South Vakoborg forest and came under the rule of King Gilgamesh and The Great Disaris council.

The Goathards would not pledge allegiance to the King, but there was great respect and friendship between the two nations.

A meeting point for the Goathards was agreed upon by the Yulis Lake, where the Goathards would reside.

The Yulis Lake was a turquoise-coloured freshwater lake perfectly round and from the skies looking down, it would appear as a perfect round turquoise blue lake in a sea of emerald green trees.

The Goathards people lived in brick-built towers; the towers would peak just above the forest canopy so they could see for miles in every direction.

These towers were of great importance and incredible lookout points, especially for seeing forest fires and camping sites. It was a defence system. All over Goathards land, these towers were situated everywhere in critical locations.

The towers were scattered around and looked like small castle folly towers. They were often covered in ivy or nestled around trees so that from afar, they could be easily missed.

The Goathards were masters of Camouflage; it was said that a Goathard could be standing in front of you, and you would not see them if they did not want you to.

People very rarely saw them; they were master tunnel folk, and at first sight of trouble or threats, they would take to their network of tunnels deep underneath the Vakoborg forest, never to be seen again.

The Goathards were excellent allies to have.

They could navigate the crusade to the Taklamakan Caves and Pinnacles in Jandar without being seen. The Goathards could do this very quickly as they often traded in Cloven town, selling emeralds in exchange for iron ore to make weapons.

As the crusaders got closer to Goathards land, the Priestess Sana Norbella cantered over to Captain Rothlan and whispered through the hood with her half-covered face, "We are being watched."

Sana Norbella looked up at the trees and looked around into the thick emerald green misty forest "the birds have stopped singing, and we are being watched." She said with great skill.

Captain Rothlan acknowledged and looked back and tapped on his saddle five times, giving the signal to draw weapons and fully form a battle-riding formation.

They carried on for several miles like this, and they came across their first Goathard folly tower.

The door was opened; it looked disused. The General gave two Disaris soldiers the signal to go into the tower to see if anyone was there.

All the while, everyone in the crusade had the sense of being watched and observed.

Oscar had gripped his wand and not his swords; he nudged Thomas and gestured for him to do the same.

Elaith nodded to the two boys, and four Tarrenash soldiers came closer and tighter to the boys to form a closer defensive formation.

The two Disaris came out of the tower and shook their heads, gesturing that nothing was unusual or anything to see.

The Crusaders went on further without a trace of the Goathards anywhere.

"They will show their faces when the time is ready," said Princess Gilgamesh as she looked back at the crusaders.

The truth was the Goathards lived so deep in the forest they never saw anyone other than Goathards.

They certainly never exchanged dialogue with strangers; if someone wandered into their lands, they would disappear like ghosts beneath their network of tunnels and caves deep beneath the Vakoborg forest and carefully watch.

As they neared Yulis Lake, small glimpses of a deep turquoise blue started to appear in the distance between the trees. The forest got lighter as the bright turquoise blue water from the lake came into view.

The crusade could now see several towers around them, so they knew they would be close.

As they got to the water's edge, Princess Gilgamesh spoke.

"Let's wait here until they are ready to come and put your weapons away; let's not display mistrust or threat. They will show themselves when the time is right for them."

The Disaris soldiers and Tarrenash soldiers dismounted and took their horses for water.

A carefully appointed perimeter of soldiers was positioned to watch across the lake and back into the forest in a defensive formation.

Thomas looked back at Elaith and said, "Now what do we do?"

"We wait," said Elaith.

The horse's wellbeing was the priority, and then food was shared between the soldiers. The crusade was still in total silence, waiting for the Goathards to show their faces.

Many hours had passed, it appeared to be wasting time for everyone, but this was planned, as this Goathard tradition was expected.

They would show their faces in their own time when they were ready, and no one would rush them.

The mixture of Disaris and Tarrenash guards stood in a semi-circle looking back in the forest when shapes and movement appeared.

It was as if their eyes refocused again, and the trees, shrubs, and bushes started to move.

Their eyes were playing tricks on them; they had been looking at Goathard soldiers. Slowly these soldiers appeared by the tens, and after only seconds almost one hundred Goathard were gathered around them.

They were short people, and they wore green and brown leathers; their faces were painted in browns and greens, and they had bushes and branches from the forest tucked into leather bands all over their bodies, camouflaged perfectly.

The crowded shoreline parted slightly, and a Goathard elder came forwards.

The atmosphere was welcoming, friendly, and calm, with no weapons drawn on each side.

The Goathard elders came forward while Princess Gilgamesh, Captain Rothlan, and Priestess Norbella walked forwards.

The Princess looked at Thomas and Oscar and gently beckoned them both over with a lowered hand.

Thomas was unsure of his role in the ceremonial greeting, but this indication would mean that he would be displayed as a key decision-maker in the campaign to reunite West Tanniv.

"My name is Lord Folred Morven of the Goathard People," said the short old man dressed in a green and brown camouflaged hooded gown.

He was old with long white hair, and his hair was woven with leaves and shrubs, which added to the camouflaged tradition of the Goathard People. The Lord spoke slowly, respectfully, and wisely considering every word he had said before it was uttered.

"Greetings, My Lord, I am Princess Gilgamesh of Vakoborg," said the Princess as she placed her hands together in a prayer-like motion and bowed slightly.

"Princess of Vakoborg, you say," said Lord Morven.

"Yes, my Lord," said the Princess.

"Why have you come?"

"This must be important for the King to send his daughter," said Lord Folred as he removed his hood to get a closer look at this most significant and important visitor to his lands.

"We have come to ask for safe passage to the Jandar Pinnacles," said Princess Gilgamesh.

"And why can't you go the normal way," said Lord Morven.

"We are also on a campaign to reunite West Tanniv, too," said Thomas nervously as everyone now had turned their eyes to Thomas.

He did not want to speak out of turn but did not want another mistake like at the Gathering of Stormhorn.

"Who are you, young man, and what are you doing with that wand," said Lord Morven as he looked at Thomas and at Oscar in the most interesting way looking both boys up and down with their perfectly cut hair.

"My Name is Thomas Marlow, and this is Oscar Williams, and we are White Stone Sorcerers from Stoney Cross."

"We are here to ask for your guidance and for your banner to consolidate West Tanniv under the great Tanniv Eagle Owls," said Thomas.

Then a squawk could be heard high in the sky; it was the Eagle Owls Tupel, Sathgang, and Yinfon circling above their heads and spiralling down.

Everyone stopped and watched these mighty birds cascade down from the skies.

The birds landed in front of Thomas and Oscar and nuzzled into the boys with great affection.

The Goathard People all looked and seemed surprised, and one by one, they all bowed and went down onto one knee.

Sana looked at the Owls landing, then looked at Thomas directly in the eyes.

Lord Morven looked at the three mighty owls standing before him with the two boys in the middle.

He looked directly at Thomas and said, "I knew your mother."

"We should sit, and you all can tell me about your quest and your reasons for being here," said Lord Morven.

The Owls then flew off into the distance, Oscar looked at Thomas, and they both looked forward, keeping calm and ever so still as the magnificent Owls flew off into the blue sky.

They all sat, and pleasantries were exchanged.

Princess Gilgamesh and The Priestess Norbella explained what had happened at the Massacre of the Leoven Abbey, along with Thomas and Oscar adding what had occurred in Stoney Cross.

They explained that no one would be safe and how Moltenwing was once again raising an army. The countermeasure for this would be to reunite West Tanniv to ensure there would be no war.

They explained that a stone circle had been removed and that The Aminoff's were behind the massacre and atrocities of the Leoven Abbey, and how no one in Vakoborg or West Tanniv would be safe.

After hearing everything that they had to say, Lord Folred Morven of the Goathard People stood up.

"The Disaris and the Goathards have had a great alliance for hundreds of years, and we have lived together in peace," said Lord Morven as he turned to look at the Princess.

"If what your saying is true, then we will need to reunite to be strong together," this time, Lord Morven turned to face his people.

"If Moltenwing could do this in Vakoborg to the Disaris, then we would be next," said Lord Morven.

"Let it be known that the Goathard People would be the first to unite under the banner of the Eagle Owls, and we will show you through the Pinnacles in the south to the Jandar Mountains," said Lord Morven as he raised his voice looking at his people and the people of the crusade.

"We shall show you through the caves to the Jandar Pinnacles, and I will leave you with two Goathard warriors to join the campaign to reunite West Tanniv."

"We will show the world that Vakoborg was a united front against any enemy that dares to enter our forest and cause such atrocities," said Lord Morven.

Everyone clapped and applauded, then shook hands and smiled at the new alliance being formed.

"Thank you, my Lord."

"We the Disaris are most grateful," said Princess Gilgamesh.

Thomas looked out at the crusade and to all the happy faces; it was not the gathering at Stormhorn; however, they were going to reunite the countries of West Tanniv on this crusade or die trying.

It was the first positive feeling that he had felt from his arrival in Tanniv and was the first real good news in a long time, and optimism thrived as the first region had agreed to reunite.

Later that day, the crusade with The Disaris, Tarrenash, and Goathard made their way to the south Vakoborg caverns led by two Goathard warriors..

The Drachen Riders

Shortly after the war council meeting of Ilihorn, the cabinet had agreed to send the Drachen Riders to West Tanniv.

Orders had been sent down to the garrisons of Ilihorn, where the Dragoons were stationed within the mountain citadel.

The command had been given to ready twelve Drachen riders on a top-secret mission into West Tanniv. The Drachen were delighted to hear this news and only too keen to engage.

The twelve Drachen riders set out on gigantic pure black enormous Shire horses. They were dressed in traditional black armour; the giant horned warriors set out for Disaris blood.

The Drachen have always hated Disaris, and for centuries. The Drachen were forced out of the forests of Tanniv centuries before.

They had been forced to live in the mountain forests of Ilihorn and always considered this to be a Disaris injustice, but now was the time for revenge.

Prince Alwin observed from his palace window and gazed down onto the dark stone cobbled courtyard and watched the Drachen warriors prepare to ride out in search of The Crusade.

The Warriors looked fierce and wicked and magnificent in their black armour and black horses. They all looked set and ready for Disaris's blood and revenge and to cut down all that came in their path.

It was the dead of night, and the darkness only added to their malevolent intent, as this was a secret mission.

They wore half helmets in a Drachen style, which displayed and presented their crown of horns on their head and covered their faces showing only bright yellow eyes and sharp Drachen teeth.

The commander roared out with pride, this was to be the first time a small Drachen platoon would be sent on a mission on their own, and they were eager to make a name for themselves.

The Drachen Riders

Content in what Prince Alwin had achieved, the Prince decided to return to Moltenwing to be as far away from these orders as possible and report directly to the Empress.

The Drachen riders jockeyed out of the dark black gates of Ilihorn and galloped down the mountain pass on route for Port Elleth where a merchant ship would take them to Qulan City across the Hiligor Sea.

They galloped through the foothills of the Ilihorn mountains heading for the warmer climates of the south.

At Port Elleth, a ship was expecting twelve riders, and they had their orders to take them across the Hiligor Sea.

They would arrive under cover of night to keep the mission as anonymous as possible.

A merchant ship named 'The Shannon', not an Ilihorn Naval vessel had been chartered and contracted to sail to Qulan City Port.

A Merchant trading ship was chosen to keep Moltenwing far from any blame of Drachen riders entering West Tanniv.

The Captain of the Merchant ship 'Shanan' was briefed and paid. The boat was run by a crew of smugglers and traders very well experienced in sailing at night with the correct forged paperwork to allow them into Port Qulan.

They also knew who to bribe for the right blind eyes to be paid off to take them through safely into Qulan easily.

The Drachen galloped down the foothills from Ilihorn, passing a small East Tanniv village called Arana.

Arana had a well-known fabulous Traven and coaching house Inn called The Whistling Beggar used by the rich of Moltenwing.

Travellers would stop for a night's rest during the voyages to Port Elleth, and it was well known by everyone for a high-end luxury coaching Inn and Hotel.

The Drachen Riders stopped there on the way to Port Elleth and demanded water and feed for their horses. When they were not met with the correct levels of hospitality and agreement, they slashed and cut down everyone in the Traven and coaching house and did not leave a soul alive.

It would later be known as the Slaughter of Arana and used by Moltenwing as propaganda to say the Tarrenash crossed the Hiligor Sea and committed this atrocity.

Almost everyone in the Moltenwing High Command knew that the perpetrators were Prince Alwin's Drachen riders, but no one would challenge the propaganda made by the Prince.

So it was known by a name and called the Slaughter of Arana.

When Empress Aminoff heard of the Slaughter, she was seen to be smirking and made a comment,

"That her son was a genius, and he always found a way to turn a situation into his favour."

At some point, there would be an inquest for the Mascara at the Leoven Abbey, and the Slaughter of Arana was the counterweight she needed when the time was right to act like a victim too.

As The Drachen riders reached Port Elleth, they cantered slowly through the dark cobbled streets. Following orders, they had been given to enter at night and not to be seen. As they reached the harbour looking for the Merchant ship "Shanan", Captain Jonik of the merchant ship waited eagerly on the dockside.

Captain Jonik of the merchant ship Shanan was a smuggler in every sense of the word, he had been a smuggler all his life, and he had made himself very wealthy trading both sides of the sea.

His orders were simple; to pick up twelve pieces of cargo from the Ilihorn Dragoons in Port Elleth and take them to Qulan City Port with no questions asked, and he would be paid handsomely.

It was a dark foggy night, and the Shanan crew stood waiting at the furthest end of the most distant pier waiting patiently.

The crew could hear the clatter of horse's hooves trip trapping along the cobbled stones slowly towards them.

The fog was so thick it was one of those nights that you could not see anything until the person was almost in front of you.

The Captain of the Drachen was called Captain Neldez; he was fierce; he stood almost two and a half metres tall and had fangs and a crown of full horns.

The Drachen crown of horns was an indication of a fully developed adult male. The horns were seen as great pride for the Drachen, and smaller stubbier horns indicated a younger male.

The Drachen Captain Neldez was tall and, with a full crown of horns, looked terrifying.

He cantered closer to the Ship Shanan and could see the crew waiting in anticipation of their arrival.

As the shapely bodies of the horses and Drachen came into view Captain Jonik of the merchant ship Shanan stood with his mouth wide open.

The Drachen rode slowly towards the terrified Captain Jonik and handed him his official transfer papers. "Nobody said that I would be transporting Drachen riders," said Captain Jonik in a nervous quivering voice.

The Drachen Captain leaned across at Jonik, the Drachen still sat on his gargantuan horse, and Jonik stood on the deck of his boat; he grabbed Jonik by the throat while his crew stood watching helplessly he squeezed.

"Do we have a problem, Captain?" said The Drachen Neldez in an intense gravelly voice putting his fanged face close to the petrified Jonik.

The Captain that was still in the claws of the Drachen's firm grasp looked down at the quayside. Only to see another eleven other Drachen come out of the mist, "No No No there's no problem let's get you to Qulan as fast as possible," said Captain Jonik as he looked around at his crew and ordered them to help and to move fast.

"That is what I thought you would say," said The Drachen Captain Neldez as he laughed, and the rest of the Drachen laughed with him.

The Crew of the Shanan hurried to get the Drachen on board the ship. Their hands shook with fear, and their voices stammered words as they spoke with terror, wilting and trembling while they hurried to ready the boat.

The mighty black Drachen shire horses boarded the ship, and the Drachen dismounted.

They each stood looking outwards across the Hiligor Sea, hungry for Disaris and Tarrenash Blood.

Each Drachen refused to sit and continued to look out at the dark foggy night.

As the ship cleared the docking harbour and sailed out to sea, the mist from the land cleared. It was a clear night, and the stars shone brightly.

The sea was silky smooth, and the Moon beamed glowingly on the velvetiness of the water as they sailed out to sea.

The Drachen stood on the decks while the horses were stowed in the lower sections of the boat deep in the hull.

Captain Jonik apprehensively sauntered over to the Drachen Captain in a much-jilted nervous way. "Would you all like some food and water?"

Neldez looked around at Jonik, who stood in front of them with his chest out, trying not to show any fear.

The Drachen Captain marched over to Captain Jonik in the most intimidating way and stood before him, looking down and cowering over him.

"How long will this voyage take us?" The Drachen Captain asked in an aggressive voice.

"One One One One and a bit days we will be there by nightfall tomorrow if the wind is right," said the nervous stuttering Captain Jonik.

"Then we will need food," said the Drachen captain in an aggressive voice.

"Ok, we will fix a beef stew with bread and water," said Captain Jonik as he hurried to get away from them as fast as possible.

The Drachen looked away, gazing out at sea into the darkness.

Each Drachen stood imagining their; very own version of revenge and devastation they would apply to the Crusade.

A Drachen stared out to sea fixed on pure revenge and roared out into the darkness of the sea. Then another roared, and another, all feeding from the energy from each other; the Twelve Drachen roared into the blackness of the night.

The crew members, all petrified and so frightened, embraced the ship's rigging. Some even recited religious prayers in a mumbled whispered narration over and over in their heads as the boat edged closer to Qulan City.

It was to be a nightmare voyage, and everyone on board the smugglers ship knew it.

The South Taklamakan Caves

The crusade was now commanded and navigated by the Goathard Warriors. The Goathards came from the far edges of the Vakoborg forest and knew the area very well.

As they travelled, the landscape changed into caverns formed from the mighty Jandar Mountains.

The Taklamakan caverns would take the crusade safely through to the pinnacles, into the Jandar mountain foothills, then onto Cloven Town.

The Riders of the Crusade paced out of the lush green forests and now down into huge sandstone caves created by water erosion over millions of years.

The caverns would go deep underground then the light would appear from breaks in the cavities as they roamed in and out of deep tunnels then into small canyons throughout the day.

These caves and tunnels were so vast and treacherous that only the Goathard people knew the way.

The stealth of the Taklamakan tunnels and caverns was the prime reason why these were chosen.

As they ventured deeper and deeper into the caves, they could see sandstone buildings carved directly into the rocks from an ancient Goathard civilization.

Thomas, who was riding next to Princess Gilgamesh, spoke of their time in The Gathering and what went wrong.

They had both grown up so fast, and The Princess was entrusted in this quest to make this work. Thomas felt such a responsibility which is why he spoke up with the Goathards early that day.

"What is Tarrenash City like?" said Thomas.

"It is a wonderful city; it is the administrative capital for trade in the whole of West Tanniv, so the buildings are huge, and the city is full of trading halls and banks," said Princess Gilgamesh.

"It's so different from Vakoborg City," she added.

"And what are the King and Queen-like?" Said Thomas wanting to gain as much information as possible in preparation for the meeting.

"King and Queen Drusunal are fair and have always ruled justly; Vakoborg and the Disaris Dynasty have always had an unblemished relationship together," said the Princess in a true regal voice while looking at Thomas.

The Princess explained that General Yeldrove and Princess Katya Drusunal had galloped on ahead to arrange and prepare for the meeting with The King and Queen and to spread the word of the Leoven Abbey massacre.

Thomas rode on thinking about this meeting in fine detail and with a simple notion that The Tarrenash Empire and The Drusunal Royals would sign and join the quest with relative ease, and it was going to be a simple meeting.

They had been travelling for most of the day, and the Goathards at the front of the quest stopped then explained that they were not far from the Pinnacles.

It was late afternoon, and a small pool of water beside a vast underwater lake was ahead and would be the perfect place for a short break for the horses.

The caverns were a strange place; they were dark with beams of light shining from the porous yellow and beige sandstone in the ceiling above. The sunlight would penetrate through at intervals, which made it feel even stranger.

Nothing lived in these caves; it was not a place for the living, and altogether most of the crusaders could not wait to get out of these peculiar caves that made everyone feel very uneasy.

The quest stopped and prepared the horses for some feed and drink.

In her fabulous green dragon scale battle dress, the Princess jumped off her horse and looked around at the cathedral-sized cave.

"I cannot wait to get out of these caves," the Princess said to Oscar.

"Yes, me too; there is something not quite right about these caves," Oscar added as he also looked around.

Looking over at Lance-Corporal Elaith Tarron, the Princess said, "How long till we get to Cloven Town."

Elaith bowed his head and said, "We should be there in a few hours just before nightfall, my lady."

"This place feels like the home of Gog and Magog itself." Said Yelfir.

"The Tarrenash Garrison at Cloven Town are expecting us," Elaith added.

The crusade was almost clear of the caves; the next obstacle would be the maze of Pinnacles, then a ride up to the Jandar border town of Cloven.

The Goathards gave the signal to saddle up and move out.

The ride through the final Cavens was almost done, and as they left the caverns, the late afternoon daylight shone back on their faces, and positivity ascended over the quest once again.

"I never want to do that again," said Oscar looking at Elaith with a smile on his face.

The Pinnacles looked beautiful in the late afternoon sun. They were gold and dark yellow and pointed at the sky like peaks on a lemon meringue pie.

Travellers could get lost in the maze of Pinnacles and would often enter in and never come out again.

Most of the people in Tanniv would avoid this maze of peaks for this very reason, further adding to the intention as to why this route was chosen for the quest to travel, as this would be an undetected route.

The Garrison in Cloven Town was based on the border of Tarrenash.

The garrison was built to keep law and order with the mountain communities.

The town was a hotchpotch of houses, Inns, hotels and shops, and an imposing granite garrison castle that overlooked the whole town.

There were much more accessible routes to take to Cloven Town, but the course through the pinnacles was the stealthier direction to take.

The two Goathards navigated their way through with ease, and the crusade followed them.

The Goathards often traded in Jandar with precious emerald stones found only in the south Vakoborg forests, and they had good trading relationships with the Turgetts of Jandar.

The trading Turgetts were everywhere in the town and found in the many Pubs, Coach Houses, and Inns.

The Turgett loved jewels and precious metals of all description, and the Emeralds brought in from the Goathards would fetch a welcome price. Green emeralds were very rare and would procure a handsome price with the stone traders of Qulan.

The Goathards of south Vakoborg would use these ancient secret trade routes, and the information of these routes would be passed down from generation to generation.

As the campaigners pushed forwards following the Goathard guides, they trotted through the mazy landscape that gradually got smaller and lesser until they were trotting upward into the foothills of Jandar.

The terrain had altogether changed now, the scenery had become grey, and the dry sandy dirt trails of the Pinnacles had given way to small shale stone pathways leading up into the mountains.

The terrain was dangerous and looked like a pathway that was less travelled or certainly less well known as it lacked the use that other trails had with shale stone littering the perilous path.

The signal was given by the Goathard guides to dismount and to walk up the first steeper pass by foot.

Captain Rothlan rushed over to the Goathard Warrior named Lulong and asked, "How much longer like this?"

"Ten more minutes on foot, then we should rest the horses for five minutes then only two hours to cloven town," said Lulong the Goathard Warrior.

"We will keep going!" Yelled General Halamar Yelfir in a deep, commanding voice as he looked back at his Princess.

"Let's take the advice of our Goathard friends and stop for five minutes before the Cloven Garrison," said Princess Gilgamesh.

The Priestess Sana Norbella kept by Thomas's side as they walked up the mountain path; her hooded Disaris robe was up over her head but, she kept alert as she walked up the pass.

Disaris did not like being out in the open like this. Woodland Disaris felt uncomfortable with the barren scenery's exposure, so naturally, the Disaris felt uneasy and very uncomfortable.

The only comfort that this path gave the Tarrenash and Disaris was that it looked like a secret path that no one had used.

Sana Norbella strolled further up the pass and looked over a ridgeway.

The Disaris Priestess looked up and could see the great Eagle Owls of Tanniv had been following.

A squawk was let out from the Owls, which were high in the sky gliding on thermals.

Thomas looked directly up into the sky; then he looked up the pass towards Sana locking eyes with her instantly; she looked back at Thomas, locking eyes with him in return.

Lulong, the Goathard Warrior, gave the signal to mount up and ride.

As they rounded the ridge of this long-forgotten path, they could see transversely across the valley and could see the Tarrenash Garrison Castle of Cloven town now only minutes away.

The castle, in its grey granite mountain rock, blended into the landscape.

The building sat on the edge of a cliff leading down into a ravine, giving it protection on two sides. The castle's rear on the far side had been built into the top of the mountain, again providing the castle protection.

The town was filled with a mismatch of houses, and the homes were occupied by Tarrenash and Turgetts citizens.

As the crusade got closer, they could see the small Cloven Town streets. The streets were crammed with the famous Inns, the famous coaching houses, and Pubs that were often spoken about in legends and folklore.

Many a good deal and underhand trade were made in this town, and it was filled with a mixture of different cultures.

A small squad of eight Tarrenash soldiers waited for crusades arrival and were spotted in the distance on horses.

They rode towards the crusade flying an Eagle owl banner of Cloven Town.

The Lord of the Castle – Lord Arel did not get many guests. He wanted to welcome the visitors personally to be as hospitable as possible; as the squad rode closer, Elaith galloped ahead and saluted the Lord.

"My name is Lance-Corporal Tarron of the North Tarrenash army," he said.

The Lord looked straight through him, wanting to get a look at Princess Gilgamesh as he pivoted his head left and right, looking over Elaith shoulders.

"Yes Yes Yes he said now where is the Princess," said The Lord of the Castle Lord Arel in a dismissive impatient tone.

"Sir, we are here for one night, and we need to come and go fast, for one night's rest only," said Elaith, this time looking up and trying to explain.

"Yes, Yes, Corporal," Lord Arel waved his hands, being dismissive and rude to the young Tarrenash corporal.

Princess Gilgamesh, with Sana Norbella, Captain Rothlan, and General Yelfir galloped over to the exchange after overhearing that the conversation was not going to any order whatsoever.

"Sir, we are here because we do not wish to be seen or be heard. Would you kindly lower your banners," said Princess Gilgamesh in a kind, considerate but stern voice.

"I appreciate your hospitality, but this formality is not needed and will compromise the secrecy of our mission," said Princess Gilgamesh.

The Lord looking dejected and disappointed, a bit like a spoilt child, looked at the floor. The flags were lowered.

"Sir, if there is a back way into the Castle, please let me know," said Elaith.

Lord Arel shrugged his shoulders and said, "No, there's only the front,"

"Some of your soldiers can stay in the Castle Garrison quarters; the rest of you are staying in the legendary White Fox Inn, and I have reserved the biggest rooms for you, Princess Gilgamesh," said Lord Arel as his child-like smile returned to his face.

The Cloven squad of Soldiers led the crusade into the bustling, busy town through the narrow streets.

The Turgetts came out to look at the procession of Disaris, Tarrenash, and Goathard Warriors.

All around the town, the local people and local inhabitants of Cloven gazed on in wonder at the warriors as they passed.

Thomas looked at Oscar, who repaid the look as they passed through the first new town since The City of Vakoborg, both trying to hide their excitement.

The town was filled with precious stone stores, jewellers, and merchant stores, all trading in metals excavated out from the Jandar Mountains. They cantered on and headed for the White fox Inn.

The White Fox Inn

They stopped outside the well-known Inn and Coaching house called the White Fox Inn. The Rooms in the Inn were large and comfortable, and the cloven castle was only small, and the keep was a grotty army castle that was not suitable for a Princess.

Princess Gilgamesh would have been fine to bed down for the night and be on their way in secrecy, but it looks like this was not going to happen as Lord Arel had gone to the most amount of trouble.

The White Fox Inn and Coaching house were huge; they entered through two gigantic wooden open doors leading into a cobbled courtyard with stables for horses on all sides.

The enormous five-story coach house and Inn had space for hundreds of guests with hundreds of rooms.

The White Fox Inn staff were a mixture of local Tarrenash, and Turgetts and a throng of stable hands came out from different doors in every direction to take the horses and bed them down for the night.

The White Fox Innkeeper and big portly Turgett named Gantar came out in his finest clothes to meet the precession. The Turgett's average height is four feet in height, with stout, broad bodies and Ganter looked every bit a Turgett.

Princess Gilgamesh turned to General Yelfir and said angrily and furiously, "Does the whole of Jandar know of our coming."

The Turgett InnKeeper Gantar stood before Princess Gilgamesh, bowed, and said, "Welcome to my most humble establishment." He grinned and beamed with his big fat rosé cheeks, looking pleased with himself while he was swinging his gold pocket watch.

Princess Gilgamesh, who was put in an absolute awkward position, nodded gracefully.

"There really is no need for fuss; we are here for one night," said Princess Gilgamesh looking down at the Turgett Innkeeper with his pretty Turgett girlfriend holding onto his arm.

"I have roasted many pigs in the Great White fox Beer Hall, and my Beer is excellent," said Gantar, almost dismissing everything that the Princess had said.

"I will get the staff to show you up to your rooms; there is room enough for everyone," said Gantar as he bellowed in every direction for White Fox Inn workers to come running.

"Dinner will be served in one hour, and I have reserved the best seats for you," he said, chuckling to himself.

The staff led Princess Gilgamesh and the others to their lodgings.

The Princess looked over at Captain Rothlan and said, "Make sure all of our horses are ready at first light."

"I want everyone in the courtyard ready to ride out as soon as possible."

The Captain nodded and said, "Yes, My Lady."

The two boys shared a room at the White Fox Inn. The rooms were nice, with two carved wooden beds, a huge rug with wardrobes, and a washroom.

The room overlooked the courtyard, and they could see straight down as the staff of the White Fox Inn were working. They had a perfect view through the criss-cross of the leading piped windows, and they could see the staff bedding the horses for the evening.

The soldiers had remained behind to ensure that the staff were doing everything correctly.

Captain Rothlan had made sure Disaris guards were posted in strategic points around the Inn, and Elaith inspected the exit points and the horses living conditions.

Elaith had posted soldiers with the Disaris too.

The Cloven Garrison Commander Lord Arel made sure that Tarrenash soldiers were patrolling the city.

The Lord had totally blundered his orders of complete secrecy; however, he had ensured that security was tight in and around the town's streets.

Thomas and Oscar rested for a while and went down to the beer hall of the White Fox Inn.

It was huge with long oak tables everywhere; each table could fit fifty people or more.

The table nearest the bar was reserved for the Princess, who had not yet arrived.

The bar was long, with twenty serving staff, all serving beer. A deafening noise came from the beer hall as conversations boomed and beer glasses clunked down on the tables.

The White Fox Inn of Cloven Town

People laughed and talked as a band with wood instruments and guitars played, all around the beer hall, where a mixture of Turgetts, Disaris, and Tarrenash and everyone seemed to have a good time and enjoy the night.

A gigantic open log fire was in the far end of the hall with six pigs being roasted and turned on a spit by Turgett chefs.

The chefs were dressed in leather aprons, and with giant ladles, they drizzled and basted the pigs in its dripping juices as another Turgett turned it while stood on a small stool twisting the spits.

The smell of pork and vegetables mixed with beer filled the air.

Thomas was guided to the Princess table, and they were given beer drinking mugs, and Turgett maidens came to fill them up when they got low.

Over in the corner near the far exit, the Priestess Sana Norbella stood with her hood up and her blonde hair coming down either side of her shoulders and with her blue eyes watching over the night's proceedings with caution, she waited with vigilance.

The Lord of the Castle Lord Arel arrived with his commanding officers and took a seat at the head of the table, saying hello to everyone.

Looking directly at Thomas, he said, "No sign of the Princess yet?"

"No, my Lord," Thomas replied.

The music played on, and more people came into the beer hall.

It was filled with vagrants and miners, as well as wealthy merchants. Everyone sat with the buyers of Iron, gold, and precious stones, all being traded under the table in cloven town.

Many of the region's small armies and towns would come to buy Iron for the smelting and making of weapons for their armies, but when questioned, they would say it was Iron purchased for farming materials that were not taxable, making the administration for this almost impossible.

Everywhere, deals were being struck with wealthy Turgett merchants, whose social system and social status would be measured by wealth, so trading, broking, and bargaining were part of the cultural lifestyle of a Turgett.

The big Turgett named Gantar came to the table with his very young pretty lady wife, who arrived with a smile and said, "No sign of the Princess yet?"

"No sir, not yet," Thomas replied.

Oscar looked over at the far end of the beer hall again at the Priestess Sana Norbella as she still stood watching over the two boys.

That night in the Leoven abbey, she had connected with Thomas, and she watched over the two boys with determination.

Lord General Yelfir, with his opposing posture, entered into the beer hall and looked at all angles of the beer hall, scanning and surveying the area. He locked eyes with Sana Norbella, nodded, and he took a seat opposite the two boys.

Lord Arel looked over at the Disaris General and said, "Any sign of the Princess."

"She will be down shortly," said the Disaris General in a very stern voice as he lowered his hooded cloak.

In truth, Princess Gilgamesh was furious and outraged that Lord of the Castle had made such a grand spectacle of everything.

No wonder this Lord had been given an assignment to this far-flung outpost in cloven town, and he had made a complete gaffe of this secret mission.

Princess Gilgamesh had been given the premium suite in The White Fox Inn, and her Disaris guards stood outside, carefully watching over the door.

She paced up and down for several minutes trying to control her anger. She stood and took a deep breath, composed herself, then gracefully she opened the door in Royal elegance while her Disaris guards escorted her for dinner.

Captain Rothlan had completed his inspection of the Disaris century points. He had ensured that the soldiers were strategically placed to watch over the settlement and the Inn for the night and decided to join everyone for dinner, sitting opposite Thomas and Oscar and next to General Halamar Yelfir.

Princess Gilgamesh entered the beer hall with her guards.

Sana Norbella glanced over at the Princess, who stood watching from the other side of the beer hall.

The Princess composed herself, and she sat at the head of the table.

The room was filled with music, laughter, and conversation.

The Inn owner Gantar, sitting next to his friend Lord Arel, smiled across at the Princess and welcomed her while boasting that this was the best establishment in Cloven Town, he bellowed while driving his stubby fist onto the table.

The Turgett Gantar yelled across the table so that the Princess could hear and anyone else of importance would hear.

He shouted across the table in true Turgett style, asking her, "If the room was to her liking, and if there was anything that she needed to him know." He said while glowing with self-importance at all the other jealous Turgetts around that did not have a Royal princess at their table.

Lord Arel, who had been drinking a lot of beer and wine while waiting for the Princess, spluttered and muttered out a sentence.

"Thank you for joining us, your royal highness; it is a pleasure to have your company."

"Be sure to tell King Drusunal of my hospitality," he said while his drunken head bobbed from side to side.

"Thank you, Lord Arel – do not worry, I will be sure to tell your King exactly how proceedings have been," said Princess Gilgamesh gracefully.

The Lord smiled at the Princess and appeared very pleased with himself as he beckoned another large beer and wine from the Turgett serving girls.

Thomas looked directly at the Princess with knowing eyes; he was reading her expressions that she was angry but was hiding it so that the night went quickly without incident.

The night went on; the music played, and the fire-roasted pig was served across the grand long tables.

The mix of cultural music and beers added to the great atmosphere in the beer hall, and everyone was having a wonderful time.

Stories were exchanged with questions being asked about the Massacre of Leaven abbey as to whether this was true.

Sana Norbella watched over the two boys and the Princess from afar without faltering.

Sana was a very quiet lady; she rarely spoke and looked a magnificent figure with extreme beauty; with the sword pommels appearing over each shoulder, she looked like an opposing figure.

Whether Tarrenash, Disaris, or Turgett, every man would gaze at her extreme beauty and grace, and many of the conversations were aimed at this phenomenal striking, stunning figure.

A drunken wealthy merchant dressed in all his fine garments sporting gold rings and a coin pouch full of money sauntered over to the Priestess and put his arms around her with drunken thoughtlessness and blind confidence, asking her to dance.

She stood firm as the drunk continued to badger her; by this time, the drunken merchant was being encouraged by his equally drunken associates that sat on the adjacent table laughing.

She stood with her beauty without a smile or to show anger. As the drunken merchant tried to pull her for a dance, he persisted as he knocked a bowl of apples and fruit off the high table next to the Priestess causing a scene.

Sana looked over at the Princess, and the Princess nodded.

The Beautiful Disaris warrior Priestess stepped back and unsheathed her two swords in an elegant wave of seamless motion, the two swords came from across her back, and she stood low with two swords in the air. Everyone watched as she looked deadly like a predator waiting for the right time to attack.

The beer hall stopped, and the band halted, and silence fell on the White Fox beer hall as everyone watched in wonder at the elegant acrobatic flair they were witnessing.

Sana gazed out at the hall, then stared back into the soul of the drunken man in front of her, sobering him with a glance.

She flicked up an apple with her foot from the floor, the apple was hurled high into the air, and with a dozen swift flicks of her two swords, apple slices rained down on the drunken man covering his face in tens of thinly sliced apple slivers with apple juice and pips, making a mess all over his face.

The drunken man looked up at the rain of apples coming down; Sana took the opportunity while he was distracted to position her two swords on either side of the merchant's red drunken neck.

The merchant froze with fear as he looked at the Disaris beauty, wondering his fate after his uncultured miscalculation.

"No one puts their hands on me," said Sana as she looked at the merchant then back across the room at anyone else wanting to try something.

Seeing this as a warning, some of his drunken friends came over to collect him, and they apologised to her while they dragged him away.

The hall applauded, whistled, and cheered at the Disaris beauty and the grace of the acrobatic swordsmanship that had just witnessed.

Sana re-sheathed her swords, removed her hood, and took a subtle bow giving the cautionary gaze to everyone in the beer hall that the next time, the apple would be the merchant's neck if another liberty was taken.

The music played on late into the night.

Princess Gilgamesh took her to leave shortly after dinner, followed by Thomas and Oscar soon after.

Everyone was to ride out at first light for the city of Tarrenash, so an early night would be the wisest way to spend the evening.

The Drachen Voyage

The Drachen were still on-board the merchant ship Shanan and were almost at Port Qulan.

They could see the lights in the distance on the shoreline of The Qulan Bastion lighthouses. The Lighthouses were the entry points to the port.

Captain Jonik, who was a little more at ease because the journey had gone so far without problems, signalled lights towards the bastion lighthouses to indicate a friendly ship was coming into berth.

These light signals would change often and were considered the correct signals to gain admission to the port.

In truth, the port and city were so corrupt that these signals would be sold to the highest paying merchants, and almost everything had become a saleable commodity in Qulan.

The bastion lighthouses gave signal back to the ship Shanan so they could enter the port, as it had done many hundreds of times before.

It was now the following night, and it was three o'clock in the morning.

Captain Jonik nervously spoke to the Drachen captain Neldez, standing on the vessel's decks looking outwards.

"We will dock in ten minutes, and I will use the pier at the far end of the harbour so not to attract attention," said Captain Jonik in his most humble pleasing voice.

"Very well," the Drachen captain replied, looking directly at him as he put his helmet back on while snarling his teeth.

The Shanan drifted slowly in the dead of night between the two Bastion lighthouses giving signals that all was well and they would be docking.

They aimed for the most abandoned and deserted end of the pier, with the crew working frantically to get the boat moored and the Drachen off the vessel as soon as possible.

The lighthouses were two huge round Martello buildings, and they had both fallen into decay and required repair, but this meant more taxes, which the Qulan inhabitants would not want to address.

These Bastions were once Shadow Warrior buildings but had not been used by the warriors in decades.

The city itself was splendid, with tall buildings everywhere, and with the principal inhabitants being Turgetts, the buildings reflected wealth and status. Given the need for the Turgetts to show off their prosperity for social status, each house had a towered dwelling, which was the city's architectural style.

The bigger the tower in width and height, the higher up the social scale a Turgett would be or sometimes even several towers; some even had ten or more, as the Turgett had an obsession with height for reasons which were obvious.

Not to say that Tarrenash and Disaris did not live in the city; there was a social, ethnic mix of many cultures. However, the Turgetts were the principal residence of Qulan and of the region.

The streets were full of Gold Merchants, Diamond Merchants, and precious stone shops, with gemmologists on every street corner.

If you wanted to buy a pocket watch regardless of East or West Tanniv, a pocket watch bought from the craftsman of Qulan would be where the finest watches in the land were made.

Fine jewellery, necklaces, rings were made from the workshops of Qulan and sold all over Tanniv on both sides of the river. Even with the barbarism of the great troubles, this trade was never hugely affected.

The Ship Shanan was docked and being made ready.

The crew of the ship was still working frenziedly to ready the Drachen horses off the boat. The team worked to get the vessel berthed correctly. The ship's crew were now taking barracking from the Drachen as they shouted for the crew members to hurry and do the work faster.

A Drachen sergeant reported to Captain Neldez, "The men are ready and waiting for orders."

The Drachen Captain turned, looking directly into the eyes of his sergeant, and simply said with a leering look, "I smell blood," as he sniffed the air and tilted his head up towards the sky.

Captain Jonik of the merchant ship Shanan and Captain Neldez both walked to the mid-deck of the vessel.

"Everything is prepared, your horses are ready, and everything is now quayside," said a very nervous Captain Jonik.

The Drachen looked at Captain Jonik and said, "You have followed your orders perfectly."

The Ship Shannon Sailing into Qulan Harbour.

Jonik smiled, "And now I must follow mine," said Captain Neldez.

The Drachen unsheathed his smaller sword and cut captain Jonik across the neck.

The rest of the crew who were lined up waiting for the traditional goodbyes were stunned, frozen with fear, and gasped with horror.

Captain Jonik died instantly, and he collapsed to the floor in a bloodied mess.

The Drachen roared up and bellowed, "Not a soul left alive," giving the order for the Drachen to begin overwhelming and slaughtering the crew members.

The Drachen smiled then, while unsheathing their swords, hunted down the crew members and systemically went through the ship, killing all on-board.

They stalked around the decks of the Shanan, Cutting, and thrusting, plunging, and swiping their dark blades into all alive.

They cleared the decks cutting and thrusting until not a single person was left.

The thinking was to leave no traces or evidence of the Drachen being there so that no one in West Tanniv would know.

So by killing them, no one would know. But now, the port authorities in Qulan City would know killers roamed West Tanniv.

If the Drachen had left the crew and Captain Jonik alive, they would have sailed back to Port Elleth asking for their money and kept this a secret anyway through fear of reprisals.

Now everyone would know killers had landed in West Tanniv, giving way to stories spreading like wildfire.

The Drachen galloped out through the small narrow streets of Qulan in the dead of night, and anyone who saw them, they cut down with their long back Ilihorn blades.

They galloped hard up into the mountains of Jandar, breaking off into two squads so that they could patrol the trade routes into Tarrenash City.

The first six Drachen went for the high road through the Jandar Mountains stopping at Inns and coaching houses, villages, and settlements looking for the crusaders causing a bloody mess as they galloped.

The second six Drachen took the valley path down through the Jandar Mountains leading through the foothills onto the Tarrenash plains with the aim to cut any crusade off on the well-known trade routes.

Each squad of Drachen would gather hostages and question them promising no harm would come to them right before they extracted the information they needed before running their guts through with their blades.

The Drachen riders were on a murderous rampage, intent on making a name for themselves with Moltenwing.

Finding the Crusade and crushing the campaign is all they would think about, and they would stop at nothing.

They galloped wildly through Jandar while causing hell for the people of Tanniv on the way. Many old scores needed to be settled, and the Drachen were finally unleashed onto West Tanniv.

The Journey to Tarrenash

The crusaders awoke at first light after the night in the White Fox inn; Oscar went down early to tend to his horse Sylva.

Elaith was already there with the horses and was tending to Leokan, the much needier of the two horses.

"Good morning Elaith."

"I did not see you last night in the beer hall," said Oscar.

"I am a soldier, and my men were stationed all around cloven guarding and gathering information about today's journey to Tarrenash city," said Elaith as he brushed his horse.

"I would not make much of a soldier, would I," said Oscar as he looked down at his feet, a little embarrassed.

"And I would not make much of a White sorcerer," said Elaith as he patted Oscar on the head.

"Did you see the Goathard soldiers last night?" said Oscar.

"Yes, they got food and slept in the stables with the horses they didn't want to mix in the beer hall," said Elaith.

"Just you boys, make sure you ride close to the other soldiers and me today; it's a dangerous path we are taking," said Elaith.

Thomas had been summoned to see Princess Gilgamesh and made his way to the suite at the top of the White Fox Inn.

He walked up the crooked, twisting square staircase up to the top floor, where notably he saw two Disaris guards outside The Princesses room.

He knocked three times and heard the Princess say enter.

"Good morning, your highness," said Thomas as he bowed his head.

"Good morning Thomas," said the Princess.

"I have a concern about today's ride; there were at least three hundred people in that beer hall last night, and each one would have gone home and told someone," she said as the Princess paced up and down.

"By the time morning trading would start in the towns market, bakeries, and tea shops, everyone in Jandar will know of our stopover," the Princess added.

"This means anyone travelling outside cloven town to other settlements, towns, and villages will tell others, and the news of our stay will be all over Jandar by mid-day and be in Qulan City by the afternoon."

"Yes, I understand, Princess; we tried to make the best of this situation last night," added Thomas agreeably to the topic.

"I need you to go with The Sana Norbella."

"Why?" Thomas said in a surprised voice.

"On your own, to the glen, the other side of the mountain and summon an Eagle Owl to get a message to General Yeldrove to ride out with his shadow warriors and meet us in the plains as we gallop to The City of Tarrenash," said the Princess anxiously.

"And I need you to do this in secret then ride and catch us up," said the Princess.

"Yes-Yes no problem, I can do this," said Thomas.

"But why are you so concerned about this," said Thomas in a soft voice.

"The Priestess Sana Norbella has a bad feeling about today's ride; she came to me this morning expressing her concerns."

"She is a priestess of the Lugella abbey, and she can see things."

"She is a special rare breed of Disaris."

"What things?" said Thomas Nervously?

"Dark things, there are dark things out there on the road," said the Princess.

A knock at the door came. It was Sana Norbella; she entered the room to collect Thomas; her hood was up, and her blue eyes peered through her dark hood.

She held out her hand and said, "Come, Thomas, we must go."

The two of them ran down the stairs and out to the front doors and onto the street. Thomas's horse Leokan was outside, Sana had prepared everything, and Elaith had been briefed.

It was still dark outside, and the sun had risen slightly, giving some morning golden sunlight in the mountains.

They mounted the horses and galloped through the narrow streets smelling the bakeries' and the fresh breads coming out of the morning ovens, and the aroma of chimneys filled the morning air.

They galloped hard through the gates and set out into Jandar and onwards to a clearing to summon the eagle owls of Tanniv.

Sana carried a note written by princess Gilgamesh asking General Lorsan

Yeldrove to bring shadow warriors.

"Sana-Sana, why shadow warriors?" Thomas asked as he galloped hard and fast.

"Because if what I think is hunting us right now, we will need them," she replied as she galloped and looked back at Thomas, who was charging behind her.

The mountain glen was an hour's ride from cloven, and they would catch up with the crusade in the foothills further down the mountain that day.

The valley glen was remote, and the message could be sent in secret.

They galloped on through huge boulder fields and with smashed rocks everywhere. It was an eerie place, and it resembled a quarry. "What happened here?" said Thomas.

"Who else would smash rocks like this? Bauk! – this is a Bauk quarry," Sana said as the gallop turned into a slower canter.

"Stay close to me," said Sana.

It was daylight by now, and there was little chance of seeing Bauk in the daylight; nevertheless, they proceeded with caution so not to wake them.

They cantered on through the boulder fields slowly and silently and around the mountain into the next valley. They trotted along until they could see the green area sloped on the side of the hill. The field was bright green, surrounded by a scene of grey mountain rock.

They reached the middle of the field where a giant megalith was located. Thomas dismounted and held his wand aloft while Sana watched vigilantly for anyone watching.

They appeared to be alone, so he continued.

He held his wand up into the air and repeated, "ibis Veni ad me" – "ibis Veni ad me" – "ibis Veni ad me" – "ibis Veni ad me," after several attempts, a squawk and hoot from an Eagle Owl could be heard be overheard.

Then a shadow formed from the giant shadowy wings flying into the glare of the sun. It was the wings of the Tanniv giant Eagle Owl that had answered the call.

"Look," Thomas bellowed as he pointed. Sana Norbella turned and looked up at the sky at this magnificent sight of a great Eagle Owl.

"Its Sathgang – Sathgang has come," shouted Thomas, and he could see the Owl spiral, corkscrewing downwards towards him.

He landed on the floor next to Thomas and purred almost like a cat while

Thomas stroked the majestic Owl.

Sana handed Thomas the pouch containing the note from Princess Gilgamesh.

He tied the pouch to Sathgangs bright yellow talon and repeated, "fly Sathgang fly to the city of Tarrenash deliver this message to Lord General Lorsan Yeldrove."

Thomas hugged and petted the Owl once more with love and much gratitude, and The Eagle Owl took off into the blue skies circling around, then over the mountain ridge.

Sana, still ever watchful, looked around for any signs of life. She grabbed Thomas and helped him onto Leokan while she jumped onto her horse and said, "Come, Thomas, let's ride; there is much danger everywhere."

They galloped down a small valley gorge at the top of the trading pass and stopped at a clearing where they could see the main Qulan to Tarrenash pass several miles away on the adjacent valley below.

Sana jumped off her horse for a closer look down the valley.

Thomas jumped down too and looked directly at Sana. For the first time, Sana looked apprehensive. She looked again, then moved and looked down the valley again. She could see clearer now, and she could see; what was coming up the mountain path. Her heart sank, and her soul was filled with dread and terror.

"Drachen," she said.

"Drachen riders," she repeated.

"What are Drachen?" said Thomas in a very concerned voice.

"Drachen are giant horned ridders from The Ilihorn Mountains. They have been sent to stop us," said Sana.

"Come, Thomas, there could be more we will have to navigate down through the Jandar forest; we can't risk any of the routes into Tarrenash," said Sana in a hurried voice.

Sana turned the horses around and went in another direction forward through the dangerous Jandar thick Forrest to try and get to the foothills of Tarrenash.

Disaris felt safer in the forest, and although this would be much slower and uneven ground underfoot, they would remain undetected.

It was the slower route for sure, and it could even take days to reach the City of Tarrenash, but they could not risk an encounter with the Drachen.

All day, the twelve Drachen riders patrolled the different routes and many trade ways in and out of Jandar.

The two groups of Drachen riders were traversing, questioning, and killing in a blood-thirsty rage as they travelled towards the main Tarrenash routes.

They were now splitting up, even more, leaving a Drachen at strategic points.

It was only a matter of time before they met up with the crusade.

The Goathards could circumnavigate down through The Jandar Mountains and the foothills without being seen, but once out onto the open plains of Tarrenash, the Drachen would be sure to find them.

Oscar rode alongside Elaith, talking and discussing local social politics.

He had read some books on The City of Tarrenash about it being the commercial centre of Tanniv. But Elaith was a simple soldier who belonged to the Border Corps, which made up the Shadow warriors and had been drafted in for this mission as an escort for the gathering but now found himself as a Lance Corporal of a crusade to reunite the banners.

"Have you always wanted to be in the army," said Oscar.

"Yes, I have always wanted to be a Soldier it was either a soldier or my parents wanted me to work on the farm with them, and there is no adventure in farming," said Elaith.

"A safer vocation to be a farmer," said Oscar.

"Yes and no," Elaith said as he smiled at the boy.

"My village was raided by an East Tanniv Brigade many years ago, and my village was burned, and my parents were either killed or married into serfdom," said Elaith.

"Oh, Elaith, I am so sorry to hear this," said Oscar.

"I was one of the lucky ones; I suppose this was not uncommon at the time. The border forces in the Bastions are not what they used to be, so East Tanniv soldiers can come and go with ease," said Elaith.

"One of the lucky ones?" said Oscar as if to ask a question.

"Well, I am still alive, so I suppose I am lucky," said Elaith.

Oscar cantered on thinking about his story.

Elaith was in his early twenties, no more than twenty or twenty-one, so the age gap was not huge. He thought about the very real threat and trouble coming from East Tanniv and how all the signs showed that East Tanniv was growing stronger and the West was getting weaker.

Lulong, the Goathard Warrior, led the crusade down the mountains. The terrain was difficult because it was wet. They cantered on by the most beautiful waterfall, and as they descended, the rocky granite from the Jandar mountain range turned to greener vegetation.

The rocks were loose and dangerous, and the riding was slow. But they were under the protection of these secret routes.

Princess Gilgamesh carried on behind the Goathards surrounded by Captain Rothlan and her Disaris General Yelfir.

She looked back at Oscar, who looked pensive after his discussion with Elaith, so she pulled her horse reins back to ride with him.

"Are you ok," The Princess asks as she smiled, looking at Oscar as the boy that used to play with her in the gardens of Tappington Hall.

"Yes, I am fine. I was thinking about Thomas," he replied.

"Don't worry, he is with Sana, and she is one of the finest sword fighters in Vakoborg," she said to put Oscar's mind at rest.

"They will be catching up with us at the bottom of the ridge down to the Tarrenash plains so, in a few hours, you will see him," said the Princess.

Oscar smiled and felt promptly better.

The crusade was almost forty people strong now, and with this being the final part of the trip into The City of Tarrenash, he looked forward to seeing the mighty City he had heard and read so much about.

The crusade was now nearing the border cross point out of Jandar and into Tarrenash. This was now as far as the secret trade routes would go and as far as the Goathard Warriors could take them.

They would now be galloping on the regular routes directly into the City as they were only five hours ride away and could now be seen clearly by anyone who would be watching.

The Tarrenash crossroad was the agreed point in which Sana and Thomas were meant to meet up with the crusade.

The Goathard warriors dropped back into formation with the rest of the warriors and four Tarrenash riders who made their way to the front of the Parade. They were now in Tarrenash, and it is the correct etiquette for the Tarrenash Soldiers to assume command of the squad and lead from the front.

They were still in the mountain woodlands and on a well-used dirt path leading to the plains. The dirt tracks were very narrow, with enough space for only two riders side by side.

Lance-Corporal Elaith Tarron, the highest-ranking Tarrenash soldier, was now in charge of the squad as Captain Norlen and General Yeldrove rode into escort Princess Katya Drusunal back to the City several days before.

The four Tarrenash soldiers cantered at the front of the crusade with caution.

The Disaris soldiers of the group felt uneasy as they ascended down the hills heading for the plains, and everyone in the group was being extremely cautious.

Elaith was not experienced enough to command a crusade like this, but he did a great job keeping everyone into formation.

Captain Rothlan tactfully rode alongside Elaith, and he diplomatically discussed putting the soldiers on a higher state of alert with weapons ready. Elaith agreed and nodded, giving the order for weapons to be at half-cock.

Later that day, the path gave way to a clearing with signposts pointing in different directions.

The clearing was a crossing point that had been used for hundreds of years. In the middle of the wooded clearing was a giant boulder that laid half-submerged in the grassy clearing and a huge carved wooden signpost that pointed into four directions. To the south, the sign said Qulan City; to the North, it said The City of Tarrenash, to the West Vakoborg, and back the way they had come, it read Jandar.

Many travellers over the centuries had made the signpost.

Trees had been felled for firewood, with the place being a campsite or stopover location for travellers.

The grass showed signs of campfires that had been used many times before, with the dusty grey residue left over from previous fires in at least five locations.

They were certainly on the main trade routes now and would be sure to bump into other travellers, traders, and oncoming traffic.

They waited for almost an hour while horses were attended to and water and food were eaten. But there was no sign of Thomas and Sana.

Captain Rothlan looked over at the Princess and explained that they must continue to Tarrenash City. The Princess agreed while looking back at Oscar as if to say it would be fine.

The Princess paced over to Oscar and said, "We have waited too long already, and Thomas will be fine with Sana as she knows the way."

"We can't risk the crusade, and travelling on these dangerous roads at night it is far too perilous," said the Princess.

Oscar dipped his head and, looking very upset, said, "I understand, Princess."

The riders of the crusade mounted their horses and took the direct route heading for the City of Tarrenash.

The Tarrenash soldiers led from the font cantering out of the forest, looking ever watchful with weapons readied.

Another clearing in the forest could be seen up ahead in the distance, so again the crusade moved on cautiously; as the squad cantered closer to the clearing. The Tarrenash soldiers at the front of the campaign could see two horsemen in the far distance.

The soldier in the lead held out an arm, signalling for everyone to stop. A Disaris soldier cantered forwards to get a better look and squinted into the distance, looking as hard as he could, trying to ascertain what he was looking at.

Feeling that they were being watched, the two horsemen in the clearing looked back down at the track spotting the crusade. The horseman tilted his head back and sniffed the air and said, "I smell Disaris." It was two Drachen scouts that had spotted the crusade.

Giving a mighty thunderous roar, The Drachen screamed out with his expansive growl, which was a signal to the other Drachen nearby that he had spotted the squad and crusaders.

General Yelfir galloped to the front of the precession and said a word he had not said in a long time "Drachen" as the blood-curdling roar of the Drachen filled the air, and the ears of the crusade, a look of horror came over the squad who knew what the word Drachen meant.

Oscar looked at these tall black horned monsters and gulped.

Captain Rothlan looked around in a hurried, frantic way; they were calling out to other Drachen; his experience had told him that this is what Drachen do.

He gave the order to charge at them, shouting, "let's charge them while there are only two as more will be sure to follow."

Some distance away, the other four Drachen in the squad who were scattered through the woods heard the faint sound. They had been looking for anyone moving in the thick trees trying to make it to Tarrenash city without being seen.

They now all stopped and heard the Drachen cry and were immediately alerted.

Now looking on at the crusade, the two Drachen stood firm on their gigantic black horses, never wanting to shy away from a challenge; the black riders welcomed the uneven odds and the fight charging towards them.

Elaith looked back at Oscar and said, "stay safe," and pointing to six of his Tarrenash men, he joined the charge. Eight of the Disaris soldiers had joined the charge, and Captain Rothlan and the Tarrenash soldiers with two Goathard warriors joined in with the charge.

Princess Gilgamesh jockeyed her horse into position with her two Disaris guards on either side of her steed; she drew out her bow and readied it for battle with a white arrow.

The two Drachen unsheathed their long black-board swords and salivated at the smell of Disaris blood and the revenge riding towards them.

The first clash of swords came from a Tarrenash blade from a young soldier charging at the giant adversary. The Drachen instinctively swung at the same time while reaching for his smaller curved sword. He steered his horse with his feet and was now in full battle posture.

The second blade clash came from another Tarrenash, then a Disaris and the mighty Drachen fought back and more than withstood the onslaught of swords thrashing and swinging in his direction.

The fighting intensified as the two Drachen managed to fight hard against sixteen Tarrenash, Disaris and Goathard fighters by this point.

A Disaris blade sliced down from behind, cutting the Drachen through his hardened armour.

Then another blade rained down onto the beast, this time cutting into the arm of the colossal Drachen's black flesh. As he let out a huge roar, his next manoeuvre was more from reaction than intention; he thrust his smaller sword behind him, piecing the stomach of the unsuspecting Disaris knocking him clean off his horse.

The Drachen then looked forwards, and with a swipe of his blade backwards, he slashed a Tarrenash soldier across the chest and neck, wounding the soldier.

More thrusts and skilful fighting came from the soldiers all fighting the two huge horsemen. Another fatal blow landed another Tarrenash that was fighting bravely but falling foul of a lethal blade that came from the Drachen attack.

The Drachens were fighting hard and seemed to be doing well despite being massively outnumbered in this skirmish.

Princess Gilgamesh, on her pure white steed, jockeyed around, but this time cocking her bow, she lifted the fletching of the arrow to her eye. She paused while furiously twitching to take aim and finally let loose her arrow aiming straight for the Drachen's head.

The arrow soared with such speed through the thick of the fighting, avoiding the brace of Disaris and Tarrenash. The arrow hit the Drachen in the throat, and it was now coming out the back of his neck with the fletching and arrow shaft coming out from his throat.

The monster looked shocked, and in a state of pure anger and rage, he dropped his swords to free his hands; with one hand, he grabbed the arrow in the back of his neck, and with the other, he held the arrow in his throat and snapped it. Pulling it out of his neck while multiple stabs and slices rained down on him from the Disaris, Goathard, and Tarrenash soldiers who took the initiative to strike and attack hard.

The Drachen persisted for a time, slowly trying to fight back; he was overrun with a volley of swords thumbing down at him.

The other Drachen was still fighting firm and strong, swinging his weapon in a pure skilful rage defeating the soldiers in front of him, and clearly had the upper hand in this fight.

During the fight, a Goathard climbed a tree near the battle and jumped onto the Drachen's horse and back while stabbing him multiple times in the back and neck. This act of bravery slowed the Drachen down.

Another arrow flew from Princess Gilgamesh's bow, this time hitting the Drachen in the thigh, pinning him to his horse as the arrow went through his leg and into his huge black steed.

The charger roared up onto his back legs knocking another Disaris off his horse violently.

This Drachen was not going down without a fight and gazed down at his fighters with a look that indicated to all that this was a fight to the death.

Two other Disaris took up their bows and fired them at the last Drachen, piercing the giant warrior again in the chest and arms, but he still stood in defiance and rode his horse around swinging his sword.

Elaith came in closer to the fight as the Drachen looked at him and smiled as if to say, "I have the measure of you, boy" the monster spat and roared then charged towards him, but the Lance-Corporal stood brave. As the Drachen came close, he swiped his blade while Elaith ducked; in return, he sliced the slower injured Drachen in his middle.

The injured Drachen, still defiant, and angry, and thirsty for more blood, looked around at the Princess on her pure white steed and galloped furiously on a suicide mission to kill the Princess and to take her down in a glorious final move before his death.

Disaris archers fired a volley of five arrows which all hit the intended target sticking into the back and side of the Drachen, but still, he roared forwards.

Still charging, a brave Tarrenash soldier swiped his sword at the Drachen, but the colossal beast still charged.

A look of panic came over General Yelfir as the creature still charged; the General was too far away. He fished around for his short sword keeping his eye on the Drachen, General Yelfir grasped his small sword and hurled his half-sword into the air hitting the Drachen in his side, but the Drachen still charged at the Princess.

The Princess had jockeyed away from her guards while using her bow, so at this point, no one was around her to protect her.

She calmly aimed an arrow at the Drachen, and with graceful ease, she pulled back and fired it into the eye of the beast, hitting him clean in the eye. Still, the mighty Drachen charged intent on bringing the Princess with him to the next life.

This time the Princess was on her own. The Disaris and the Tarrenash soldiers galloped hard and tried to reach her in time.

The Princess pulled out her silver Disaris sabre sword, and stood firm ready for the fight, and was prepared to die fighting. Ready to meet her newly fated early visit to the afterlife, she glared hard at the Drachen, and she prepared herself for both scenarios to fight or to die fighting.

The Drachen roared up, baring his fangs intent on plunging his dagger and his fangs deep into the Disaris Princess, and as he got closer, he made a last leap.

Oscar held out his wand and shouted "praesidium umbraculum," "praesidium umbraculum", "praesidium umbraculum", and aimed his wand at the Princess.

A massive ball of light appeared, and a vast blue and white bubble protected the Princess in a defensive shield, and as the Drachen hit the force field, he was thrown back several metres flinging him from his horse, leaving the Princess completely protected and safe from harm.

The Drachen half dead lay in a pool of his black blood as Disaris and Tarrenash ran to finish him off.

Princess Gilgamesh looked over her shoulder and at Oscar and smiled.

General Yelfir rode over to the Princess, checking to see if she was ok, then looked over at Oscar and saluted him; the entire Disaris guard held up their swords and saluted Oscar in recognition for his bravery and quick thinking.

The Gotthard warriors were also commended for initiating the quick thinking that helped bring down the mighty Drachen.

There was no real-time for any appreciation or gratitude or thanks. There was no time for discussions by anyone; many Disaris laid dead, and many Tarrenash soldiers laid dead too, with many injuries in the depleted squad.

Elaith looked over at Oscar; he nodded his head and again said, "stay safe."

If this was the devastation two Drachen could do, then a platoon of Drachen would defeat the crusade with ease.

They could hear Drachen Roaring in the distance and the sound of their reverberations getting closer as they tried to find their contemporaries.

Captain Rothlan, who was bleeding from the fighting, shouted, "let's move!"

"There will be more Drachen coming, and we need to move fast," he added.

The crusade gathered up the dead, and they moved out quickly, galloping hard across the woodlands in the hope to reach The Tarrenash plains.

More roars came in from the Drachen as they found their fallen dead combatants.

The small squad of Drachen led by Captain Neldez had taken the southern route down from Jandar and was riding hard. By luck, he was on a direct collision course with the crusade without knowing it.

They could hear roars from the other Drachen who were chasing the crusade from the rear. As they moved through the woodland, the weather turned, and it began to rain while the mid-afternoon skies turned grey and dark.

Thomas and Sana were still slowly riding through dense forest on the safest route down from Jandar.

The Drachen had been expecting this scenario, and the other four, who were now chasing the crusade from the rear, had changed tack.

This was good news for Thomas and Sana, giving them a clear run onto the Tarrenash plains. They would have met up with four Drachen in the bottom of the valley, but now the route was clear for them to ride on.

Sana, not knowing this, still proceeded with extreme caution, ensuring that they took the safest route.

As they reached the lowermost part of the gorge, they were now in Tarrenash and almost in the woodlands leading out onto the great plains.

Oscar, Princess Gilgamesh, and the Crusaders were galloping hard for the City of Tarrenash; they were being hunted by four Drachen who would be gaining on them. The Drachen Captain Neldez was galloping hard to cut the crusade off at the pass leading down onto the plains.

It was an unplanned manoeuvre from the Drachen; however, the timing would mean they would meet at some point on the main track leading to Tarrenash City.

The four Drachen would roar at intervals signalling to Captain Neldez and the other five Drachen. These primaeval roars and growls were communications and indications helping them pinpoint each other's positions.

Captain Rothlan was ridding badly but keeping up with the expedition as they galloped hard, but he had been hurt in the fighting.

The Captain was trying his best to conceal his injuries to the rest of the crusade and to disguise that he was most certainly mortally injured; he was especially hiding this from Princess Gilgamesh. But blood was dripping down his arm, and his left hand was soaked in blood.

The Captain's face and skin had taken on the look of a dull grey complexion he had donned his helmet to hide his injuries further to mask his face. But the other riders and Disaris soldiers could see that he was not ridding well and struggling to keep up, and his breathing had become heavy and uneven.

Several more miles later, the Drachen roars got closers the Captain slowed.

General Halamar Yelfir halted and shouted for everyone else to stop.

The General looked at his old friend, the Captain, who looked back at him with a look and a pause, and with the most minuscule nod of the head, General Yelfir understood what needed to be done.

The Disaris Captain was now buckled over in pain, and princess Gilgamesh jogged over and nodded at the Captain.

"Come, we will help you," she said to the stricken Captain.

"Not this time, Princess," said The Disaris Captain.

"You go; I intend to bring at least one more Drachen down before I reach the mighty Disaris gods," said Captain Thalland Rothlan as he smiled with blood now showing in his mouth and teeth.

General Yelfir looked at his Disaris Princess and said.

"We must ride."

"Its soldiers' way, my lady."

"Goodbye, my old friend," said Lord General Halamar Yelfir griping his Captain's forearm.

Another expansive roar came in the distance, this time sounding closer.

"Go!" yelled Captain Rothlan.

The rest of the crusade nodded while the Captain remained, and the crusaders rode off into the distance.

The Captain selected a spot near some bushes so that he would be less seen and prepared himself.

The Captain organised his bow, loading the string with an arrow in readiness.

He repositioned his pouch of arrows near the horse's neck so that he could get at them easier. He pulled his two swords from their sheaths and again positioned them so he could draw on them with simplicity. Then the glorious Disaris Captain waited.

Oscar had felt sad, so many lives had been lost, and Thomas was still out there. It appeared the crusade was falling apart, and he had never seen such ferocity from another being. The pure hate and willingness to kill from the Drachen left the boy unsure about everything.

If West Tanniv could not agree on simple matters like taxes and defence and East Tanniv could summon such hate and determination, what hope would the crusade have.

Elaith looked over at Oscar, grabbed his leg, looked at the boy, and said, "Ride with me - ride with me." his head and heart lifted as he instantaneously felt improved and more fixed on the task he focused on.

Captain Thalland Rothlan sat in wait on his horse until the Drachen came into focus on the brow of the track.

The Captain had a clear shot from his vantage point; he had chosen a position of a deadly nature, the brow of the hill opened up onto a clearer part of the track. The Disaris Captain's choices were no coincidence or mistake; these were military decisions based on forty years of Disaris military training. All this training was now coming to his instincts and senses one last time.

He carefully lifted his bow as he was in pain and held his arm up to his cheek, and closed one eye to focus on his target; he waited and waited until the timing was perfect. The Captain unleashed an arrow that flew straight and true and plummeted into the hard riding Drachen's shoulder.

The Captain's injury hampered him as he aimed for the Drachen's eye; nevertheless, it hit its target.

The Drachen jolted back slightly, looking into his shoulder at the newly embedded arrow; he roared and dug his heels into his horse to ride harder.

Reloading in pain, the Captain got off another arrow which this time missed and missed by a long way. The Captain reloaded again and got off another shot. The Drachen rode harder, now charging at the Captain, and he hit another Drachen in the chest.

The Captain now knew that the bow was out of this fight; he then threw his bow to the floor and went for his swords while gasping in pain.

The Drachen had slowed at this point as they prowled and skulked towards the injured Captain like an apex predator.

The Captain unsheathed his two swords as the Drachen roared and salivated at the sight of the injured Disaris.

They grumbled and growled their throats and voices, tilting their heads down, looking through their furrowed brows with their yellow eyes, and trotted towards the Captain as they came ever closer, still drooling at this most wonderful time.

The Captain delayed any movements; the longer he kept the Drachen, the further away the crusade was getting. This was an act of pure Disaris courageousness and bravery.

The Drachen looked deep into the Disaris Captain's eyes, "It's been a long time since I have tasted Disaris meat," he said while laughing at the ill-fated Captain.

The Captain stood firm, mustering up the energy to grip his two swords with his blood-soaked hands one last time. If he was going to die today, he was going to die fighting.

The first Drachen unsheathed his swords and cantered towards the Captain, and moved in for the Kill. The beast swung his broad sword as the other Drachen sat on their horses laughing.

The Captain blocked the swing with his sabre, and again and again, the Drachen beat his sword against the Captain's blade until the Captain could defend no more.

The Drachen swung his blade one last time, and the Captain once again found the vigour to block the hit. But this time, the Captain was completely finished. He slumped forward with his head down on his saddle.

The Drachen calmly jockeyed closer to clutch the Captain around the back of his neck to show to his counterparts the measure of his success. This was a sad sight to see for such a brave, selfless magnificent warrior who was now finished at the hands of pure evil.

The four Drachen sat laughing on their horse's savouring every moment in the humiliation of the Captain when the Captain gript his smaller sabre tightly had thrust it into the Drachen's neck and up into his brain in one wildly thrusting motion.

The Drachen grasped his own neck with two hands while holding the blade that was now completely submerged upwards into his chin.

The Drachen looked back at his comrades with a look of shock and confusion as he slumped to one side and fell off his horse.

Captain Thalland Rothlan looked up at the remaining Drachen with his exhausted eyes, knowing that this was his final moment, said, "Who is next to die today and smiled?" This infuriated the three Drachen, which sent them into a wild sword wilding tempered rage as three of them cut the Captain down, and the Captain fought back the best that he could.

The blows came from all angles finally ended in a sword thrust into the Captain's side, which came out the other side of his body.

Captain Thalland Rothlan died that day but took a Drachen down with him and bought time enough for the crusaders to escape. It was a true selfless act of bravery that would always be remembered.

The Tarrenash Cross Roads

Princess Gilgamesh and the Crusaders were galloping hard to the cross point of the Tarrenash plains, knowing that they were being chased by the Drachen they had encountered only hours before.

They were not aware that they were riding into a lethal situation.

The Drachen captain Neldez was riding hard with five Drachen soldiers on a southern Jandar path and would shortly arrive at the same point.

The three Drachen's who had finished killing the captain now galloped up from the south and were chasing down the crusade hard. The crusaders neared the crossroads, which was a natural trade route from Tarrenash to Qulan City. They could see riders up ahead in the distance, in the dark, dull skies as the rain poured down from an angle.

Cautiously they approached the horseman in the distance, unsure who they were getting close to; they approached slowly to within a few hundred metres they could now see who the riders were.

Five huge Drachen gawked across at them as captain Neldez smiled and said, "well-well-well, we have a Disaris Princess."

The Drachen snarled and roared up at the crusaders as the campaigners looked up, evaluating their every move.

Looking behind them, they could see the Drachen riders coming up from the rear in the distance. The Crusaders were now trapped, and captain Neldez could see that they were ensnared.

The hooded Disaris, including the Princess, loaded their bows with half-cocked arrows in readiness for the orders.

General Yelfir looked everywhere, galloping up and down, assessing the situation, then organised the troops to fight.

The three Drachen's in pursuit could now see the precision in the distance and could see the squad of five Drachen in the expanse ahead of them.

The Drachen had the advantage with the high ground; they all roared up to signal and communicate to one another.

The Battle of The Tarrenash Crossroads

315

The tension was now thick and the air filled with a whistling wind coming off the Tarrenash plains. As the grey skies blackened and the rain fell harder, everyone could feel the pressure.

Elaith positioned his Tarrenash soldiers in two flanks, one small force to the rear and the larger group facing the five Drachen riders who were now trotting slowly, expecting a volley of arrows.

The Disaris legion pointed outwards into four directions with Princess Gilgamesh and Oscar in the middle.

The two Goathard Warriors stood proud alongside their Vakoborg cousins, ready to fight, and everyone had weapons in hand.

There was a strange deathly silence as the wind howled and whistled in the late afternoon from the Great Plains as the heavy rain set in and the light faded under the black clouds that blocked the sun.

Everyone could feel the power and pressure in the air as each side measured and assessed the situation.

The three Drachen's that came up from the rear stopped. Then a Drachen threw a round ball that bounced and spun towards the Tarrenash and Disaris. To everyone's disbelief, shock and horror, it was Captain Thalland Rothlan's head rolling towards them.

Princess Holly Gilgamesh

The Princess looked over in horror but keeping calm; she shouted, "no one fire until I give the word," she looked at Oscar through her helmet and gave him a look of ease.

Captain Neldez sat smiling and laughing at the head tossed towards them; he sniggered at the thought of this skirmish as a bloody victory.

Impatiently Captain Neldez ordered three of his men to charge straight at them. He then roared up, calling the two from behind to do the same.

The two Drachen from behind were not in excellent condition as they had been wounded in the first clash and injured by Captain Thalland Rothlan's arrows.

Five of the Drachen's in two directions, charged at the crusade.

The Princess ordered the crusade to fire their arrows, adding, "Show no mercy as they will show you none in return."

Oscar looked apprehensive and nervous; he held his wand in one hand and a sword in another, expecting to fight. He sat on his horse, memorising and thinking of spells that could be needed. He had now proved himself many times to be a quick thinker in these situations.

The Drachen's were building up speed.

The Tarrenash warriors held their swords, and the Goathards posed in a battle stance, ready for the Drachen's to come and welcomed them to fight.

The Disaris fired, giving a volley of fifteen arrows toward the Drachen with most hitting them. The Drachen considered the bow and arrow a cowardly weapon. They took the volley of arrows, and still, they came racing hard.

The battle formations held firm as the Drachen's now met with the crusades, the first flanks connected with swords hitting everywhere with the sound of metal hitting metal ad sparks flying.

The Drachen's were significantly outnumbered, but these enormous warriors had the power of five men and were filled with the hate of thousands.

The swords clashed, and the swords plunged. Two Tarrenash soldiers who were sadly amongst the first to die in the fight collapsed.

A Drachen swung his sword, slashing a Disaris soldier's chest, killing him instantly, and almost every swing was now maiming or killing one of the crusades.

The battle looked terrible for the crusade, and the Princess knew it as she was loading and firing her arrows at point-blank range into black Drachen's Flesh.

The Drachen captain Neldez looked on at the battle, and liking the way the encounter was going, he gave the final order for the remaining Drachen's to charge.

Captain Neldez pointed at the Disaris Princess and said to his men, "I want her head to take back to Ilihorn with me," and then set them to charge.

The Princess looked up from the middle of her defensive circle and fired arrows towards the newly charging Drachen, hitting one in the eye killing him stone dead as he fell from his immense black steed.

A Drachen roared at his fallen comrade and skilfully threw a dagger aiming for the Princess directing the blade for her neck; the knife spun and flew true, silently spinning in the air towards the Princess with lethal accuracy. The Princess was unaware of the peril as she was reloading another arrow into her bow.

Oscar looked around and swung his sword, and with more luck than skill, he diverted the blade. Hearing the sound of metal on metal so close to her face, she thanked Oscar and recognised what had just happened.

Captain Neldez was now well and truly in the fight as all formations turned to complete fighting disorder and chaos with mayhem everywhere.

Blades hit with blades, steel hit with steel, the blood-curdling cries of men being stabbed or wounded filled the air with Drachen roars rumbling as they reverberated across the battlefield. Blood and rain fell in equal measure as the screams and cries filled and haunted the air.

It was clear that the Drachen were making headway and winning the battle; each could fight three or four of the West Tanniv fighters; as blood was spilt in every direction, another two Disaris fell, adding to the losses.

General Yelfir thrust his blade into the neck of a Drachen as he protected the Princess at all costs.

The Princess was now fighting with her swords, and Oscar was swinging his blade too. The lines had now been broken, and the defences were shattered as hope faded and dissolved, and the Drachen captain knew it and could taste victory.

Among the fighting, Oscar tried to blind the beasts with beams of light from his wand, but this only slowed the Drachen for seconds.

Elaith was now off his horse and dug his blade deep into the back of the Drachen next to Captain Neldez.

Elaith looked directly at the Princess and then at Oscar and shouted, "ride-ride now!"

He had created a punching hole in the fight; the Princess reared up on her white horse, grabbing the reigns of Sylva, Oscars horse, as they thrust through the battle riding and galloping up to the crossroad high ground escaping.

A Drachen spotted this and gave chase; they disappeared from view over the ridge. Elaith looked up, feared the worse, and could only look on as he was heavily engaged in combat.

The Princess and Oscar re-appeared; General Halamar Yelfir looked up in a state of confusion and could see Oscar and the Princess looking down at the battle and not moving.

A horn was sounded.

The Tarrenash men fleetingly stopped to hear it was a Tarrenash battle horn; they became more motivated to fight in the rainfall and mud.

They could now see charging from the high ground an entire battalion of Tarrenash guards galloping into the fight with one hundred Tarrenash soldiers sounding horns and shouting. It was a relief battalion from the City.

Captain Neldez could now see the battle was lost, but he refused to stop fighting in the true Drachen style of death or glory.

One by one, the Drachen fell but not before they wounded or maimed a West Tanniv soldier.

The Drachen captain looked up and ordered his small squad to ride south, with four remaining Drachen wounded but in tacked and battle-ready.

One of the Drachen was still in the foothills of Jandar and was stalking the woods, looking for anyone coming through the forests.

Captain Neldez decided to link up with him and regroup and try again once they had recovered.

General Lorsan Yeldrove stood at the top of the ridge, looking down at the blood and the skirmish from the battle that had taken place.

He looked directly at Elaith and the Princess with disappointment at his late arrival; everywhere laid dead Disaris and dead Tarrenash.

There would be time to report this blunder and ascertain what had happened to the crusade, but a regrouping would now need to be implemented.

The Regrouping of the Crusade

Lorsan took time to evaluate the situation; his old friend General Yelfir covered in blood, shook his hand while looking at Lorsan with a look of contentment and relief.

Elaith, ever the soldier, rode to Oscar to see if he was ok.

General Yeldrove looked around, accounting for the dead and the wounded.

"Where is the Marlow Boy," said Lorsan.

"He is with the Priestess Sana Norbella and are somewhere in the foothills or Tarrenash coming down from Jandar," said Princess Gilgamesh.

"We must ride out to them; it was Thomas who sent the Eagle Owl to alert you," said Princess Gilgamesh.

General Yeldrove gave the order for the wounded and the dead to be taken back to Tarrenash.

The new reinforced soldiers and crusaders would follow the Drachen to ensure safe passage for Thomas and Sana, who was now coming down the mountain.

"The Drachen are now seeking revenge; we must stop their murderous rampage," said General Yeldrove.

Lorsan suggested that Princess Gilgamesh went to The City, but Oscar had refused to go to Tarrenash and the Princess stood firm, not wanting to split the crusade.

The remaining Disaris soldiers, the new Tarrenash soldiers, Elaith and General Halamar Yelfir, and The Goathards all agreed to ride back to get Thomas and Sana.

"This crusade will not fail a reign of terror was tumbling on West Tanniv now, and this crusade must reunite and not fail," said the Princess in a speech to all that agreed to ride on.

The crusade was now under the command of General Yeldrove; he gave the order to follow the Drachen and head back south towards Jandar.

They galloped hard on full alert heading back to the forest crossroads. Everyone in the Crusade looked shabby and battered but still galloped firm with a passion for the crusade and hunger for Thomas and Sana, for which they owed so much for getting the message to Lord Yeldrove.

Thomas and Sana were still under cover of the forest. They had done well to go this far undetected, now only a few miles from the woodland crossroad. They both felt confident of linking up with the crusade and ridding into Tarrenash City.

They had seen the Drachen earlier that day, and Sana was an excellent tracker, and she could read the forest.

There were no signs of anyone patrolling this ridge down to the Tarrenash Forest crossroads, so they proceeded with caution.

A lonely scout Drachen had been left to prowl the woodland looking for anyone using the forest to travel through undetected. He had spotted an old forest mountain ridge that had not been used in some time and decided to lay in wait.

Sana and Thomas wandered down this ridgeway and would encounter this loan Drachen at some point.

Sana stopped and removed a bow from her saddle harnesses, flipping a leather flap and revealing the beautifully carved white Disaris bow and a pouch full of arrows.

Thomas watched on and saw her adjust herself and prepare for this style of battle. Her swords still crossed her back, and now she rode with her bow loaded and half-cocked.

Thomas felt confident in Sana after seeing her display of swordsmanship and acrobatics only the night before in the White Fox Inn.

Lord Yeldrove and the crusade were ridding hard tracking and chasing the Drachen down.

They came across the site of Captain Rothlan, and everyone stopped and had a short moment of silence in commemoration for the brave Disaris Captain.

A Disaris soldier jumped off his horse and covered what was remaining of the brave Disaris Captain.

Princess Gilgamesh looked down and said, "We will come back for the Captain later he will get his warriors burial, for now, we must ride."

The Princess grabbed the reins of her horse and galloped on desperately hunting down the Drachen.

The Drachen horses were much faster than West Tanniv horses, but they would still get sluggish and have to slow at some point.

Sana and Thomas were now manoeuvring their way out of the forest and down on the ridge leading to the woodland crossroads.

The prowling Drachen had now spotted them both and commenced stalking them in the late afternoon covered by the rain and the darkness of the grey skies, the sun only randomly appearing between each black cloud for moments at a time.

Captain Neldez and the four remaining Drachen soldiers had almost reached the crossroads.

The Drachen Captain roared up, and the stalking prowling Drachen that was fixed on Sana and Thomas could hear but did not respond.

Sana halted upon hearing the cry from Captain Neldez. She pulled back her bow, turned in the opposite direction, and fired an arrow blindly deep without thinking or looking into the green vastness of the thick forest into nothing.

Thomas looked at the priestess in confusion as the white arrow flew true into the forest, hitting the prowling Drachen deep into his chest.

A thunderous roar let out from the confused and surprised prowling Drachen as he clasped at his chest, wondering what had happened.

Thomas looked into the eyes of Sana in total magnificence and wonderment at what had just happened and what hit witnessed. "How did you know?"

She looked at him and said, "Just ride – ride now!"

The cry from the stricken Drachen alerted Neldez and his small squad, and they rode towards the din.

The Captain of The Drachen and his four soldiers arrived to see the Drachen with an arrow through his chest and was pinned to the tree as the arrow flew straight through him and left him unable to move, dying and immobile pinned to the barky tree.

Captain Neldez got off his mount and said to the dying Drachen, "point" the dying Drachen could barely lift his blood-soaked black arm and pointed in the direction of where Sana and Thomas were travelling.

Neldez looked at his men, then back at the stricken Drachen that lay dying, and he thrust his sword into his neck to finish him off callously. Captain Neldez, with no sorrow, gave the command to give chase.

The four Drachen turned their horses around and galloped through the West Tanniv woodland to pursue them both.

Thomas was looking brave, galloping, and Sana looked remarkable as she thundered through the woodland in her black hooded robe, alert to the dangers around her.

They were ridding frantically, and they could see rocks to the left and then a clearing to the right which led up to the woodland crossroads.

Sana glanced back, and she could see four horsemen following them deep in the wooded scrub. Knowing that they would be exposed and unprotected in the crossroad clearing, she veered off to the left behind the boulders. Her plan was simple to pick them off one by one from a vantage point.

They cantered behind the boulders to a piece of higher ground which looked down onto the clearing she loaded her white Disaris bow. She pulled it back and rested the tense bowstring on her face while looking down the arrow shaft, ready for the fight.

The four Drachen trotted into the clearing cautiously; they looked left and right down the crossroads.

It was only a matter of time before Sana or Thomas's horses would make a sound, or they would be alerted. The rain fell hard, and thunder could be heard in the distance coming from the Tarrenash plains.

They cantered behind the boulders to a piece of higher ground which looked down onto the clearing she loaded her white Disaris bow. Sana pulled it back and rested the tense bowstring on her face while looking down the arrow shaft, ready for the fight.

The four Drachen trotted into the clearing cautiously; they looked left and right down the crossroads.

It was only a matter of time before Sana or Thomas's horses would make a sound, or they would be alerted. The rain fell hard, and thunder could be heard in the distance coming from the Tarrenash plains.

Sana had a Drachen in her sights, aiming for his eye. There was every chance they would ride off, so maybe there was no need to fight. Or there was every chance they would locate them and charge.

Sana did not panic, she remained composed, she focused on the sounds of the forest, the birds and the breeze and the rain, and her concentration was on the Drachen that she had selected to die, which was dead in her sights.

In Sana's mind, she knew she would get off another shot, perhaps bringing down two Drachen before the fight turned into swordsmen combat.

Sana's thoughts were being; calculated, with her eyes dancing and tracing the Drachen as they trotted around in the wet long yellow grass of the clearing.

Thomas put his hand on Sana's leg and whispered, "it's ok, Sana – it will be ok, I believe in you."

Sana looked through the corner of her eye; she smiled and seemed pleased at the gesture as if this small indication had helped her make up her mind on what to do.

She unleashed her arrow, which zipped through the air in silence, hurtling towards its intended target, striking the Drachen in his eyeball, killing him dead instantly.

Captain Neldez looked to his right to see his fallen comrade, and with a fit of rage and anger, he gave out a mighty Drachen roar.

Sana instantly, in one swift motion, loaded her bow again, firing another arrow, this time hitting Captain Neldez in the shoulder, leading to another Drachen roar.

Again the three remaining Drachen looked around as another Arrow hit another Drachen before they identified where the volley of arrows was coming from.

She loaded up one last time, hitting another Drachen in the side. Totalling three arrows fired, all hitting their target, she went for her swords.

Thomas did the same unsheathing his swords and holding his wand.

The Drachen brought the fight to them as they located the rocky Stoney ground and aimed straight for them.

Sana looked around at Thomas and said, "Stay with me." She galloped straight for them, which the Drachen did not expect, and Sana dashed between them, yielding her two swords slashing both Drachen in the mid-drift as she fled.

Thomas galloped around the fight, not really knowing what to do. This helped by adding to the confusion as a Drachen made a decision to follow him.

There were now three very angry, injured Drachen that would stop at nothing.

Sana faced two of them, including the angered Captain Neldez, who roared amongst the sword fight said, "I am going to eat your Disaris body once we are finished as I did in the Leoven Abbey," he said while laughing.

Sana heard these words and instantly stepped up her fighting style. She was now fighting two Drachen simultaneously, and her extraordinary fighting style kept up with the two Drachen with ease.

Thomas disappeared from sight, so she battered down the swords again, and again, and again until she found a gap in the fight to charge in the direction of Thomas.

Thomas was handling the Drachen with a combination of magic and a muddle of sword fighting as he created a protective bubble with one hand, then

The Capital City of Tarrenash.

King Drusunal & Queen Drusunal of Tarrenash

a thrust of his Disaris sabre in another.

Sana again rotated back at the Drachen and prepared to charge at the two pursuing malevolent warriors; she stormed towards the two monsters as they prepared for the charge with their long swords once again.

The three of them charged towards each other faster and faster, all trying to jockey for the initiative.

Sana leapt from her horse, swiping and thrashing her blade, cutting the neck of the Drachen as she landed on the grass in athletic style, watching her kill as he gradually stopped ridding, sliding from his saddle and fell from his horse dead.

Captain Neldez was the next Drachen, and he was readying himself for a charge at the Disaris Priestess who was now on foot.

The Drachen was bleeding from the skirmish with the crusades on the plains and now wounded from the arrow that sat deep in his chest, he looked on, and he welcomed death or glory.

The Drachen breathed heavier, and he adjusted his muscles and garment to make him more conducive to a more typical fighting style; he threw away anything weighing him down.

He coiled himself up for a charge at Sana to either cut her down with his sword or trample her with his horse. He charged and charged hard.

Sana stood strong and stood tall, waiting for the Drachen to approach; he charged harder than he had ever charged before, the swords finally clashed together in an array of sparks and violently sounding clashes of metal, knocking her to the ground.

Thomas, who had got free from the Drachen pursuing him, galloped over to Sana and jumped off his horse Leokan, who ran from the fight. "Run Thomas, run," cried Sana.

"No, I can't just leave you," cried Thomas thinking that it was now all over.

Captain Neldez and the other Drachen circled back around; they now had the upper hand and charged again at Sana, who held her blades above her head. The rain was now coming down on their wet faces, and with beads of water dripping down, she looked death in the eye and welcomed the afterlife.

They galloped from either end of the clearing and got faster and faster. Thomas, who was now next to Sana with his sword and wand, closed his eyes, and as the Drachen swords swung down at them, he shouted out a spell "vis ager" "vis ager," and a giant bubble and protective sphere appeared protecting them, both and knocking the Drachen to the floor.

The Drachen stood up and laughed as they marched towards Sana, and a mighty sword fight ensued with swords clashing and metal sparking; they fought as Sana cut down another Drachen, killing him with her mesmerizing style of combat yielding her two sords.

Thomas charged, but the enormous captain Neldez knocked him several metres striking him with a backward thrust of his sword pommel; his eyes were fixed on eliminating Sana.

Sana charged in again to protect Thomas, which put her in a venerable position. Then the captain lifted his sword to kill the Disaris priestess; as she dropped one of her swords which had become too difficult to yield in such close-quarter fighting, she pulled out a dagger and thrust it deep in his huge muscular thigh, which slowed him only for a few seconds.

The Drachen Captain looked down at them and lifted his sword to bury into her head; she held out her Disaris blade to block this mighty clash of weapons in the hope that the advantage may swing in her favour.

The Drachen smiled and lifted his sword to kill her with a confident swing of his blade, but he stopped and jolted, then jolted again and again and again as black blood dripped out of his mouth and down his fangs. He held his blade and lifted it again and swung it down at Thomas and Sana, and again, a jolt and another jolt stopped him.

He had been hit by nine Disaris and Tarrenash arrows, and as he fell to his knees. Sana and Thomas rolled away in the muddy chalky wet grass as the colossal malevolent Drachen finally fell to his death ending his bloody rampage and the Drachen Warrior's murderous voyage into Tanniv finally came to an end.

Princess Gilgamesh, General Yeldrove, and General Yelfir galloped into the crossroads to assess the situation with the rest of the battered crusade. "Where are the rest of the Drachen?" said Princess Gilgamesh.

"Sana has killed them all," said Thomas, covered in mud, black blood and rain.

The rest of the soldiers and warriors looked around in amazement that Sana Norbella had killed five fully grown Drachen males and were all astonished.

In the second wave of troops to arrive, Oscar jockeyed in with Elaith and some other Tarrenash soldiers, jumped off his horse and ran towards Thomas and Sana.

"Are you ok," said Oscar.

"Yes, I am fine," said Thomas as they both embarrassed each other.

Sana raised her hooded cloak back over her head and collected her bloodied weapons and horse; she then went back to blending into the background with the soldiers.

The Tarrenash and Disaris troops bowed their heads in salute, calling her Norbella the Drachen Slayer as she mounted her steed.

This was not a name that the priestess cared for. She sat on her horse with her cloak and hood up covering her face. She straightened out her black robe with the red rings on it and went back to being silent.

Thomas looked over at the Disaris beauty; he bowed his head and looked directly into her eyes with a look of gratitude and appreciation; as the rain poured down his face dripping from his nose and chin, he had a look of sadness and thankfulness in his eyes as they exchanged a long glance.

The crusade, albeit bruised and battered, was now back-on-track, it was a sad day, and everyone gazed at each other with a sense of sadness and relief.

It took heavy losses with the loss of so many Disaris and Tarrenash soldiers.

Oscar had saved the Princess from a Drachen using his fast-acting magic.

His actions had been noted with princess Gilgamesh exchanging a look of extreme love and affection for the young sorcerer which, would bond them forever.

The newly reformed crusade headed back down the track on the road to the City of Tarrenash, riding out of the foothills and heading for the open grasslands in the thunderous pouring rain.

After an hour's ride, they could see the Tarrenash City. It was immersed in a sea of open grasslands, farms, and wide-open plains, and as it came into view, the boys could see the enormous City with its giant impregnable walls, this booming central hub of trade would leave a lasting impression on them.

Thomas looked across the savannas and could now see the City on the horizon. He cantered over and nudged Oscar beside him to look. The enormous Capital was coming into view with its vast onion dome-shaped towers and castles truants everywhere it looked glorious.

The epic castle's walls looked gigantic; it was a monumental city indeed. It could be seen for miles around in every direction.

The City of Tarrenash is the biggest in West Tanniv, and millions of people live there.

Oscar became excited about a new place that he had read so much about, and it was now becoming a reality.

The central trading hub of West Tanniv was growing ever more prominent as they came closer and closer to the City walls. It was a city in a sea of grass plains as far as the eye could see.

The first thing that struck the boys as they got closer was the colossal walls that looked solid and impenetrable; it was a sight to behold.

The newly reformed crusade slowly cantered through the checkpoint into the main castle walls then into the citadel.

The City of Tarrenash

It was a citadel like no other; it was built into a cliff canyon, the only high ground in the Great Plains. Houses built together over hundreds and hundreds of years, peasant housing, shops, Inns, coach houses, market squares, and rich, affluent areas as well as super-rich neighbourhoods.

Banks and accountants were everywhere, which was all part of the Tarrenash Empires' mighty farm community.

It was said that all money flowed to the City of Tarrenash; well, in fact, eight out of ten coins spent in Tanniv would be administered first in the City of Tarrenash.

The main castle's inner walls were still massive, much like a smaller castle that you would find in England. As they entered through the main gates into the parade square, they could see armies and troops of different coloured forces and soldiers in their military pageant on parade.

Thousands of troops were marching in the main procession square, which was vast.

The Tarrenash had an immense army that was made up of farming communities. But at harvest time, the military would shrink by as much as seventy percent because the soldiers would return home to farm and harvest the fields, which was the Tarrenash way.

An army of stable workers came out to greet the riders, and the garrison masters came out to organise sleeping quarters for the night.

A smartly dressed man tall and handsome with a moustache was standing on the castle steps waiting to greet them. Stood beside him was Princess Katya Drusunal.

The smartly dressed man walked a few steps down the grand marble stairway and introduced himself; "I am the Prime Minister Fadan Perra, and I welcome you to The City of Tarrenash."

Princess Gilgamesh, Thomas, Oscar, Lorsan, Halamar, Sana, and Lulong all dismounted and headed up the grand staircase to greet them.

Princess Katya looked down at the voyagers and said, "My father, King Vanidon Drusunal, and my mother, Queen Magrith Drusunal, are expecting you."

The Drusunal Dynasty; were a fair, kind, and considerate family, and the Drusunals royal bloodline had ruled the vast Kingdom of Tarrenash for over seven hundred years.

The Kingdom stretched into the West, bordering the Forrest of Vakoborg, and the Northern Mountains of Stormhorn, down to the Jandar Mountains in the south, then out to the mighty River Ailmar in the East. It was by far the biggest Kingdom in West Tanniv.

The crusade leaders marched up the grand steps and into the great halls of Tarrenash.

The crusaders walked down the long corridors, and everywhere around them, they could see huge doors for the administration to tax and quantify commodities. Farming, crops, harvests, troops, and other trades were all mathematically accounted for here.

This city was the central administration for the whole of West Tanniv. Some shrewdest minds would work directly in the palace alongside the minsters to run the mighty Empire and its powerful landlords and state leaders.

The Prime Minister and Princess Katya came to the main palace doors, where two Tarrenash Elite sentries protected the doors.

Princess Katya nodded, and the guards opened the doors, leading to the most beautiful gold-gilded room.

The floor was black and white marble-like a chessboard, and at the head of the large long room where twenty ministers, in black cloaks with white wigs, sat in two royal thrones, the King and Queen waited for the crusade to enter and proceedings to begin.

The Crusaders entered and marched close to the raised thrones. Everyone bowed, including Princess Gilgamesh, who did not have to but saw this as a way of showing her gratitude.

The King spoke, "Welcome your Royal Highness Princess Gilgamesh! I welcome you to my Kingdom," said King Vanidon Drusunal in a deep, strong voice while the Queen Magrith Drusunal also nodded, and Princess Katya nodded too with a smile. The King had a short beard and a kind face and wore a simple crown; the Queen sat still and had a gentle nature and wore a small crown.

"And welcome all of you," said King Drusunal looking at Thomas, Oscar, and the rest of the precession.

"Thank you, my lord," said Princess Gilgamesh.

"You have my deepest sympathies for what happened in the Leoven Abbey; we are all still in shock," said the great King.

"I sent a message to your father, King Gilgamesh," said King Drusunal.

"I know my Lord, and he too sends his appreciations," said Princess Gilgamesh.

The King stood up and walked closer to the crusaders and closer to Thomas as he spoke.

"You must be the Marlow boy," said the King looking directly at him.

"Yes, my Lord," said Thomas as he bowed his head.

"I knew your mother very well, and we still hold a seat in our council for a Marlow," said the King as he pointed to a vacant chair behind him; the chair was red velvet with a brass plaque with the words inscribed Marlow.

"And who are you?" said the King while looking at Oscar.

"I am from England, and I am a white sorcerer from Stoney Cross," he said in a hurried voice.

"Oscar is a very brave one too, my Lord he saved Princess Gilgamesh and fought bravely and true in the battle of the Drachen's," said General Yelfir, who wanted to credit Oscar with such Courageousness.

The King looked and nodded, then gave Oscar a long smile as if to recognise his bravery, especially for saving a Princess.

"And what have you all come to ask, my Queen and I today," said the King with a knowing tone.

Princess Gilgamesh spoke, "we are here to Unite West Tanniv under one banner and reform the old alliances."

"My father, the King of Vakoborg, has set forth this crusade to reunite West Tanniv, and this is what we intend to do," said Princess Gilgamesh as she walked around talking proudly as only a royal would do.

"I have come to do everything I can do, to help unite the banner to my lord, I am a Marlow and a stone keeper, and I know it is my job to help unite the forces of West Tanniv," said Thomas.

I am a Marlow and a stone keeper, and I know it is my job to help unite the forces of West Tanniv," said Thomas.

The Great King understood what needed to be done. Tarrenash knew more than most, the pressure Moltenwing was now applying to the Kingdom, and it was directly affecting everyone. Most would suffer from the adverse effects; however, people would still be making huge profits somewhere.

There was talk of illegal trading, and the Tarrenash bankers, accountants, and analysts could see the economic impact of this illegal trading coming from Qulan and flowing directly to Moltenwing.

Reports on violent raids in the far northern territories had slowly made their way back to the King. Accounts that Elec City was now fully controlled by the Aminoff's too was very clear to see.

The King looked back at Thomas and looked away only to return his gaze to the boy as he looked at him with great interest.

"Your mother holds a seat in the Elec trading council and in Qulan City and here in Tarrenash and Jandar," said King Vanidon Drusunal as he looked at Thomas.

Alina Marlow was the only person in Tanniv history, both sides of the Alimar, to hold such titles. This is why Thomas would become so important, and the shrewd King knew it.

"Did you know this, Thomas?" Repeated the King.

"I know most of this, but not everything, My Lord," He said while bowing his head.

"The Marlow seat is in the name of Marlow, meaning you could rightfully take this seat," said the King, who was very knowledgeable of all trading laws.

The Expansive Tarrenash Empire had many towns and villages, and the economics were mainly based on the farming communities. Each village and town had conscripts into the Tarrenash army. This vast Empire and its farming community were a symbol of its tremendous power. They could fight, they could farm, and they could trade.

The young men would work within the farming communities as boys, then at the right age, would serve national service and be conscripted into the Tarrenash army until old age.

The Village life of the Tarrenash farming community was a communal life. They would work the fields and the orchards as a village and bring the product to be bought and sold directly in the City of Tarrenash.

These goods would be sold and distributed all over East Tanniv. This way of life was at the heart of the National Tarrenash identity. "If you scratched a Tarrenash underneath, you would find a farmer."

Moltenwing was now bearing down on the Empire, begging the question of what was going to happen to this way of life and the Tarrenash identity itself. More trade flowed directly to Moltenwing in the East and its free slave labour economics, and who could compete with the lower prices spawned out free labour.

The City ministers would administer the plans for cultivating land; administer a rotational system of the land to prevent overworking, turning each field or plot into arable land or grazing land by rotation.

This was all administered by the parliamentary system in the city.

A great many super-rich, wealthy Lords, and wealthy Barons would own the land and the villages, and many would sit on the trading council in the parliamentary system in Tarrenash City.

Eighty percent of the population would live on the great farming plains of the Empire and belong to the agriculture communities. Everyone could base their routes back to the farming communes of Tarrenash.

A village Elder ran each village with council members, and all commune decisions would need to be agreed upon with the Village Elders in this diplomatic way.

Thomas's mother, Alina, would sit on the trading councils looking after the fair trade for everyone. She would often visit these farming communes and sit with the people of Tarrenash to understand their beliefs and problems, and this is why King Drusunal was interested in Thomas.

The Disaris of Vakoborg signed the agreement to reunite the banners along with the Goathards of South Vakoborg, and the Princess had now come to ask the King of Tarrenash to do the same.

The King stood up with the Queen and spoke, "Vakoborg and Goathard have signed the treaty to reunite West Tanniv so the Tarrenash will do the same," said the King as he gripped his wife's hand.

The great King Vanidon Drusunal and Queen Magrith Drusunal together spoke of this signing as a great day, and the Queen added, "The Day will come when we shall unfurl the great banner of the future. This future is to reunite West Tanniv and fly once again this symbol of peace."

This was of great relief to Thomas; he had long since endured the burden of the collapse of the Gathering of Stormhorn. Although the newly formed crusade would be a long-drawn-out process, three of the great nations of Tanniv had now joined the reunification, and others would now surely follow.

The campaign was now gathering momentum, with three of the nations of West Tanniv signed. Stormhorn had failed, but each nation would sign this time, and the banner would be reunited.

The crusade would now need to stop at the many towns and villages of Tarrenash on a quest to educate the communities on their way to the border Bastions of West Tanniv along the River Alimar.

The powers of self-government with the towns and villages would need to understand and be educated to enhance the crusade further.

King Drusunal signed the treaty with his Prime Minister Fadan Perra, who signed on behalf of the people, and the newly formed reunification had begun.

A great map of Tanniv was laid out on the floorings of the Tarrenash City hall while its ministers and the Crusaders decided on a further plan to move and navigate. This route would end with a signing in Yelcan with the Bastion high command, leading to a second Crusade into Jandar and Qulan City.

King Drusunal spoke to Thomas and Oscar with his daughter Princess Katya and Princess Gilgamesh. They sat at the far end of the hall while the ministers and crusaders discussed the routes.

King Drusunal was a wise King, and he identified early the power of a Marlow returning into Qulan City to sit at his mother's seat.

The people of Qulan City and Jandar regions were peaceful neighbours to the Tarrenash Empire, and they were also diplomatic traders of Tarrenash.

However, the greed and corruption now coming from Qulan made it a very dangerous place. The Long arm of Moltenwing played on the greed of the Turgetts, and the culture of money and trading in the city made it easily corruptible.

Qulan was ministered by a democratic trading system made up of the merchants that ran the city. The Turgetts, Tarrenash, and Disaris that sat on the trading council would decide everything from planning permission to military and naval strategies to simple everyday local issues like sewage and housing.

The main topic of any meeting was trade and money and the more money made, the more satisfied the trading councils would be. Almost every one of the trading council was corrupt. Almost everyone had merchant agreements with Elec City or Port Elleth, and some would even have holiday homes in Port Elleth.

King Drusunal knew all of this corruption.

The Tarrenash banking analysts could see that things were not right, and the uneven disproportionate wealth now coming into Qulan was not coming from

Tarrenash or the overworked Jandar mines.

Prince Alwin was an excellent trader that knew and understood the power of a good bribe. He would often remark that: "Once you paid a bride, you had the person bought – But the value of this bribe was worth far more by extorting the person even further from fear of the truth ever being revealed."

The Prince also held a seat on the trading council in Qulan but had not taken a seat in the Qulan trading council for many years.

The Empress knew that Qulan had fallen, and her son the Prince took this city without blood being shed or troops being deployed.

"So Thomas, you will need to ride into Qulan and take your seat at the next trading council; even if you say nothing, this will send the right message," said King Drusunal.

Many more plans were made as the route for the reunification campaign was decided, but the following signature needed for the reunification would be the Bastion of Yelcan's high command.

King Drusunal, much like the Disaris King, sent his daughter Princess Katya to join them in the crusade. She would play a very different role in the campaign, adding diplomatic strategy by sending two Princesses.

Princess Katya would join the crusade going from town - to town to the farming commune towns convincing the lords and elders that reunification was a peaceful method and would ensure harmony and prosperity. Having the Tarrenash princess would add significant weight to any counterarguments that may play out and add to the importance of the campaign.

The Princess would then break off before the crusade got to The Bastion of Yelcan and head to Qulan City to soften any opposition that may lay in wait.

After visiting Yelcan, The Crusade would then follow the meeting with the Qulan Trading council linking back up with Princess Katya.

By now, the spies in Tarrenash City would have reported that the crusade was again well underway. Qulan would already be receiving information on the campaign and the skirmish of the Drachen crossroads.

The Bastion of Yelcan

General Yeldrove of the Shadow warriors would need to sign the treaty with the Shadow Warrior Command in the border Bastion of Yelcan.

Lorsan was every bit a Shadow Warrior and had proven himself loyal to West Tanniv and Tarrenash hundreds of times. He was known as the hero of Ilihorn during the great chronicled battles, which had lasted many years.

However, his name Yeldrove was a Moltenwing name, and his parents and family were part of the Moltenwing elite and aristocracy. He would never hold the authority to sign such a treaty. It had hampered the loyal General all his life which made his rise to such a prestigious position within the Shadow Warriors a meteoric rise.

The Border Bastion of Yelcan was on the shores of the river Alimar. It was a grand Bastion made from granite rocks brought down from the Stormhorn Mountains many centuries before.

The Yelcan Bastion had stood rooted for hundreds of years. It stood with a central rounded Martello keep with four rounded walls which stood as arches volley points for any oncoming attacks; it was surrounded by a deep moat and had many miles of tunnels.

It was rumoured that each Bastion was linked via an underground network of tunnels, creating a labyrinth of communication and defence unlike anything else in Tanniv. The central hall is where the high command would deliberate, and it had the most amazing views at the top of the Martello, with the sights stretching across the Ailmar River and into East Tanniv

It sat amongst the marshes and fog of the river, and with its small harbour and port, it severed as a shadow warrior garrison that defended West Tanniv.

The Marshes and fog added to the Bastion's defences as it prevented an attack, and armies marching around the sodden marshy grounds had never been successful. It housed a grand Stone circle with huge stones that had been well maintained with a very rare central stone unlike anything else in Tanniv.

It had the most beautiful, well-maintained gardens with a longhouse where the practice of magic was once done in the stone circle hidden in the gardens.

Yelcan was the central Bastion where the high command would distribute its orders to the warriors, soldiers, and the other Bastions.

The Bastions themselves were spread across the whole of the River Ailmar, stretching to the far north of Tanniv down to Jandar, Qulan and beyond extending down to the Hiligor Sea.

They were positioned every few hundred miles, were in drastic need of repair, and were underfunded, lacking Warriors and money.

They had proven difficult to maintain in recent years.

Each Bastion was run by a Bastion commander, who would keep an arcuate and meticulous log of information. This information would vary from each day. Information on how many ships are in the river. Or vessels at sea, how many ships had been in port, the different cargos, and a census of the local area.

Then more common in recent years, a log of raids and illegal trading activities that were now becoming more frequent.

This knowledge was shared with a complex system of communication and postal delivery between each Bastion. All ended up in Yelcan to be processed and assigned in the Shadow Warrior High command.

This information would be shared in a series of weekly and quite often daily high command meetings.

The Bastion security and defence system were financed with taxes coming from The Tarrenash City Banking system; the taxes collected came from everywhere in West Tanniv, including Vakoborg, Goathard, Jandar, Qulan, to name a few. However, the distribution of funds into The Bastion of Yelcan was outdated and not in line with its needs. It was vastly underfunded in all areas, and each Bastion had forty percent fewer Shadow warriors needed for an effective defence system.

The fully practised Shadow Warriors were now only numbering a few. These practices would be centred on the Stone circles and the ability to move between them using localised portals.

The Shadow warrior rank structure was indicated with brass metal pips on the sleeves of the Warrior. A Shadow warrior with five brass pips on each sleeve was a fully practised shadow warrior who could move between stone circles. In recent years due to the underfunding and the lack of expectations to practice and learn such an art, the more common brass pips seen on a Shadow warrior would be three or even four.

Lorsan, despite his vast experience and commitment to the practices of the

Shadow warrior way of life, would only have four pips again due to his Moltenwing family name. He would never be allowed to escalate to the five pips, which would enable him to learn the art of The Stone circles portal abilities, and this was of much disappointment to him.

Lorsan fell in love with the idea of becoming a Shadow Warrior decades before, and as a small boy, he left his aristocratic Elite lifestyle to become a shadow Warrior. Running away from his Moltenwing Palace life at just fourteen, he joined the exclusive guard.

Then over the years, during proven campaigns and recognitions, he had made his way up to General and Lord. Nonetheless, his Moltenwing name had prevented him from becoming a Yelcan High commander or advancing to the practices of portal movement.

The crusade would now leave him once again proving himself to the Yelcan High Command that he could reunite West Tanniv and the difficult times he knew that would come ahead.

The Great Basiton Of Yelcan.

The Signing of the Bastion of Yelcan

As the crusade made its way through the meandering marshes of Yelcan, Thomas could see high in the skies that afternoon the Eagle Owls had been following them. Sana, who was riding close to Thomas, pointed into the skies as they looked up; Sana was equally fascinated by these great owls and captivated by Thomas's affiliation with these majestic creatures.

The Yelcan marshes were foggy and damp, and the problematic land was vast and fed from the river Ailmar. The long, thick, hard-wearing grasses poked out from the marshy waters and could be seen as far as the eye could see.

The Yelcan Bastian was strategically placed on the bend in the twisting Alimar River and had a small harbour, which was extremely important.

On a clear day from the Bastion, the soldiers could see the faint outline of Port Elec and could see down the river in both directions. One of the Bastion's key objectives would be to monitor, count, and record the shipping going up and down the river and trap and constabularies smuggling.

Over recent years the Shadow Warrior border force were not seen as any real threat to smugglers or illegal traders because of the lack of funds and support.

As they trotted across the marshlands, they came to a more solid path, this trail led down to the Bastion, and the Stronghold could now be seen in a dense mist of fog.

The crusade waited outside the great moat waiting for the draw bridge to be lowered.

The draw bridge lowered, and one by one, the crusade entered a small courtyard with a stable garrison waiting to collect the horses.

Lorsan Yeldrove, who arrived days before, had come down personally to walk the crusaders in.

The small coaching courtyard had a colossal oak and metal-studded door at the far end, further adding to its defences. Once the door was opened, the crusade was ushered into a rounded alley footpath were high upon the balconies; the shadow warriors looked down at them from windows.

This was another defensive feature of the Bastian as Oscar imagined a volley of arrows raining down on them.

Once through this part of the Stronghold, very surprisingly, the fortress opened up into beautiful green gardens. The soldiers and warriors maintained the Gardens. The Yelcan gardens were seen as a sense of pride for the Bastion of Yelcan and were extremely beautiful, with vegetables and fruit orchards everywhere.

The boys understood that the Shadow Warriors were self-sufficient with the fish from the river and fruit and vegetables from the garden.

General Yeldrove led the crusade through the gardens and up the stone steps to the castle walls, onto a terrace that looked directly out onto the river Alimar.

"So there it is," said Thomas as he gazed out onto the mighty river.

"Yes, and you can see Port Elec in the far distance," said Oscar.

Suddenly everything that they had been studying had become a reality.

The countless dinners in Stonecross with maps of Tanniv under dinner plates and books about the river everywhere, but the one consistent thing that the maps would always have is the mighty river Alimar, the natural divide from East to West.

The two boys sat on the stone benches on the terraces, looking out at the river in the late afternoon sun.

Oscar felt a sense of achievement seeing the great Bastion of Yelcan and the mighty river Alimar. This would leave a mark on him for the rest of his life.

Thomas sat too also with a sense of success that they had accomplished something this time. Everyone was signing the treaty. He was confident and sure that the Yelcan treaty would now be signed, and Qulan, then Jandar, would be next to follow. With the late afternoon sun on their faces, they sat for a while talking like friends, like friends back in Stoney Cross where a Marlow meant nothing. It was good to feel ordinary again.

Princess Gilgamesh looked over at her friends and could see them for the two boys in Tappington Hall that she once played with. Not two soldiers fighting Drachen and Bauk and being brave for the sake of being brave. She walked over to the two boys to join them.

Oscar looked up at the beautiful young princess "take a seat, Holly er er er, I mean Princess Gilgamesh – please forgive me," Oscar blurted embarrassingly.

The Princess looked down at the two boys with Oscar going red, gave them a stern look, and then burst out laughing. Then Thomas laughed, then Oscar too. "It's ok, my friend, don't worry," she said as she continued to laugh.

General Yeldrove looked over at the laughing filling the sunny afternoon air and smiled at the small part of normality he was observing.

"My Lady, Thomas, Oscar, it's time to go in," he said, looking over at the three of them.

The Princess got up and entered through into the grand Martello with her Disaris General with Sana, then Lorsan, and the two boys with the Goathard Warrior Lulong.

Oscar had been told about the shadow warrior pips indicating rank and who had the ability to use the stone circles as portals and could only spot three of the high command with five pips.

The crusade was offered seats around the opposite end of the long desk. So that everyone could speak and be seen. Sana stood at the back against a wall with her dark priestess robes covering her face.

Princess Gilgamesh spoke first, communicating about the treaty and the reunification and the importance of defence. She mostly talked about what had happened at the Leoven abbey.

They listened without interruption.

The high command Lord Marshal Vaymar spoke first. The Lord Marshal was the highest-ranking commander in the Border force, and the Shadow warrior command and all military decisions would require his signature. He also had five brass pips on each sleeve, indicating that he was a Stone circle portal traveller.

Lord Vaymar was unpredictable people never really knew what he was going to say. He glanced across at the Goathard Warrior and said, "Did Lord Folred Morven send you young man?"

Lulong, the Goathard Warrior, looked up at the Lord Marshal. "And said yes, my Lord the Goathard believe this treaty is of benefit to everyone."

"Yes, well, if the Goathards believe this, then they have a better understanding than most in Tanniv," said the Lord Marshal.

The Goathard warrior looked him in the eyes and nodded with great respect. Lulong felt proud that he was thousands of miles from his home, and he was recognised as was his leader.

The Princess continued to talk as the discussions turned to the great crusade and how most regions had signed the treaty to unify West Tanniv again.

The high command listened and would stop to deliberate and talk between them during the course of the conversations, the Lord Marshal being the spokesperson, would address the crusade.

"We intend to sign the treaty; this is not in question," said the Lord Marshal.

"Our questions are how many troops would all the nations of West Tanniv send to us? And when will the troops will be sent?" said the Lord Marshal.

"Plans are being drawn up regarding recruits coming to you from the Tarrenash plains, my Lord. I can say the Disaris Legions would be sent immediately," said Princess Gilgamesh.

"The Goathards will send our warriors too; just tell me how many are needed," said Lulong.

"I have word from King Drusunal and Princess Drusunal that The Tarrenash Armies would send troops too," said General Lorsan.

"We will draw up what is needed and send this information to the members of this new League of Nations," said the Lord Marshal.

The conversations went on into the night. How many Bastions there are, the troops needed, and the funds required to make the Bastions strong again.

General Yeldrove desired to reopen the Shadow Warrior academy once more and begin recruiting young would-be shadow warriors to work in the Bastions.

Restoring the borders would make the Bastions strong and the borders strong and would give economic strength back to West Tanniv.

Lord Marshall went on to speak about Qulan, and he feared that Moltenwing had now corrupted the cities officials so much that it would be impossible to get the treaties signed.

The Bastions kept arcuate records of the merchant shipping with Elec and Qulan, and the records would show ships arriving from Port Ellet in the southern Hiligor Sea, all linked to trading in Qulan.

These types of lucrative secret trade agreements were not so easy to break.

Elaith Tarron was called to bring the treaty scrolls that now had tens of signatures, and now Field Marshal Vaymar signed on behalf of the Shadow Warriors and the Border Bastion forces.

There were now only three more signatures needed. Jandar and Qulan would need to sign and the mountain region of Stormhorn that made up the Northern kings and Nomad tribes.

The Crusades stayed the night in the Bastion of Yelcan then followed the river for a full day's ride into Qulan City in the morning.

Moltenwing Refutes Claims of Barbarity

The government refuted the claims that Moltenwing had engaged in the atrocities from the Leoven Abbey Massacre.

Rumours began to circulate that it was an order that came from Moltenwing and that East Tanniv guards had robbed and killed the Nuns.

These actions have been put down to the savagery of the Moltenwing Elite Guards, and they had been well primed with instructions from the Empress herself.

These acts were described as warring policies designed to panic and cause unrest through performances of pure barbarity. However, the Moltenwing Regime denied all knowledge of these actions and put the Massacre down to raiders from the north of Tanniv.

A hearing was set up by Moltenwing officials so that the Empress could send this examination back to Tarrenash.

The investigation for the Massacre of the Leoven Abbey was farcical. Moltenwing had commissioned an investigation into the Massacre, and evidence-based on knowledge coming from Vakoborg and Tarrenash was heard, and a vote from the Moltenwing government was given. The vote was simple and unanimous; it was a vote that Moltenwing refutes claims after a long and lengthy inquest. The messages were sent back to the Tarrenash council, then to Vakoborg, and the matter was closed.

Shortly after the enquiry, the Empress summoned her warring council along with her son Prince Alwin to the council halls of Moltenwing.

By now, the stories of the Drachen raids on the crusaders were beginning to surface. So other investigations would now need to be held in a similar style. However, the Empress had grown bored of these explorations and gave these investigations to her son Prince Alwin to organise.

The Drachen had not exactly been subtle. They had galloped through Qulan and the Jandar Mountain towns, cutting down everyone in their path, causing a trail of destruction, devastation, and misery as they rampaged across the mountains and foothills of West Tanniv.

The small Drachen Detachment had been lost, but this was not seen as a defeat by Moltenwing but an essential piece of propaganda to be used at the warring council meeting.

The administration would deny all knowledge of the Drachen, saying that Drachen's were notoriously difficult, and they must have come down from the Ilihorn Mountains to cause trouble.

Messages were also sent to The City of Tarrenash that the Drachen had caused equal amounts of problems in East Tanniv too, citing 'The Whistling Beggar' Coaching Hotel and "the Slaughter of Arana" that had happened only a week before.

Prince Alwin had written to the Prime Minister of Tarrenash PM Fadan Perra, asking him to attend a meeting in Port Elleth. To participate in a discussion and investigation into the Drachen sightings to unlock the three instances; the first was the Massacre of the Leoven Abbey, the second would be The Slaughter of Arana, and the third would be the Drachen Battle of the Tarrenash crossroads.

Prince Alwin also wrote to the Qulan head of state, Turgett Lanlith Jaclar, asking him to attend this meeting.

The Qulan head of state, Lanlith Jaclar, wrote back to Prince Alwin's administration, adding a further mystery asking for another incident to be added to the agenda called the slaughter of the merchant ship Shanan in Port Qulan.

In truth, none of this meant anything. These were political games being played by the Empress, and Prince Alwin intended to test the West Tanniv system to see if any aggression would start or any threats would happen.

Any aggression or threats would fall into Prince Alwin's hands, which would give The Prince further need to manoeuvre Ilihorn Dragoons into intimidating locations. But to do this, the Empress would need to get the vote from her warring council in Moltenwing.

The Empress had called a meeting with her warring council, and within the halls of her magnificent palace, one hundred of her generals, advisors, lords, and noblemen would be amassed.

The people were enticed with a personal invitation from Empress Aminoff herself. The Empress had arranged a grand Ball and Banquet in honour of the warring council, and to ensure everyone would turn up, she made the offer that gifts would be given out to each of her council in recognition of this celebration.

The warring council meetings commenced in the grand palace.

The Empress addressed her council with her normal brand of beauty, grace and etiquettes. She spoke softly about the blame coming from the West and how they were now applying pressure for investigations into East Tanniv matters, and how Moltenwing would take the blame for these things.

She then spoke about the West Tanniv revival, the gathering of Stormhorn, and the newly formed crusade.

The Empress produced evidence of letters coming from Tarrenash and Vakoborg demanding answers into certain incidents that had been happening, blaming Moltenwing and East Tanniv.

The Empress produced evidence of other trading deals coming from Qulan and Port Elec, along with trading agreements that had been happening in Ilihorn, further enhancing that Qulan wanted peace and to trade with Elec more freely, which was the truth.

The Empress Aminoff spoke for hours. It was the longest anyone had seen or heard from the Empress as she spoke of the noises coming from the West, accusations being made, and complaints and claims of kidnapping adding to the serfdom economy.

She spoke of West Tanniv and their ambition to bring down the serfdom economy. This distressed the warring council gravely as these were the super-rich of Tanniv, and they had been made super-rich from the exploitation of free slave labour.

The very thought of serfdom ending would bring the warring council in line, and the Empresses knew it. So she touched on this point many times during her speech. The very idea of bringing down serfdom brought fear into the room with the Lords, Nobleman, and landowners, as many of them were wealthy from the serfdom economics.

The Empress spoke in detail, playing the victim and using the reunification crusade adopting propaganda to bring the warring council onside.

The Empress finished her many hours of speeches with a simple end. "Reunification means that they intend to unite against us."

"We must manoeuvre our troops to display that we will not be invaded, and we intend to stop anyone coming across the Alimar River."

Prince Alwin and Empress Aminoff had done a fantastic job in rebranding the crusade to unite West Tanniv into an act of aggression.

They took incidents like; the Leoven Abbey and the Drachen and used this to appear the victims.

The Empress asked her warring council to sign an agreement to maneuverer troops into critical locations along the river Alimar.

The Empress elegantly and gracefully asked her warring council:

"I am not here to ask you to go to war."

"I am asking you to defend the East Tanniv way of life, to defend the East Tanniv economy, and to defend what the West was trying to take from you."

"They are trying to end our way of life and our serf economy."

"This was not war; this was defence," she shouted to her council, this time looking at every member.

"To commemorate this day."

"The day that we stood up against the enemy that threatened our way of life."

"I give each of you my loyal subjects, more lands, more power, and a small gift of diamonds, emeralds, and rubies with gold in a box marking today's date, so you remember the day we stood up against our oppressors."

The assembly clapped and cheered, and everyone stood up, patting each other on the back and looking so contented.

The contract agreeing the management of troops had started.

The Empress and her son, the Prince, played this amazingly well, and everything fell into place.

The Aminoffs arranged a grand palace ball that night, and everyone in the capital was in great spirits. This ball would be a night to remember.

Most of the nobles and aristocracy on the council are relations or cousins of the Aminoff, so half of the signatures would be easier to obtain.

Champagne ran freely, music played, and the beautiful ladies of Moltenwing had turned up in all of their fineries, with stunning dresses, diamond necklaces, and diamond earrings. Grand golden gilded coaches had poured into the courtyard of the Moltenwing palace.

Magnificent entrances were made by Lords, barons, noblemen and merchants, and their beautifully dressed wives as each aristocratic Lord entered, with each highborn trying to look more magnificent than the other.

The treaty was passed around the table that night, with each Lord basking in the beautiful gifts of diamonds, rubies, emeralds, and golds showing their wives. While servants bought the new certificates of new land ownerships to show each council member how much richer they had become.

They each signed the treaty dismissively as if it was an interruption to the night. The Aminoff Empress was always the most beautiful lady in the room, and she was now the most popular. The treaty was signed, then passed around the room; she stood on the upstairs balcony looking down at the party with her son, the Prince.

They had ordered fine wines and champagne to be poured all night; while the music played loud, they were ushered up to dance with patriotic Moltenwing songs being played. This was a well-orchestrated strategy the Empress looked on as the last of the signatures were signed. She then wandered around the ball, looking beautiful and bowing her head gracefully at her subjects.

The handsome Prince wandered the ballroom halls ever the bachelor as young eligible Moltenwing beauties gazed upon his power and beauty while he majestically walked the halls shaking hands and smiling.

They had all been deceived, and their greed was used against them; within the defence treaty contract was a small clause naming The Empress as the Supreme Commander of all troops in East Tanniv, giving her the full rights to control the armies as she saw fit.

It was a glorious day for Moltenwing and the Empress Aminoff, who was now every bit an Empress.

She wandered sophisticatedly around the party, chatting to everyone. She ensured she spoke and flattered everyone.

She chatted to the ladies of the warring council, the wives, and the young mistresses.

One young lady who was almost as beautiful as the Empress bowed and remarked how beautiful the Empress was in real life and was spoken to for some time by the Empress.

She wanted to use this chance to ensure her popularity was well embedded within the culture and memories of this incredible night.

As the night fell, a magnificent display of fireworks engulfed the whole city.

Guests were invited out to the Palaces Grand Terrace that overlooked the entire city. Fireworks burst into colours everywhere, and more champagne was served.

Staff came out from all entrances wearing red finely gold-gilded uniforms, white gloves, and white wigs, with tricorn hats forming a long train of servants carrying silver treys with what seemed to be hundreds of beautiful blue and red velvet boxes. The staff led out onto the terrace, and once the fireworks ended, they handed out more gifts to the guests. Gold fine pocket watches, with the date, engraved made from the finest Turgett jewellers in Qulan. The ladies were given the brightest glowing diamond earrings mined and made from the fine jewellery merchants of Jandar, all engraved with the date.

The streets of Moltenwing were lined with food stalls and souvenir stalls, all handing out street food with music playing, intended for the working classes and middle classes of Moltenwing to enjoy the celebrations.

The Pubs, Traven's, and Inns of Moltenwing were given free beer and wine for the night's celebrations. Moltenwing for this night would be the finest place to be in Tanniv.

As the night's celebrations came to a close, the sense of being a Moltenwing citizen meant something to protect.

The Empress was now loved more than ever, and the economy in East Tanniv was booming. The Aminoff's had played their hand beautifully, and they now had the whole of East Tanniv eating out of their hands.

The Road to the City Port of Qulan

The road to Qulan City was a simple day's ride following the mighty river Alimar down to the mountain pass which overlooked the City.

The crusade set out at first light. All of the provinces and districts that the crusaders encountered had signed the agreement for the reunification of West Tanniv, and a union was now well underway.

The Lord Marshal of Yelcan sent messages to all the signed regions requesting troops, taxes, and resources to restore the Bastions and re-troop the Strongholds back to capacity.

King Drusunal from Tarrenash had already begun to send troops and resources, and a sense of achievement was once again shrouding the Crusaders as they rode onto Qulan.

Princess Katya was already in Qulan City under the mask and disguise of an inspection visit to the Tarrenash garrison. But she was really in Qulan to aid the signing of the reunification agreement. Princess Katya had prepared for the Tarrenash City Palace to be opened up and receive the crusades once they arrived.

The Princess inspected the Tarrenash Navy, which was only around twenty vessels strong. The fleet was made up of merchant ships, patrol boats, and a soldier carrying ships.

The small Tarrenash naval garrison was in the harbour of Qulan at the far end of the central city port. Everyone in Qulan knew of her coming, so the Tarrenash knew there would be spies everywhere.

The City was busy with the small Turgett people wandering everywhere. Turgetts were very secretive because the main Turgett and Qulan business were fine jewellery making, diamond and gold necklaces, as well as earrings.

They tempered any animosities towards others in Tanniv, and instead of getting angry, they would deal with things in a Turgett way. For example, the Turgetts knew with their small size and stature, they were often the butt of most jokes in Tanniv.

So they tempered this with a non-violent practical approach by exploiting certain loop wholes and contacts. They would levy extra hidden taxes on deals and often looked down on all non-Turgett people.

Qulan had a mix of cultures, and while Tarrenash and Disaris people lived in the city, the official Turgett ministers would treat them unequally in many ways. They would segregate the town so that Disaris and Tarrenash could only live in certain districts.

As long as foreigners submit to Turgett authority, they let people live in the city, especially spending their money in Qulan.

Turgetts made excellent Lawyers and outstanding accountants, and the jewellers and diamond merchants were the best in Tanniv.

To wear a Qulan made pocket watch or to wear a Turgett made piece of jewellery was something that only the elite in Tanniv could wear or afford.

As long as foreigners submit to the Qulan authorities, then schooling, education, or the justice systems could be used, and providing adequate tax collection would be collected, foreigners would be acceptable.

It would result in a healthy Tarrenash and Disaris population in the city. But still, ninety percent of the Qulan citizens would be of Turgett origins.

So too, now see Ilihorn Dragoons in Qulan would fit the Turgett public system providing they were benefiting the community and paying the correct taxes and behaving and especially spending money the Turgett ministers and authorities would have no problems.

Nowhere in Tanniv was this more apparent if you had money and were prepared to spend it, you could become a citizen of Qulan very quickly.

As the crusaders got closer to the Jandar mountain ridge, they began to see Turgetts scurrying past the foothill trails that stretched down to the River Ailmar. The crusade would ride up and over a small well-used trading path up into the smaller hills, then get the most magnificent views of Qulan City as they rode down into the town.

The city was every bit as beautiful as their books described; the huge merchant harbour was full of hundreds of ships.

The ships were busy with goods being loaded and merchandise unloaded while seagulls followed fishing vessels, hoping for scrapes tossed aside, and it was a sight to behold.

The West Tanniv Empire appeared to be collapsing after the Gathering of Stormhorn; here in Qulan was a very different story.

The Turgett houses looked stunning with their small doors and windows;

these towered dwellings all seemed to be as fine-looking as the next.

The system of segregation appeared to be evident from the view down on the city; they could see the larger houses of the Disaris and Tarrenash in the different city quarters.

The crusaders meandered down the trading path into the city, passing Turgett miners either heading down into Qulan or heading back into Jandar.

All looked secretive and suspicious like they had diamonds or gold about their person; they scurried along either on foot or on horses with their heads down, paying no attention to the crusaders as they passed.

Thomas and Oscar came from a small village in England where you would often see people waving or chit-chatting in the street or the occasional toot from a car horn, with shopkeepers and postal workers eager to say good morning or comment about the weather. But here in Qulan City, there was no time for small talk, no time for chit-chat, and it was as if everyone had a secret and no one wanted to talk.

The Crusaders made their way down into the city port. Elaith had spotted the Ilihorn Dragoon uniforms from some distance away, but because of his amazement, that Dragoons were in Qulan to be sure he needed to take a closer look.

The crusade cantered through the narrow streets of Qulan, observing the Dragoons sitting in the mid-afternoon sun eating lunch and drinking in the pubs and restaurants of the port. Very edgy looks were exchanged from both sides, but nothing more than looks to each other as the crusaders passed the gothic part of the old city.

They made their way up the narrow, steep streets to the Tarrenash quarter of the city and into the Drusunal Palace, which nestled into the mountainside overlooking Qulan.

It was a stunning place with massive white colonnades and huge terraces with flowers and hanging baskets everywhere.

The climate in Qulan was very agreeable, and it was protected from the Jandar Mountains from any rains coming from the Tarrenash plains, and the weather was generally good. Although the winters could be harsh on occasions, the city typically experienced mostly sunshine and nice warm weather most of the year.

There was a small garrison of Tarrenash soldiers numbering around fifty stationed in the barrack quarters at the far end of the courtyard.

The Tarrenash Colonel in charge of the troops ran a flawless operation.

The overall reporting in the Palace was seen to always be in order, and they could see around the Palace, the grounds, and gardens that everything was well maintained.

Colonel Tobas Jorona kept the place in order, and the garrison was well-kept, with Princess Katya was well-informed when she arrived.

Colonel Jorona explained that the Ilihorn Dragoons had arrived only the night before. In keeping with correct protocols,' he immediately put the garrison on red alert, doubling the guard's, patrols and security in the Drusunal Palace.

The Colonel had also sent a rider informing King Drusunal and the Prime Minister Fadan Perra that the Ilihorn Dragoons were in Qulan and further reports would follow. The message would take two days to reach Tarrenash city, and the Cornel had done his job.

Princess Katya came out to greet the crusaders as they entered the courtyard of the Palace.

Princess Gilgamesh jumped down from her mount and hurried over to the Princess, saying, "we have just seen a squad of Ilihorn Dragoons in the city."

"Yes, we saw them yesterday; they are causing no harm, and from the reports I have had, they are being very well-behaved," said Princess Katya.

"Do we know how long Ilihorn Dragoons have been coming into Qulan," said General Yeldrove.

"Yes, Colonel Jorona, who is stationed here, has said they arrived yesterday – these are all questions to be brought up in the Trading council assembly tomorrow," repeated Princess Katya.

"Lanlith Jaclar has a lot of explaining to do tomorrow," said Princess Gilgamesh in an angry voice.

Thomas and Oscar were introduced to Colonel Jorona, and the Colonel had been briefed to treat these two with the highest amount of security.

The Colonel had written to The Head of state Lanlith Jaclar asking for a meeting that morning and had no response yet.

The Head of state, Turgett Lanlith Jaclar, the Prime minister of Qulan, held some jurisdiction over Jandar, and he was a strange fellow even by Turgett standards.

The Tarrenash Colonel in charge of the troops ran a flawless operation, and he often spoke with Lanlith Jaclar, but he had kept the news of Illihorn dragoons in Qualan a secret.

The overall reporting was seen to always be in order, and they could see around the Palace, the grounds, and gardens that everything was well maintained. There was a small garrison of Tarrenash soldiers numbering around fifty stationed in the barrack quarters at the far end of the courtyard, which had been assisting with the reporting.

Lanlith Jaclar always had a full security team and bodyguards with him everywhere he went. He was undoubtedly now one of the richest men in Qulan city and boasted the most enormous Palace in the region. While Turgett were naturally skittish and boastful by way of showing off their dwellings, they were also secretive; Lanlith Jaclar looked like he had many secrets, and again even by Turgett's standards; he seemed like he had a lot more to hide than the average Turgett in his position.

The trading council was assembled the next day in the Turgett council hall.

The hall was a vast round white building with hundreds of colossal marbles pillars from the Jandar mountains, and with a dome at the top, it could be seen from everywhere with its cathedral-like status, especially from out at sea.

It was positioned in the very north of the city, at the towns highest point. It was only reachable by foot, and hundreds of steps would lead up to the trading council hall.

It was rumoured that certain Turgetts of significance had secret tunnel passageways leading into the trading council from their mansions and palaces, but everyone would need to walk for now.

Thomas woke that morning with the smell of the fresh sea air and the warmth of the sun coming through his window. Oscar was already awake in the corner of the room, readying his uniform.

Thomas often thought that all eyes were on him because of his Marlow status and was now glad that Oscar was building his reputation as a white sorcerer and now hero. He had been awarded the highest medal one can get for saving the princess on more than one occasion that day at the battle of the Drachen crossroads and was given the "Hero of the Federation medal" for bravery in action, and no higher award could be given.

"I can't believe we are here in Qulan," said Oscar.

"I know after everything we have been through in the past," said Thomas. He looked out of his window onto the port at the many hundreds of ships in the harbour with numerous ships anchored outside the walls waiting to get in.

He looked out at the Hiligor Sea and could see the importance of this trading

The Turgett City Port of Qualan

port for Tanniv and the importance of the reunification signature.

The boys put their boots on and headed down to the palace dining hall for breakfast. The dining hall was long, with the windows open with everyone enjoying the warm summer breeze and fresh fruit and pasty breakfast.

Princess Katya sat at the head of the table with Princess Gilgamesh sat beside her. General Lorsan and General Yelfir were sat discussing Qulan politics with the garrison commander Colonel Jorona.

Oscar looked out into the courtyard expecting to see the hustle and bustle of horses and stable staff, and he especially looked for his horse Sylva. But the square was quiet, and no such hustle could be seen.

"Good morning Thomas and Good morning Oscar," said Princess Katya, the first to see them as the two boys walked in.

"Are you ready for today?" she added with a smile.

"Yes, your highness," said Thomas while Oscar nodded enthusiastically.

Princess Gilgamesh smiled at the two boys while they took their seats at the table, and good mornings were exchanged.

Lorsan spoke about his plans to reorganise and restart the Shadow warrior academy again, which had long since been his dream to resume the academy. The conversations were mainly aimed at Princess Katya as her father would need to consent.

The conversation changed, and Lorsan looked at the two boys. "I hope you have your best walking boots on today, boys," he said with a smile.

The two boys looked shocked and looked confused.

"There will be no need for horses today; there are hundreds of steps to walk up in order to get to the trading council," said the Colonel while smiling.

Breakfast was eaten, and plans were discussed, and immediately after breakfast, they would take the long walk up to the trading council.

The Colonel had arranged for ten guardsmen to escort them up to the council chamber that morning, and the Priestess Sana would insist on joining too in order to add protection to Princess Gilgamesh and Thomas.

The walkout of the Palace took them down a short hill, then a diagonal walk up some steps through a narrow alleyway between two houses, which then opened out onto the grand steps leading up to the council hall. The marble steps were at least eight metres wide, with hundreds of steps walking up to the hall.

All around them were Turgetts and wealthy Tarrenash merchants, all with ceremonial robes making their way up the steps to the trading assembly.

Thomas looked up at the steps in complete wonder and glanced back down at the cities trading port. They could see the whole of Qulan from the top with the turquoise blue of the sub-tropical Hiligor Sea and palm trees everywhere; it was a beautiful sight to see. They walked up the steps and into the great vaulted hall, which was round and circular like a stadium.

All around them were wooden benches going around the whole hall with gold plaques on the seats indicating whose seat it was.

Princess Katya pointed to The Marlow seat, which was high up nearer the larger chairs; these chairs indicated that these were more official or held a more significant meaning. The hall was almost full, and Thomas made his way up to the Marlow seat.

Oscar was instructed to wait with the Terrenash guards and watched from the public gallery.

Princess Gilgamesh and Princess Katya took up their royal seats which, were spread in different directions in the hall.

As Thomas walked up the stairs, many of the Turgetts looked at him and whispered as he walked past, observing him for where he was going to sit.

Sana had followed Thomas and decided to stay on the back wall behind his chair. He looked around and found his seat with the gold plaque reading Marlow. He took his seat and looked at the Turgett council around him and felt very scared and intimidated.

The view down into the hall was fantastic by this time; the hall was filling up, and what seemed to be hundreds of Turgetts now created an echoing din from the many whispered conversations.

He looked around and could see doors to the left and the right.

The doors opened behind him, and high-ranking Turgett officials poured out to take their seats, all looking at Thomas with great confusion.

He looked a few rows to his left and could see Princess Gilgamesh in the Disaris section, then a few rows down Princess Katya.

The head of state, Lanlith Jaclar, had not yet come from his chamber door. Thomas looked around the halls; it was now almost full, with a few seats waiting to be filled.

A tremendous knocking thumbing sound came from the gallows where two Turgetts were thumping two ancient oak timbers together suspended on ropes to create an echoing noise that ran through the whole hall, signifying that the gallery should now fall silent. The doors were locked, meaning that no latecomers could attend.

The Qulan head of state, Lanlith Jaclar.

A master of ceremony spoke, "The head of state Lanlith Jaclar will now be entering," said a deep official voice coming from a very old Turgett dressed in dark blue robes and a floppy hat.

The hall then fell silent, and in walked Lanlith Jaclar.

He was robust-looking, with a short beard. He wore blue robes and wore a monocle eyepiece. Immediately upon entering, he looked directly at Thomas in the Marlow seat with great interest and looked over at the dark hooded Disaris standing behind him against the wall.

He looked over at Thomas again and looked out at the great hall, took a deep breath to address the whole gallery, and as he exhaled to talk, he stopped. He looked over at Thomas again, all in a fluster.

"Who are you, young sir?" he said, peering over at Thomas. The whole hall gasped and murmured.

"My name is Thomas Marlow, and my mother is Alina Marlow, who created this trading assembly, and I am here to take up her work once again," shouted Thomas in a clear and strong voice.

The Turgett was taken back; he was once again in a flutter.

"Why was I not told about this?" He said to his chamber peers beside him in an annoyed voice.

"I only arrived yesterday, and I believe Colonel Jorona from the Tarrenash Palace here in Qulan wrote to you," Thomas said with a strong voice so that all of the galleries could hear.

Princess Katya looked over at him with a smile and a nod as the boy was holding his own in front of the Turgett council.

General Lorsan looked up at Thomas with a proud smile, and Oscar Almost giggled, while Princess Gilgamesh looked at him and smirked.

Thomas gripped his wand under his cloak and, in his mind, called Tupel or Sathgang or one of the Great Eagle Owls until a feeling of absolute delight hit him inside, and a great eagle owl appeared as Thomas stood up to address the crowd. The owl flew in from the belfry windows high up in the dome roof, and it was Sathgang; he flew in the hall to the crowd's amazement.

No one knew how the owl would come to Thomas, and this would be a secret that only Thomas knew.

Sana was standing behind Thomas, but he felt the need to look back into her blue eyes; peering over his shoulder, they locked eyes, and a moment of supremacy was exchanged between them, giving Thomas the strength to carry on.

The Great Owl circled the hall and landed on the back of Thomas's chair, towering about him as he took his seat. The Turgett in the crowd all knew the stories of Alina Marlow creating the trading council, and now they could see this great Oman happening before them.

Lanlith Jaclar was lost for words, as was the rest of the hall.

Thomas stood up and addressed the trading council. He turned and stroked Sathgang, who perched on the back of his chair.

"My name is Thomas Marlow. I have been on a great campaign with Princess Katya Drusunal and Princess Holy Gilgamesh, along with Lulong of the Vakoborg Goathard People."

"I am here to ask you to sign a treaty that would reunify West Tanniv under the Great Eagle Owl banner once again."

The crowds muttered and murmured after his speech and as the din thickened. The Head of State, Lanlith Jaclar, spoke to the great hall. He spoke about the prosperous times and the peace and wealth they were already experiencing.

The Qulan and Jandar Turgett only cared for prosperity and had signed a treaty to limit their contact with Ilihorn and Moltenwing directly after the Ilihorn war. But most Turgetts felt that this agreement was outdated and was never really agreed upon in Jandar, and Qulan and this created many counterarguments for this treaty to be annulled.

To advance Qulan trade, the Turgetts had established and developed direct links with merchants and financiers in East Tanniv and have found consoles in the major trading cities in Port Elec and Moltenwing. In recent years the Tugetts had taken a direct hand in Moltenwing politics and had made no secrets in promoting their prosperous interest.

Princess Katya stood up to address the hall and looked directly at The Head of State Lanlith Jaclar.

"The Port and harbour of Qulan is a West Tanniv port."

"The Turgetts have been entrusted to manage this port and are custodians of the port for the Benefit of everyone in West Tanniv," she said, shouting at the hall.

"The port is not yours for prosperous personal gain. The decisions on this port are for West Tanniv to decide not for the wealthy of Qulan to decide based on illegal trade agreements," the Tarrenash Princess said, sounding every bit like her father, the King.

The Turgett halls filled again with mumbles, but this time with angry murmurs coming for the colonnades.

Everyone in this hall was now so corrupt and was now so entrenched into the East Tanniv economy. Princess Katya could feel that this was a lost cause.

Princess Gilgamesh stood. "Thomas Marlow stands in the halls today wanting to reunite West Tanniv not for war but for defence."

"Why would this hall not want to have extra protection and extra defences and extra insurances for peace?"

"I rode through Qulan harbour yesterday, and I could not believe my eyes when I saw Ilihorn Dragoons walking freely in the City," said the Princess demanding an answer.

"They have been no trouble, and they have spent money and have been well-behaved," said a member of the Qulan trading council.

"Qulan has begun to issue passports to East Tanniv, and wealthy financiers are coming from Port Elleth and Moltenwing to invest," said another Turgett Merchant.

Princess Katya Drusunal stood up again in a fury, "Because you are using the protective powers of Tarrenash and Vakoborg to negotiate such deals that are out of the taxation and jurisdiction of West Tanniv."

"You have been developing Hiligor Sea commerce under the protection of the authorities in West Tanniv to prosper," she said again in a loud, angry voice, looking and aiming this at the whole court.

The Turgetts could not fight a war, nor could they crew ships; they were using the benefits of the West Tanniv typography flying ships flags under Tarrenash banners to ward off any harm from other boats.

As the hours passed, it came to light that a very clever Turgett official had fashioned a secret agreement called the "league of friends," The League of friends had been established between Port Elec and Qulan, creating trade. The Port Elec trade agreement would create the loophole needed to trade directly with The City Port of Elec under the league of friend's contract created by knowledgeable Turgett lawyers.

The trade agreement was simple if their cargo was stopped, it was Port Elleth cargo bound for Elec. Then if Elec Cargo was coming into Qulan and checked, it was coming from Port Elleth under the league of friend's agreement, thus creating the loophole.

Princess Katya could talk all day, and Princess Gilgamesh could speak of the Leoven Abbey Massacre, but the league of friend's agreement was so riddled with Moltenwing corruption it could not be stopped or unwritten without solid political arguments.

The Lord Marshal Vaymar of the Bastion of Yelcan appeared to be correct.

To get the Qulan's signature would be impossible now.

Thomas stood up to address the court in one last attempt "I have read my mother's work on creating this council today, and I have had the information passed down to me."

"without the Marlow agreement to create a trading network with the Turgett's, the people of this city would still be trading their wares in the markets today," said Thomas looking at some of the more wealthy Turgett merchants.

"It was a Marlow that saw the exploitation happening and the unfair treatment happening to the Turgetts, and a Marlow helped, we are asking for a new defence agreement not to go to war a defence agreement," said Thomas in a strong pleading voice.

The Turgett Lanlith stood up.

"We are in a time of peace. We are in a time of prosperity; yes, it was a Marlow that created this fair trading council, and this is why you are still here today," he said, looking at Thomas.

"But we have grown, and we have evolved, and I see no reason to sign this treaty today," said Lanlith Jaclar.

Oscar looked up at Thomas with thoughts that he had done his best. Everyone had done their best.

In truth, the league of friend's agreement had placed Qulan under the joint sovereignty of Ilihorn and Port Elleth, which meant that Ilihorn Dragoons could roam freely in Qulan.

The meeting came to a close with no real headway gained on either side.

Princess Katya walked up to the Turgett Lanlith Jaclar. She said, "You do realise you have created a state where Dragoons and Moltenwing Imperial Guard can come freely in direct contact with Tarrenash Soldiers, Disaris Legions, and Shadow warriors."

"I hope you have an army strong enough to deal with the mess you have created here," said the Princess with gritted teeth.

"League of friends! You have no friends now!" said the Princess as she turned her back.

Lanlith Jaclar, with his bodyguards around him, hung his head in shame then hurried back into his chamber.

Thomas stood up and looked at the Great Eagle Owl Sathgang stroked him and said, "Thank you for coming, my friend."

Princess Katya walked over to Thomas. "You did well; the problems here run deeper than just defence."

"Strings are being pulled here from Ilihorn," said Princess Gilgamesh.

"Keep Sathgang around. I need to send messages to King Drusunal," said Princess Katya.

The hall was emptying at a rapid pace.

The crusaders left and walked back to the Tarrenash Palace for a meeting with the Colonel.

Princess Katya and Princess Gilgamesh sat with General Yelfir, General Yeldrove, Colonel Jorona, and Captain Norlen. Instructions and orders were given. One hundred Disaris troops and one Hundred Tarrenash troops would need to be deployed and sent to Qulan.

The Tarrenash Barracks would now need to be on red alert, ready to receive more troops.

The Tarrenash Garrison Castle of Cloven town would need to hold an additional five hundred troops on amber alert, ready to come to the aid of the Qulan Garrison if required.

Thomas summoned Sathgang and Tupel, the two Eagle owls, to deliver the messages to King Drusunal and King Gilgamesh.

The reunification has been signed by everyone apart from Qulan. Jandar would be the next stop. Most of the officials in Jandar were at the trading council meeting, and there was little or no chance of this being signed, but they needed to try. The Jandar Turgetts and Tarrenash had a different relationship than the Turgetts of Qulan. During the Battles of Ilihorn, the Dragoons carried out reprisals against the Turgetts, and the Tarrenash came to the aid of Jandar. Princess Katya was hoping that this would be remembered.

As news spread of Qulan's refusal to sign the reunification treaty, a sense that things would never be the same again clouded the city and the population that lived there.

The Qulan head of state, Lanlith Jaclar, returned to his chamber, and a further surprise would come apparent.

Prince Alwin Aminoff was sat at Lanlith Jaclar's desk with his feet up, gazing out the chamber window.

"You did well to keep the league of friend's treaty," said Prince Alwin Aminoff. Suddenly it had become clear why Ilihorn Dragoons were in The City Port of Qulan.

"It was not easy," said Lanlith Jaclar while puffing and panting.

"You did the right thing; there will be prosperous times for everyone," said the handsome Prince as he stood up to cower over the Turgett.

"Now tell me what you know about this Marlow boy," said the Prince as he wandered around the Turgett chamber.

Changing of the Winds

The following day the crusade was still in resident at the Qulan diplomatic palace; a meeting and plans were being discussed for the next move in reunification.

To hear that Qulan had now broken away from West Tanniv was a considerable blow. However, four of the most powerful nations had now signed the reunification agreement, so all was not lost.

Thomas spoke of the power of the Marlow seat and how he could feel that some members of the trading council were ready to vote in favour of a new reunification agreement. He thought that there was still hope and that the Turgett Lanlith Jaclar could be persuaded.

The Turgetts were superstitious, and while they were not openly religious, they did believe in omen, and seeing was believing. That day in the great hall, they did see the Tanniv great Eagle Owl fly down to the founder of the city councils son, and seeing the owl with a Marlow perched upon his seat as he spoke did create a stir, and the news of this omen was spreading throughout Jandar and Qulan fast.

The annual City Port of Elec regatta week was coming up; this was a congress week much like Moltenwing's annual assembly but would involve a regatta and a flotilla of vessels all on display. This was a time for The Royal Aminoff's so they could see their naval power and superiority.

The neighbouring warlords in the north would traditionally come down for wrestling matches in the town's wrestling arenas. Gambling would occur; political discussions would take place among the many sporting venues, grand dancing balls, and parties.

The City port of Elec had a trading council much like Qulan, and it was a chance for Turgett merchants and East Tanniv traders from Moltenwing to get together for this event each year.

Now that Qulan had broken off diplomatic relations with Tarrenash, many merchants would travel to Elec as it would be a chance to make money.

General Yeldrove and General Yelfir had devised a dangerous mission in response to the league of friend's agreement, and the heads of the crusades sat and listened to the plan as it was divulged.

The Marlow name under Alina Marlow still held a seat in the Elec trading council. Because Alina Marlow created this trading council again and in part by Alwin Aminoff, a small team would sail across the river Ailmar and into The City Port of Elec for Thomas to lay claim to this seat.

It had been decided that Sana Norbella, Thomas Marlow, Princess Gilgamesh, and Captain Norlen with Elaith. They would sail to Port Elec to take up the Marlow seat in the Elec chamber during the celebrations of the annual regatta.

Oscar listened to the meeting discussions and looked extremely disappointed not to hear his name mentioned. A look of sadness came over Oscar's face as he locked eyes with his best friend Thomas then looked over at Princess Gilgamesh.

Lorsan looked over at Oscar and patted him on the knee.

"We have something to do between us," he said, looking at Oscar. Detecting that he was disappointed, Lorsan stood up and asked Oscar to stand too.

"I will be travelling back to the Bastion of Yelcan."

"I will be setting up the New Shadow Warrior Academy, and I will be doing this with Oscar Williams, the White sorcerer, and hero of the Drachen Crossroads."

Lorsan looked down at him, then held out his hand and said, "Will you do this with me, my young friend?"

He looked at Thomas with a teary look and smiled at this opportunity; Thomas smiled back.

He knew that Oscar was the stronger of the two in the art of magic, and they somehow knew that this was a fantastic thing to do.

"I will do it," said Oscar.

He smiled at the opportunity of becoming a shadow warrior and also had experience in Stone circle portal travel. Lorsan shook his hand as everyone smiled and clapped.

The annual congress would provide the perfect cover for a boat to sail across to Elec City under cover of nightfall and the mask of the flotilla happening that week. Hundreds and hundreds of boats in and around the harbour that week would make the perfect cover for the mission. The Port would be impossible to manage the security that week, so the new mission would be the perfect opportunity to slip into the City.

The mission was extremely dangerous to attempt, but there were still many friends of Tarrenash who lived in Elec that would help.

The Disaris General Yelfir was not happy about Princess Gilgamesh going, but he knew she would be in good hands with Sana Norbella the Drachen slayer, and he also knew he would not be able to stop her.

The Shadow Warriors had a network of spies in East Tanniv, and from the information being gathered in the Bastions, they were now reporting large-scale troops manoeuvring around critical locations along the river and the coastlines of the Hiligor Sea.

The Elec Regatta would be a chance for the Prince to show off his Navy that he had built over many years to his mother. The Empress would be shown the magnificent ships that now made up the East Tanniv Navy.

The ships would sail backwards and forward from key locations close to Elec. Grand aristocratic balls and terraces party receptions would be taking place that week, showing off the fleet to the high society of Moltenwing and Elec.

It would be an advantageous time for discussions on any battle plans or manoeuvres with the Generals.

Princess Katya was now reinforcing her troops in the Qulan garrison and would ride into Jandar to speak to the Turgett Elders in the small town of Erlen, deep in the heart of the Mountains.

Jandar did not have a main town or City; most Turgett inhabitants lived underground in the mountain mines. A trading network of towns and villages would run through the mountain range down to Qulan City.

The Jandar elders held a commission in Erlen Town, and all Jandar decisions and information would be administered in the small town.

This commission that Princess Katya and the crusade would need to meet with for discussions regarding the reunification of Jandar.

So she dispatched two riders to arrange the meeting so that things would go smoothly. Many of the Jandar Turgetts and merchants would have been at the trading council meeting and would have heard the discussions.

Especially that Qulan had broken away from the laws of West Tanniv under the newly revealed league of friend's agreement.

However, Princess Katya would ride into Erlen Town with the crusaders the following day, which still had the two Goathard warriors as representatives of South Vakoborg, the Disaris General Yelfir, and the Tarrenash and Disaris troops.

The Manoeuvring of the Troops

The armies of East Tanniv had been manoeuvring into crucial positions along the river Alimar for many weeks now.

The Lords of Moltenwing were increasingly united in the prosperous economy, and state officials shared such ideas of a new Empire.

Moltenwing nationalism was at an all-time high, and the love of the Empress was being spread across East Tanniv far and wide, with statues and memorials for the Empress springing up in every village, town, and city.

The new defence agreement in East Tanniv was now well underway. The Empress was now manoeuvring troops freely, and she had full consent from her generals.

It was late summer, and five thousand soldiers had been deployed to the City Port of Elec. Many thousands more had been positioned in strategical places along the river Alimar.

The Ilihorn Dragoons under the command of Prince Alwin was now stretched from Port Elleth along a new five hundred-mile defensive front.

The Moltenwing guard under the command of Marshal Rhorn Fadan controlled all the forces south of Elec City, linking up with the Ilihorn Dragoons further south.

Port Elleth was the summer destination for the Moltenwing super-rich. The Port now had five thousand combatants stationed in and around the area. Many of these soldiers were serf conscripts, which the Empress did not fully trust, so an equal measure of Ilihorn Dragoons and Moltenwing Elite guard would be sent alongside the conscripts.

The armies were sent back from skirmishes with the warring tribes in the far-far east of Tanniv, and around forty thousand soldiers were now stationed along the river.

Marshal Rhorn Fadan was now in-charge along with the newly called Alimar front. The Marshal was tall with no hair; he had long sideburns linked to a big curly moustache and a military man. He was a huge fat man who wore the most magnificent military commanders' uniforms with fifty medals. He had severed in almost every campaign, and conflict Moltenwing had ever fought in.

He loved his soldiers and troops and often spent his time in his grand Moltenwing house around an enormous table with lead soldiers and figurines with his generals playing at war and military manoeuvring.

He was now in his sixties, and he was excited at the chance of building a new front and commanding troops again in a field of battle.

The Empress Anastasia Aminoff and Prince Alwin had decided to make the Qulan agreement official and send a government leader into Qulan to create a legislative body and a Moltenwing Embassy in Qulan City to make everything official.

The Empress had a sister called Baroness Asmira Darbella, and she had a single son too, Prince Alwin's cousin. The Empress often talked with her sister and her son Archduke Merith Aminoff who lived in the shadow of Prince Alwin's achievements and was considered a joke compared to the mighty prince Alwin.

The Archduke was a politician, a nobleman, a wealthy landowner, and a commanding general. He held many of these titles due to the persistence of his mother pleading and begging her sister Empress Anastasia Aminoff on his behalf to give him such tittles and grant him such riches.

Even his name Aminoff was chosen to make him even more important due to the Archduke's weak nature. So Asmira once again begged her sister, the Empress, to let him take the name Aminoff.

He was a short and skinny pale man who had a funny walk and was always looking down at his feet and wore magnificent uniforms with medals and epilates to make himself appear significant.

He always blamed others for his lack of achievements and always held a grudge against someone in court. But what he wanted more than anything else was to achieve something or to be remembered for something.

The Empress often made fun of her nephew openly as he always appeared to be in a mess or sick or carrying a hanky sneezing.

She would then look back at her magnificent handsome son Prince Alwin and smile, much to her younger sister's Baroness Darbella's jealousy.

The Baroness heard the news that a new Moltenwing Embassy was to be opened up Qulan. A state official would need to sail across the Hiligor Sea to agree on the league of friends' agreement, then sign an Embassy contract to create a new delegation. A state official would be needed for the grand opening of the new Moltenwing Embassy palace in Qulan.

Prince Alwin had unofficially been there many weeks before and had already established the new Embassy palace and the Embassy agreement. This was very much a signing and ceremonial mission to smile, put ink to paper, cut a ribbon, and return home. The most difficult decision would be which furniture to choose to have in the Embassy palace.

The Empress did not want to attend a Qulan City Embassy opening and nor did Prince Alwin. Both were preparing for the more important Elec Grand Regatta.

It was agreed to send the Archduke the Empress's Nephew. The Archduke carrying the family name Aminoff would have its uses, and sending Merith Aminoff to do this simple job would be fine and would send the correct message.

Several days later, the Archduke was in Port Elleth preparing his ship for the mission to open the Embassy in Qulan.

He began the day in Port Elleth in his grand home accompanied by his mother, the Baroness. She sat and spoke to her son over breakfast that morning, advising him on what to say, do, and even what to wear.

The Archduke sat back in his chair, going over the contract and making amendments to the league of friend's agreement.

"What are you doing, my handsome son?" Asked the Baroness.

"I have been reading the league of friend's agreement and the Embassy agreement, and I am going to get East Tanniv a better deal and make a name for myself, Mother!" Archduke Aminoff said in a high-pitched voice.

"This time, everyone will see that I can also be a strong person for Moltenwing," said the Duke in a childlike manner.

"Yes, that is a good idea, my son; go and make a name for yourself so that you will be known for getting a better deal than your cousin the prince. This is your time to shine," said his mother, the Baroness.

"I have also decided to go with three thousand troops and not just one thousand to really show I mean business," said the Archduke.

The Archduke collected his magnificent parade uniforms with his many medals, gold epilates, and highly decorated brassards; he got into his coach, kissing his mother goodbye that morning.

He made his way down to the port to inspect his three thousand troops and the four ships that would set sail for Qulan that day, and with his newly amended league of friend's agreement, he would go and negotiate a better deal for himself, and for East Tanniv.

The troops looked glorious in their parade dress, all in dark blue with their white parade webbing and shiny boots; they stood on the dockside being inspected by the Archduke and his Captains. It was a bright sunny morning, and the weather was fair with a breeze coming from inland.

The Archduke looked out at sea with his seafaring captains as they made sail for Qulan City, commenting, "That this was the perfect day for sailing as they had the wind on their side." The ships set sail and would be in Qulan by mid-morning the next day.

Return to the Bastion of Yelcan

Thomas and the newly appointed partisans on the secret mission to the Port Elec galloped back to the Bastion of Yelcan.

Thomas, Sana, Princess Gilgamesh, Captain Norlen, and Elaith would be assigned to this mission to sail across the River Ailmar to Port Elec to take up the Marlow seat in the Elec chamber during the celebrations of the annual congress and regatta.

Oscar and General Yeldrove also rode to Yelcan with the chosen riders to begin their mission of restoring the Shadow Warrior academy, which had long been a dream of the General.

Lorsan could not return to East Tanniv with the mission through fear of being recognised, and now that things were heating up in East Tanniv, he could not go through the fear of endangering the operation.

General Lorsan would be better served to prepare for the troops arriving from Tarrenash and the City of Vakoborg.

As they rode back into The Bastion of Yelcan, the high command had been waiting for them. The Yelcan high command was sorry to hear about their failed attempt in the ratification of Qulan.

The High command was told of the new mission and for Thomas to take back the Marlow seat in Elec. The High command listened and arranged to lend a ship to help them cross the river.

Later that night, Thomas stood high up in the ramparts looking out at the river as the red sunset on the mighty Alimar. Oscar could see him, and after his meeting, he walked over to talk to his friend.

"I can't believe we are both going in different directions," Oscar said to Thomas as they both stood side by side.

"I know it seems so strange that we are now going to be apart in Tanniv."

"It's ok, Oscar. I will be back in a day or two, and now you have Shadow warrior training, I am jealous," said Thomas. Oscar smiled and gazed out at the river.

"Are you happy to become a shadow warrior?" said Thomas making sure his friend was ok.

"Yes, of course, it's the most amazing thing in the world, Thomas – I just never thought we would be apart," said Oscar.

"I will be back in two days or three, I am sure of it, so don't worry," said Thomas as the two boys stood chatting on the Bastion ramparts watching the sunset over Tanniv with a sense of the unknown.

Princess Gilgamesh saw the two boys and wandered over. "Hello boys, how are you both."

"We are fine, Princess; this will be the first time Oscar and I will be apart," said Thomas.

"I know, we will win out, and be victorious there is no doubt about this," said the Princess.

The three warriors and friends stood on the ramparts together for one last time before they set off; they each pondered what was going to happen next on this journey. It had taken so many twists and turns already, and nothing was ever clear, and things very rarely went to plan.

They had been largely successful with the reunification. So they concentrated on positive things, and they watched the sun go down before bed that night.

The Mission to the City Port of Elec

The following day, the Bastion soldiers prepared a small sailing boat for the voyage over to Port Elec.

The port was further up the river Alimar and would take a whole day to sail there, and they would enter the port waters around nightfall.

They would then wait for the cover of darkness, anchor, sleep the night in the harbour, and disembark as the port got busier for the day.

Oscar woke early and had walked down to the quayside to say farewell to Thomas, Princess Gilgamesh and the rest of the small squad.

He was now dressed in full black shadow Warrior uniform with an emblem of the stone circle and the Owls of Tanniv on his chest.

He looked like a magnificent young warrior' and had a single brass pip on each sleeve. Looking at Oscar dressed like this made Thomas happy as he could see that he was pleased too.

Thomas and the other participants of this mission all wore regular clothes, and Sana had opted for ladies working clothes, leather trousers, boots, and hair down to cover her face.

Princess Gilgamesh opted for a similar dress style with her hair down to cover her face a little in case she was recognised.

Elaith and Captain Norlen wore regular peasant clothing, but everyone wore a hooded cloak to hide their weapons. They looked like ordinary working-class people so, they could walk through the busy streets undetected.

General Yeldrove walked down to the docks to wave them goodbye as; Elaith and Captain Norlen pushed off the small sailing vessel to begin the voyage.

The harbour of the Bastion of Yelcan was shallow and small, and before no time, they were sailing outside the arm of the Port.

Thomas waved back, and Oscar signalled back with enthusiasm. Oscar did not leave the quayside until they were a spec on the horizon.

Lorsan put his arms on his shoulders and said, "come on, let's get some food; we have a lot to plan, and I want to begin your training right away."

The ship manoeuvred out into the middle of the river while Elaith and Darfin hoisted the mainsails.

The Disaris did not like to be on the water or open land, and they only trusted the forest. So while Sana and the Princess said nothing, Thomas could tell that they were uneasy about the voyage and did as much as he could to comfort everyone.

They talked throughout the voyage up the river, going over the plan to walk through the city to visit the main commerce assembly galleries.

The commerce assembly building was huge; it was a long red-bricked building with pointed towers on it. It would be a ten-minute walk through the harbour, and the streets would be busy with the celebrations, so it would be easy to walk undetected.

The voyage up the river was slow and steady, they were against the flow of water, but the wind was on their side. It was not windy, but a steady late summer breeze blew up the river this time of the year.

Elaith took to the helm and rudder, then steered the ship up the river, tacking left to right to take advantage of the wind.

The boat had a small cabin area with bunks. Food was made and passed around by Captain Norlen. Everyone tried to stay out of view, and a rotation of only two on deck at any one time was maintained.

Thomas sat up with Elaith, talking as they meandered up the river.

"Have you ever been to Port Elec?" said Thomas.

"No, I haven't, but I hear it is amazing," said Elaith.

"I bet you are missing Oscar," said Elaith as he looked down at Thomas while steering the ship keeping his eyes on the horizon.

"Yes, he is the one person that has been with me everywhere," said Thomas.

"I am missing him to Thomas – but he is in good hands and to be chosen to be a shadow warrior is an astonishing opportunity," said Elaith.

He spoke to Elaith for several hours while they sailed up the river, and he did various jobs; tying ropes down and moving sails around.

Sana kept on her bunk and sat cross-legged, reading from what was thought to be religious scripters. While Princess Gilgamesh lay in her bunk, resting for the next day.

The Princess thought about the League of friend's agreement that had been signed by Qulan City.

She thought about the trading council along with Moltenwing. In years gone by, the often elitist nature of the East Tanniv residents would terrorise the Turgett community for their height, appearance, and skittish nature and poke fun of them. Now the Empress would have a Turgett trade agreement, and they would now walk freely with the merchant port residents, much like in Qulan.

The thunderer, a Turgett merchant ship, had been spotted by the Princess on the horizon that day.

It was travelling up from Qulan and had been seen previously that day.

The Elec Trading assembly was exceptional, and the annual City regatta made this a wonderful week of celebrations.

The Princess wondered how beneficial the Elec trading council had become now decisions were now being made in Moltenwing for everything. More could be achieved in a single conversation to explain one's feelings and motives at these meetings than could be achieved in a whole host of letters going backwards and forward between the trading ports.

Thomas Marlow and Princess Gilgamesh would need to take up their seats and be vocal to strike up opposing views about how to deal with the League of friend's agreement in the event of its collapse.

Princess Gilgamesh and Thomas discussed options on the boat that day, and it was agreed to be as outspoken as possible to disagree with everything on the agenda.

The Princess was not deterred by this strategy and convinced Thomas not to be afraid.

Once you had a voted seat in the Elec Trading council, it would never be abolished, and Vakoborg City had a prominent seat which Princess Gilgamesh would take up. Marlow had a hereditary seat passed down from his mother because Alina Marlow and Alwin Aminoff created the council.

As they navigated up the river that day, many settlements could be spotted on both sides of the river. The river was wide and, in some places, several miles wide and was wide enough to create the natural border between East and West and the many cultural differences.

The sun started to set on the river, and the reds, golds and amber, colours of the sun setting, appeared in the sky. The Port of Elec could now be spotted in the distance with its piers and towers. Its distinctive look was now coming into focus. The port was far bigger than in Qulan City, and the instantly recognisable towers could be seen very clearly.

The two towers were defensive barbicans that housed two entire soldiers' garrisons in each tower, with cannons pointing in all directions to defend the port.

The cityscape was now coming into view, and as they drifted closer, hundreds and hundreds of ships were now being seen anchored outside the harbour walls. These ships were for the regatta happening that week and vessels coming from everywhere for the trading congress.

The Ilihorn Navy, with its vast ships, looked colossal, and the noises from each ship carried its own brand of sound and racket, as some vessels partied, some crafts sang songs as they cleaned the decks and some ships simply made noise from cooking and dining. It seemed like the whole of the Alimar River had turned up to be part of the flotilla.

As Elaith and Darfin steered the ship closer. They decided that hiding in plain sight would be the best option. The theory is that if they were too close, it would not arouse suspicion, and if they were too far, it would provoke mistrust. So they navigated the ship into the harbour walls to find a suitable mooring.

As they entered into the port, rounding the harbour arm, they were hit with ships everywhere.

The supper rich of Tanniv had turned up in their thousands with ships sailing up from Port Elleth and beyond.

The high society of Elec and Moltenwing would be arriving at the grand parties and palaces that would be taking place that week.

Elaith made anchor while captain Norlen readied the ship for the night. Once the boat was made safe, everyone came into the ship's galley to eat dinner.

The mood was silent as most of the plans had been discussed that day. Everyone knew what needed to be done; there was also an air of nervousness.

A beef stew was dished out onto metal plates, and with wooden cutlery, a massive cut of bread, everyone, no matter royal status or army rank, sat together and ate.

Thomas decided to go and look outside at the city.

By this time, it was dark, and he could see a million lights all bearing down at him from the many tall and beautiful buildings around him.

Princess Gilgamesh walked outside to take some fresh air before bed too.

The Princess looked over at Thomas and could see that he was thinking deeply about the day ahead of them.

"It will be easy enough, Thomas; we will attend the meeting just to show everyone that we can."

"Then we will send the right message to Jandar and to Qulan," said the Princess.

"That is it? That is all we are here to do," said Thomas.

"Yes, we need to show our faces and let everyone know we are here to take back our seats, to send the message, to the makers of the league of friends, and to the instigators of the Leoven abbey," repeated the Princess.

The Princess explained that the League of Friends is a fragile agreement and that it will break down. Another ballot for the reunification of West Tanniv will take place again in Qulan, and next time the vote will be in our favour.

So Princess Gilgamesh and Thomas Marlow attending the assembly in Elec would be spoken about and will further soften the opposition who would not sign the agreement.

"Come on, Thomas let's get some sleep; we will need to be in the Elec hall by morning," said the Princess as they both walked below deck to sleep for the night.

The ships beds were quite comfortable, built like a wooden box that they climbed into. The bunks were stacked three high, one on top of each other.

Thomas climbed up to the top bunk and laid on a bed of duck feathers in a hard thick, robust cotton mattress and within minutes was fast asleep.

Early the following day, everyone woke to the sound of the neighbouring ships all waking up at different times.

Thomas got up and had a wash in a basin as fast as he could, wetting his hair down and straightening himself out for his first visit to Elec and the assembly hall. He couldn't wait to step outside to finally see the famous city port.

Elaith and Captain Norlen were already awake, working on the ship to ensure all the mooring ropes and anchor had not moved overnight. They readied the ship's `rowing tender in preparation for going into town.

Thomas looked out with the sun on his face, the first thing he could see was the famous twin barbicans of the harbour, and they were huge with huge tower rooves with the most enormous flags flying from each tower.

Everywhere around him stood hundreds and hundreds of ships ranging from all sizes, and everywhere the cities, merchants trading piers were hauling cargo on and off of the vessels that lined the wharves.

He then turned his head to view the city.

The city streets bustled with horses and carts, coaches and restaurants, Inns and bars were being readied for the day's trade.

The buildings were beautiful; each building looked like a townhouse and was painted in reds, peaches, pinks and even light purple. Each building had a fresco painted on the outside depicting a time from long ago, all were decorative monuments of architecture, and two were never the same.

Captain Norlen readied the ship's tender, and Sana, the Princess, Thomas, and Elaith climbed down the rope to board the rowing tender.

The captain took up the oars while the two Disaris and Thomas jostled for position to even the boat in the water. Elaith took the tiller while the captain rowed to the piers main jetty.

Sitting this low in the water made the Disaris particularly uneasy as the enormous naval and merchant ships looked even more menacing from being so low in the water. As they paddled, other maritime workers would look over at them, making everyone feel uneasy.

There were now hundreds of other tenders around in the harbour, making things difficult to navigate all rowing towards one of the many unloading jetties in the port.

Captain Norlen disembarked first while Sana and the Princess went next Elaith tied the tender down, and as they approached the jetty, they leapt out of the boat, then sauntered up the jetty careful not to slip on the lime green fine seaweed, which made the walkway slippy. A huge fat official man in a dark blue harbour masters uniform stood at the top with a clipboard and a pencil asking people to state their business.

Thomas looked nervous but would smile when people caught his eye.

"State your purpose," said the official-looking harbour master.

"We are here for the celebrations and to watch the wrestling for the week," said Captain Norlen.

The harbour master looked suspicious and squinted at the captain and then looked hard at the small group, and with that, Sana Norbella took down her hood and, with her immense Disaris beauty, looked at the man with her blue eyes. The man stopped, stunned by her magnificence and said, "Ok, be on your way and enjoy the week."

Sana smiled at the man, and the other men in the harbour masters management looked on at her beauty.

"Have you ever seen such beauty," said one of the harbour master administrators to another.

"Let's keep walking," said Captain Norlen in a lowered tone, smiling and talking through his teeth.

The City Port of Elec in East Tanniv.

The streets looked lovely; decorations in Blue and white had been laid out all over the city with flowers hanging from baskets and lanterns on every street corner.

Ilihorn Dragoons and Moltenwing guard patrols everywhere on every street, marching for security as the Empress was coming into town.

The shops, with their café, Inns, and coaching houses with Pubs were all opening up for a day's trading as the sun shone on the streets.

Earlier that week, Marshal Rhorn Fadan of Moltenwing had sent thousands and thousands of troops into the city as part of the defence strategy that the Empress and the Prince had decided on. So the city was awash with Ilihorn Dragoons, Moltenwing guards and elite hussars.

The five of them walked down through the wide streets while the Captain led the way.

Everywhere was the hustle and bustle of city life. The city was so beautiful and clean, and it looked even more splendid with its celebratory decorations.

The Elec Assembly Hall was at the far end of Ropemaker Street, and it was a wide street that ran down from the main port.

The small group strolled through the crowded streets, making their way down Ropemaker Street steadily.

In the distance, they could see a bulging mass of people huddling around a doorway waiting to get through small doors; it was the entrance to the Trading assembly hall.

It was not magnificent from the outside, the streets were uniform in style, and every building was the same shape. The huge oak door had a hanging sign which simply read The City Port of Elec's Trading Assembly Hall, which let you know that you were in the correct location.

Captain Norlen and the group got to the entrance and joined the masses of Officials, Nobleman, Merchants, and Ministers, funnelling into the small doors and joining the line to get into the hall.

Security was at an all-time high everyone was being questioned as they entered. Each seat holder was allowed, one assistant. Elaith opted to stay outside and watch from the other side of Ropemaker Street, waiting patiently for them to return.

The Princess and Sana still had their hoods up while Thomas and the Captain tried to blend in.

Through the masses, they were now being corralled into the buildings main entrance. Thomas could see Turgetts and finely dressed men coming from Moltenwing and Ilihorn.

He had the distinct recognition that he was now in East Tanniv, and the cultural differences were now showing.

The main entrance was small and had an enormous chandelier hanging from an ornate fresco plastered ceiling. At the end of the entrance hall were four staircases going in different directions, with girls standing with seating plans showing everyone the correct chairs and ushering them to the suitable stairs.

Princess Gilgamesh walked to one of the ushers and whispered her name. The young girl looked at her with a gracious look and pointed her silently in the right direction.

The Princess and Captain Norlen were through and were now walking up the stairs. Thomas hustled his way to the front with Sana and said "Marlow" in a low voice to the same girl. She looked at Thomas with a kind smile, checked her seating plans and pointed to the stairs to the left, which led in a different direction to Princess Gilgamesh.

They were now through the security point too.

The Princess looked at Thomas with a knowing nod, and they each walked in their respective directions to their seats.

The stairs wound upwards, reaching four stories high leading to ivory white doors. The white doors had huge brass shaped handles and were opened by the girls who worked in the Assembly Hall.

The ladies were friendly and polite and moved in a lifeless fashion. This was Thomas's first experience of serfdom as these girls were clearly slaves.

The doors opened out onto a huge room with hundreds of people in every direction.

These were the nobles, traders, merchants and the wealthy of East Tanniv, and everywhere; Thomas looked, he could see extreme wealth.

Another usher walked over to Thomas and Sana and asked for their names, and Thomas whispered "Marlow", and a girl walked them directly to his seat.

Sana stood back and kept herself at a safe distance against one of the walls and waited.

Thomas was looking out into a sea of people looking for Princess Gilgamesh. He was unaware that she would be so far away, and he continued to look until they spotted each other; then, looking for more comfort, Thomas looked over his shoulder behind him to see Sana looking at him.

The view looked amazing; he had never seen so many well-dressed, wealthy people in one place.

The military uniforms looked magnificent, the Nobleman looked tall and strong, and everyone in the room had an air of superiority.

He took his seat, a black wooded ornate chair with a green leather cushion for comfort. Everyone around Thomas's proximity was looking at him while whispering and muttering, but he was trying not to notice.

A trumpeter played a few notes to signify the start of the assembly when Prince Aminoff walked in to take his seat.

He sat to the right of Thomas and one row behind. The rest of the Ilihorn courtiers walked in and took their seats, shielding Thomas from the direct view of Prince Alwin.

The Qulan ministers walked in and took their seats to the right of Prince Alwin. The head of state, Lanlith Jaclar, had attended with his ministers. One of Lanlith Jaclar associates looked down to see Princess Gilgamesh in her Disaris seat and nudged Lanlith to let him know that the Disaris Princess was in attendance.

Lanlith Jaclar looked to his left, knowing roughly where the Alina Marlow seat would be and gasped quietly. Alina Marlow is the most respected name in Qulan with the Turgetts. She had dedicated her time to helping the Turgetts, and without Alina Marlow, the Turgetts would not have a trading council or a seat in the Elec Council assembly. To see Thomas Marlow in her seat dealt Lanlith Jaclar a huge blow, and with an immense notion of shame, he hung his head.

The room was now silent, and Prince Alwin stood up to speak.

"I have brought you here today to celebrate the League of Friends," said Prince Alwin as the whole hall erupted into applause and cheering.

"I have brought you here today as we intend to continue trading with our Turgett brothers in the West."

"And I have brought you here today to celebrate a more prosperous time."

"And I have brought you here today for more trade, to earn more money and to open up the gateway for an open trade agreement with Qulan City."

Once again, the hall erupted into clapping and cheering.

"Distrustful people will say the Moltenwing Empire means war."

"But I say that the Empire means peace and wealth for everyone."

Everyone in the room hailed and applauded again.

The words peace, wealth, happiness did apply to everyone in the room but did not apply to the slave economy that ran the farming and industry in the country.

The Prince talked about the agreement being signed tomorrow for port treaties and ships to flow freely in Elec. Everyone fell silent and thought about the many opportunities that this deal had now opened up.

Prince Alwin looked out at his assembly and smiled at everyone in the room. Then as he sat down, something caught his eye to his left.

He could see a person's head sat in the Marlow seat; the Prince looked sharply in the direction of Thomas. Thomas could feel his eyes gazing at him and could feel the energy for the Prince staring in a confused way.

The Prince, who would never lose control, looked directly at Thomas and sat down, thinking he would deal with him later. He clicked his fingers, and his chief of security came to him; Prince Alwin whispered into his head of securities ear, "make sure you detain that person in the Marlow seat. I want to speak to him in my private chamber after the assembly."

Sana could see the exchange in communication and feared the worst and prepared for everything; looking everywhere for escape opportunities, she devised several plans in her head.

Princess Gilgamesh also saw the glance from Prince Alwin and the exchange in conversation with his security chief and feared the worse, but she remained calm. The congress went on for many hours. There would be no grand speech from Thomas nor Princess Gilgamesh, and they both achieved what they needed to do.

The hall was filled with Turgett's and Merchants who could see the Princess, and the task was now done.

As soon as the congress finished, they would hurry out with the masses, return to the ship, and sail back to Yelcan.

As the congress came to a close, the masses filtered out.

Sana walked past the busy rows of seats and hustled past the members who were all leaving, making it difficult to walk against the tide of people walking to go. Four of Prince Alwin's guards began shuffling towards Thomas from the opposite side. Sana got to Thomas first and said, "Come, let's go."

Thomas got out from his seat, seeing that four of Prince Alwin guards were approaching him. Sana put Thomas under her cloak and looked frantically for options. Prince Alwin was standing in the back row calmly watching this scenario play out and was half enjoying watching what was going to happen with anticipation.

Four more of Prince Alwin's guards approached from the other side, making eight guards now coming on each side.

Sana removed her hood and looked at the four guards approaching from the left, then looked behind at the four guards coming from the right.

The men stopped and gazed at her beauty and majestically stunning blue eyes; this bought those precious seconds as they manoeuvred down to a row of seats closer to the balcony.

A further two guards now approached from the other side, coming up from the balcony's left; they were now completely closed off and stood still looking for options.

Prince Alwin's chief of security came over to Thomas and said, "Prince Alwin would like to speak to you in his private chamber."

He nervously looked up at Sana, and she looked directly at Thomas, without saying anything, and he knew what Sana was saying.

It was at that strange moment he understood everything. Sana and Thomas had built a telepathic bond and could communicate without talking, which was rare even by Disaris standards.

Sana was trained in the telepathic arts but had not managed to connect with another being until now. It was why she kept close to Thomas; they had developed a scarce, almost extinct telepathic connection.

The guards walked Thomas and Sana up the eight rows to the chamber door. Prince Alwin was now in his chamber sat behind his desk.

As Thomas walked in, the Prince instantly recognized him. The Prince kept calm, and not wanting to show his emotion, he spoke in a polite, relaxed manner.

"So we have met two times before," said Prince Alwin as he leaned back in his chair.

"And you, young lady, please remove your hood," said the Prince, now looking at Sana.

"Arh, very rare indeed," Prince Alwin said.

"I see that you have Vupear," said the Prince looking directly at Sana, jumping out of his chair to take a better look at her.

Thomas looked around at Sana and wondered what a Vupear was.

A Vupear is a very rare form of Disaris so rare that only a few were left in Tanniv. A Vupear was so beautiful and so mysterious to all men that they could hypnotize men and even ladies with a simple look of their beauty.

"I have read about the Vupear Disaris, but I have never actually seen one; you are indeed magnificent! – I should show you to my mother," said the Prince as he gazed upon Sana looking her up and down, making her feel uncomfortable.

"But let's talk about you, my young friend; what is your name," said the Prince, now turning his thoughts back to Thomas.

"My name is Thomas Marlow from Stoney Cross," he said in a firm voice.

"Marlow, you say, and your mother was Alina?" said the Prince as he wandered around his room looking out at the cityscape of Port Elec.

The Prince looked out at the window so that everyone in the room could now only see his back. "I knew your mother – I knew your mother very well, young Thomas! Some would say we created these councils together," said the Prince, still looking out at the window.

"So now that we have a Marlow returning to his seat in Elec, what is it you intend to do?" said the Prince, now looking at Thomas.

"I just wanted to attend to see the Grand Assembly in Port Elec, and I intend to continue my mother's work," said Thomas.

"You intend to continue your mother's work?"

"And have you not heard of the league of friend's agreement?"

"I assume that you have, given that you were also in the Qulan Trading council meeting last week," said the Prince with an air of superiority and dominance that he knew everything.

"Yes, I have heard of the league of friend's agreement which I consider to be a narrow document that needs work, and I am here to listen and to learn," said Thomas in a firm voice surprising the Prince.

The Prince sat back down in his chair and looked at Thomas with a small and subtle smile.

"What are you doing tonight?" said the Prince.

"Traveling back to West Tanniv," said Thomas.

"Nonsense, you will be my guest at the Empress Regatta Ball tonight," said the Prince in a tone that would not leave Thomas with much room to say no.

The Prince looked at Sana Norbella and dismissed her.

Sana clenched at her sword under her cloak, but sensing that now would not be the time. She turned and nodded at Thomas again, the two locking eyes with each other with a deep connection. Again she spoke telepathically, "I will link up with the Princess, and we will get you when the time is right."

Sana walked out of the door, leaving Thomas with the Prince.

"You can stay in my Palace here in Elec, and I will have to organise some new clothing for you for tonight," said Prince Alwin.

The Prince clapped his hands, and a team of people came out to take care of Thomas and to escort him to the Aminoff Palace in Elec.

"Thomas, you have nothing to fear; I merely want to show you some East Tanniv culture; it's not every day we have a Stone Circle sorcerer in Tanniv, and I want to introduce you to a few people," said the Prince as he smiled.

The Prince knew that the boy was of great value and would be an asset as a hostage for now. But a hostage masked in hospitality.

He was escorted to the Grand Aminoff Palace by horse and coach.

Sana had now connected back with Elaith, who was waiting outside.

"Where is Thomas?" said Elaith to Sana.

"The Prince has taken him; he is to attend the grand regatta ball tonight," said Sana speaking to Elaith.

"Where is the Princess and Captain Norlen?" Sana asked.

"They have returned to the ship; the Captain is worried about the Princess; she is a far too bigger prize for the Aminoff's to claim," said Elaith.

The two waited only to see Thomas escorted into an Imperial coach with fifty Moltenwing Hussars.

Again to Sana's frustration, now was not the time to break Thomas out from his situation.

Sensing that Thomas was in circumstances that he would not want to be in, she could also feel that he was not in life-threatening danger. The Prince wanted to show him something which would mean he would stay alive for now.

Sana and Elaith returned to the ship. Captain Norlen and the Princess were in the galley talking about the next plan.

The Captain spoke, "I need to get you back to Yelcan, my lady; it's far too dangerous; we can't have a killed or captured princess. You are far too valuable," said the Captain in a demanding military tone.

"And what about Thomas," said the Princess.

"We will set sail now and return with a squad to diplomatically barter for his release the Prince has no right to keep him here," said the Captain, whose main concern was not to lose a princess under his watch.

"For now, I need to get you back to the Bastion of Yelcan," said the Captain.

The Princess acknowledged that the Captain was right and reluctantly agreed.

Sana and Elaith both looked down with immense disappointment but again unenthusiastically agreed. No one knew that the Prince would take such an interest in the Marlow boy.

"Yes, we will need to create a diplomatic campaign to get Thomas back; this is now the only way," said Princess Gilgamesh.

Sana stood up and said, "I will stay, I will stay and track his movements and keep watch over him."

Princess Gilgamesh looked at Sana and gave her a look to say thank you.

"We need to leave now," said Captain Norlen.

Sana climbed down to disembark the ship and onto the tender, then paddled off back to the quayside with her hood up; she rowed back, docking the small boat, and ran off into the night.

Elaith and Captain Norlen readied the ship and sailed out of the port for the Bastion on Yelcan.

The Archduke's New Deal

The Archduke Merith Aminoff was now anchored in Qulan harbour.

A grand Qulan ceremony was taking place in the harbour as the Archduke turned up in the port with more troops than expected.

The head of State Lanlith Jaclar was at the Elec Annual Regatta, and most of the Qulan ministers were there too.

The Governmental leader assigned to watch over Qulan was a Turgett called Alock Fardell, and he had been given orders to show The Aminoff Archduke the new Embassy.

He was then to ceremonially wave the Embassy agreement and the new League of friends' agreement to the celebrating crowds and give a short speech that day.

He had orders to show the Archduke the new Embassy and Garrison and to close the day with a grand dinner that night.

Much like Archduke Aminoff, the Turgett Alock Fardell had been given this simple ceremonial job because he was considered a useless entity.

Alock was a son of a significant Qulan super-rich trader and had been given the job of social affairs minister as a favour from his wealthy father.

Even Alock Fardell had not expected to do anything as part of his duties, and receiving the Archduke that day would send him into a fluster.

The Archduke Aminoff arrived among scores of rowing tenders, much to the panic of Alock Fardell as he was only expecting one thousand troops.

The crowd massed, and people waved white hankies from the windows of almost every house in Qulan in celebrations for the day.

The skinny Archduke came ashore with his officers looking superior and masterful in his gleaming uniforms as he landed.

Alock Fardell stood on a raised stage, and he welcomed the Archduke Aminoff into Qulan City, shaking his hand for all to see.

"We were only expecting one thousand troops, my lord," said Alock Fardell as he smiled at the crowds hiding his confusion.

"Well, I suggest you find a solution and find one fast," said Archduke

Aminoff, very offensively to the small Turgett treating him appallingly in a disrespectful and challenging tone.

Alock Fardell looked back at the Archduke in a perplexed way but called upon his staff to find a resolution for this very remorseless order.

The Archduke strolled about on the raised podium with arrogance. He was not influencing the crowds, and the masses of Turgett could sense this by his body language; there was something wrong.

Alock Fardell turned to the Archduke and whispered, "I am meant to take the two agreements from you and wave them around at the crowds," he said, looking up at the Duke.

"No, we are going to amend a few things, and we need to go to my new Embassy to talk about this," repeated the Archduke in an aggressive tone.

"I had not been made aware of this, and I do not have the authority to agree on anything like this," said the poor confused Turgett.

"Then find the authority," he barked while gritting his teeth.

"Everyone is in Port Elec right now," said Alock looking ever more distressed.

"Then we will agree on these amendments. Do you realise I have three thousand Ilihorn Dragoons in Qulan City now?" said the Archduke threateningly while grasping his sword pommel, intimidating the shocked bewildered Turgett.

The proceedings were stopped abruptly. The other Turgett Officials, alongside Alock Fardell, equally looked shocked and upset with the tone exchanged.

They made their way up through the narrow streets to the new Moltenwing Embassy.

"This will not do whatsoever; we need something bigger," repeated the Archduke offending the senior officials that were with the convoy walking together.

"This is what has been agreed on, my lord."

"An Embassy Palace with a garrison for one thousand troops," said Alock Fardell looking ever more confused.

"I don't like it; find me another!" said the petulant Archduke as he looked at the building with total disgust.

The Archduke entered the inadequate Embassy to find an office; the Turgett officials and the Archduke's Officers all entered.

Archduke Aminoff opened up the agreement and read out his amendments.

The league of friend's agreement had said explicitly that only One thousand East Tanniv soldiers could be in the city at any one time.

The Archduke wanted this amended to an unlimited amount.

The agreement had laid out a contract of berth places for ships signifying no more than two ships at any one time.

Again the petulant Archduke wanted this amended to an unlimited amount.

Again another contract point was scrutinized in the agreement for trade profit percentages to be increased in East Tanniv's favour.

More unrealistic terms: one hundred more seats are to be made available for the Qulan City Trading council to be opened up for East Tanniv residents to take.

The list of impractical terms was now being read out in a naive manner.

The governmental leader Alock Fardell and his administration listened on as the Archduke and his Officers were bullying them.

"I cannot agree to these terms, my Lord; I do not have the authority," said the deeply saddened Alock Fardell.

"You are the highest-ranking official in Qulan, and I am the highest-ranking Official from East Tanniv here; we can sign anything we want," said the Archduke who stood up to tower over the Turgetts.

"I also have three thousand Ilihorn dragoons who could take this city by force if I do not get this signed today," said the Archduke as he looked at his officers.

The Archduke dismissed the Turgett officials and said, "I expect you to return to me in three hours with a signed agreement or a declaration of war, and these are your only choices."

Alock Fardell and The Turgett officials hurried out the door rapidly and back to the Grand Turgett trading council, feeling deflated, threatened, and swindled.

Culturally and socially, you could not threaten a Turgett.

If you threatened a Turgett, then a Turgett would spring into action with a counter plan.

By nature, you could only discuss or negotiate with a Turgett passively.

Many Turgetts would have security plans in their home life with secret escape tunnels under their houses, money put into many banks, hidden hoards or jewels, second homes and so on.

The problem with Turgett Escape tunnels had reached alarming proportions, as many of the tunnels would burrow into another escape tunnel as every wealthy Turgett had the same way of thinking.

The whole of Qulan had a very well-rehearsed plan as a city too, and this

Archduke Merith Aminoff

plan could be put into action at any time.

If Archduke Aminoff had studied Turgett Culture, he would have learned that threatening, intimidating behaviour like this would force a Turgett to go underground and counteract any aggressive behaviour.

The Qulan ministers left the new Embassy in a hurry, and a defence plan was put into action.

Turgett horns were sounded all over the city, giving the signal for the army to blockade certain strategical streets.

They raised chains across the harbour denying access in and out of the port and for the secret tunnels to be put into use which mobilized ten thousand Turgett soldiers and conscripts into place.

Streets were blocked, creating a well-rehearsed defensive line, windows boarded up, and while the city fell back to these defensive lines using the network of tunnels, The Archduke looked pleased with himself as he spoke with his officers.

The Ilihorn dragoons looked around and watched as each shop, Inn, coaching house, and bar emptied and boarded up without seeing anyone move on the streets.

The streets seemed to empty, and everyone disappeared into their tunnels, falling back to their defensive line.

The Turgett Officials were now in the Qulan trading council safe as ten thousand Turgetts were manned and dug in on the defensive line.

All this had happened without the blundering Archduke knowing as he was having lunch with his officers drinking wine and laughing.

Colonel Jorona of the Tarrenash army garrison could hear and see what was happening.

The Tarrenash Barracks was already at red alert status due to the Archduke's visit that day. The Tarrenash army garrison sat safely behind the Turgett defensive front line.

Colonel Jorona took a walk up to the trading council hall to meet with the caretaker governmental leader Alock and was granted a meeting.

Alock took the meeting with The Colonel, believing this would benefit the current situation.

Alock Fardell explained what had happened earlier that day and that the Archduke had given demands that his newly amended agreement would need to be signed, or he would declare war in three hours.

"So I have locked the city down, and the defensive front line has been formed," said Alock Fardell.

"You have done the right thing," said Colonel Jorona.

"You do realize that we can no longer help you and all I can do is look on and aid you with unofficial advice," said the Colonel in a regretful tone.

"Yes, I understand," said the skittish and nervous Alock Fardell.

"We will wait this out until Minister Lanlith Jaclar returns from Elec City," said Alock Fardell.

"I will need to send a message to Tarrenash City and to The Bastion at Yelcan," said the Colonel.

That afternoon the Archduke walked around looking pleased with himself sat in his new office chair with his feet up, looking at the clock waiting for the new agreement to be signed.

He sat pronouncing to his officers "that Prince Alwin was no deal maker and that he would have all the glory this time."

What had actually happened was a blockade, and the siege of Qulan City had now commenced.

It had begun without the signing of this agreement without the Moltenwing high command, and it had commenced without the blundering idiot Archduke even knowing about it.

After the three-hour deadline had passed, there was no sign of the Turgett minsters or Alock Fardell.

The Archduke walked out onto the streets to see an empty environment.

No people, no movement, even the shops, the Inns and the Pubs were empty.

He walked down to the port, and there was nothing. The second-biggest trading port in Tanniv was empty.

He took a squad of one hundred dragoons and walked with his officers in the streets. His officers gave the order for the streets to be inspected.

As the Archduke and his officers walked up the steep, narrow streets, they were met with blockades in every road.

Reports had begun coming in from the dragoon officers in every direction, explaining that the city had gone into some sort of lockdown.

The small thin pale Archduke was not good at hiding his feelings, so he screamed in a childlike manner blaming everyone around him.

"I am going back to my office, and I want a plan of what to do about this," he said in a juvenile rant.

The Archduke walked back to the safety of his unwanted Embassy and hid in his quarters.

He was surrounded by his officers, and he vented at them again.

"What is the Empress going to say?" he cried.

"What is the Prince going to say?" and he yelled.

"You have all let me down", he screamed at his officers, over and over again.

He called a meeting gathering everyone in.

The Archduke gave the orders to organise five separate attacks on the defensive line.

He was going to show the Turgetts what Ilihorn Dragoons could do.

One of his officers advised on not charging at the well-orchestrated and rehearsed Turgett front line, indicating that the Turgett obviously knew what they were doing and had done this before.

The petulant Archduke dismissed the officer for being a coward and sent him back to the ships for punishment later.

The Archduke ordered the five attacks to take place, still believing that this was going to be a victorious day and that the Qulan Turgetts would sign his agreement.

The five attacks took place as hundreds of Ilihorn Dragoons marched in lines bravely. This was to scare the Turgetts into running off.

Then with their swords drawn, they walked to the newly formed front line.

As they got closer, they could see nothing, not a Turgett insight.

They marched with great confidence, and as they got closer, a volley of arrows came from every tall building in every street, firing and raining down thousands of arrows onto the dragoons. The Turgett are not great archers, but the Narrow streets had funnelled and condensed the troops into bottlenecks while the Turgetts rained thousands of arrows and boulders down on them, killing hundreds of soldiers.

The order was given to retreat, and the wounded and dead Dragoons laid everywhere littering the streets of Qulan.

The messages were sent back to the Embassy to inform the Archduke.

"It has been a massacre, my lord," said an officer puffing and wheezing.

"Oh, has it indeed," said the Archduke as he smiled and smirked at the officer jumping around with joy.

"You don't understand, my Lord, we have been massacred."

"We could not see the enemy, and then thousands of arrows rained down from everywhere, my lord the streets are so narrow it's impossible to move," said the officer.

The Archduke stood up screaming at everyone, "You've let me down – You've let me down get out of my sight."

One of the officers ordered the Ilihorn troops to create a defensive line and not to attack again.

The Dragoons dug in and created a counter protective line, ensuring that they would be safe.

The Archduke went to his bedroom to lie down while he thought about his next move in this complete and utter blunder he had found himself in.

If you asked the Archduke's mother, Baroness Darbella, she would have recognised this bout of depression as the Archduke would take to his room with these episodes of tantrums for much of his life.

The Empress Regatta Ball

Thomas was now in The Embassy Palace in Port Elec.

He was alone but had been given a grand luxurious suite.

He sat on the bed thinking about Princess Gilgamesh, Sana, Elaith and the Captain.

While Thomas felt like he was under room arrest, it was a luxurious, comfortable room, but two guards outside prohibited him from leaving.

The door opened, and a man and two ladies arrived in a very stylish fashion; all three were very stylishly dressed, and all three looked at Thomas, sizing him up looking at him with heads tilted and glancing at him.

The man stood in front of him and clicked his finger; a squad of ladies arrived with racks and racks of clothing.

"Why are you here," said Thomas.

"We are here, young sir, to get you ready for the Grand Ball tonight."

The three stylists looked Thomas up and down and began to thrust fabrics at him, draping them over his shoulders while looking at his eyes and hair colour while another measured his feet and his legs.

Some more ladies walked in with three needlepoint sewing wheels.

The material was cut, and the ladies sewing wheels stitched clothing together while the room filled with the noise from the whirling sewing pedals. Gold buttons were chosen gold stitching was chosen.

"What are you doing?" repeated Thomas.

"We are creating a black and gold uniform, so you look the best you have ever looked," said a very flamboyant lady who revelled in the task of getting Thomas ready.

A bath was drawn, and Thomas cleaned himself with very little privacy.

Another lady came into the room to trim his hair and fingernails, and even toenails.

Another lady approached, covering him in talcum powder while spinning around to spray him with perfumes.

A royal jeweller turned up with fifty pocket watches, and a ribbon medallion style medal was chosen to hang over the uniform.

Gold buttons were selected, and satin lines for the trousers all matched to create a masterpiece uniform that was being fashioned.

The seamstresses finished, and the gold Moltenwing emblem buttons were sewn onto the uniform.

Thomas was told to stand in the centre of the room while the ladies dressed him.

A further knock came from the door; a man with glasses and a leather apron arrived and a leather carrying case. He walked in looking directly at Thomas and unbuttoned the case, and opened it out.

The finest leather boots, all gleaming looking new, were displayed while the man and the two ladies deliberated on which pair to choose.

"We will keep them all," the man said with a swish of his hands.

Thomas stood still while a thin white cotton shirt was put over his head and arms; the two ladies bent his elbows and fed his arms into the sleeves.

The trousers were made from thin, light wool but were hard wearing and had a thin black satin line down the outside of each leg.

The black jacket was placed over the shirt, which showed a little white collar and the gold buttons that fastened the blazer looked splendid. It had sixteen gold buttons, eight on each side with gold twine woven around the buttons for design.

The black knee-high boots were put on each foot and fastened while the jeweller fitted Thomas with a gold Qulan made pocket watch.

Then the medal was placed over the uniform. White gloves were given to Thomas with an ornamental short sword with a white belt and a white leather strap that went over his shoulder diagonally.

The man addressed Thomas again, "we will make another ten or twenty uniforms like this in different colours; they will be ready by the morning," then he flamboyantly walked out.

The other two ladies bowed and said, "Have a wonderful night."

Thomas looked back at himself in the mirrors, and he had never looked better.

He looked dashing and handsome and strong and intelligent all at the same time.

He walked around the room, not really understanding what was happening; he looked at his new pocket watch while pacing up and down.

Twenty minutes later, another knock on the door came.

A young girl came into the room and said, "The Prince would like to see you down in the reception hall in ten minutes, my lord."

"My name is Thomas; what is your name," said Thomas with a smile on his face.

"My name is Kristina, but I am not meant to talk to you, my lord," said the nervous young girl.

"OK, I am sorry, do you work here," said Thomas.

"Yes, I work here, my Lord, I am one of the serfs that run the Palace here in Elec," said the young girl.

Thomas remembered the serfdom of East Tanniv and how it was run by slave labour.

"OK, thank you," Thomas said politely.

The young girl looked back at him, remembering if anyone had ever said thank-you to her – her whole life.

"Kristina!" Thomas yelled.

"Yes, my Lord," said Kristina.

"Can you walk me down to the front entrance so that I don't get lost," Thomas asked.

The young girl was shocked again as she tried to remember if anyone had asked for help and not ordered her before.

"Yes, my Lord, please follow me," said the young girl.

Thomas went out onto the enormous hallway landing on the upper floor of the palace townhouse and could see paintings everywhere.

Then looking down onto the townhouse ground level, he could see the fine marble floor with a grand chandelier entrance.

Prince Alwin's voice could be heard from another room as his voice echoed while Thomas walked down the stairs trying to identify where the sound was coming from.

The young girl nodded her head and said goodbye; again, the girl looked oddly at Thomas for saying goodbye and having such manners.

He stood in the middle of the entrance while looking at himself in the mirror. He stood up straight and tall. The prince's footsteps got louder, and his voice became louder as he spoke to the butler of the palace.

"Thomas Marlow! You look very dashing like a young Moltenwing Prince," he said with his arms wide open, smiling at Thomas as he walked in.

"Our coach is almost ready," said the Prince as he put on his white gloves.

The two guards that were stationed outside the door also followed Thomas down the stairs. The Prince looked at the two guards, nodded, then explained to Thomas that they were his personal security and would follow him everywhere.

The coach arrived with eight black horses, around twenty hussars in front of the coach, and twenty guards behind all wearing parade dress with gleaming swords, polished boots, and hats with red and white hackles upon magnifying-looking shiny black horses.

It was late afternoon, and the sun was still bright in the sky.

They were on their way to the imperial waterfront palace, which had the most magnificent terrace that overlooked the river and the port.

The house was dressed for a grand ball and dinner in honour of the Empress herself.

The Princess sat opposite Thomas and spoke to him the whole way.

They did not speak about Stoney Cross and their encounters in England, or about Mr Griffins or anything important.

Prince Alwin spoke with excitement about the nights' activities. The night would begin in the Imperial Palace, a drinks' reception would be held to watch the Ilihorn Navy go by.

There would be fireworks and then a grand dinner.

"When we arrive, I will introduce you as Thomas with no last name, just your name," said The Prince; Thomas nodded and agreed.

He was not sure why he agreed, but he thought it was best to agree with him and not say much at all.

"Introducing you with no last name will create a stir with the other guests."

"If anyone asks your last name, you must say ask the Prince because they would not dare," said the Prince as he smiled at Thomas.

The coach slowed and then almost ground to a halt.

Thomas could hear the shuffling of horses all moving out of the way for a Royal coach and its guests.

He could see out across some perfectly mowed green lawns, the Imperial Palace. It was huge, and they could smell; they were near the riverfront too.

The coach pulled directly outside. The driver jumped off the stagecoach and spoke to the master of ceremony, "The boy's name is Thomas."

"Thomas who?" said the Master of Ceremony.

"Just Thomas," said the coach driver as he walked away.

The doors opened, and Thomas was propelled into the aristocratic high society world of the super-rich Moltenwing elite.

The master of the ceremony called out, "His Royal Highness Prince Alwin Aminoff and Thomas," he shouted in a deep voice.

Most of the aristocrats in earshot turned their heads when they heard the name Thomas; they could see this well-dressed young man in the most expensive uniform with the most costly Turgett made watch and jewelled medal on his chest with the most important person in the room.

Thomas looked handsome, sophisticated and now mysterious as he was with Prince Alwin, and he had no last name.

The room led out onto an enormous orangery garden where drinks were being served in a colossal greenhouse, which opened to an outdoor summer terrace.

All dressed in the most beautiful silk and satin ball gowns, the ladies looked on at the Prince and Thomas as they walked past. They all wore sashes of different colours that indicated which family or part of Tanniv they were from.

The ladies wore fine Turgett made jewellery, and they looked like the most beautiful girls in the world.

The men, all of whom looked much older than their ladies, all wore the most impressive military uniforms designed to astonish any onlooker.

Prince Alwin wore a black uniform with a black satin line down the trousers with gold buttons. He had nothing fancy on the uniform but was a handsome man; all the ladies liked to watch as he sauntered around.

As Thomas and the Prince walked past the mirrored wall in the orangery, Thomas could see that they were dressed in a similar style, and everyone in the party was watching them with sideways glances.

The terrace opened up onto the most outstanding view of the river Alimar. The house was positioned on the bend in the river; it overlooked the Navy that was on display for Tanniv to see.

Prince Alwin walked through the thick of the party to a quieter area of the terrace in the colonnades, where the Prince took the time to show him the ships of the Tanniv Navy.

Thomas could see thousands and thousands of troops further down the river and camps and soldiers as far as the eye could see.

"Are those soldiers down on the river," said Thomas as he pointed towards the thousands of troops based along the river. "Yes, they are Ilihorn Dragoons and Moltenwing Guards; this is part of the East Tanniv defence system that will ensure peace in Tanniv," said the Prince in a stern regal voice.

"Peace, you say," said Thomas.

"Yes, Peace."

"Look at the wealth and the happiness at this party."

"We created the league of friend's agreement based on peace."

"This is, so we could all prosper together not, so we can destroy each other in war," the Prince said while smiling at the boy.

"I will take you for an inspection of the troops tomorrow – you can see for yourself, but first, let's enjoy the night," said the Prince.

A string orchestra played in the late summer evening.

Champagne and wine flowed freely while conversation and laughs were being had everywhere.

Thomas followed the Prince around the party and grounds while they both spoke of politics and of peace.

The parties conversation and din changed to a happier louder tone when Prince Alwin stopped and, without looking, said to Thomas, "That is my mother, the Empress Anastasia Aminoff; when you meet her, call her Empress or your highness," said the Prince.

Thomas instantly got nervous; he had heard so much about this lady and about the horrors she had bestowed upon Tanniv.

As the party got slightly louder, the Prince and Thomas waited for the crowd of people saying hello to the Empress to thin out.

Thomas then got his first glimpse of the Empress.

She looked beautiful; in fact, she looked like the most beautiful girl in the room, and she looked so young, not what he had imagined at all.

The Empress looked like a young lady, tall and elegant, and looked gracious and stunning, and she glided around the party saying hello to everyone she met.

She did not wear lots of jewellery like the other ladies and was a simple, elegant lady simply dressed in a white satin dress with an orange Moltenwing sash.

The Empress spotted her son; she smiled then glided towards the Prince with a smile on her face.

Thomas stood perfectly still, with his hand behind his back as the Empress got closer.

"Hello, Mother," said Prince Alwin.

"Hello, my handsome son," said the Empress of East Tanniv, smiling radiantly.

"And who do you have here with you tonight," she said with a smile and an elegant manner while she tilted her head down towards Thomas.

"This is Thomas Marlow from Stoney Cross," said Prince Alwin to his mother.

"Oh, so you're a Marlow, are you," said the Empress.

"We should keep that a Secret for tonight," said the beautiful Empress.

"That will keep the tongues wagging," said the Empress as she winked at Thomas with a smile.

Thomas looked and smiled, being as polite as possible.

He started to talk, but an almighty great bang echoed as everyone laughed and cheered a joyful noise. The fireworks had begun.

The sky lit up with so many beautiful colours.

Thomas looked around and watched up at the sky in amazement.

Everyone turned and faced out to the Ilihorn Navy while the fireworks crashed and banged above them.

The staff kept everyone's glass full of champagne while the orchestra played in time with the fireworks.

Thomas had not seen anything quite like it in all his life.

The fireworks pounded, and the sparks lit up the skies.

The feel-good atmosphere was contagious as Thomas felt more relaxed too.

He could see the contented beaming smiles on the faces of the aristocracy, and it felt good to be in a positive atmosphere.

Over the past year in Tanniv, he had seen the arguments and the discontentment from the many regions. The failing of the Gathering of Stormhorn, the Leovan abbey, the disputes between Qulan, and Tarrenash, the Drachen warriors, and even the dangerous atmosphere in Jandar and Cloven Town. This was the first night that he had felt a sense of balance in society.

The grand dinner was called by the Master of Ceremony, and a gangway was created so that the Empress, Prince Alwin and now Thomas could walk in first.

Thomas walked in with his head held high in his smart Tanniv uniform and felt a sense of importance.

The grand imperial dining hall was huge; it was dressed in white table cloths and flowers with the most expensive silver cutlery and beautifully painted with the Moltenwing coat of arms on the crockery.

It housed a long oak table that could fit two hundred guests easily.

Empress Aminoff sat at the head of the table, the Prince sat to her left, and Thomas sat on the opposite side to the Prince on the Empress's right.

The rest of the glamorous guests flooded in while each guest took their seat.

Everyone was looking at Thomas or pretending not to look. But everyone was interested in whom the new boy at the table was.

Thomas and Prince Alwin had not left each other side all night.

Over dinner, the Prince commented, "That we must get you back to Qulan tomorrow, and he would figure something out." This comment from the Prince put his mind at rest because he knew he could leave at any time, and he felt like this was a diplomatic meeting.

"I can just return to my ship tomorrow," said Thomas.

"Yes, that would be fine; however, my sources tell me the ship left with your small squad almost instantly after the assembly," said the Prince in a very relaxed manner.

"Not to worry, my young friend, I can arrange a ship to take you back," said the Prince as he sipped his glass of wine and winked at Thomas.

The music played, and the food was served.

He felt strange that everyone had left him and could not quite believe it.

It was a strange but comforting feeling as he felt safe and was having a great time. He would treat this as an ambassador's trip, and he would make the most of the excursion to find out as much information as possible about East Tanniv.

The Empress said very little she would smile at the guests around the table and occasionally speak to her son. Thomas felt very nervous about being in her company.

She smiled at Thomas and said, "How do you like things in East Tanniv?"

"Everything is amazing, my Lady, and everyone is being so polite," Thomas said again in a very edgy tone.

The Prince looked across at Thomas, held his chin high, and sat up straight, gesturing to do the same. He recognised the helpful motion and sat up and raised his chin.

"If you like Elec, then you would love Moltenwing," said the Empress.

"Moltenwing is the most beautiful city in the world," said added.

"Have you ever been to Moltenwing?" said the Empress.

"No, your highness, I have not," said Thomas, this time remembering to sit up straight and raise his chin.

"Then you must come one day as my personal guest," said the Empress as she smiled across the table at one of her generals.

"There you have it, Thomas, an invitation from the Empress herself," said Alwin.

Thomas smiled and said "Thank-You" as he continued to eat and watch the magnificent Ladies and Gentlemen of Moltenwing.

After dinner, the guest filtered their way through to the grand ballroom for dancing and waltzing to the beautiful orchestra playing in the grand Imperial ballroom.

One of the staff dressed in a brilliant Imperial butler's uniform approached Thomas asking for permission to speak. "There is a young lady over there asking if you would like to dance with her," said the serf Butler.

Thomas looked at the Empress and at Prince Alwin, not knowing what to say. Prince Alwin gazed at Thomas and said, "go on - you can't refuse a ladies offer."

"But I don't know how to dance correctly," he said as he went bright red in the face and very embarrassed.

The young lady looked over at Thomas with a smile. She was around the same age as him and stood with five other girls of the same age who were all admiring the handsome boy in the Moltenwing uniform.

The young girls' name was Olya Enbella, and she came from one of the Moltenwing Noble families and was related to The Empress and the Prince somewhere along the line.

"You will be fine, Thomas; go and dance," said the Empress.

Thomas stood up, feeling very nervous and walked over to the girl.

"My name is Thomas, and I would love to dance with you," he said while holding out his white-gloved hand.

The other four girls all giggled as they ushered Olya forwards, and she accepted his hand, and they walked towards the dance hall.

"My name is Olya Enbella my father is Lord Enbella."

"Hello Olya, I am so sorry I am afraid I do not know how to dance," said Thomas, still very apprehensively.

"That's OK. I will teach you," she said in a soft voice.

She took his hand and placed his other hand around her waist.

She looked at Thomas and said, "Just close your eyes and feel the music."

Olya was pretty; she was the same age as Thomas and wore a beautiful pale blue ball dress, with a pale orange sash around her shoulder and waist with the coat of arms and emblem of her region on the strap.

She had blue eyes, a pale complexion and flawlessly made hair in a tiara. The rest of the girls looked on as Thomas tried to dance.

"I am sorry about my dancing," said Thomas.

"No, no, you are fine," the young girl said; they both danced slowly while the young lady led Thomas in time with the music.

The song finished, which Thomas felt relieved about.

He said thank-you and returned to the Prince, who was now in the ballroom stood talking to some official military men in the corner of the room.

Thomas walked around the ballroom and could feel all eyes were on him as he walked around with Prince Alwin smiling at everyone.

The night went on, and the dancing continued late into the night.

The Prince said good night to the Empress as he decided to get Thomas back.

The two rode in the stagecoach back to the Palace.

Thomas was silent on the way back and remembered all the elements of the night.

It was a fantastic night and one that he would never forget.

They got back to the Palace, and the staff escorted Thomas to bed.

"I will arrange a vessel to take you back tomorrow," said the Prince as he said good night and thanked him for his company.

Thomas got back to his room and was given hot water in the bathroom and satin bedclothes for the night.

He lay on his bed, missing Princess Gilgamesh and Sana, and especially Oscar. But also he felt no threat coming from his current situation in the Palace and found the Prince and Empress to be very friendly, polite and kind.

The following morning Thomas woke up to breakfast in bed and morning clothes laid out for him.

This time the clothes were like a military royal style uniform but less decorative.

The new uniform was brilliant and very striking but not as elaborate as last night's.

It was around nine in the morning. Thomas was given hot water in the bath and his new set of clothes. Without thinking about this, he put on his new clothes while the serfs of the house served him breakfast on silver plates with fine cutlery on a table assembled on a white table cloth brought in by an army of staff who waited to tend his every need in the suite.

A short while later, the Prince knocked on his door and said, "Good Morning, Thomas."

"I have an idea," he said.

"Rather than go back straight away, there are wrestling matches and horse races happening today in the grand Elec arena."

"Why don't we go and watch and have a gamble?" Prince Alwin said.

Thomas stood for a while, looked at the Prince, smiled, and said, "Yes, my Lord, that sounds like fun."

"Excellent, then I will organise a coach," said the Prince.

Jandar and Erlen Town

Princess Katya and the Crusaders were now high up in the Jandar Mountains. They were crossing the main mountain trade routes.

The fifty strong crusaders were without Princess Gilgamesh, Oscar, and Thomas; nevertheless, the determination of Princess Katya still remained.

They cantered through Jandar, passing Turgetts as they travelled, spreading the message to everyone about the plans for reunification.

The Princess of Tarrenash was well primed and prepared to meet with the Erlen Town Elders of Jandar.

The Elders of Jandar had been gathered to meet with Princess Katya and the remaining crusaders and were well aware of the campaigners coming into Jandar that day. But now, the Turgett Elders were receiving new news as by this time updates of The Ilihorn Dragoons creating a battlefront in Qulan had reached the Jandar Mountains.

A squad of Tarrenash soldiers had been spotted that morning galloping hard up the mountain path and sent by Colonel Jorona from the Garrison at the Embassy in Qulan City.

As the Squad of Tarrenash soldiers came closer up the mountain path, Princess Katya decided to wait to see why they were ridding with urgency.

So the Crusaders waited and sat with the Tarrenash Soldiers as they rode up from Qulan; they explained what had happened with the league of friend's agreement that day and that the Ilihorn Dragoons had set up an invading front on Qulan City under Archduke Aminoff.

The news was spreading far and wide. It was now all over Jandar that Qulan was in trouble. Rumours were circulating that a skirmish had broken out between the Dragoons and the Turgetts. Also that Qulan had gone into lockdown.

This was not the whole truth; the real news was that they had not invaded; this was a complete Blunder from Archduke Aminoff. Once Princess Katya heard the news, she became more determined than ever.

"I knew it – I knew it," said the Princess looking at General Yelfir and the rest of the Crusade. She was hesitant to ride back to Qulan, but she decided to gallop hard into Erlen Town to meet the Turgett Elders.

The Jandar inhabitants mostly lived underground in the mountains' mines and in small villages and towns along the Jandar trading routes.

The houses were made with thatched roofs, and thick brick and plaster as the winters high up in the Jandar Mountain were particularly harsh.

The Crusade now spread the word of what was happening in Qulan to anyone they passed that day. The information was now travelling fast throughout the region that Qulan was in trouble.

The Jandar elders held a commission in Erlen Town waiting to receive the Crusade and were now getting messages coming directly from Qulan City via messenger pigeons.

Courier pigeons were how the Turgett's interconnected, and they had set up an effective communication network using the birds all over Jandar.

All Jandar decisions and information would be administered in Erlen Town, and now talk that Qulan city had gone into a lockdown was on everyone's mind as the news was now coming in from all corners of the region.

Princess Katya and the Crusade were now riding hard into Erlen town to have discussions regarding reunification.

The campaign entered the town, and the crusaders were ushered to the towns main street.

The Turgett locals pointed them in the direction of the Town Hall at the far end of the village. The town hall was half-submerged and built into the side of the mountain.

Erlen town was quite a large town. It had several large coaching houses and Inns and was famous for the rough gold and rough diamond trade that would go on behind closed doors.

Nothing about this town high up in the mountains was particularly welcoming; it took on the look of an industrial town built for the purpose of mining.

Princess Katya and Lulong and the Disaris General cantered into the town hall where forty Turgett elders from the Jandar regions and mines sat in the conference. With her long blonde hair and dark eyes covered in dirt and dust from an arduous ride, the Princess wandered into the room passively with a smile bearing the emblems of the Tarrenash Empire.

They all sat around a central fire roaring hot while hot meat and potatoes were being prepared.

Each Turgett looked old with a long beard and smoked a pipe sitting around the fire, all deliberating. They each had tough skin and looked weathered while they sat close to the roaring fire. They would sit in group conversations while running and governing Jandar for hours like this.

They had suspicious-looking faces, and all would glance at each other for approval when speaking.

As the crusaders entered, they sat opposite the Turgetts, assembled in a semi-circle on wooden benches around the fire.

Princess Katya spoke about the reunification and the Leoven Abbey Massacre. She had seen first-hand that Drachen riders and Ilihorn Soldiers now patrolled Turgett land too in Qulan.

She spoke about the importance of peace and how regions of West Tanniv had grown apart over the years.

An Old Turgett who sat centrally in the middle of the Elderly Turgett council called Fardi Dorcane raised his hand politely to the young Princess Katya and spoke.

"Princess, I do not mean to be rude; you have my respect."

"The Tarrenash and the People of Jandar had always lived in peace."

"But please allow me to speak."

"I was in Qulan City at the trading council meeting, and I heard you speak, and we have been expecting you," said the old wise Turgett.

"We are now getting reports that Qulan City is overrun with Ilihorn Troops, and the Qulan Turgetts have now gone into lockdown," he said with a worried look on his face.

"I believe that the trading council in Qulan have been foolish."

"They have been foolish to sign the league of friend's agreement, and now Ilihorn Dragoons have overrun the city."

"I fear the worst for Qulan and my many friends who live there."

Princess Katya tried to talk again.

"Please, Princess, I am old, and I will forget what I am going to say. Once I have finished, you may talk," said the old Turgett.

"We have gathered today to say we will sign the reunification agreement, and we will once again fly the Eagle Owl banner of Tanniv," said the old Turgett as the others all sat and nodded while smoking their pipes and playing with their long beards chewing on salted pork.

Princess Katya smiled and exhaled with relief, and the rest of the Crusade smiled along with them.

"My father the King will be happy to hear this news," said Princess Katya.

"What are the plans now?" said the old Turgett Fardi Dorcane.

Princess Katya explained that troops were already being sent to the Bastions all over Tanniv from Tarrenash and Vakoborg.

Then how they will be going back to the Qulan Embassy to observe. To try and put a peaceful end to this dispute that is happening in Qulan.

"We will send a regiment of Turgett soldiers to aid our Qulan Brothers," said the Turgett Fardi Dorcane, as he looked around at his Jandar Elders, who all smoked their pipes and nodded.

"Then we shall ride with you as combatants and under one banner of the great Eagle Owl," the Princess said, and she shook the hands of the Turgett elders.

The atmosphere in the Hall was excellent and positive.

The reunification was now complete.

The northern tribes in Stormhorn would be the next stop.

This would be a one-week ride and would need to wait until the Qulan dispute would be settled.

So, for now, the Crusade and the Turgett regiment would ride into Qulan City.

The Yelcan Plan

Oscar awoke in the Bastion of Yelcan; he had been given his own room, which overlooked the river.

He had now been training in the Art of Shadow Warrior fighting and had been doing very well.

He missed Thomas dearly, and every morning he would wake up and look out on the horizon for the ship to return.

He wore his black uniform with pride, and before breakfast, he would walk up to the battlements to see if he could see the ship in the distance.

A small vessel was spotted that morning, and although the glare from the morning sun was masking the boat from being fully identified, he could see it was Thomas now returning.

Princess Gilgamesh, Captain Norlen and Lance-Corporal Tarron all looked back at the shoreline from the small vessel and navigated towards the Bastion of Yelcan.

The atmosphere on the boat was one of sorrow and disappointment that Thomas and Sana had not returned.

The council meeting had gone to plan, and the message of Princess Gilgamesh and Thomas Marlow being present at the meeting had sent the correct meaning to the Ministers of Qulan.

However, Thomas and Sana had not returned, and Thomas was now in the Aminoff's hands.

As the small ship navigated the shallow marsh deltas and got closer, Oscar was standing high on the ramparts and could not see Thomas as the boat came in, and he had a feeling that all was not well.

He looked and looked again. Oscar knew that Thomas would be on the vessel to wave back, and he could see from the body language of the crew members they looked dejected.

Captain Norlen was a soldier through and through, and while the decision to leave was a challenging, difficult decision to make, he knew it was the correct thing.

Keeping the Princess of Vakoborg safe was the most important thing.

The ship got closer, and the soldiers of Yelcan came out to secure the boat alongside the small harbour wall.

Oscar ran down to the anchorage detecting something was wrong.

General Yeldrove, who watched the ship from his room, went to the Quayside to hear the news.

While Oscar and General Yeldrove stood patiently, Captain Norlen walked off the ship first, then the Princess and Elaith.

"We have no Thomas or Sana," said Captain Norlen.

Oscar looked directly at Princess Gilgamesh with an immense sense of upset and disappointment.

"You had better come inside and explain everything," said General Yeldrove.

The five of them walked into General Yeldrove's office chambers which overlooked the River Alimar.

The General organised some food and some hot drinks to be prepared.

The Princess spoke first. "The meeting went well, and everyone saw us; this sent the correct message to the diplomats from Qulan who saw Thomas, and it was the perfect message," said the Princess.

"But something unexpected happened," she added.

"Prince Alwin took an interest in Thomas and asked him to attend a private meeting in his chambers," She said again with a sense of sorrow.

"Sana went in with him, but she was dismissed and ushered out of the chamber."

"Then what happened," said Oscar in a desperate voice.

"Sana came back to us and explained that she would stay and track Thomas."

She explained that he had been invited to the Imperial Empress Ball that night.

Captain Norlen went on to explain that "he needed to get the princess back —to Yelcan and how it was far too dangerous."

"You did the right thing, Captain; having Princess Gilgamesh safe is the most important obligation," said General Lorsan Yeldrove.

"It is not ideal we will need to send a diplomatic letter from King Gilgamesh or King Drusunal explaining that Thomas is an ambassador of West Tanniv, and he must be kept safe," said General Yeldrove.

The General turned to Oscar and explained that Thomas would be given an ambassadorial lifeline with a diplomatic letter sent from both Kings in West

Tanniv. This would mean that his safety would be guaranteed.

Princess Gilgamesh looked at Oscar and said, "He will be ok; he will have the ambassadorial title, and Sana Norbella will be watching over him."

Oscar felt better and started to come to terms with what had happened to his best friend.

Princess Gilgamesh sat down immediately and wrote the letter to her father, the King of Vakoborg, and General Yeldrove wrote the letter to King Drusunal.

The messages were to be sent using a team of riders, and in a few days, Thomas would be given an ambassadorial title.

Then the message would need to be sent back to Port of Elec.

Princess Gilgamesh would now wait in Yelcan and take up residence. She did this for two reasons she wanted to stay with Oscar, and tactically the Princess was in the best place to make military decisions.

The Princess was given a room and would be waiting for news.

She remained to see if the reunification of Jandar was accomplished.

The Disaris Reinforcements and Tarrenash troops would be arriving any day now into Yelcan. New strategies would be made with the Bastion High Command to distribute these troops along the Bastion fortifications.

Oscar would spend his time training with his magic and learning to sword fight and ride horses correctly.

The other shadow warriors and Tarrenash soldiers had all taken a liking to the young apprentice, and he trained hard every day in the longhouse in the Yelcan Gardens with a wise wizard named Ovidel Ildore, who had been training shadow warriors for decades.

Yelcan was the central hub for information coming in from all the Bastions up and down the river. So it would only be a matter of time that the information regarding the reunification successes of Jandar and the invasion of Qulan City would reach everyone in Yelcan.

Every day, Yelcan Patrol ships would patrol the water and halt Tanniv ships asking for paperwork and general information that each Bastion required.

So information was always quite up-to-date and relevant.

As the days past the Disaris Princess would spend her time writing and devising strategies, and she would often train in the gardens with Oscar and the rest of the soldiers and recruits.

Later in the afternoon, several days after the Princess had returned to Yelcan, a ship had moored in the harbour with word from Qulan City.

The ship's captain went straight to the Yelcan High command and explained that Qulan City was now under siege and that thousands of Dragoons had taken the harbour and the lower parts of the city. The Turgett had dug in deep and still held the high ground and had gone into lockdown.

This, of course, was in part the truth. The Dragoons did hold the lower part of the city. But it was a blunder from Archduke Aminoff; information of the invasion was now spreading through Tanniv like wildfire.

Reports that Ilihorn troops had taken the city by force through a military tactic were now increasing as the story morphed a hundred different ways from its origin. Only the Archduke and his officers knew that this was a complete mess, and it was more of a predicament and stalemate.

The stories were well-founded as The Archduke did arrive with four times more troops than expected, and his demands were in its self an act of war.

But now, the Archduke found himself in a siege situation, without military support, or food, or previsions.

In the current situation, the High Command nor the diplomats in Moltenwing knew anything about this act of war.

Princess Gilgamesh and Oscar were in the gardens practising sword fighting when the news had come in. They both ran to the High Command assembly hall to receive this information.

General Yeldrove and the High command were all deep in thought; about what to do.

The Princess entered, and Lord Marshal Vaymar asked the Princess and Oscar to take a seat.

"I have three bits of information to tell you," said Lord Marshal.

"It appears that Qulan City is under siege, and we are trying to understand what has happened."

"It seems strange to us that days after the League of Friends becomes official, they would plan such a strange invasion tactic," the Lord said, looking around at his other Marshals in a confused way, as it made no sense. They had no backup, provisions, food, or military strategy that would typically be associated with a siege or invasion of this type.

"The information is fragmented; we intend to send ridders to the Embassy in Qulan to get a better understanding," said Lord Marshal Vaymar.

"The second piece of news is that Princess Drusunal was successful and that

Jandar Turgetts have signed the reunification agreement," said Lord Marshal Vaymar with a happier tone.

Oscar looked at Princess Gilgamesh and smiled.

"The Third piece of information is that five thousand Disaris and Tarrenash troops will arrive here in Yelcan to collect their orders to join the Bastion border force," the Lord said gain.

There was a lot to think about everyone was in utter disbelief that Qulan City was under siege.

Princess Gilgamesh would wait to receive the troops, who are now attending the reunification agreement, to maintain the border defences.

Then after receiving the troops, she would take a small squad back to the Qulan.

Oscar and the Princess returned to training in the gardens and continued for the remainder of the afternoon. It was a strange atmosphere while they both thought about all the information and the peculiar times they were experiencing.

The Princess left Oscar to practice while she took up another meeting with the High Command.

General Lorsan Yeldrove summoned Oscar to his chambers that afternoon to talk about all the reports coming in.

Everyone everywhere was preparing for the reinforcing of the Bastions.

As he walked across the castle grounds that day, there was a real buzz in the air with people organising all sorts of things in every area of the Fortress.

He marched across the parade grounds and could see Lance-Corporal Elaith Tarron in the stable taking care of the horses. They both saw each other and waved.

Oscar looked a fantastic sight to see in his new Shadow Warrior uniform. He wore this uniform with Pride along with his medal for bravery that he received at the battle of the Tarrenash crossroads with the skirmish they had with the Drachen.

He marched across the parade grounds and up into the main building of the Yelcan Bastion to General Yeldrove's main office.

Captain Norlen was also in the chambers discussing the new information and creating strategy, and they had both summoned Oscar to the office.

"It appears that Princess Gilgamesh will be returning to Qulan to link back up with the crusaders along with Princess Katya," said Lorsan Yeldrove.

"The letter for Thomas Marlow's ambassadorial immunity would be well underway now and will be sent to the Moltenwing administration." Oscar was relieved to hear this.

"Princess Gilgamesh is putting together a small squad to ride out tomorrow for Qulan, and the Princess has requested that you attend," said Lorsan Yeldrove.

"It is your decision you can stay here in Yelcan, or you can re-join the crusade," said General Yeldrove looking down at the smartly dressed young shadow warrior.

"I think I know what I want to do, sir," he said as he stood up straight, looking dead ahead.

"I would rather stay here to continue my training and to wait for Thomas and to help with the reinforcements coming in from Vakoborg, Jandar, and Tarrenash."

General Yeldrove and Captain Norlen smiled; Oscar was turning into a soldier and was beginning to think like a warrior.

"Sir! Would you mind if I speak to Princess Gilgamesh before I make my decision," said the young soldier.

"Yes, speaking to Princess Gilgamesh would be the best thing to do first," said General Yeldrove.

Oscar said thank-you to the General and Captain and marched out to find the Princess.

He marched out of the main Bastion keep, through the walkway, then across the moat bridge into the gardens.

He could see the Princess practising sword skills. She looked impressive in the late afternoon sun with the stylish athletic moves she was practising in the shade of the trees.

"I have just had a meeting with General Yeldrove," said Oscar.

"He has said that you would like me to go with you to Qulan City to link back up with the Crusaders," He said.

"Yes, I would like you to come with me again." said the Princess.

"I would like to come, but I must think about how useful I am in West Tanniv."

"My name holds no value in Tanniv, and I would like to continue my training as a shadow warrior here in Yelcan," said Oscar.

"I also think I would benefit and serve West Tanniv more by helping to reorganise the tens of thousands of new troops arriving," said Oscar in a lowered tone.

"You know Oscar, that is what I thought you were going to say," said the Princess.

"You look at home here, and you look especially at home with your Shadow Warrior Uniform," said Princess Gilgamesh.

Oscar stood up tall; every one that knew him before could now see how well he had done over the past year.

He looked handsome and imposing in his new uniform.

The Princess explained that she understood how he wanted to stay, and she commended him for becoming a shadow warrior.

The Princess had made arrangements to leave after the first intake of Disaris warriors and would stay for another week or maybe two.

The two friends sat in the afternoon sun talking about Thomas and discussing the politics of Tanniv until the sunset on the Bastion gardens. The grounds had never looked so beautiful, and while the golden tones from twilight drew the day to a close, they both sat thinking about Thomas and the uncertain times ahead.

Return to Moltenwing

Thomas was still in Port Elec; he had been staying in the Embassy Palace.

He was a guest of Prince Aminoff, and they had been discussing the policymaking for Tanniv; they had attended the wrestling matches at all the stadiums. Betting and gambling and having a great time.

Wrestling was part of the festival of Elec that week.

Wrestlers from Tanniv had been coming to Elec for hundreds of years competing and gambling and had become part of the traditional celebrations.

Thomas went everywhere with the Prince, and they gambled and went to the wrestling festivals during the day and then attended the aristocratic parties by night.

Everywhere Thomas went, the Nobles of Moltenwing wondered who the boy was.

Thomas's uniforms were dashing, and he walked everywhere with Prince Alwin, and he was always by his princely side.

Each day the Prince would ask Thomas if he wanted to go back; the Prince would also find an alternative thing to keep him in East Tanniv.

The following day Thomas was invited to see the troops manoeuvring down by the river for a full Royal inspection.

The Moltenwing guard under the command of Marshal Rhorn Fadan had been relocated just south of Elec City.

The soldiers had been strategically placed on a hundred-mile front to link up with the Ilihorn Dragoons further south, and a sea of pitched white pointed tents lined the grasslands of the river as far as the eye could see.

A grand general called Marshal Fadan was Tanniv's longest-serving officer, and he had been placed in command of the troops along the new front.

He had been a soldier since he was a boy, and he loved military life. He was one of the richest men in Tanniv, with a massive mansion in the northern regions near the Rovalur Mountains.

He was a strange chap, and in his mansion, he would sleep on the floor and had his room made up and dressed like his mobile military tents, so he did not

Lord Marshal Rhorn Fadan of Moltenwing.

lose touch with the army life when he was at home.

He loved moving his troops around, so the current deployment of troops along the Alimar River was his perfect life.

However, the Quality of the troops had declined significantly as most were now conscripts from the Tanniv serf system.

These conscripts came from the farmlands and plantations, so many serfs would be sent back as harvest was now in season. These were not ideal fighting troops, and the Marshal knew it.

Thomas awoke that morning to find a new uniform on his bed, this time in dark military green with a matching tunic style jacket and gleaming riding boots; each uniform looked more magnificent than the next.

He got dressed with the exciting prospect of a packed day and Royal inspection of the East Tanniv Army and their encampment.

Marshal Rhorn Fadan of The Moltenwing guard was meeting them at the Embassy Palace that morning.

The servants came into the room that morning to ready a hot bath for Thomas and bring him a breakfast of pastries and fruit.

He put on his new uniform then looked in the mirror at himself, looking magnificent.

He then spotted an addition that he had not seen before.

It was a military hat with a peaked visor and a Moltenwing Brass badge in the hat's middle.

The hat also had a gold-style rope around the rim, making Thomas look like a soldier.

There was also a leather belt that went around his waist and over his shoulder.

He looked so official and so handsome.

No wonder the whole of East Tanniv was talking about this striking young man.

He went down the grand staircase to meet with Prince Alwin and Marshal Fadan that morning.

He looked down at the Prince as he walked across the upper floor landing, and he was wearing the same uniform as Thomas.

Thinking that this was a parade-style of uniform, he dismissed this as it made him feel remarkable.

Prince Alwin was standing in the main hallway reading letters when he looked up. "Arh Thomas, you do look like a smart young man," said the handsome Prince.

Marshal Fadan stood with a cup of tea in his hand, waiting while wandering up and down the hall admiring the paintings.

His colossal personality echoed through the gallery as his boots trip trapped around on the marble floor. At the same time, he admired himself in the mirror, looking at his magnificent commander uniforms with at least fifty medals that jingled around his uniform.

They waited in the hallway, waiting for the footman to announce that the Royal coach was ready.

Thomas felt so important like he was a general himself.

The coach arrived, and the footman came to the door, and the three of them got into the coach bound for the plains just south of Elec.

A hooded figure stood opposite the street, looking over at the coach.

It was Sana Norbella; she was trying to communicate with Thomas telepathically.

As Thomas got into the coach, conversations were going backwards and forwards about who was sitting where flustering Thomas.

He pinched the bridge of his nose to close to his eyes as if something was being said but, he couldn't entirely focus on it.

Then before he could concentrate, the coach and the eight horses pulling it charged off down the cobbled street, and Sana had missed her chance.

Sana had stayed close the whole time, and she intended to keep nearby until the time was right to get him back.

She would never stop because of the connection between them both.

The coach rumbled against the cobbled stones and through the sometimes wide and sometimes narrow streets, with one hundred imperial guards galloping around the coach in a tight formation, making an enormous din as they galloped.

The journey through the cobbled streets would not take long before they were outside the main city walls and out to the city limits.

The surrounding countryside was flat and bright green, and Thomas could see the tents from the thousands of soldiers in the distance.

He had a rough idea of where he was going as the soldiers could be seen from the Imperial riverside palace, and he saw them at the party several nights before.

The Prince and the Marshal continually spoke about the army, the Dragoons, Hussars, and the Royal Guardsman. The Prince proudly talked about his Navy, from which Marshal took a dislike.

The Marshall was a soldier through and through, and any talk of Navy would bring the Marshall to a grumpy state with the odd comment about "land soldiers being the best combatant Moltenwing has to offer."

The Prince would smile at Thomas and tilt his head towards the much older Marshall, and they both sniggered at his grumpiness.

Finally, they had arrived in the flat land down by the river.

Thomas got out and could see hundreds and hundreds of tents with thousands and thousands of soldiers in rows on parade, all in their pageant dress uniforms.

He looked on and thought that this was the best sight he had ever seen.

Two Generals rode over on horses, and some horse handlers walked around with the reigns from three horses that jockeyed with them.

The Prince was given a giant black horse, Thomas was given a horse slightly brown but in a similar style with the Marshal's horse who had been given his usual trusty grey steed.

Prince Alwin led the way while Thomas jogged next to the Prince and Marshal Fadan cantered beside them, both talking about the troops as they slowly trotted down the line.

It was a perfectly straight line of men wearing what looked like perfect uniforms, highly polished boots with gleaming swords and brilliant white belted webbing.

The Marshal took the Prince and Thomas over to the high ground several hundred metres away, where they were given a display of manoeuvres.

Watching the soldering of thousands of troops all forming different formations was a marvellous sight to see. They moved to the sound of trumpeters, drummers, and flutes and other coloured flags waving from Marshal Fadden and his generals.

"What do you think, Thomas?" said the Princess as he gazed out with an ambitious face and a sparkle in his eyes.

Thomas had not seen this leering look from the Prince before, it was as if a mask had dropped, and he could see a side to the Prince that he concealed to everyone.

"I think it looks amazing," said Thomas with a beaming smile on his face, but looking at the Prince with a more detailed look.

Some soldiers carrying baskets of wine and picnic food set up tables in a sun-shaded marquee with chairs and tables laid out.

The manoeuvres happened all afternoon as all the different regiments showed a well-rehearsed array of battle formations.

Prince Alwin could see his ships in the distance, and Thomas could see the happiness in the Princess face looking out at his army as if he were playing with his soldier's toy set as a boy.

Thomas looked on with equal interest as drummers drummed and flags waved and trumpets sounded; the troops manoeuvred into many different battle formations that afternoon.

Later that afternoon, a small squad of Moltenwing cavalry Hussars approached the Marquee.

These riders looked like they had been on the road for days; they were covered in dust and looked pale and exhausted.

They ask to see the Prince with direct orders to give the Prince the message they had carried.

As the dusty, dirty Hussar cavalrymen approached the Prince, the Moltenwing guard tried to block the Hussar's path.

The laid-back Prince who sat stubbornly in his chair drinking wine and watching his troops looked over and waved his hand with a tiresome voice said, "Oh, let him through if he has a message."

The tiered exhausted cavalryman handed the Prince a note.

Prince Alwin opened it up while keeping an eye on the manoeuvring troops in the distance.

Then averted his eyes onto the dusty letter. His eyes widened, and he spat the wine out that he sipped only a second before, then he jumped to his feet "that stupid little blundering idiot."

"What is it, my lord," said Marshall Fadden.

"Ready my horse," said the Prince.

"But what is it?" repeated Marshall Fadden, this time with more persistence.

"That idiot cousin of mine."

"He has started a war against Qulan City," said the Prince as he paced up and down."

"How has that stupid man managed to start a war with a peace agreement," he said, smashing his fist down on a table.

Marshall Fadden looked shocked, as did the other Generals and Thomas.

"He only had a thousand men and a peace agreement; how did this happen," said the Marshall.

"Read the letter for yourself; he's taken three thousand and amended the league of friend's agreement," said the Prince as he handed him the letter.

Thomas listened to the news. He could now see that East Tanniv did want peace, and this was an accident. Prince Alwin jumped on his horse then looked at Thomas to do the same.

"Come with me, Thomas; we ride to the imperial palace to see the Empress."

They galloped hard back up the hill towards Elec City to the short distance to the Imperial Palace.

The Prince got to the main entrance when slaves came running to his aid to open the door "where is my mother? He shouted," in an aggressive voice at the serfs. Where is my mother? The impatient Prince shouted once again.

Some slaves pointed towards the west wing of the grand imperial palace.

The Empress was in the Orangery surrounded by plants and flowers.

She had a letter on the table too among the flowers and the greenery from the Orangery. Thomas could see that she was distressed.

"Have you seen what that no good cousin of mine has done," said the Prince in an angry but slightly softer voice as he slammed the dusty letter on the pruning desk, among stems and flower petals.

"Yes, my son, that blithering idiot has made the biggest blunder of his life," said the Empress in an angry voice.

Before she got too stressed, she spotted Thomas.

"Hello Thomas," said the Empress in a soft, elegant tone with a beautiful smile.

"Hello, my lady," said Thomas.

"This is just boring Politics; why don't you go and wander out in the gardens? We will come and get you," said the Empress.

Thomas nodded, then sauntered outside in the late summer afternoon air looking back at the river.

"We need to return to Moltenwing," said the Empress.

"I agree; when I get my hands on that weak little Darbella, I will wring his neck," said the Prince.

"We have some time to think about this; let's not be too hasty," said the beautiful Empress in a soft tone to her son as she unfurled his fist-shaped hands from the desk, soothing him like only a mother could.

"We need to get back to Moltenwing and assemble the warring council again," said The Empress.

"Yes, Mother," said Prince Alwin.

"One last thing, what are you going to do with that Marlow boy?" said the Empress looking directly into her son's eyes.

"He will come with us, of course," the Prince said while smiling at his mother.

"I will leave that to you," said the Empress as she turned around, swishing her royal dress and gown as she hurried out of the Orangery to get ready.

Prince Alwin wandered outside to find Thomas.

He was sat in the gardens looking south at the troop's encampment.

It was late afternoon, and the sun was getting ready to set.

It had been a clear blue sky day, and the late afternoon sun was beating down on the boy in his military uniform.

"I need to return to Moltenwing, my young friend," said the Prince as he found Thomas.

"I am sorry that this ambassador's trip has come to an abrupt end," said the Prince as he sat down beside the boy.

"You can see some of the problems that I have to face running such a large state, and it appears some errors have happened in Qulan City that we need to fix to ensure peace," he said.

"I understand, my lord; this trip has helped me understand more about East Tanniv, and I now appreciate that you have a quest for peace and not war now," said Thomas in a stern voice, looking back at the Prince.

"I will arrange for a boat to take you back tomorrow," said Prince Alwin.

"It is my wish now to convince the warring council in Moltenwing that war is not what we need," said the Prince.

"You know I knew your mother very well; this is the precise situation she would have been excellent at. She could have come to Moltenwing to ensure peace would prevail," said the Prince looking down at Thomas.

"Then I have an idea," said Thomas with bounds of energy.

"Why don't I come and continue my mother's work."

"I have always wanted to see Moltenwing, and I could help you," said Thomas as he jumped up.

"But don't you need to get back?" said a very cunning Prince Alwin.

"Yes, but peace is much more important," said Thomas.

Prince Alwin smiled at him and agreed that he would go to Moltenwing.

Moltenwing is five days ride by coach, and we will need to stop at various Inns on the way and, there is now much to organise.

The Prince and Thomas spent the rest of the afternoon walking around in the garden discussing Politics.

The Empress looked down from her bedroom window at The Prince and Thomas walking around the gardens. She had a smile on her face as she watched from afar.

Alwin looked back at the window and nodded, and the Empress nodded back, with a knowing look, as they both strolled around the grounds. They both knew what an asset Thomas was to keep in East Tanniv.